unattainable

BY

MILOSH ZEZELJ

First Paperback Edition: September 2016

This is a work of fiction. Names, characters, businesses, places, events and incidents are either the products of the author's imagination or used in a fictitious manner. Any resemblance to actual persons, living or dead, or actual events is purely coincidental.

Published by Golden Ribbon Publishing

Library of Congress Control Number: 2016914691

ISBN-10: 0-9979583-0-8
ISBN-13: 978-0-9979583-0-0

2 4 6 8 10 9 7 5 3 1

www.unattainablebook.com
info@unattainablebook.com

to mom,
my angel on earth

to dad,
I love you without limit

to Nenad, my other half,
I don't know what I would have done without you

to Jelena,
I love you more than my own life

to Braco,
the Sun in my life

to Jo Rowling,
Thank you for the lifelong inspiration and magic—you make this world a
better place

CONTENTS

Driven by the forces of love, the fragments of the world seek each other so that the world may come into being.

Love alone is capable of uniting living beings in such a way as to complete and fulfill them, for it alone takes them and joins them by what is deepest in themselves.

—Pierre Teilhard de Chardin

PREFACE

Death had come for me unexpectedly, brutal and unimaginably fast, and I knew in that moment I had lost everything I had been fighting for in the past few days of my life.

The air felt razor-sharp as I involuntarily drifted into death, far away from the person I loved the most. Letting go hurt more than my broken bones, and there was nothing else that I wished but for it to be over fast.

My lips curved into a weak smile when I saw the warm light somewhere in the distance, and I knew the aftermath was going to be peaceful.

Even though the solid matter my body hit against was hard, when I spotted my enemy, strong and not human, only steps away from me, I knew it wasn't the end yet.

He stepped closer, and I said my farewell to earth.

THE ACCIDENT

"Adam, are you ready?" my mother called from the kitchen. I raised one eyebrow and looked at the clock on the wall. It was exactly seven-thirty in the evening—; a reminder enough to hurry up if I didn't want to miss our flight. I had spent the past three hours in my room packing my most necessary belongings.

It was almost the end of summer break, and my mother and I were getting ready to move from Switzerland to Serbia. At the time, it felt like a simple decision for both of us, and we decided to make it as smooth as possible. She was offered a position at the National Bank of Serbia, and I was accepted to the University of Applied Linguistics in Belgrade, which I had dreamed of attending since high school. I was raised multilingual and spoke a total of five languages. Both my mother and I thought it was the right time to invest in my skills. Hence, our decision to move.

I gave my empty room a last glance—one of those good-bye looks—and checked the cupboards and closets to make sure I wasn't leaving anything behind. We had already sold the house with some of the furniture and got a good enough price to provide for both of us for some time.

I proceeded to pack some picture frames that I had left untouched until the very last moment, out of procrastination. I was trying to trick my mind not to think about moving and therefore left the frames out much longer than I had intended. I paused briefly to look at the picture in the biggest frame. It was taken only a few days after my birth and showed my smiling parents. Together.

I had very few memories of my father. My last name, Christakis, was an omnipresent one. And obviously his looks were too—brown eyes, brown hair, thick eyebrows, edgy jaw and small ears—and one of the reasons my mother had signed me up for modeling competitions since I was young. Her efforts weren't always in vain. I did win a few of those, including the *Mr. and Ms. Teenie Contest* at the age of thirteen, even though the memory of that one felt slightly embarrassing as I grew older.

My mother, Maria, whom I nicknamed May, was one of the first words I ever spoke. She had never been secretive about her breakup with my father, which happened when I was two, even though they never spoke after he moved away to Greece. I encouraged her to date, which she did sometimes, but most of the times, she ended up making excuses and said she was too busy with work. Since she had me at eighteen, we theoretically grew up together, and had established a friendship-like relationship that most kids could only dream of having with a parent.

I stared at the old photograph for another moment and slipped it into the pouch inside of my suitcase and went downstairs to the kitchen where I found May with a checklist in her hands.

Some inches shorter than me with black shoulder-length curly hair, May was in her early forties and her skin had more of a brown tone than mine. Her femininely round face featured some irregular pigmentation sprinkled over her nose. She narrowed her eyes and sighed, but finally released a loving smile.

"Did you get everything done, love?" she asked with her musical voice.

"All done," was my quick dry answer. The nervousness snuck up on me, and all of a sudden, I had mixed feelings at the sight of our empty house.

"Perfect. Olga should be here any minute to give us a ride to the airport," she said, leaving the now-empty kitchen. "That's it."

Mom would always give me some privacy when needed, and she was excellent at knowing when that time was. I allowed my eyes to wander through the empty room, trying not to overthink our decision; hoping to be able to start a new life. She had partially given up hers for mine, and I promised myself to make sure she was going to enjoy our decision as much as I was supposed to.

The doorbell rang.

"That's Olga," mom said and opened the door rashly.

"Maria, hi. All packed?" Olga greeted her with an unusually deep voice for a woman. She was always out of breath due to her obesity.

They kissed on the cheek.

"Sure we are, come on in," mom said.

"Oh, listen, it's rush hour and I think we should leave as soon as possible." Olga wiped away a thin layer of glistening sweat from her upper lip. I caught mom make a face.

"That's okay, I just have to bring our luggage down."

I helped May carry our heavy bags downstairs, and Olga greeted me with a manly high five that almost broke my fingers. She was an impatient driver and on the way to the airport honked at everyone who was driving too slowly for her.

5

I fell asleep once we reached the highway, trying to prevent my mouth from popping wide open and drooling all over myself.

It was just past eight when we got to the airport in Zurich. Despite the fact that the sun had already disappeared from the horizon, it was still hot. The airport was crowded, giving me the usual feeling of travel fever, with mixed sadness and excitement.

We said good-bye to Olga and made our way through the crowd in a rush. When we checked our luggage, night had already covered the sky in a dark layer of gray clouds. And finally, we boarded the plane.

I sat next to the window and drew the blinds down since May was scared of flying. I didn't feel like eating anything and started listening to music. When we took off, I fell asleep.

Mom woke me up as the plane began to descend toward Belgrade. The cabin crew prepared for landing while information about connecting flights was announced.

It was past midnight when we got off of the plane. The night was still warm—Serbia is known for its intense seasonal climate. I was born there; but at the age of two, after my parents got divorced, May moved to Switzerland with me. We used to go back every now and then during school breaks to visit, but this was actually the first time ever that we moved back to live there together.

We took a cab to our new apartment, which was in the center of Belgrade, not far away from the *Nikola Tesla* airport. Mom had found us a nice furnished apartment, which I immediately liked. It consisted of two bedrooms, one bathroom and a small kitchen that was connected to the living room. It also had a balcony with a view of the city. Belgrade was shining beautifully in the darkness tonight.

"Home, sweet home," mom said and opened the balcony, inviting a humid, warm breeze to fill the room. In order to avoid an emotional conversation, I went into the bathroom, brushed my teeth and put on my pajamas.

I wished her good night and went to my room. Although it was a little bit smaller than the one in Switzerland, it was still nice, with big windows and heavy curtains, a huge wardrobe, a bed and some cupboards. That was totally enough for me. I fell asleep very quickly and had a dreamless night.

I was awoken by the sun the following morning. It was a bright day, and the rays of sunlight shone freely through my big windows, as I had forgotten to draw the curtains the previous night. I blinked myself awake and slowly began my morning routine, which consisted of taking a shower and having breakfast.

May had already left—I didn't know where she had gone—so I decided to make myself some toast, only to realize that we didn't have any groceries at all. Being left with no other choice, I decided to go get some. Before I left, I started unpacking my bags, stuffing my clothes into the drawers and the wardrobe. I also made sure to put out my picture frames, placing them on the chest of drawers. It sure would take me some time to get used to this new place, I thought.

It was a warm day, and the streets were crowded with people. I couldn't resist the temptation of walking around to get to know Belgrade's streets a little better. I first went down to my most favorite pedestrian zone in the city, *Knez Mihailova,* a handsome historic shopping mile surrounded by stores and cafés, and enjoyed the idea of playing tourist.

After spending some time there, I decided to go check out my new campus—and to get the groceries later on my way back home. The fact that I didn't have any plans for the rest of the day and the desire to spend as much time outside as possible strengthened this decision. I asked some people if they knew where the campus was, and apparently it was well-known in that area. A random pedestrian told me it wasn't far away and I followed her directions.

I was convinced that it was noon, for the sun was on its highest position on the horizon and burning the back of my neck. The morning breeze had disappeared. After half an hour of walking around, I had to admit, to my disappointment, that I couldn't have walked in the right direction (so, that much about playing a tourist rang true). I was facing an apartment building in front of a highway, which curved its way behind some trees in the near distance. Annoyed as I was, I decided to turn around while passing a playground where some children were playing to get the groceries.

What occurred next happened so fast, that I had no chance to react, though I perceived several things at once.

A dog ran across the street, a jogger who was running bumped into me, a dove flew above my head, and a child on the playground began to cry.

Enough distractions for my human eyes to miss the coming car, which was approaching from the right side of the road.

Even if I had seen the car, it was already too late. All I could hear was a crash of splintering glass as I was scooped up into the air by impact. Immediate pain was followed while intense panic ran throughout my body. Then I lost all physical consciousness.

***

I was dead. I was sure without a doubt. I felt it. And even though I didn't want to believe it at first, it was obvious. All the things I felt, saw and heard indicated my death. The warmth, the colors, the endless white light and the muffled voices. I had always associated death with pain, but there was none. It was as if I had never hit my head. I thought I was dreaming, but at the same time it felt as though I wasn't. Suddenly, a spark emerged from the white light, bearing an abnormally beautiful person.

She had the most irresistible appearance and looked radiant,

8

like liquid sunlight. Her hair was long and light-brown. Her face was a true masterpiece, marked by indescribable beauty. Thin eyebrows decorated a perfect set of gold-brown eyes, behind which I could see beaming sunlight shining through. She was dressed in white and was moving toward me fluidly, in a light and graceful way, as if floating.

She knelt next to me on the hard pavement and looked deeply into my eyes without ever saying a word. We were surrounded by pure white light; the street, the pavement and the car all disappeared. I couldn't speak. Even if I tried, I knew I would fail. I felt a desperate urge and need to ask who she was. The first sight of her had numbed my body, making it impossible for me to move. I was trying to find a rational explanation for where I was and who she could be. The experience felt like a dream, but so real and vivid at the same time. The light was so blindingly strong. I had to squint and narrow my eyes.

At the same time, I could feel a sensation of warmth that ran through my veins and flowed into my chest. And then, only a short moment later, my heart felt as though it was expanding. It felt open, as if it had burst in pieces, an overflowing wellspring, that was pouring a warm, electrifying current. The feeling was absolutely climatic, and as it expanded even further, I felt an unconditional sense of caring and compassion well up in my body. With every moment that passed, I felt more complete and more alive. It was as though I was part of something larger, something I never knew existed before. The feeling kept flowing freely and I felt joyous and safe. The unifying explosion in my heart was uncontrollable, like a volcano erupting, fast, unexpected and mysterious as it expanded to my arms and hands, which were moist from the heat. I felt in complete balance, and my skin had a tickling sensation.

I felt as if I had left my body, light and airy, and in the next moment there was a broiling fire in my heart.

And then, all of a sudden, she unexpectedly leaned forward and gave me a soft brief kiss on my lips.

I could feel the warmth and the adrenaline rushing through my veins. Her lips felt like the softest rose petals washed with the glory of dawn. My heart started racing; a massive explosion shifted my chest into irregular rhythmic movements, and a sense of excitement in my body suddenly doubled, as if she had injected life back into me.

My lips felt tingly even after she broke the ephemeral kiss.

The fire in my heart spread violently fast, burning my insides with a healing sensation. I became tired and fought to keep my eyes open, to enjoy her seraphic face for another moment. Suddenly, and simultaneously I was falling through empty space, into a soft, safe place.

And then, I woke up.

I don't know how long I was unconscious. At first, I didn't dare open my eyes as I tried to sense my surroundings. I thought about blood, but the only thing I could feel was my heavy aching head. I moved my hands to figure out where I was lying, but had to wince immediately. I could feel a stinging pain in my left arm and opened my eyes blinking slowly—a catheter. Crap.

I was lying on a hospital bed, my left arm was tied to an infusion, and my head was wrapped in gauze wrap. My head felt heavy, and I could only move with great effort. I sighed. I could hear something move and then someone carefully gave me a big hug. It was May.

"Love, are you alright? What happened to you? Where have you been? Do you hear me? Can you speak, can you move? You don't know how worried I've been all this time. They told me that everything would be alright."

She was hysterical and didn't look well at all. May was restlessly touching my face, my head and my hands. The dark circles under her eyes were immediately noticeable. Worry was painted all over her face.

"I'm fine," I managed to say. I winced at the sound of my weak voice.

She was frantic. "Don't move, I'll get the doctor." She left the room quickly and for a brief moment it was quiet before she came back followed by a doctor.

"Hello, Adam, my name is Dr. Vidan. How do you feel?" he asked, checking my infusion.

I groaned and tried to speak. "I think I'm okay. I only have an awful headache, that's all. I think." My mouth was dry, which made talking even more exhausting.

"That's normal. That should be gone in a few days, don't worry. You are a very lucky guy. Even though the car hit you quite hard, you only have a mild concussion." Dr. Vidan proceeded to check my eyes for sensitivity to light and asked me silly questions in order to rule out I wasn't experiencing any loss of memory.

At last he smiled, squeezed my shoulder and led May out of the room to talk to her.

It took me a good minute to actually realize what he had said. And then I remembered the car hitting me. Only I could cross the street without turning left and right to check for coming cars. Now I had to deal with the consequences of my clumsiness. Great, I was beyond annoyed with myself.

The door opened, and May was by my side so fast it took me a moment to realize just what she had asked, "How are you?"

"I'm fine, really, don't worry. I'm just tired. Go home and get some rest," I lied. I felt really bad for making her worry about me. Our moving transition should have been much smoother.

"They can't find the bastard who was driving the car. I am so sorry," she apologized. Finding him wouldn't have made any difference, I thought. I would still be here tied to this bed.

"Mom, it's okay," I insisted.

She ignored me. "Should find him…lock him up. People like that should not be allowed to drive." Her eyes were teary.

"Mom," I tried again, "I'm okay. I promise. Nothing is going to happen to me."

"I'm staying with you," she insisted before I could even try to convince her to leave. "The doctor said they gave you some painkillers. You might feel sleepy."

"I'd be glad to pass out."

I felt better when she left the room and headed down to the restaurant for some coffee. I was still feeling bad for making her worry and didn't want her to see me all covered up in gauze wrap. I could finally let myself *feel* bad. My thoughts drifted away trying to find a rational reason of how the accident might have happened. I couldn't even remember how I had gotten to the hospital. Someone must have called the ER.

And then I remembered my dream. I remembered the girl's sublime face. I had never had such an intense and vivid dream before. It was as though I could still feel her lips on mine, her beautifully intense eyes locked on me, followed by the warmth of her body. I touched my chest with my free hand. It felt normal. I *must* have hit my head really bad, I thought in silence. That was the only rational explanation my mind could come up with before the meds knocked me out.

The next day I felt better and annoyed at times. They came five times during three hours to check in on me. I couldn't stand it, and May's presence added to my stress by causing great effort on my part to convince her that I was fine. I was glad to notice when she was feeling much better and wasn't freaked out about the situation anymore. They started to give me only mild painkillers, and to my surprise, I felt much better by the end of the second day. The third day was the best: I got rid of the IVs and the gauze wrap.

"Take care, and come back should you feel any sort of pain," Dr. Vidan advised, handing me my release papers.

"I'll make sure to do so," I said.

"Thank you, doctor," May said as I handed him the signed documents. I was glad when I finally got to leave the hospital with her.

Time passed. Before I knew it, the last week of summer break had come, and I was nervous. One week left until the start of the term. After my accident, I spent the rest of the week at home, not being active at all, just to make May happy. The weather worsened halfway through the last week, casting a dark gray cloud over Belgrade that was followed by a late summer rain.

On Monday, May gave me a ride to campus, which was surrounded by nature. Somehow, they were able to find a rural-looking spot in the central-eastern part of Belgrade to build the campus on.

"Take care and call me if you need anything," she said as she dropped me off.

I loved the campus immediately. It was enormous, consisting of three main buildings and the dorms. There were classrooms and lockers on each of the four floors of all three main buildings, A, B and C. I was assigned a locker on the second floor of building A. The cafeteria and the library were on the first floor of building A.

As I entered building B, I pulled out a letter from my backpack, which I would have left at home had May not reminded me to bring it with me. It said that the introduction for new students would be held in the auditorium. I wandered around for a couple of seconds until I found a sign pointing toward the entrance and headed in what I hoped would be the right direction. Only when I was entering the auditorium did I realize how nervous I actually was.

There were a lot of young people sitting inside, and some were already talking to each other. The auditorium was huge and could easily fit up to 500 people. When I realized that I was awkwardly standing in the door blocking the entrance, I hastily moved away, and almost tripped before steadying myself on an empty chair. One thing was sure: My clumsiness had not abandoned me. The guy next to me was having a hard time suppressing his laughter. I sighed and forced a crooked smile on my face.

The door of the auditorium closed and an elderly man made his way onto the stage. Judging by his thinning hair, I believed he had to be in his sixties. He wore a gray suit with a pair of square glasses sitting on the tip of his nose.

"Welcome to the University of Applied Linguistics," he said, beginning his speech in a raspy voice. "My name is Mr. Hugentobler, the president of this university, and I am honored to give yet another welcome speech."

As he was speaking, a couple of professors entered and sat in a row on the stage behind him. He then introduced them in a polite way, though I immediately forgot their names as soon as he said them.

After a while, we were given our schedule and a campus map. We were also told to go to the registrar's office to sign some papers during our first day to confirm our attendance. I sheepishly glanced at the schedule in my hands. I had my first class—Spanish—in about ten minutes.

"Excuse me, can you tell me where the registrar's office is?" the guy sitting next to me asked. "I can't find it on the map." His English had a slight accent.

"Sure, let me have a look," I said and checked the map.

"There," I pointed to an almost invisible spot on the paper. "Building C, second floor."

He looked relieved and said, "Thank you."

"Make sure you don't trip," he added while shoving his papers into his backpack.

I replied with my best sense of humor, "I can't help it. I was born on Friday the thirteenth." He looked up and laughed.

"That's a good one. I'm Teo by the way. I just moved into the dorms," he said, stretching out his hand.

"I'm Adam," I said. "Nice to meet you."

"Likewise. I'll see you around," he replied as he trekked to the exit.

I almost made my way to Spanish with comforting, stress-free thoughts. I self-studied Spanish at home for over seven years and had made it my third native tongue. The classroom was already crowded with students when I entered and I proceeded to a free seat next to the guy from the auditorium.

The professor, Ms. Arrigoberta, arrived only a short moment later.

"*Buenos días,*" she said.

A young woman with blond hair, she was wearing a blue skirt and a white button-down top. We were handed a list of the books we would need for the first semester, which she said all the students could buy during the lunch break, in the auditorium. Shortly afterward, we were given a placement test to find out what level of teaching was best suited for our class and to determine if anyone needed to go back to Spanish for beginners.

By the end of the lesson, I knew more about Teo than Spanish grammar. He had the entertaining quality of not being able to stop talking and told me he had recently moved from Mexico and was planning on moving to Italy after the completion of his studies in Belgrade. He was the first to be done with the placement test and left after half an hour.

I took my time with the test and left a couple of minutes before French class with Mr. Auberson, asking some students passing by where his classroom was.

Mr. Auberson was an elderly man who reminded me of my

English teacher from Switzerland. He wore glasses and a black suit and smelled strongly of cigarettes.

"*Bonjour. Je m'appelle Monsieur Auberson,*" was his opening sentence.

French passed in the same way as Spanish. We were once again given a placement test, and I was the first to complete it.

"*Vous pouvez maintenant faire la pause déjeuner,*" he said to me before I left. Then I made my way to the cafeteria, following the arrows on the map that led me to the first floor of building A.

"Adam, over here!" I turned my head to the right.

It was I'll-babble-you-to-death, Teo. He was sitting at a table with some other people and was gesturing to the free seat next to him.

"How's is it going so far?" he asked.

"It's going well. French was easy," I said.

"Yikes, can't stand French. I chose Portuguese instead," he rambled while he was reading the menu. "Have a look. The menu's great."

I was really hungry, but kept it simple, ordering the chicken and vegetables.

"They really try to make you feel at home," Teo said to a Chinese girl next to him who looked like she didn't understand a single word he said.

"So, tell me, where are you from?" he asked me, turning away from the Chinese student.

"I was born here in Serbia. I moved to Switzerland at the age of two when my parents got divorced. I hardly remember my father though. I have lived alone with my mother for most of my life, and we just moved back here," I told him in a nutshell.

The waitress approached our table with our orders, and then we dug in. We were all so hungry that we didn't speak until we finished. Lunch was good, except that Teo kept talking to everyone at the table as if he knew us from long ago. After I was done, I grabbed my schedule from under the table just to have something to do. Next was English with Mr. Slipper.

I was about to order a soda, when all of a sudden a heat wave hit me and my hands began to sweat. My heart started racing, and I felt dizzy for a second, grabbing onto the chair. For a moment I thought some of the meds I had taken were giving me anxiety, but it was then when I saw *her*.

The long, light-brown hair, the intense eyes and the golden face. She looked fragile, but yet so perfect. The rays of sunlight that came from the huge windows were painting her hair honey-gold. She was carrying some books in front of her chest, looking somewhat out of breath, her soft rose lips slightly parted. Her eyebrows gave away a visible hint of worry. As she looked around the cafeteria, a strand of hair fell to her forehead. That right there was beauty summed up in the human body, I thought, an appearance that simply and totally pleased my sight. I couldn't believe my eyes. She moved in a graceful way, scanning the cafeteria as though looking for something—or someone. It took me a moment to realize where I had known her from before. But by the time I did, she had drifted away.

I realized that I had been paralyzed, staring at her with my mouth wide open. My hands were still sweaty and I was still warm, but the dizziness was gone. For that brief moment I forgot my surroundings; in fact, it was as if I was waking up out of a trance.

The smell of fried food, the taste of chicken in my mouth, the chatter, the sound of knives and forks against the plates, my hands on the table, and the feeling of clothes rubbing against my skin. All my senses were back.

"I need to get some books for French," I said unthinkingly, threw some cash on the table and grabbed my bag from under my chair. I was up on my feet within a blink.

"Give me a sec, I'll be right there with you!" I heard Teo complain, but I was already halfway out the door. I sort of managed to look back and give him an apologetic look.

Now I knew that she actually *existed*. I had seen her while I was awake in my physical body. Hadn't I? My rational mind was racing, going back and forth from explanation to explanation, weighing and debating them. This must be real; I had seen her among the crowd in the cafeteria. A physical, live experience right in front of my eyes! But why had I seen her in a vision before? Was this even possible? Or was this indeed a side effect of the meds they had given me a week ago at the hospital? I tried with great effort to shut off my mind, finding myself in a long hallway.

From the corner of my eye, I could see her head toward the exit. I hurried after her.

It was very hot outside; the sun was burning the pavement. Some students were lying on the grass, while others were having their lunch under the shades of the trees. I needed a good minute for my eyes to adjust to the bright light. My head was turning to all possible sides, scanning every single face. I ran to the middle of the court, already convinced that I had lost her, when I spotted her in the near distance on her way to the auditorium. Now I was running, bumping into students who cursed at me. I finally reached the entrance of the auditorium and pushed the door wide open in a violent way.

All I could see was a huge crowd of students—all of them buying books for the semester. Large tables had been set up in the middle of the auditorium, forming a line that slithered from one side of the room to the other. I found myself desperately elbowing everyone around me, trying to spot her in the midst of the crowd. I cursed, annoyed with myself. It was impossible; I had lost her.

My body and mind were going crazy, something that had never happened to me before. I was more than curious to find out who she was; it was as though I had just run through the desert and had encountered a mirage. My body acted up even more; the hair on my arms stood up, with a sudden thirst in my mind, the one only she could quench, fogging up all my other irrelevant thoughts.

I raced between the tables and spotted her on her way out. I hurried after her. Once outside, I could see her disappear behind a door right next to the auditorium. Without hesitating, I slammed the door open and found myself in the restrooms.

"Wait!" I yelled. I looked around. There was absolutely no one in there. I lay flat on the floor, peeking under the doors, making sure that no one was actually there. I could swear I had seen her enter through that same door.

How could she have disappeared from a closed place without windows large enough to climb through? Lying on the floor in the restrooms, following someone I had only seen in my dreams, I really needed a reality check: What in the world was I doing? Never before had I behaved like this. It was definitely not my usual behavior. If delusions were one of the side effects of my concussion, I would make sure to check back in with the doctor. Realizing how silly and actually how stupid I looked lying on the floor, I got up and headed outside.

Back in the auditorium, I could see Teo waiting for me. "Where have you been?" he asked.

"I needed to use the restroom. I ate too fast," I lied to him.

"You're alright now?" he asked, his eyes trying to read my expression. He was probably wondering what issues I had.

I tried to calm my breathing. "I am. Let's get our books. Lunch is almost over," I said, and we made our way to the large tables.

I was looking for a distraction, but nothing helped. I couldn't stop thinking of her. At that moment I wasn't even sure if she was real or not.

Teo and I headed to English after finally getting our books. The afternoon seemed to last forever. As in the previous classes, we were given a placement test. After English, we went to German with Mr. Rosenberg. I wasn't sure if I was annoyed about the fact that Teo had ended up in that class with me as well or if I was just disturbed by the girl I saw earlier.

After this test, we weren't allowed to leave for the day. Mr. Rosenberg seemed like a very boring professor. He was also the first one to throw homework at us. Then he wished us a nice afternoon and dismissed the class. I checked my schedule and was relieved to find that I was done for the day.

A smooth summer rain was trickling down as I made my way to the bus station. I didn't mind. It was the least harmful part of my day.

DÉJÀ VU

When I woke up the next day, I sort of felt fine, though my brain hadn't stopped looking for another rational explanation to sort out the happenings from the previous day.

The night felt long and I was still awake even after three in the morning. Only when the obsidian sky outside started to brighten and the traffic sent rattling noises up my windows did I manage to fall asleep.

I procrastinated as I lay in bed, hitting snooze on my alarm and rolled onto my back to stare at the ceiling. I made myself remember her and was surprised how little effort it cost me; my heartbeat accelerated and my body acted up in an unexpected way.

My hands felt warm and turned sweaty as I opened my mouth to help my breathing. My throat felt dry, and weirdly, I felt thirsty, but not for anything to *drink*. It was as though I had been blind until then and, for a brief moment, had had the chance to see something that I never knew existed before. It felt as if I was on a quest and she, that girl, was the mystery of it.

I wouldn't have made a big deal about it if I had only seen her while I had been unconscious. But shortly after that, I really saw her on campus, and that's what had me puzzled. I asked myself how many people dream afterward about someone whom they had only met once before. Not many, or hardly any, that I was sure about. So maybe it was just some weird coincidence or she just incredibly resembled the girl from my dream.

But then again, why was I so startled by her appearance? I decided to play and take it a step further, envisioning her again. The warm pinch in my chest was unexpected, but nothing close to unpleasant at all. It felt as though I had spilled some warm liquid all over myself, which excited my body as it traced down my skin.

I closed my eyes and there I saw it, her hypnotic face. Her warm eyes, her smooth skin and her parted silky lips. Her features were feminine and, above all, provokingly beautiful. Too perfect, really, to be touched by anyone, I thought. I pictured her like a draft of summer breeze or sparks in the night—impossible to be held, touched or captured for purposes of pleasure. And there it was, that thirst again, like a drought in my body, and all my senses left my skin prickling. I didn't know who she was. I didn't know where she had come from, but I knew that for some unknown reason I was drawn to her. She was beautiful, but there was something more behind that beauty. I could almost feel it.

All of a sudden, she appeared to me like an untouched flower, with bright vivid colors just waiting to be picked, discovered and explored. Something behind her appearance, behind those sunny eyes, was calling my attention, was distracting me internally—and I knew before I had even realized it, that she had turned into an unfinished desire, a previously unfelt longing that already had me idolizing her.

And there I was, turning some unknown girl into something so irresistible. And as I lay there voluntarily intoxicating myself with the memory of her, the feeling in my chest evolved, staggering and fleshly.

A pleasant feeling, I told myself, as my lips curved into a smile and I found the motivation to get out of bed.

"Good morning," May greeted me from behind the morning paper. "How did you sleep?" she asked, raising her head to look at me.

"Fine," I lied, forcing a crooked smile onto my face, grabbing a full bowl of cereal. I didn't want her to know that I almost hadn't slept at all. Furthermore, what was I supposed to tell her was bothering me? A girl from my dreams?

"I have to get going," she said on the way to the shoe rack. "You'll find some cash for lunch on the table. Call me if you need anything."

I went to the bathroom, brushed my teeth and checked my schedule, realizing that I had forgotten to go to the registrar's office to sign the papers yesterday. I would have to make sure to do so before class today.

The University of Applied Linguistics was only a 15-minute drive from our apartment. The green crowns of the trees were waving at me from the bus station, and some squirrels were sprinting from tree trunk to tree trunk. Following the campus map, I made my way to the registrar's office. I knocked on the door and entered.

Her face hidden behind a computer, an elderly woman was sitting at a table; only a fine bush of her gray hair was peeking out from behind the screen.

"Good morning. My name is Adam; I'm a new student. I started yesterday but I forgot to sign the papers we were told to," I explained. She looked at me with a polite smile, red circles drooping from under her tired eyes.

"Sure," she said. "We can take care of that here." She dug through some papers on her desk and handed me a clipboard with an attendance sheet for that semester.

"Thank you, and have a nice day," she said, sitting down to resume her work on the computer.

I grabbed my backpack and was on my way out when my hands suddenly began to sweat, again. I felt warm, really warm. I grabbed onto the desk without the woman noticing my dizziness. That was it; I was going back to the doctor tomorrow, I told myself. While I stood there waiting for it to wear off, the door opened. I widened my eyes. There *she* was.

I stepped away from the desk and leaned against the wall. My heart was racing, I felt as if my feet were going to give in any moment. The feeling in my chest was back, this time more intense, unexpected and enticing.

She let her eyes wander through the office, her hair dancing in a gentle way behind her shoulders. The hidden hint of a worried expression was almost invisible, but still decorated her golden face. She noticed me, giving me a minute nod with a slight curve of her rose lips. Her eyes didn't lock on mine; in fact, it was as if she tried to ignore me. She made her way to the desk in a graceful way, not looking at me at all. I saw how she put her hair sideways in order to cover her face. I was still pressed against the wall, unable to move.

Her voice was barely a whisper, soft and graceful, just like her slender figure, and it sounded like an orchestral symphony to my ears as she said, "Good morning, I haven't signed my forms yet."

"You can do that here," the woman answered and handed her the clipboard, while giving me a questionable look. I forced an apologetic smile on my face, stopped pressing my body against the wall and managed to make my way out of the office. People were definitely going to think I had some serious mental issues.

24

With my hands still sweaty and my heart racing, I tried to pull myself together. I decided to wait and confront the girl.

The door opened.

I took a deep breath and cleared my throat; my voice was failing me.

"Excuse me, is this yours?" she asked with the same whisper in her voice.

She handed me a campus map and a schedule, which must had fallen out of my backpack, but I just stared into her intense eyes. She was only a few inches away from me, but I was already gone, consumed by the unfairness of her beauty and numbed by the warmth her body radiated. I was in trance.

"Your map," she tried again to call my senses back to reality.

My mind was fogged. "Mine. Thank you," was all I managed to say. For a fraction of a second our eyes locked, and I could see the hidden worried expression more clearly. As if she was uncomfortable with our encounter, as if she was trying to tell me something more through her eyes.

She smiled briefly, almost rushed. The chemical reaction in my chest felt like a monster releasing as I stared at her, unable to speak. I didn't even get a chance to blink; she had already made a right and was heading down the hallway. I followed her as fast as I could, but couldn't spot her anywhere. Where could she have gone so fast?

She *is* real, my rational mind told me. Relieved, curious and irritated at the same time, I sank down on a bench at the end of the hallway. *Breathe,* I was telling myself. My surroundings reappeared—I was awakening from the trance.

"Adam!" It was Teo. He was walking toward me.

"How's it going today?" he asked and sat next to me.

"Fine, thanks. Yourself?" For once I was glad he had appeared, hoping that talking to him would be enough of a distraction.

"I'm good, let's go. We are running late."

I had completely forgotten about the time. I looked at my schedule, which I was still holding in my hands, and we made our way to Spanish together.

It seemed that the day couldn't get any more confusing. I was beyond puzzled, with sweaty hands and a racing pulse. Then I saw *her* sitting in the back of the classroom.

The seat next to her was already taken; otherwise I would have sat there. I locked my eyes on her, but she avoided my look. She kept staring at her hands, her hair bouncing down on both sides of her head. When Teo realized that I had been looking at her, he tugged on my shirt and I had a seat. He smirked and gave me a *you-are-nasty* look. At least I was more than convinced that she *was* real. He had seen her as well.

I couldn't help staring back every now and then, but she still kept her focus on the table, not raising her eyes at all.

Ms. Arrigoberta started the class as soon as she entered the classroom, though I had a very hard time focusing. My hands were still sweaty, but the dizziness was gone. Why would this always happen when I saw her? I grabbed onto the table, preventing myself from turning back and staring at her. I just wanted to make sure she was still there, sitting motionless behind me. I wanted my eyes to sink back into my skull and pop out at the back of my head just so I could look at her. Where had she been the other day? And why was she avoiding me? I wanted to ask her all these questions, to sit down and talk with her. I needed to clear my hopeless mind.

It felt too soon when Ms. Arrigoberta dismissed us for the day. The class had passed what seemed to me in only a second. I hadn't even grabbed my books from the table before she was gone. To my surprise, I was sort of upset by her behavior. Ignoring all my existing urges to get up and follow her, I started gathering my books together and shoved them very slowly into my backpack.

"You're coming?" Teo was already on his feet hovering over me.

"Sorry," was my quick response, and I finally got up. I noticed from the corner of my eye that he had given me a strange look. I had to contain myself if I didn't want him to think I was a weirdo. I couldn't let this get to me. In fact, this must have been only coincidence. What if she had never appeared in my dreams? What if she only looked very much like the girl I had seen after the accident? Yes, that was the explanation I decided I wanted to stick to.

Teo greeted a girl in the entrance hall.

"Hi, Natasha. How are you?" The girl was short and wore a blue T-shirt and ragged jeans. Freckles were sprinkled over her nose and cheeks.

"Hi, Teo. I'm fine. How about you?" she asked, smiling a bright smile that revealed some yellow teeth.

Teo gestured in my direction. "Fine. Natasha, this is my friend, Adam."

I shook hands with her.

"Did you choose Italian too?" she asked.

"No, I didn't. I have French now," I answered and glanced at the clock in the entrance hall. It reminded me that I was running late, and I was glad to have a reason to leave, making my way to French in a hurry.

The door of the classroom was open when I darted inside, only to be surprised yet again. *She* was sitting *alone* at a table in the middle of the classroom. I hurried and immediately sat down next to her, realizing that I had completely failed in my plan to stay away from her. There they were again, the sweaty palms and the warmth.

"Hello," I said, roughly with the intention of confronting her.

"Hi," she greeted back with a whisper. She had an apologetic look on her face, which was hard not to notice. I was trying to

27

meet her eyes, but she had only quickly raised them and was locking them back down on the books in front of her.

Mr. Auberson entered the classroom and asked us to have a look at page five, in the chapter about business French. He instructed us to work in pairs today and to focus on improving our vocabulary. I tried to ignore all my excitement, but failed drastically. The other students had already started, while the girl and I just stared awkwardly in silence at the pages of our books.

I cleared my throat.

"Would you like to go first?" I asked, surprised how my intention of confronting her had completely changed. It felt *wrong* to confront her. After all, I didn't want her to feel harassed.

I listened to her even breathing. She pressed her soft lips together for a second and exhaled through her mouth.

"What does a 'fixed rate' mean?" she asked, with her eyes completely focused on the words in the book.

My eight years of French seemed to have completely abandoned me. The French meaning was sitting on the tip of the tongue in my dry mouth. I knew it was going to be hard to concentrate sitting next to her. I shook my head as an answer.

Her voice was still a whisper. "It's *un prix forfaitaire.*"

Of course, I should have known. I could feel how I blushed slightly.

"Do we know each other?" I blurted out unthinkingly.

I could see an almost invisible twitch in her body. For half a second I could see her body tense, but then quite immediately, she changed her posture, released the tension, straightened her back against the chair, and raised her eyes from the book.

When she spoke, her eyes were locked on mine. "I'm sorry?"

"You look very familiar to me," I tried to say without sounding silly.

Her answer came very fast, almost instantly. "I would know

if I had met you before." And there it was again. That apologetic expression.

I was suddenly ashamed. "Of course." I dug my face into the book. I couldn't figure out what was happening to me.

"How about 'We acknowledge receipt of your offer'?" she insisted, fixing her eyes back on the textbook. My nervousness was growing with every question. If I could only explain to her what was going on with me. If I could only make her see what I saw, make her feel how I felt. Then, maybe then, she would understand. Maybe then she would give me a satisfying answer.

"It's *Nous accusons réception de votre offre*," she said, breaking the awkward silence.

Of course it was, I told myself, trying not to look stupid.

Her finger moved on the page. "What about 'the expiration date'?" she asked, not giving me a chance to ask further questions.

I tried hard. As hard as I could. My brain was just not cooperating at all. She then raised her eyes for a brief second, her soft lips curving slightly, giving me another worried look. Her eyebrows were perfectly parted above her eyes and her forehead looked as smooth as fresh fallen snow on the top of a mountain.

"*La date d'expiration*."

"I'm having a hard time focusing, actually," I said to my defense. I felt defeated.

"You better repeat the vocabulary, otherwise you'll fail," she added in a gentle way.

She took her eyes away from mine so fast it left my head spinning and for a moment neither of us said a word. I felt an incredible urge to take her by the hand out of the classroom, to go somewhere more private, to shake her and make her confess that we had indeed met before.

"Have you ever felt as though you have seen someone before but couldn't remember if your encounter had actually happened?

Or felt as if you've seen something before in the past and you were having that same experience again?" I couldn't help asking.

She hadn't moved at all. She listened politely to my questions, blinking behind a silky strand of hair. Her skin looked so soft that I was wondering for a second if my fingers would actually leave dents in it if I touched her.

"I have," she began with a soothing expression on her face, "it's a phenomenon of having the feeling that whatever you are experiencing in the present moment has already been experienced in the past, whether or not it has actually happened." She added, "It's called déjà vu," giving me the perfect answer. Was that the explanation for what was happening to me? I scowled at her. She had surprised me with her quick answer.

"Makes sense," was all I said, feeling as if I had found the answer to my suffering.

"Whether or not it has actually happened," I repeated after a couple of seconds, as my brain was digging deeper looking for another realistic explanation. Why couldn't I be happy with her simple answer?

She nodded politely, as if to let me know I had understood what she had said, though still not making eye contact for longer than a second. "Exactly," she said.

"But how do you actually know whether or not the experience has indeed happened before?" I pressed.

"It depends. Sometimes you can figure it out, and sometimes you can't. You can start by trying to look for physical evidence that is perceived by others besides yourself," she explained. She made it sound so easy. It almost felt as if she had prepared herself for my questions with that answer. As far as I knew, she was the *one* and *only* physical evidence linked to my dream, but then there was no one besides me who could agree with that. No one I knew had ever seen her before. I must have met her only in my dream, I told myself, convinced at last.

"I like your theory," I said.

Her lips smiled. "It's a proven fact," she added in a confident way. Whether she was good at pretending or whether she wasn't bothered by my insistent inquiries, she actually didn't seem to question my sanity, and I was relieved by that.

I realized that my hands weren't sweaty and that my heart wasn't racing as much as before. I suddenly had the urge to move closer to her with my chair and touch the back of her hand.

"May I ask for your name?"

She raised her eyes for only a brief moment. I couldn't see the hint of worry on her face anymore.

"Caroline," she said with her musical voice.

"I'm Adam. It's very nice to meet you. I like your name, Caroline."

I liked the taste of her name on my lips, and its sound clung supernaturally in my ears.

This time she looked up from her book to meet my gaze. "Likewise," she said, "and thank you." Her soft lips were curved into a complete smile now.

"Make sure you repeat the vocabulary," she advised me as she put her books away. "I will see you around," she said just before Mr. Auberson dismissed the class by announcing an exam the following week. She was gone before I could even blink.

I just kept staring after her, not even making an attempt to follow her. Where had the time gone? No possible measure of time would be enough for what I spent with her, I told myself, allowing the conversation to sink in. She was smart, and I was irresistibly drawn to her in the most innocent way possible.

Alone in the empty classroom, I had a look at my schedule and quickly gathered my books together, sprinting to German. The class had already started when I entered. I closed the door, trying not to interrupt Mr. Rosenberg, and hurried to a free seat

Teo had saved for me. Mr. Rosenberg gave me an annoyed look, but didn't say anything.

Not for a moment did Caroline escape my thoughts. I felt much better after I had talked to her, and was relieved to finally know that she did exist and that I would see her on campus again.

After German, we made our way to English, trying to stay awake through Mr. Slipper's talking. The rest of the morning was uneventful, and I couldn't help scanning campus for Caroline's face.

Teo and I had gotten two seats at the far end of the cafeteria and were halfway done with our pasta when Natasha came to sit at our table.

"First semester?" a female voice asked, and we turned to see a small woman wearing an apron. The three of us nodded yes.

She responded: "The University of Applied Linguistics is celebrating its fortieth anniversary this Friday night. We are looking for volunteers to help with the event and still need some help in the kitchen. If you're available to help, you can sign up with me. You can earn some extra cash." She waved some papers in front of us.

I had no plans for Friday night and thought volunteering would be a good excuse to keep myself sane and busy.

"I'm down," I said, and she handed me a sign-up sheet.

I didn't mind when Teo reached for the papers as well. "Me too," he said.

"I'm busy," was Natasha's way of saying no.

"Thank you for your participation," the woman said and walked away.

The afternoon seemed to last forever. I didn't see Caroline in the hallways, which made me slightly uneasy, and I was happy when I was done for the day.

INEXPLICABLE

I was dreaming.

It was not a usual dream for me—I was trapped and couldn't escape. It was foggy, but I could recognize with effort where I was. The building looked like a huge church or an old school building with huge windows. The light was muffled, and all I could hear were my own steps against the cold marble floor as I paused for a second to allow my eyes to adjust to the darkness. It was very cold, and I had the feeling that with every step I took the floor was turning into slippery ice. My teeth began to chatter, and I could feel goose bumps covering my skin as I slowly went down the long hallway. At the end of it, I made a left into another hallway, where the light flickered above my head.

A dead silence was lingering in the air as I continued walking slowly until I came to a set of large white marble stairs. I went upstairs and came to a long, dark hallway, which had less light and no windows at all on either side. I walked past some open doors and glanced into the rooms. Although there wasn't any light in them either, I could recognize that the building I was in must definitely be a school. I could make out a huge blackboard, tables and chairs in the darkness, though the classrooms were completely empty.

I was about to keep on walking, when all of a sudden I heard a child's hum in the near distance and felt the temperature drop immediately. I slowly turned my head sideways and faced a little girl I had never seen before. Cutely dressed in a late-sixties style, she was holding a red ball in her hands. Her appearance was somehow eerie, and she seemed to be translucent. When she saw me, she stopped humming and looked up at me.

"Who are you?" I heard myself ask.

The little girl didn't answer; she just kept staring at me. I took a step closer to her and knelt down. "Could you tell me where we are?" I asked further.

She continued to stare at me until she suddenly began to hum and play with her ball again. Then, she started to skip away.

"Wait! Where are you going?" I yelled as I followed, trying not to lose her.

She went downstairs, along more icy hallways, and although I was running, I couldn't catch up with her. She kept humming and playing with the ball, leading me through another slippery hallway until we came to the entrance hall. The massive wooden door there was locked from the inside, and I had the feeling that the darkness was going to swallow us. She stopped skipping and humming and turned around to face me.

Speechless, I returned her gaze. She didn't move a muscle. She just kept looking at me with a blank expression. I slowly took two steps closer to her, upon which, she proceeded toward a closed door on the left and ran straight through it.

I followed her and found myself again in a long hallway and spotted her at the end, playing with her ball and waiting for me in front of another door.

I was growing impatient. "Where are you taking me?" I asked.

Her expression was blank, as if all joy had been sucked out of her.

I waved with my hands in front of her face, yelling, "Do you hear me?"

She just raised her eyes from the ball and looked at the door that was behind her and I followed her through it. She skipped through another hallway and started humming again. I listened more carefully to the melody, but couldn't make out any meaning to it. She had led me into a large room full of mirrors and I followed her to the largest one. While she was looking into one of the mirrors, her blank expression changed into a sad, painful one. I felt bad for her. I wanted to comfort her, but suddenly realized that she didn't have a reflection. I froze for a moment, horrified.

When the girl saw my expression she dropped the ball, which fell to the floor without making a sound, began crying and ran out the door.

"Mom, mommy!" she cried in a hurt child's voice while running down the hallway. She was sobbing.

"Wait!" I shouted in vain. She kept running and darted through a door that I hadn't seen before, where, out of breath, I witnessed a horrific event.

A woman was bent over a lifeless body lying on a bed.

"Honey, wake up," the woman said, crying.

I realized that the body belonged to the ghost of the girl whose soul I had been following through the school building. Her body was dead. The woman must have been her heartbroken mother.

I felt my body tremble as I stared at the scene unable to help. Then, out of nowhere, someone entered the room.

The person who entered wore a long white cloak with a hood

covering her face. No one seemed to have noticed the person in the cloak, except me. While the mother was helplessly crying, the person who entered pulled back the hood.

It was Caroline. Here she was in my dreams, again. Her beautiful face was marked by traces of profound worry.

"Sweetheart, it's alright. Come here," Caroline said with a soothing voice to the girl's ghost that was hovering by her dead body. The girl's ghost wiped the tears from her cheeks and grabbed Caroline's hand.

"Caroline, what's going on?" I asked, my voice drowning. Her head turned in my direction and I caught her golden eyes. It looked as if the sun in them had completely set.

"You shouldn't be here, Adam. You better leave right now," she warned, her beautiful face frowning. I didn't understand anything and kept staring at her with an insistent expression.

Her eyes were pleading. "Please," she begged, hugging the ghost of the little girl as she knelt down. "We're going for a walk, okay?" she explained and gently pressed her soft lips against the child's forehead to give her a kiss. And then they started walking away.

"Wait." My words were only a whisper.

What just happened? Why was Caroline there, and what had happened to the little girl? The building started to tremble and I began to run as fast as I could, slipping on the icy floor. The ceiling caved in on me, I hit my head, and the darkness swallowed me.

I woke up sweating and gasped.

My sheets were soaked and my fingers were digging into the mattress. I could hear the beat of my heart and the rush of blood in my ears. I swallowed and wet my dry throat. It took me a good while to realize I had just woken up from a bad nightmare.

Still panting, I took off my pajama top and glanced at the alarm clock. It was five-thirty in the morning; I was so overwhelmed with the nightmare and my experience with Caroline in it that it was impossible to fall asleep again. I decided to take a cold shower.

That was the second time I dreamed of Caroline. There was definitely something triggering those vivid dreams, and I was desperate to find out what it was. The image of the little girl's face was still ever-present in my mind as I tried to figure out if the dream was supposed to have some sort of significant meaning to it.

After my shower, I tiptoed to the kitchen, ate a bowl of cereal and went back to my room to put on some clothes. I was relieved when I remembered that it was Friday.

The university was celebrating its fortieth anniversary, which would bring some relief to the boring routine of my day. I checked the paper. It stated that all volunteers had to be there by 7:00 a.m. at the latest, which would give me a chance to walk instead of taking the bus. I washed the dishes, grabbed my backpack and opened the window, inviting a warm morning breeze into my room. *I really need to get myself together,* I thought, and left the apartment.

The morning walk through Belgrade's streets had done me good, and I got to campus early. Many students were already standing in front of the entrance door, waiting for someone to let us in. I spotted Teo in the middle of the crowd. He was typically talking to a group of people.

One of the event coordinators approached our group, handing out our daily schedules and explaining the time slots and our positions.

"Looks like we won't be working together," Teo noted after having a look at the schedule.

I made my way through the cafeteria to the kitchen, where the short waitress with the apron from the other day was already talking to a small group of volunteers.

"Good morning, folks," she said enthusiastically. "It's a pleasure to work with young people like you. I'd like you to form a line so I can sign you in and pair you up in groups of two."

"You'll be working with me," she said nicely after I told her my name. "I don't have anyone to pair you up with yet. One person didn't show up."

"I'm fine with that," I replied. She smiled at me and led me to the back of the kitchen.

"My apologies for running late," someone said from the door. The voice was very familiar to me, bringing a sensation of warmth with it. In it, I felt every single one of my cells, and it filled my heart with excitement. In fact, it was as if that voice had pinched my soul, in a soothing way though.

I slowly turned my head to the door, wondering if my mind was playing a joke on me. But there she was, standing in the doorway with her firm and intense expression, the sun clearly visible in her eyes. Her lips were again slightly parted, and her hair was touched by the wind. My palms were sweaty, but the dizziness was controllable. I watched her in astonishment as my jaw dropped wide open. My entire life situation needed some serious in-depth examination, I told myself.

The waitress checked the list in her hands. "Come on in, right on time," she said. I was still paralyzed, my feet unwilling to move.

"Don't give each other such looks," she added once she realized that we both were intensely staring at each other.

"I simply cannot understand today's youth," she said. "Come on this way." She waved with the clipboard in the air. I finally managed to move and followed her into the back of the kitchen, with Caroline directly behind me.

The back of the kitchen was bigger than I had imagined and

had several different kinds of kitchenware hanging on the walls. The short waitress led us to a huge sink by the window and told us that we would be peeling potatoes for the first part of the morning.

"I need to go check if the delivery is here," she said, making her way to the back door in a rush. "I'll be right back."

I spoke before the waitress was out of the kitchen and broke the electrifying silence: "Good timing." There was no way I was going to let Caroline go without an explanation this time. I had a hard time containing myself and needed to figure out a way to approach her without sounding insane. I wasn't even sure *what* to ask her.

"Thanks. Actually my alarm didn't go off this morning," she said, slightly out of breath, while gracefully brushing a strand of her honey-golden hair out of her face.

"I didn't know you had signed up," I said in a challenging tone, wondering if there could be any explanation for her knowing that I was going to be there.

Her eyes seemed to smile as she said, "It was actually a last-minute decision." I realized that she wasn't avoiding my eyes as much as she had the other day. For a brief moment, I was wondering if she was going to leave abruptly again, but then her expression softened and her rosy lips curved back and revealed her teeth as she formed a perfect smile.

"This way, please." The waitress's voice broke my trance. She was gesturing at three guys who were carrying wooden boxes into the kitchen and putting them next to the sink.

The waitress looked content. "It's about time. I see the stares are gone," she said, handing each of us a potato. "They won't peel themselves, you know."

"I'll be back to check in on you. Make sure you soak them in water after you peel them," she ordered and darted out of the kitchen.

I was excited to find myself alone in the same room with Caroline and could feel how my chest heaved like an unleashed monster. This time it felt red-hot.

"You're good at it," I complimented her for being several potatoes ahead of me after only a short while. The peeler moved gracefully in her hand, softly and tenderly taking away the first layer of the potato.

"Don't apply too much pressure. Just let the peeler glide softly," she said, advising me and smirking when I dropped my potato into the sink.

"Laughing is not allowed," I said to my defense. Her laugh was contagious and addictive—the sweetest one I had ever heard. For a fraction of a second, I forgot all of my inexplicable experiences of her.

She looked free of worries in that moment, almost like another version of herself. "Laughing is good for the soul," she mused with the same smile on her face and helped herself to another potato. If laughing was indeed good for the soul, then I never wanted to stop laughing. Especially with her.

"Another one of your theories?" I asked, finally grabbing another potato.

She looked up with a confident expression, almost entertained. "Theories and facts."

I had the feeling that I was getting hooked on the way she spoke. I had, for some reason, always been drawn to the intellectual side of people. During another silent pause, I was trying to let go of my thoughts and to just gracefully embrace the moment with her. But the burning desire to mention my thoughts and dreams was making me tense.

"Where are you from?" I asked, breaking the silence. I considered that overly basic question as a very innocent and sanely safe way of approaching any kind of topic.

With a graceful movement, she finished peeling another potato and dropped it into the water while the ends of her loose hair tickled my bare arms. The fire in my chest erupted.

"From far away. I moved here from Spain with my family," she said. "Actually, very recently." She allowed herself to lock her eyes on mine for a quick moment and then focused back on the peeling again.

"Spain is awesome," I said, trying not to sound silly. "A couple of years back I went to Madrid with my mother." She looked up at me briefly. Talking to her for the time being was easier than I had imagined, and it felt like we had known each other forever.

"Did you like it?" she asked, seeming to have no assumptions about where I was trying to lead the conversation.

I dropped my potato again. "I did. It was pretty cold though. It was winter when we went."

Her smile seemed to stupefy me. "Winter gets pretty cold," she noted with another smile on her face.

The following couple of seconds I was clandestinely observing her from the corner of my eye. Every single one of her movements were so graceful that they seemed to follow each other like a flowing waterfall. A strand of hair was dangling in front of her eyes while she was bending over the sink. Her sunny eyes were perfectly placed delicately in the sockets on her face; her lashes followed the blinks of her eyes with pride, and her skin looked so very soft, as if someone had actually woven her in silk. I was mesmerized not only by her looks, but also by the feelings she caused deep inside of me.

"How about you?" she asked, almost catching my stare.

I looked down at my hands quickly. "I was born here, lived in Switzerland and just moved back."

She seemed to understand. "Being new is not always easy." At least we had one thing in common.

"Tell me about it," I said, grabbing another potato. I was weighing out my possibilities of bringing my intentions into words.

I drew a quick breath. "Back to the theories," I said, speaking slowly. She raised her perfect eyebrows at me.

"Do you have any theories on dreams?" I asked, phrasing my question carefully. For a brief moment she wrinkled her smooth forehead, but then relaxed completely.

"There are many theories on them. Most of the time dreams are perceived involuntarily," she explained in her confident way. I was eager to hear more and kept staring at her questioningly.

"They can be caused by many different reasons. Furthermore, there are many different types of dreams," she said. She narrowed her eyes for a fraction of a second, as though trying to find out the reason behind my questioning.

"Different types?" I asked.

"Sleep paralysis. Just to name one," she answered my question, giving me another beautiful look. I felt as though I was talking to a wise person who knew everything about life. Even though I had been asking her silly questions, her intellectual capacity seemed to be limitless.

I was confused. "Never heard about it. But it sounds creepy," I said, putting the next potato in water to soak.

"It can be pretty uncomfortable," she responded. "It is an incident in which a person briefly experiences the failure to react or move. Most of the time it is followed by horrid hallucinations of an intruder to whom the dreamer can't react due to the occurring paralysis."

Her latest theory made my stomach twitch, even though it only had a little similarity with my most recent dream about her.

Now I was being careful. "Any theories on recurring dreams?" I asked, recalling my dream of last night and because I had dreamed of her twice now.

42

She stopped peeling her potato for a second, brushed a strand of hair from her forehead with another graceful movement and looked at me once more. And there it was, the questioning look on her face; I knew she was trying to read me and was hoping she wasn't going to ask me any questions, and I was relieved when she didn't.

"Those are actually much more complicated and can be caused by anxiety that occurs during times of stress or by post-traumatic stress disorder, among other things." She was speaking slowly, as if out of compassion toward everyone who was experiencing those kinds of dreams. "Some of the theories say that recurring dreams represent the person's current state of psychic imbalance," she added with a mixture of concern and apology written on her absurdly beautiful face.

I was nervous, though I wasn't completely sure if I was uneasy about what recurring dreams meant, or what they were saying about the dreamer.

I noticed a minute change in her posture, only visible in the way she held her shoulders. Her arms were still slightly bent in a perfect angle, and it looked like she was applying another peeling technique. The movement of her peeler had accelerated slightly, gliding over the potato from right to left. For a second I thought about telling her about my recent accident, but decided to dig deeper into her own theories.

"And what's *your* theory on them?" I asked, hoping that whatever she was going to tell me would not in any way be related to a person's sanity.

Her expression softened. "Sometimes I do think that they have a meaning. Away from the world, though," she claimed neatly. The movements of her wrist slowed down and she gave me another quick look.

I felt stupid. "How do you mean?" I was convinced that she definitely was a very smart person, way ahead of me.

43

"I think their meaning must simply be found beyond our outer reality and separate from all possible logical thinking. But then you would have to access a whole other level of thinking, which most of the time results in confusion and despair."

I was trying to let her theory sink in. "Like thinking outside of the box?" I asked, trying to keep up with her intelligence.

She nodded, saying, "Exactly."

How was I supposed to approach any of my recent experiences from another mind-set if everything that had happened already went against all my logical thinking? Sometimes I preferred facts and figures over trying to believe in the supernatural.

"One box down," she announced excitedly, putting her latest potato in water to soak and interrupting my racing mind.

I heaved another box onto the sink and tried to make up my mind in silence.

Firstly, I was overwhelmed with the definitions of her theories; secondly, I was convinced that she could dish out a PhD-level essay on any topic I could ever possibly think of; and thirdly, I had one last chance left to confront her with my recent dream.

"You look like someone I dreamed of. Very much like her indeed," I blurted out unthinkingly, waiting for her to burst out laughing. I was expecting a sudden change in her behavior, but she only looked up at me and gave me a warm smile. There was absolutely no trace of surprise or any sort of questioning look on her face. I was almost disappointed.

"I have a theory for that as well," she said with her words leaving her lips in a very exquisite way that almost looked planned to me. I was completely taken by surprise by her answer and could feel that my desperation was visible on my face.

She spoke slowly: "Synchronicity—to give it a name." My mind was completely blown.

"I've never heard about it," I admitted. It really seemed to me that she could have a theory on anything I could possibly ever ask her. I started to feel defeated.

"It's a set of events that's also known as meaningful coincidences," she defined.

"Meaningful coincidences?" I quickly asked, sounding completely surprised. Those two key words got my full attention. "In what way?" I added, my body tensing.

"Let's take your case as an example. Let's say you have a dream at night and the next day whatever you dreamed of, either a person or an object, shows up unexpectedly. Those events may be casually connected, but they also may be connected by meaning," she explained, this time not looking at me at all.

Connected by meaning; isn't that what I had been looking for? Her words had definitely triggered a form of excitement in my body, and I was more than convinced that I had met her before—and was hoping she was finally going to admit it.

That feeling in my chest was coming back, a boiling-up sensation, as I came closer to my confession. "How do I know if the events are connected by meaning?" I asked hastily. I was growing impatient all of a sudden.

Now she looked slightly nervous, as though she hadn't expected that question. "Those details are usually called to your attention by your subconscious mind and in most of the cases end up not having any meaning at all," she responded, speaking slightly faster than usual, as if trying to straighten out what she had just said. Even the movement of her wrist accelerated. She looked as if my last question bothered her and locked her eyes on her hands. She was once again avoiding my eyes.

I summoned up all my courage.

"You know, actually, the first time I dreamed of you was after I got hit by a car," I said, speaking very fast. My heart was racing and throbbed in my ears. I simply couldn't explain what was happening to me and why I was so drawn to her. The aftermath of my confession happened in what seemed to me a flash.

From the corner of my eye I could clearly see how the peeler glided off the potato and, with a very harsh movement, rigorously parted the flesh of her left hand. She winced immediately, throwing the peeler and the potato into the sink and covering the cut with her right hand. She turned her body away from me quickly.

It took a second for me to react. "Take this," I said perplexed, handing her some paper towels. She grabbed them out of my hands with her back to me.

"I'm sorry," she said stuttering, her smooth voice almost a whisper, and left the kitchen in a rush without looking at me. I couldn't move; I wasn't even able to analyze what had happened.

I stared after her, still very shocked by the harm my confession brought about. Not willing to let her escape one more time, I managed to move my feet and run through the kitchen to the cafeteria. But she was gone, of course. I cursed and kicked a chair.

My adrenaline was rushing, my mind was racing, and my body was out of control. Could it be possible that someone you recently met would have such an intense impact on you?

I clasped my hands to my face as if trying to wake myself up from a nightmare. She had cut herself; I had clearly seen that. My confession must have definitely triggered something inside of her; of that I was convinced.

And now she was gone. She had escaped once more, causing even more questions to arise in my mind. My desperation turned into fury, and the fury transformed into hate. Hate toward myself and toward everything that had just happened.

I found myself walking back and forth among the tables and chairs in the empty cafeteria, waiting for her to come back. But I knew she wouldn't return. I hated myself even more for not running after her, for not grabbing onto her arm, for not apologizing, and for simply having failed.

Furious, I picked up the chair I had knocked over only to discover that she had dropped the paper towels under the table. I picked them up unthinkingly and made my way back to the kitchen, where I grabbed my peeler and approached a potato in a very violent way, chopping it into pieces. I was counting from one to ten, and then backwards, naming all the existing colors I could come up with, and trying to remember the last thing I ate. I was doing all of that just to keep my mind safe, to keep my thoughts locked in the back corner of my brain, and to keep myself busy. I was breathing very loud, which seemed to calm me down. I was going to talk to her the next day, I told myself. I had already done too much harm talking about my dreams.

I managed to get through the second box of potatoes by myself and started on the third one, more than convinced that I was running behind. I grabbed the potato Caroline had dropped into the sink and took away the remaining layer of skin with a harsh movement of my peeler.

I'm not sure how the next thought came to me. Quite absentmindedly, I snatched the paper towels out of the trash can.

The revelation felt like fire and rain, burning the insides of my yearning mind, causing a war between everything irrational and its antidote; surprising, unfair and yet very provocative at the same time. The paper towels were clean; there was absolutely no trace of blood. I flipped them around several times in my hands, examining them thoroughly. No matter where I looked, the fact remained the same: There was no blood on them.

My heart exploded and a broiling heat overcame me as I was facing yet another inexplicable situation. My mind could not have played a trick on me; I had undoubtedly seen how she had cut herself. I needed answers, and I very much deserved them.

47

"Not done yet?" the waitress asked, interrupting my thoughts. She was approaching the sink in a rush with a sour expression on her face. I threw the paper towels back into the trash can.

"Almost," I said, trying to sound convincing.

She looked around in the kitchen. "And the girl?"

"She left. Felt sick," I lied. It was the best answer I could come up with.

She looked annoyed. "She should've told me," she said, wrinkling her forehead. "You two should've done more than just these. I'll give you a hand," she said scolding me, and grabbed Caroline's peeler and a potato.

I felt sick and had the feeling that my lungs weren't getting the amount of oxygen I needed. After we had peeled the potatoes, we cooked and mashed them, adding some spices and poured out the creamy paste into glass bowls. I was relieved when she dismissed me from the kitchen and sent me to the second floor to help decorate the hallways. I couldn't help looking for Caroline's face among the students. I was miserable.

I spotted Teo at the end of the hallway where he was hanging up some posters on the wall and approached him. Everything felt so irrelevant. The hallways had been decorated with balloons and garlands in many colors, and it looked as if someone was about to throw a huge party.

"Looks nice," I complimented him.

"Adam, haven't seen you the whole morning," Teo said, taking a step back in order to check if his poster was crooked.

"Been very busy in the kitchen," I said. "Tilt the left side an inch down." I was completely unwilling to mention anything that had happened in the kitchen.

He seemed overly excited. "Me too," he said. "Looks great, don't you think?"

"It does," I said, trying to sound as excited about the whole decoration thing as he was. I was glad when we were called to gather in building C. We were told there wasn't much work left to do until the actual celebration and to make our way to the reception area to collect our cash. I lingered around there for as long as possible, trying to spot Caroline's face. I wasn't surprised that she didn't show up.

"You joining the party?" Teo asked on our way outside.

"I have to run," I lied. Even if I wanted to, I couldn't enjoy the day anymore.

"There's going to be free food."

"I'm okay. I really need to leave," I lied again, this time slightly annoyed with him.

"I'll see you on Monday," he said before making his way to the auditorium for the start of the celebration.

The day was cooler than the one before and I walked very slowly to the bus station. The sound of my steps against the pavement was followed by the sound of the leaves that danced in the wind. I couldn't help throwing a last glance at the campus, hoping that I'd see her before the bus made a left and trees blocked the view.

DOMINIC

It was Saturday evening, and I was crouched on the bed in my room listening to the heavy raindrops that bounced off my windows while May prepared dinner in the kitchen.

It was a gloomy day, and the shades of gray in the sky looked exactly the same as they did the day before, making it hard to tell if the sun had risen or set throughout the entire day. It was remarkable where my experiences from Friday had led me.

I grabbed the dream interpretation book, which I had bought the previous day, out of my backpack. I left it in there for almost an entire day, trying to ignore it out of fear of being judged for buying it. Frankly, the only one who did judge me for getting it was myself.

I sighed and, against my mind's will, opened the little book and began to read the words on the first page. I did believe that dreams could sometimes have a meaning to them, but I had never considered actually looking them up in a book.

I had to admit to myself that it definitely was my desperation that forced me to buy it as I let my eyes wander throughout my room, squeezing in another sigh before figuring out which particular part of my dream to look up. I recalled both dreams about Caroline in my mind, and that led me to pick the first noun. I was looking for the word *face* and flipped to the indicated page.

Face. Seeing someone's face
The face symbolizes the waking life. Any dream involving a face usually refers to your tendency of hiding from a normal life.

I actually had to smirk about that first one. I clearly had absolutely no intention to hide from a normal life. In fact, that was the only thing I was asking for. I wanted my dreams to be explained, to be stopped, and allow me to lead a normal, logical life.

Seeing faces that don't involve a happy expression could mean that you are hiding some type of disapproval or that you possibly hold some sort of shame for a specific situation.

I could surprisingly relate more to the latter interpretation. I was definitely wholeheartedly disapproving of my experiences and actions that involved Caroline. Since I had actually met her, I hadn't behaved like my old self. Her appearance had somehow changed my whole persona. Lastly, and truly, I definitely was ashamed of how silly I had acted in the last couple of days. Furthermore, I still couldn't forgive myself for what had happened in the kitchen the other day.

Beautiful face
A beautiful face represents a restless mind and soul.

51

Caroline's beautiful face indeed had cursed me, if not innocently and unintentionally, with a restless mind and soul. It was
as if a part of my soul, quiet and unknown to me, had been in
some way disturbed by hers, though I was still not sure if she had
disturbed me in a positive or negative way.

Tear-stained face
A tear-stained face means that someone is hiding something from you, which
can also be accompanied by misery and desperation.

As much as I disliked believing in these interpretations, the
previous two had definitely been the most accurate ones. I was,
without equivocation, convinced that she was hiding the truth
about our encounter. Her intellectual capacity was limitless, that
I was sure about. But she definitely was not very good at hiding
the truth. Or something. My revelation had undoubtedly caused
her great harm; she was upset, startled or surprised by what I had
said the other day.

The more I dug into it, the more I was convinced that I had
met her before. It was just a matter of time before she was going
to finally admit it. I simply couldn't see anything bad about our
encounter and the reason for hiding it.

Ice
Ice is derived from water, which is a reflection of our inner emotional state.
In some cases, we might have cut off some emotions, thoughts or informa-
tion, freezing them, so that we don't feel them anymore.

I couldn't decide if I was pleased with that explanation. Was
I approaching the whole situation in a cold way? I knew for a fact
that I wasn't. I was more than desperate to find out the reason behind all the events that were linked to Caroline. But, on the other
hand, I was trying very much to suppress and avoid the sudden

interference of my dreams with logic and reality. These thoughts led to one mysterious, if not fundamental, question—to which I didn't have an answer: Was Caroline in any way trying to avoid reality?

To walk on ice, slip
Walking on ice represents our knowledge of taking a risk, and that we,
most likely, should be careful.

I rolled my eyes at that interpretation. Wasn't slippery ice always supposed to represent some sort of threat? The scenes flashed through my mind, and I remembered Caroline saying that I wasn't supposed to be there. Could she, in any way, be aware of any possible risk or danger I was about to bring upon myself?

A loud thunderclap sent some light vibrations through my windows. I had been so consumed by the book that I hadn't even realized the storm picking up outside. What a perfect setting for a dream interpretation session, I told myself.

School, building
Dreams about schools are generally always linked to a specific learning pro-
cess. The type of school building points out a particular state of conscious-
ness of the dreamer. Happy and colorful settings relate to positive, cheerful
reflections of the dreamer's current life situation. Whereas dark, misty and
gloomy settings relate to life-changing situations, feelings of being misunder-
stood, pain and misery, as well as the perception of being indoctrinated.

I reread that paragraph twice before I allowed my gaze to lose itself in the wet darkness behind the window. If this was true, and I had a very hard time thinking it, then my current life situation definitely wasn't the happiest it had ever been.

What learning process was I going through? And was I really being indoctrinated by something, or someone, trying to make me unthinkingly accept a set of beliefs? And if so, hypothetically, what set of beliefs would that be? The fact that phenomenon existed and the human race could somehow make their dreams into reality? I had hoped that I would have a much brighter, maybe clearer picture of what was going on in my current life, but all these interpretations had just upset me. My life seemed to me like scattered pieces of a big puzzle that didn't fit together.

I decided to put the book away since all the explanations seemed to be linked to my various levels of consciousness, awareness and belief systems. Almost instantly, I grabbed my laptop from my desk. I thought for a moment before doing a Google search for the *"meaning of the name Caroline"* and waited with much curiosity for the results to pop up. The list started with a link to a site with female baby names where I read in pink letters that one of the most famous bearers of the name had been Caroline of Ansbach, who was Queen of Great Britain as the wife of King George II. I returned to Google, scrolled down to another search result and clicked on it. The following site showed the name of Caroline Bingley centered in the upper part of the tab and I paused, as I knew that name from somewhere. I continued reading and before I even knew it, I was somehow entertained. I was first introduced to Caroline Bingley when I read Jane Austen's *Pride and Prejudice*. Austen had described her as attractive and elegant. The personality of Austen's Caroline differed from my Caroline very much, but at the same time it was amusing how I would describe my Caroline's appearance with the same adjectives Austen used for hers. Royal, even.

I opened another tab and landed on a website with the meaning of Latin names and scrolled down until I found hers.

Caroline, origin: Latin
Caroline, meaning: beautiful woman

As I read those words, I imagined Caroline as a mythological Latin heroine, an incredibly tempting, dissolving fairy tale. She was very beautiful, that I had already established for myself, and I suddenly felt the simmering heat turning up in my chest. She had turned into something appealing, almost forbidden, and I found myself trying to solve the riddle behind my feelings for her. She was physically attractive; but at the same time I felt, and knew, that there was more to her than that, something that penetrated far beyond than just the physical. It was as though I was attracted to her on also a nonphysical, inner psychological level. The harder I tried to come up with an explanation for it, the more difficult my attempts became. She was a riddle; something not even my body seemed to understand. Sweaty palms and a racing heart weren't anything I had ever experienced with anyone before. But then I also grew annoyed and hopeless as I remembered I might possibly not have another chance to talk to her. She may have decided to ignore me after the incident in the kitchen.

I would find out, eventually, I promised myself, for this feeling was impossible to ignore. I drew the curtains against the flashes of lightning and the storm, and made my way into the kitchen to join May for some late dinner.

On Monday the rain hadn't eased. On the contrary, it picked up, with hefty winds that blew everyone's umbrellas inside out and upwards and drenched their fall clothes.

It was the second week of October, and I had a very accurate feeling that winter was going to hit Belgrade pretty early that year. I disliked winter more than anything.

Due to a lack of sleep, I found myself among the first to arrive on campus that morning. I unloaded my backpack, stuffing some of my books in my locker, along with my umbrella. To avoid wandering around campus hoping I'd run into Caroline, I made my way downstairs to the library with the aid of my school map, intending to dive deep into a book in order to slow down my racing mind. I told myself that it definitely was time for a good read, though at the same time I was sure that no distraction would be enough to help me forget the past couple of days.

I liked the library; books had always had a soothing effect on me. The curved wooden reception desk was artfully placed in the middle of the library, surrounded by numerous books on the shelves. This ocean of books stretched over two more floors that rose upward, decorated as well, shelf after shelf overloaded with books. Several round tables were spread throughout the library where small table lamps had been placed. Huge mosaic glass windows allowed a muffled light to illuminate each part of the building. The whole place had sort of a medieval feeling to it, which I really liked. What amazed me the most, though, was the silence.

The librarian, a young woman with reddish hair, greeted me politely as I made my way to one of the bookshelves where I allowed my gaze to wander over the shabby and dusty books. I was one of many people who liked the smell of books, but never openly admitted it.

As I grabbed the first book my hands could get a hold of, the annoying voice in the back of my head started to heap more misery on me. I tried to shut it off by holding the book up to my nose. I spotted a table all for myself, took off my wet jacket and settled in there. I hadn't even read the first page when someone cleared their throat behind me.

"Excuse me, are you Adam?"

When I turned around, I saw someone whom I'd never seen before on campus. He spoke with a firm voice. We were of equal height; he had coffee-brown skin, short dark-brown hair and light-brown eyes. Although he appeared lean to me, he still looked pretty sturdy. Or at least he was trying to look that way.

"Yes, I am."

His eyes darted from left to right as though he was making sure no one had followed him.

"Can I talk to you for a second?" he asked suddenly.

I gestured to a free chair across from me. "Sure, go ahead," I said, asking myself what this was all about. I wondered if perhaps volunteers were needed for another event. The guy took a seat and pressed his hands down on the table. He looked nervous.

"Do you know who I am?" he asked.

Realizing then that the conversation wasn't going to be about volunteering at all, I just gave him a blank expression.

"No, but I certainly know that you know who I am," I answered sarcastically.

He didn't smile, but remained serious. From close up he looked somehow familiar to me.

"I am Dominic, Caroline's brother. I think you know who she is," he shot back at me with his serious face.

Hearing her name so unexpectedly, I felt time stop for a fraction of a second. Simultaneously, an incredible amount of pinching warmth shot through my body, rushing down my spine causing a feeling of both relief and tension. I had the sensation, for some unknown reason, that I could sense how my sympathetic nerve fibers produced epinephrine.

"Yes, I know her." A lump started to lodge in my throat.

"Good. Because I want you to know that you made a mistake," he said with his firm voice, not missing a single syllable and narrowing his eyes.

Now I could see his resemblance to Caroline much more clearly. Even though he seemed to be giving me attitude and I felt the urge to lunge forward and hit him in the face, his eyes still seemed full of life. Both Caroline and he seemed to have a rare ability to speak through their gaze.

"A mistake?" I asked, worried he knew about the scene in the kitchen.

Dominic leaned forward in his chair. "You're a threat to her," he warned me, speaking slowly.

He took me by surprise with this. How in the world could I be a threat to Caroline? She had cut herself in the kitchen because of my words, not because of my actions. I never intended to cause any harm to her.

"Secondly, you're harassing her," he added, his eyes darting in all directions.

He wasn't giving me a chance to speak. And he had hit a raw nerve in me. All of a sudden, I was furious.

"Hang on. First of all, it's none of your business whom your sister is talking to," I said, my hands forming into fists. "Second, she can gladly discuss my supposed mistake directly with me— I am not discussing this with her little brother. Third, she knows where she can find me."

"It might not be my business, but your behavioral cusp is bothering her," he responded with another firm expression on his face. I had no clue what he meant by *behavioral cusp*, which annoyed me even more.

With shaky hands, I grabbed my backpack and my jacket. I wasn't going to listen to him any longer. I knew I needed to get away or I would punch him, and I had already caused enough damage to Caroline.

"She said that, not me," he added aggressively.

Irritated as I was, I turned around. "Said what?"

His response came as if shot out of a gun: "That she doesn't want to talk to you again."

Without knowing what to say I just turned around and walked away. I was confused, angry and hurt, all at the same time. Had she really told him to come talk to me? Many questions arose in my mind. Was she really lacking that much courage and couldn't

58

confront me, or had she chosen to ignore me once and for all? I had made a complete mess out of my life, I told myself. A lake of disappointment and desolation overcame me while I made my way to Spanish absentmindedly, elbowing anyone out of my way that came too close.

Dominic had injected his words into my mind very unexpectedly, and I would have a very long, if not painful, time getting them out of my brain.

Teo and two other students caught up with me in the hallway and added greatly to my annoyance.

"Morning," Teo greeted me, trying to catch up with my fast pace.

"Hi," I said tonelessly. I forced a smile onto my face, telling myself that none of what had happened was their fault.

"How was your weekend?" he asked while we made our way to the middle of the classroom and took our seats. My eyes immediately scanned the whole room searching for Caroline.

"It was okay. I spent most of the time watching TV," I lied.

I was glad when Ms. Arrigoberta silenced the class and called for our homework.

Monday had never been my favorite day, even taking into consideration that I was distracted and couldn't pull my mind together. I found myself forgetting some of the simplest Spanish vocabulary I had learned many years ago. I was more than relieved when she dismissed the class early and I was to make my way to French alone.

The classroom was still empty, and I intentionally avoided the seat where I sat next to Caroline, just a couple of days ago. Deep down though, I hoped that she would show up. I was making up stories, telling myself she might have overslept and was about to walk through the door any minute. But that was in vain, of course, and she didn't appear.

Lunch was just another tasteless part of the day. I didn't eat anything, but instead kept my eyes locked on the door of the cafeteria, recalling the first time I had actually met Caroline. The scene felt so vivid, that I almost thought she was actually standing in the doorway.

Tuesday felt the same as Monday, if not even worse. I struggled through the French exam with difficulties, even though I had spent a whole lot of time going over the grammar and vocabulary beforehand. Frankly, I had skipped page five for obvious reasons, which could have been a potential reason for failing the exam.

On Friday I began to doubt whether I would ever see Caroline again. The following week I spotted Dominic three times on campus, though he refrained from talking to me, which confused me even more. I spent most of my breaks in the library, trying to think of a way to straighten things out.

On a cold gray day, I almost made my way to the table in the back of the cafeteria where he sat alone. I wanted to confront him, in a nice way though, and ask him where Caroline was. I wanted to know if she was alright and if there was any chance I could talk to her. I ignored that thought and found myself drowning in more misery. I didn't know what to do.

Two weeks later I summoned up my courage, went to the registrar's office and asked for information about her.

"I am sorry but we are not allowed to give any information about other students for privacy reasons," the short woman explained, leaving me in the dark.

"Please, I'm a good friend of hers," I insisted. "We're working on a paper together that is due by the end of the week and I can't get a hold of her."

"I am sorry," she said, shaking her head. "I have to follow the policy." I left the registrar's office feeling defeated since I thought this was my last chance to reach her. I silently headed to lunch with Teo, who after noticing my sudden mood swings lately, kept himself from starting a conversation with me. I sort of felt bad, but definitely couldn't share my worries with him.

One of the following nights I had another short, if not disturbing, dream about Caroline.

I dreamed that we were together on a field of flowers, holding hands while her light, silky dress danced gracefully in the warm breeze. The flowers tickled my bare feet as we walked across the field, and the sun was playing with the colors of her hair, changing its shades from honey-gold to dark brown, depending on the angle I looked at her. Caroline looked stunning in the dream. She was marvelous. Her skin looked, even smelled, exquisite, and her aphrodisiacal collarbone made me feel passionate.

Followed by the song of birds, we ran past large trees, the leaves of which were a bright juicy green. The humming of bees deepened the feeling of summer.

We didn't speak for quite a while, but rather observed our surroundings with a mutually silent gaze. We kept walking until we reached a meadow by a little lake with a small wooden bridge upon it. The dream would have actually been pleasant if pitch-dark clouds hadn't blown in, completely filling the sky.

The water of the lake turned dark, and small motionless fish popped up on its surface. I immediately pulled Caroline a step backward.

"What's going on?" I asked, suddenly alarmed.

But she kept smiling. "What do you mean?" she asked, clearly not startled by the sudden change in our surroundings.

I tightened my grip around her wrist. "Can't you see the clouds and the dark water?" I questioned.

"Adam, you shouldn't be scared. There is nothing bad here," she tried to reassure me.

"Let's go." I pulled softly on her arm just to be confronted with another dark part of the dream.

It was the sight of our hands, which astounded me. My hand

was colorless, like in a black-and-white movie, while hers was a normal color. Looking down at my body, I realized that I was *completely colorless*. I was growing uneasy and let go of her hand. Everything behind me was colorless too—the birds, the flowers—it looked as if a disease had broken out.

"Caroline, what's going on?" I demanded with a weak voice.

She just slightly shook her head and covered her mouth with one of her hands.

"I'm sorry," she whispered while tears filled her golden eyes.

"Tell me what this means!"

"I said you were a threat to her," a firm voice said behind my back.

The hurtful intent of the voice rang in my ears. I turned around and faced Dominic, and even though he was behind me, he still appeared in color. He began to move toward us while the dark clouds descended from the sky and swallowed me.

I opened my eyes and gasped.

Another nightmare. I kept lying on my bed staring at the ceiling with no strength left to move. I was exhausted and felt as though all my energy had been sucked up by my dreams. I wasn't sure what was more devastating, the fact that she had disappeared or the recurring dreams I kept having. One thing I was absolutely sure about: I had to find a way to stop all of it. I wasn't myself anymore and needed to help myself before I went completely crazy.

The days passed very slowly, and breathing began to hurt. It was a cold November morning when I dragged myself to my locker and found a Post-it with the following message:

She's out of the country.
Don't search in vain.
D.

I needed to read the note three more times before my brain could actually take in the meaning. I could feel the last bit of hope leaving my body as I scrunched up the little note and leaned against my locker.

She was gone.

ICE-COLD

I opened my eyes. Another morning.

From where I was lying on my bed I could see the fog that appeared like a heavy misty cloak of agony lingering in the damp morning air of Belgrade. I moved only with great effort; I had been frustrated ever since I found Dominic's Post-it note.

Going to class didn't make sense anymore since I knew I wouldn't see Caroline. I was disturbed by how much that knowledge hurt and caused me pain; it felt as if someone had unexpectedly taken away a part of me, maybe that one and only specific missing ingredient I desperately needed to survive.

I took a deep breath and exhaled through my mouth, my pain growing with each breath.

At moments I thought it was wrong to feel such a high level of attraction toward someone I barely knew, but at the same time I knew I couldn't control it. She had come into my life abruptly, without any sort of forewarning, and she had also left in almost the same way. I felt wounded, not physically, but internally. My chest felt shallow and cold, as though her departure had pierced it with a cold blade.

I rubbed my chest to ease the pain and forced myself into the shower before having breakfast and heading out.

I spent the 15 minute ride on the bus going over some Spanish vocabulary since exam season was in full swing before Christmas break. I was nervous about break; I needed to be busy and distracted all the time and couldn't allow my thoughts to consume me.

When I got to campus, there were Christmas decorations everywhere. There was a huge Christmas tree in the entrance hall of the library. There, the bookshelves, still my safe haven, had been adorned with simple, but thoughtful, holiday motifs.

"How did it go?" Teo asked after the Spanish exam.

"It wasn't actually that bad," I answered, surprised that I had been able to focus at all.

"Way to go! See you in English."

French was still a hard one, though. I avoided the seat in the middle of the room where I spent time with Caroline and tried to focus on the class, and I intentionally ended up repeating each of Mr. Auberson's words in my mind. For some reason, I was able to shush the voice in the back of my head. And, to my relief, I passed the previous French exam.

"Where are you two going to spend your winter break?" Natasha asked during lunch in the cafeteria. She was always rambling on and joining me and Teo every time she spotted us on campus.

"I'm going to see my family in Mexico," Teo said while having a bite of his burger.

"How about you?" she asked, scowling at me with green pieces of lettuce between her yellow teeth.

"I'm staying here," was all I said. I tried not to let her bother me, but failed when she started fishing the pieces of lettuce out of her mouth with her fingers and proceeded to place them on a napkin next to my plate. Natasha was one of those people who had no filter and was not embarrassed in any way about sharing her private life with anyone.

After lunch, we made our way to text analysis, the sixth class on a Tuesday, my longest day of the week. All the first-semester students had been invited to the auditorium. I couldn't help but allow my eyes to wander, glancing at everyone's face, hoping that I would see Caroline's. I was glad we could stay in the auditorium for the last class, phonetics with Ms. Mori, as well since that prevented me from unconsciously looking for Caroline in the hallways.

Ms. Mori was a young Japanese woman who was, in my opinion, the only teacher who was able to keep us focused throughout the entire class, which contributed greatly to quieting my mind.

All my classes had become much more complicated and complex since the beginning of the term. Exams were held almost every day. We even had a nerve-wracking paper due right after we returned from Christmas break.

On Thursday I said good-bye to Teo, who was flying to Mexico the following morning.

Friday was a very slow day. Some of the classes had been shortened or completely canceled. One of the best things about the university was its international orientation—we often ended up celebrating international holidays, too.

I paid the library another short visit, loading up my backpack with the books I needed for my paper, and then made my way in slow motion to my locker to unload some of the books I wouldn't need during the holiday break.

When I opened my locker, another little Post-it note, which someone must have thrown through the slits, fell to the floor. I froze for a second and held my breath. With sweaty hands and racing heart I picked it up.

Tonight at 11 on the large square.
Take the BG706 seven stations from campus
and then follow the light.
Please come alone; it's very important.
D.

My fingers automatically tightened around the paper and I could feel hope growing inside of me. The note had triggered a sensational spark that shot all the way up my spine, making me stand taller. It was as if someone had snapped me out of a lousy state, grabbed me by the shoulders awakening all of my five senses. There it was, another note from Dominic, but this time I was very much relieved.

After the last couple of miserable weeks, I finally had something to look forward to. Maybe Caroline had asked him to apologize and wanted to straighten things out. But then, my thoughts changed: *What if he was about to tell me that she wasn't coming back at all?* I was too excited about feeling alive again to let that thought overcome me. It was time to figure things out, and I was really looking forward to doing just that.

On the ride back home I was thinking about what I was going to tell May. She had noticed that I had been spending a lot of time on my own lately and hadn't been going out. I didn't want to tell her about Caroline, at least not yet. In the end, it came down to the fact: I had to lie to her.

Once home, I rushed to my room and unloaded my heavy backpack. Adrenaline was rushing through my body, and I felt much more energized than I had been in a long while. I grew impatient when I realized that May had already prepared dinner. I couldn't just leave without any explanation—that would be unfair.

67

That's fine, I told myself, *just a little bit longer.*

"Perfect timing," she said with a smile on her face when I entered the kitchen and helped her set the table. Her hair was tied back with a few uncombed strands pointing in all directions. I knew she had just woken up from a nap not too long ago.

I tried hard to suppress my sudden excitement and said, "I've been hungry all day long."

I ate dinner quickly, spooning the hot soup into my mouth with rapid movements and burning the back of my throat.

"Mom, I'm going out tonight with my friend, Teo," I said, trying to sound as convincing as possible.

She raised her head from her bowl with a surprised expression. "That's nice," she said. "I didn't know you had made plans."

"He's flying home tomorrow, and wanted to meet for drinks before he leaves," I said in a confident way. The soup finished, she served us some paella.

"I'm glad you're getting to spend some time with friends. You've been so busy with classes lately," was her happy response. I could see how she had lightened up, clearly happy for me, and I felt bad for lying. But Caroline had become my own personal mystery, and I took all the responsibility for whatever was required to solve it by myself, alone.

I helped May with the dishes and lingered in my room until, finally, it was 10 p.m. I was off my bed in a second, grabbed a flashlight from our emergency kit in the hallway and ran out the door quickly.

The night was very cold and I tightened my scarf around my neck while waiting impatiently for the bus. The 15 minutes it took to get to campus seemed like a never-ending eternity. My mind was racing as I was thinking very hard about a rational way to talk with Dominic. I wasn't even sure what he was about to confront me with. I would, I had promised myself, be nice and contain myself, because I just couldn't screw up another chance. I needed to know where Caroline was.

When I got off of the bus, it started snowing. Fluffy white crumbs were peacefully falling from the dark sky and, very much to my dislike, were sticking to the streets. I was hopping from foot to foot, waiting for the next bus as I glanced at the Post-it note in my hands that I took with me, mostly for my own sake. It was a piece of proof, a personal trophy that would allow me to see her again. And that nice thought helped to keep me warm.

The wind picked up and I was relieved when I got on the bus, which felt like a much-appreciated shelter from the snow.

Except for two people in the back, the bus was completely empty. Once past campus, we made a sharp left into the darkness. Naked trees with white crowns flashed past the windows as we drove into a part of Belgrade I was sure I hadn't ever been in before. I was wondering if I'd be able to catch a bus back at a decent time before dawn while I was counting the stops on my fingers. I was the only passenger on the bus during the last mile.

Then, finally, the seventh stop.

I got out of the bus in a rush, and the cold bit every uncovered part of my body. I immediately grabbed the flashlight in my backpack and pointed it in all directions. I had been dropped off in a rural-looking area of Belgrade, which was very poorly lit. There was no one else on the streets, and this made me question why Dominic had chosen this part of the city as the place for our reunion.

I spun around in a circle; trying to make out what street I was on, for the signs of the bus stop were worn.

Follow the light, he wrote, I told myself, and blinked a few times until my eyes adjusted to the darkness. It was still snowing, and to my disadvantage, a thin layer of fog was lingering on the streets. I could make out some trees in the near distance and started walking away from the bus stop. *Follow the light,* I kept telling myself, assuming that I was walking through an empty park.

He could have at least given me some more detailed directions, I complained to myself in silence. I wasn't even sure if I was headed the right way. The cold snuck into my body and I couldn't feel my feet anymore. I was about to make a right when, all of a sudden, a light flashed up in the distance, across what seemed to be a meadow.

I paused for a second to figure out if I had imagined it and kept staring into the black distance waiting for some kind of proof. There it was, again. It flashed up very quickly, as if someone was switching on and off a flashlight. *I'm not far away from our spot at all,* I told myself, and sent back the same light signal with my flashlight. My heart was racing, making me forget about the cold.

And then, fearlessly, I started walking across the field toward the light. I fastened my grip around the flashlight, determined to talk to Dominic, and this time I wanted all the answers I could get. I quickened my pace and was almost running across the field. I nearly stumbled a couple of times, but that didn't matter to me, I was running toward the answers that I deserved to receive.

The thick fog swallowed the path I had come from, and I paused for a fraction of a second waiting for another sign from the light. This time it didn't come quite as quickly as previously, and it seemed further away. My heart was pounding louder, causing a drum-like noise in my ears.

I flashed my light back, soaking up the wetness in my eyes from the cold wind with my gloves. After another brief moment, the light flashed again.

This happened again and again, three consecutive times. Whenever it flashed, it seemed further away. It was like Dominic was moving away, heading further east. At one point it appeared very muffled, almost invisible, and I had to stop for another couple of moments until the fog wore off. I kept trying to follow it until finally it looked as if he had stopped moving away. I was out of breath when the light caught my attention again, this time only a couple of feet away within the darkness.

I ran toward it.

"Caroline?" I shouted into the black emptiness and paused.

This was exactly the spot where the light had come from. I was completely sure about it. I walked around the huge fir tree that I had come to face, my eyes darting left and right.

Nothing.

"Dominic?" I tried again.

The only answer I received was the whisper of the wind in my ears. I was growing very impatient and had absolutely no intention of playing hide-and-seek with him.

"Hello, anyone there?"

No answer.

This was the moment I had been waiting for so long, the moment I would finally straighten things out with Caroline, but Dominic seemed to be playing a game with me.

A growing feeling of anger was notable in my voice when I said, "I'm here! Hello?"

Silence.

It slowly came to mind that this might well be his own form of revenge. As my thoughts began to turn negative, I started feeling the cold again. My jeans felt like nothing more but a layer of icy razor-sharp fabric against my skin; my feet, ears and the tip of my nose were numb.

The hope that this meeting had initially given me was slowly but surely fading away. I felt tricked, defeated, confused and angry at the same time. Did they lack the basic respect and courage it took to talk to me? Why were they playing with me? I hadn't caused them any harm. In fact, I had apologized to Caroline right after the incident in the kitchen.

I kept flashing my light back and forth in all directions as I moved between fir trees, finally completely losing my patience and temper.

I kicked the closest trunk and walked back across the field when a cracking noise made me stop.

I immediately turned around, but was even more annoyed when I didn't see anyone. I was sick of this game and wanted to get away from the park, go back home and allow my desperation to overcome me in the safe shelter of the four walls of my bedroom.

I started walking faster when I heard the cracking noise again, this time it was louder and closer. I turned around instantly, holding up the flashlight in front of me with my shaking hand, only for its light to be swallowed by the fog.

The fir trees in the distance were almost invisible; there was no one behind me. I froze for a brief moment, listening to whatever kind of noise my cold ears could perceive. Once again I signaled with my flashlight, hoping that this time I'd get an answer. After no signal was returned, I turned around determined to walk away, when I heard the cracking noise again.

This time I realized, it wasn't coming from behind my back, but rather from under my feet. In slow motion, I tilted my head down to my feet. No further explanation was needed for me to understand what was going on.

In that moment I realized that *I* had caused the cracking noise because I was walking on ice. What I first thought was the white field must be a frozen lake, and Dominic had certainly been playing a game with me all along. A very unfair one, indeed.

This realization gave me a slight panic attack as I started to calculate my chances of running back to the fir trees without the ice cracking open under my weight. They weren't far away, that much I was sure about. I remained motionless for a moment, trying to somehow equally balance my weight on both of my feet.

72

It felt as if time had stopped, and my blood seemed to freeze as I slowly took off my backpack and dropped it in front of me. It gracefully slid a few inches away before coming to a stop. From the corner of my eye it looked like a curled-up dead animal.

I turned back to face the fir trees when a cracking noise reminded me of the seriousness of my situation. I was terrified and threw the flashlight across the ice, hoping it would land directly in front of the fir trees and allow me to make out how far away I was from them. But instead, it landed facing the opposite direction. The movement of my arm caused another audible crack.

Run, I told myself, realizing that I was left with no other choice. I took a few breaths and decided to count to three.

One.

Crack.

Two.

Another crack.

I didn't count to three. With all my remaining might, I threw myself forward trying to run as fast as I could. The cracking of the ice was a faithful companion as I sprinted, but I wasn't fast enough. The ice completely caved in under my weight, and I held my breath.

Darkness.

The water was ice-cold and numbed every single muscle of my body, freezing the blood in my veins as it forced itself in, like an intruder through my eyes, nose, mouth and ears. As I fell into the cold water, I could feel a piece of sharp ice deeply cut into my right cheek. The frigid water gnawed on my fresh wound as I swallowed both water and blood. I had bitten my tongue. Horrified, I tried to swim to the surface, but was hindered by the weight of my wet clothes.

Another shock overcame me as I realized that the surface had frozen back together above me, pronouncing the sentence of a slow death. I desperately started hammering with my fists against the icy wall above me over and over again, but all was in vain. I ran out of oxygen in just a couple of seconds. And somehow, in the midst of everything that was going on, I realized in the next second two things happened at the same time.

Someone, or something, grabbed onto my ankle and pulled me down into the pitch black depths. Terrified, I started kicking my foot to loosen the grip, and in only a fraction of a second, I heard someone shout my name.

It was *the* sweet voice that soothingly touched my soul and warmed my dying heart. She was there; Caroline was on the surface of the ice screaming my name and I couldn't get out to see her before I died. I wanted to swim up, break through the ice, and apologize and confess that I was purely and wholeheartedly drawn to her.

The sound of cracking ice reverberated in the dark water, a sudden wave of effervescence caused a sparkling sensation on my skin, and I lost consciousness.

I never thought I would escape death several times—twice, to be exact. And I was afraid if I started counting them that I might attract another near-death experience. I slowly opened my sticky eyes and blinked a few times. The strong light I encountered triggered a self-defense mode, forcing me to shut them right away. I tried to move, but my head spun.

I exhaled through my mouth.

As I finally opened my eyes again I realized, with much disgust, that I was lying on a hospital bed. While everything was a visual blur, I could hear more than two voices speaking at the same time.

"Adam, love, are you alright?"

May was leaning over the bed and was restlessly touching my cheeks and forehead with her shaky hands. The hysteria in her voice revealed that she was beyond concerned, which only served to make me feel worse for giving her a hard time once more. I had been such a failure.

I tried to say, "I'm fine, don't worry." My throat was sore and itchy from the cold water.

"What happened? I was so frightened when I got the call that you were in the hospital," she said, squeezing my hands.

That was a good question. What exactly had happened, and how much could I tell her about? Even before I opened my dry mouth to make up a lie, someone interrupted me.

"We found him with Teo on the frozen lake. They were ice-skating and didn't see the warning signs. They sure are lucky that we passed by right at the moment when the ice collapsed."

My eyes flew to the door in a blink, which made my head spin even worse, and I had to lean back on the pillow. The voice was soft and was touching my heart in its unique way. It was Caroline, and she was right there. Dominic was standing next to her to my great surprise.

I didn't understand anything. Why were they there? And why had Caroline mentioned Teo?

"Teo…where?" I asked confused, keeping my head on the pillow.

"He helped us pull you out of the water. Nothing happened to him, and he's on the plane back to Mexico," Caroline added, a concerned expression on her silky face.

I rubbed my temples. *A lie,* I told myself, after the exhausting minutes it took me to recall what had actually happened. She was telling May a lie. For whatever reason.

I locked my eyes on Caroline; she was still standing in the door wearing a white knit sweater and tight pants with high-heel boots. She answered my gaze with a soft and lovely look. The feeling in my chest was pure ecstasy.

May was dabbing her teary eyes and hugged me by almost throwing herself completely onto the bed when a familiar face appeared in the door.

"Good morning, Adam."

While Dr. Vidan was walking toward the bed, he took a small flashlight out of his chest pocket. Its light was unpleasantly blinding.

"I think I'm okay," I said and turned my head to see Caroline still standing in the doorway. I was afraid she would disappear at any moment. I couldn't let her go this time; I needed to talk to her at last.

"You owe your friends a lot," he said, checking out my head with his hands.

"Does it hurt?"

I winced. "It's tolerable."

My eyes were still focused on Caroline. The usual brightness in her eyes was almost invisible, and though she didn't appear to be tired at all, I could sense her exhaustion.

"I'll have them X-ray you just to make sure we don't miss anything."

A nurse approached the bed, helped me get into a wheelchair and took me a few floors up.

I had never liked hospitals. The biting institutional odor made me nauseous, and my dizziness grew with each passing overhead lightbulb on our way down the long hallways.

Ignoring the dizziness, I kept turning my head back just to make sure Caroline was still behind me. And indeed, she was—followed by Dominic, whose expression was a mixture of guilt and confusion. She responded to my gaze, but he kept his eyes focused on the floor. He owed me an explanation.

I was relieved when we finally reached the risk-of-infection-looking X-ray room, where the nurse helped me lay down in what seemed to be a tube, after I stumbled a few times on my own. Caroline and Dominic waited outside while the X-rays were taken.

I was glad when the nurse pulled me out of there and helped me back into the wheelchair, even though an orchestra of drums was playing in my ears. While the nurse was pressing some buttons on a machine, my eyes darted to the door where I saw Caroline talking to Dominic. It appeared as though they were arguing about something; she was leaning against the wall while he was talking to her in a low voice, his lips making fast movements and his hands dancing in the air in front of her face.

May snuck into the room to check in on me. Her hair looked messy, and with teary eyes, she gave me a tired smile. "I can't find words to express how grateful I am that these two lovely people helped you."

"They're from the same university, Mom," I said, exhausted from the X-ray procedure.

She looked toward the door.

"They are? This is so kind of them."

"Yeah," was all I managed to say before the nurse started wheeling me out of the room again.

"Am I leaving?" I asked her on our way down the long hallway.

She looked down at me. "You have to talk to the doctor first, though we would prefer it if you stayed over-night."

I didn't like her answer at all; no way was I going to spend another night at that hospital. When we finally got back to my room, Dr. Vidan was waiting for us. The nurse handed him my X-rays, which he then examined patiently. I was feeling worse after the ride through the hospital and felt I could throw up at any moment.

"Your X-rays don't show any damage to your skull or other parts of your body," Dr. Vidan explained. "I will give you something for the headache, but would like to keep you for at least one more night." May nodded in approval. There it was: another night in the hospital. I had already caused May too much worry and pain; so complaining about this now would be very disrespectful.

"We have to make sure your body temperature goes back to normal," he said, speaking more to May than to me.

"I would appreciate it," she said with a relieved expression on her worried face.

May was hovering over me the whole time, clearly not willing to admit that she was about to pass out any moment.

"There is no need to worry, Mom. I'm okay. Please go home and rest. I'll be leaving tomorrow and will be alright, I promise."

It took a good 15 minutes to convince her to go home, and to my great surprise—and confusion—Dominic offered to accompany her, which she finally accepted.

The realization hit me like a wrecking ball causing stirring excitement in my whole body: I was being given another moment alone with Caroline and she didn't appear as though she had any intention of running away.

She drew the partition between me and the other patient with an elegant movement of her arms so we could have some privacy and then took a seat next to me. My chest was filled with a sweet current of hope that made me feel all warm. And there was that thirst again, but this time it felt more intense, more like a feeling of inexplicable longing. I was puzzled, my hands were sweaty, and I didn't have a clue about what to say.

"Hi," she said with her beautiful soft voice breaking the silence.

I cleared my dry throat.

"Hi." I rested my eyes on hers. She wasn't avoiding my gaze at all; in fact, she looked more comfortable being in the same room with me than ever before. I couldn't afford to lose any more time.

I sat up.

"Can I ask you some questions?" I pressed politely, unwilling to sound rude at all. Even if I wanted to yell at her, grab her by her shoulders and shake her, I couldn't. She had a subtle ability of easing all my anger and physical pain.

"Yes, go ahead," she said, nodding and alluringly brushed a wavy strand of hair from her forehead. Her eyes were warm, and I had the feeling that she had prepared herself for my questions.

I spoke very slowly: "Where have you been all this time?"

She moved in her seat, giving a slight sign of being uncomfortable. "At home," she whispered.

"For almost two months?" I asked in desperation.

"I had some family issues," she responded, giving me an apologetic look.

She was being unfair. "Such as?" I shot back at her, only to realize how rude that question was. She blinked a few times, a layer of glistening tears filling her eyes.

"Believe me, I wish I could tell you."

"This is much more complicated than I would have ever thought," she added, breaking her gaze while tugging softly on the sleeve of her sweater.

"It doesn't matter to me how complicated it is," I said. "I believe that I deserve an explanation." I didn't want her to cry, but I couldn't help asking for more.

"You ditch class and don't talk to me. All I know is there is something happening to me, something...," my eyes flew to the ceiling as I was looking for the appropriate word, "...something *otherworldly*. And it started from the moment I met you."

She remained quiet for a moment, her head tilted down to her lap. I could see how a single tear escaped her eyes and smoothly ran down her silky cheek, a drop of silence.

She was off the chair within a blink, saying, "Try to sleep. We'll talk tomorrow."

I sat up, ready to grab her hand.

"I promise," she assured me with a blissful expression on her perfect face.

Somehow, strangely, deep inside, I knew that she would keep her promise. It was as though she had put me in an obedient state with her words.

"I will see you tomorrow," she whispered, moving to open the partition.

Knowing that she was about to leave, I couldn't help asking one last question.

"We've definitely met before," I said, more as a fact than a question. She paused for a second, her hands resting on the curtain. Then, she slowly turned around to face me. The proof I had been waiting for was clearly painted on her marvelous face.

My soul was at rest and free. I interpreted her look and silence as my long-awaited confirmation.

THE SECRET

I couldn't remember when I last slept as well as I did that night. I rubbed the sleep out of my eyes and glanced out the window. It was snowing. To my surprise, seeing the white flakes didn't bother me; in fact, they seemed like a peaceful aftermath.

Breathing wasn't painful anymore, and I was very much looking forward to the day ahead. Caroline had promised that she would talk to me, and I was more than ready to hear whatever she had to say.

"Good morning," a hovering nurse said as she looked at the clipboard on the foot of my bed.

"Headache?" she asked, her eyes scanning the paper.

I shook my head no.

"That's good. Dr. Vidan wants to see you before you leave. He'll be here in a few minutes."

She took my temperature. "Back to normal."

I was surprised by my quick recovery, that I felt fine and energized.

Someone opened the partition.

"Morning."

Caroline had pulled her hair back into a ponytail, its ends dancing on her shoulders, and wore a white winter coat. She looked as though she was made out of snow; pure, smooth and absurdly beautiful.

"Hi," I responded immediately, surprised by her sudden appearance.

"You look a whole lot better than yesterday," she mused and sat down next to me. The craving feeling in my chest was back.

"Thank you. I do feel much better," I said, trying not to sound too nervous. She had come back for some reason, maybe because she cared. I had no idea why. In the end, she kept her promise and that was all that mattered to me.

"Are you allowed to leave yet?" she asked, her eyes locked on mine.

"I think so, though I have to talk to the doctor first."

I was ready to jump out of bed and talk to her—I had waited so long for this precious moment. She smiled a warm smile, her soft lips curving back in a delicate way.

Dr. Vidan appeared in the door. "I have been told that you are feeling better today," he said, grabbing my chart.

I sat up in my bed as if to show him how *good* I felt.

"I do."

"No headache, no fever, no pain. That sounds good," he said this more to himself than to me.

"Let's have a last check. Follow my finger."

I did as I was told; trying not to look at Caroline, as I didn't want him to think the accident had given me a lazy eye. From the corner of my eye, I was almost sure that her face looked amused, as though she was smiling behind a strand of hair.

"Seems to me like everything is fine. I'll give you some mild painkillers in case the headache comes back."

I was embarrassed to expose myself in the hospital gown they made me wear and encouraged Caroline to wait outside. I was glad to discover some fresh clothes that May must have brought with her the previous day.

I found Caroline outside the door. "Can we leave now?" I asked. "I think I'm getting sick."

"I'd like to introduce you to my father," she said serenely.

She caught me off guard with this announcement and I paused in the hallway.

"To whom?"

"My father. He works here in the maternity ward," she said with a soft smile on her lips. "He's an obstetrician." Her face had a pleased expression. I was impressed; she had been raised by a doctor, no wonder she was so smart.

Even though I was nervous and couldn't quite figure out why she would want me to meet her father, I somehow still wanted to greet him. I wanted to know every single detail about her. Once we reached the fifth floor, she walked me to the reception desk.

"Good morning," she said to the receptionist, who raised her head from the screen and smiled a tired smile. "We are looking for Dr. Spes."

"I think he just started his break," the receptionist said. "Just go that way." She gestured to the right. As we were walking down the hallway she directed us to, a sliding door opened at the end of it and a man walked out.

"Dad, good morning," Caroline said and hugged him.

The appearance of her father surprised me completely. He was a really young-looking man with dark-brown hair, which was combed to the right, with exactly the same skin as hers. Only his eyes were different; they were a darker brown.

"Caroline, what a surprise," he spoke in a firm rhythmic voice. I could instantly make out Dominic's resemblance to his father.

"This is Adam," Caroline said, introducing us and making gestures with her hands.

"Nice to meet you, Dr. Spes."

His handshake was firm, somehow dominant.

"The pleasure is mine. Are you feeling any better?"

"I am, thank you. I owe a lot to Caroline and Dominic."

I was debating whether I should tell him the incident had been Dominic's fault. I shook that thought off though; it sounded immature and childish to confront a father for his son's actions. I would wait. There was still plenty of time to confront Dominic directly.

"Are you busy?" Caroline asked.

He smiled and said, "The breath of life always greets a newborn day." I could tell he was one of those people who draws you into his being by the way he speaks.

"Well then, we don't want to impose. We were passing by and I thought we'd say hi."

Caroline hugged her father good-bye.

We shook hands, and I said, "It was nice meeting you."

"Likewise. Take care you two," Dr. Spes said, and just before he disappeared behind the same sliding door, I could almost make out the way he gave Caroline a slight nod of his head.

My mind was blown. Why was it that everything linked to her was so appealing? Almost in a provocative way, I longed to know all possible existing details about her.

"He's nice," I said on our way to the elevator.

"Thanks," was her quick response. "Hope you didn't mind that I introduced you to him."

I shook my head. "Not at all," I said, pleased, but still confused by her sudden proposal.

Her beautiful face was serious again. "I'm going to take you home," she suggested once we were outside and walking toward the bus stop.

My stomach clenched. I looked at her in protest.

"Caroline, no. I thought you were going to talk to me." I couldn't let her get away this time.

"But you have to take it easy now and get some more sleep. Your mother is probably waiting for you."

She waited for me to get on the bus first.

"Not before I've talked to you," I said, speaking fast. "You owe me a lot of explaining. You promised," I added desperately.

This time I was actually tugging on her sleeve. May didn't have to know I had already left the hospital. The bus was already in the center of Belgrade, and I was growing impatient.

"Would you mind if we went somewhere quiet to sit instead?" I suggested while she remained quiet. Her eyes were zipping from right to left as she took in the moving landscape.

At last she looked at me. "Only because I promised," she said with a concerned look on her face.

I was relieved and still had hope—at least for the time being.

"Thank you," I said, trying to convey how much I appreciated her cooperation.

We got off at *Knez Mihailova* and made our way to a small café. The warm air inside was welcoming, and we headed upstairs to a private corner by the windows. I ordered a hot chocolate for each of us. She was seated directly across from me. I could somehow perceive that she was uncomfortable all of a sudden.

"Thanks again," I said. "Really."

The waiter placed two cups of hot chocolate on the small table in front of us, and keeping her head down, she grabbed hers right away.

After a quiet moment, she allowed her eyes to wander somewhere in the distance for a quick second and then locked them back on mine. Her hair was still perfectly tied back. Her forehead still had that silky touch to it, and her golden eyes were piercing in a mesmerizing way. I felt as if she was trying to make me see the situation through different eyes. Hers.

She was tense, but my gaze was insistent.

"It's okay," she began. "You are right; you deserve an explanation." I nodded, encouraging her to continue.

"It's just…complicated," she said, her eyes lowering down to her cup.

I tried to be gentle.

"How complicated can it be, Caroline?"

She looked up at me. "Very. I just don't want you to be freaked out or *afraid*," she spoke slowly. I was absorbing her being through her beautiful eyes. From close up she looked like an immaculate illusion.

"I will not be afraid of you," I said. "Ever." I slowly moved my hand away from my cup and rested my fingers on the back of hers. They felt silky and warm—gentle, to be exact. The electrifying current in my chest returned. She didn't move her hand away.

She sighed. "Some emotionally fueled experiences can cause an excessive cortisol release that can damage the human brain," she said with a serious expression.

It was most likely the doctor's daughter in her who said that, but I didn't understand a word and stared at her blankly.

"You won't cause me any harm," I responded. "That much I know."

I couldn't let this moment slip by. I had come this close—farther than I ever imagined—and letting her go without an explanation would mean the complete annihilation of my existence to me.

"What if *I'm* the one who is afraid?" she asked, breaking the silence. I perceived a slight twitch of her hand, and her golden eyes narrowed for a brief moment.

I leaned over the table closer to her. "Don't be," I said. I realized how my fingers automatically intertwined with hers, as if to let her know that she was safe.

But she looked like she felt confronted.

"What if I can't help it?"

Though her forehead was smooth, she still wore a frown on her face.

"Then let me speak and you won't have to be afraid," I suggested.

She remained in silence for another brief moment, not even breaking eye contact when she slowly blinked. The sunlight was touching her silky face in a captivating way, and it occurred to me, once more, how perfect she was.

She nodded yes.

I drew a deep breath. My time had come, and with it, my hope was reborn.

"I never thought that I would ever be attracted so innocently to someone I had just recently met. Someone so beautiful and noble in their way of being. And I never imagined it would happen in this way. I remember exactly the day last summer when I was looking for the campus and got hit by a car. I can still feel the impact. What I'm saying is, I never imagined or thought it possible that I could actually meet someone—you—while I was unconscious. I still remember your kiss."

I paused to look at her.

Her face shifted. "That was the first time you ever saw me?" she asked surprised and narrowed her eyes.

"The first time," I replied and had a sip of chocolate.

"Not even if I was crazy would I have imagined that I would see you again at the same university," I paused again and looked for half a second through the huge window. It was snowing.

I spoke slowly recalling each scene in my mind.

"I was really surprised and disturbed when I entered the same restroom just a minute after you only to realize you weren't there. That was the first time you disappeared. Coincidence?"

She remained in complete silence, an apologetic look forming on her face.

"What really surprised me was that you showed up at the registrar's office exactly at the moment when I was filling out my forms. Coincidence? I don't think so, Caroline. And I don't think that it was nice when you disappeared, again, shortly after our encounter there."

She just kept listening patiently to me. I couldn't help talking, for the cry of my heart needed to be heard.

"I sort of could handle all those things better than the dream. When I woke up from it, I was panting. Even today I can't find an explanation for why I dreamed of a dead girl who was humming, playing with a ball and running through an empty, cold school building. I was more than puzzled when I realized that she was dead, that I had actually been following her ghost. And then; you appeared. I still remember exactly how you kissed her forehead and told her that everything would be alright. Before you left that dream, you told me that I wasn't supposed to be there. Coincidence?"

Her apologetic look had deepened, and I could make out a glistening crystalline layer in her eyes. She nodded gently, encouraging me to keep talking.

"I have still not found a way to forgive myself for what happened in the kitchen," I said cautiously. I could feel her soft hand wince at the mention of that incident.

"I am, I know for sure, not crazy. I clearly saw you cut yourself. I don't know if you can explain how someone can be cut and not bleed. Or is this just another coincidence?"

Once again I finished with the same question. The snow had

picked up. She looked out the window and in silence contemplated the people passing by. Her hand was warm and I freely allowed my fingers to loose themselves in her silky touch.

"Then, your long, painful disappearance, which still hurts."

I stopped to swallow the lump in my throat that prevented me from talking.

"You just disappeared without any warning. What hurt more was Dominic's Post-it note, telling me that you were out of the country. That was the most pain anyone has ever caused me."

She blinked some tears away, her eyes revealing how sorry she was.

"And then that dream. We were on a beautiful meadow on a sunny summer day. It was actually a very pleasant dream until I discovered that my body had no color. Everything was dead, and Dominic showed up all of a sudden. What's your theory on that dream? Coincidence, that I dreamed of you again?"

My heart was racing and the blood was rushing in my ears.

Her eyes focused on the winter sky outside.

"And then, months after that dream, my recent accident on the frozen lake. I have to admit that I was really surprised, confused, but very relieved when you and Dominic found me struggling for my life under the frozen surface. I had given up all my hope of ever seeing you again and had already accepted my death. But then, you two found me."

"Coincidence?" I asked for the zillionth time.

From the corner of my eye I could see how she was slowly, almost invisibly, shaking her head.

"And what about my scar? Is it coincidence that my scars disappear when you show up?"

A tear escaped her golden eyes.

"What about Teo? How could you have known about the lie I told my mother? Another coincidence?"

I was shaking.

Another tear rolled down her plush cheek and I squeezed her hand.

"You disappear when I want to talk to you," I pleadingly said. "You don't bleed, and you heal wounds. How is this possible?" I was breathing fast, the desperation in my voice noticeable.

"There has been something so irresistible about you from the moment I met you. Why am I so attracted to you, why do I dream of you? Why does my heart feel as though it's about to explode every time I think of you?"

My lips were vibrating and I could feel my pulse racing in my temples.

She took a sip of her hot chocolate and sighed.

"You won't let it go, will you?" she asked, hoping that I might somehow change my mind.

"Please," I begged.

She slowly put her cup aside and, with an elegant movement, held both of my hands in hers. Her gentle touch was firm, safe and comforting.

"You asked me a lot of questions which I will answer. But before I can tell you anything, I have to ask you some fundamental questions," she said, looking deep into my eyes.

I nodded. My heart was racing.

"I am asking you right now, Adam. What would you do if you fell in love with someone who wasn't human? At least not entirely. And what would you do if that person was an angel? Your own guardian angel. How far would you go to save a love that is so heavenly that it's almost unattainable?"

Time stood still as she spoke.

I could feel the way my whole body began to tremble. It was as if something had started crawling through my veins, shooting up my spine directly into my heart. My breathing increased, my heart rate accelerated, and my blood pressure rose. I was panting as I devoured every single one of her words. I could feel my heart beating in my throat as my hands began to sweat, my very being startled by her confession. Her questions had provoked a burning sensation in my body, making all of my senses—sight, hearing, taste, smell and touch—long for her addictively.

If her words were poison, I prayed for her to be as venomous as possible. Caroline had opened the door to her soul and unveiled her mystery. And deep down I knew I was face to face with my own guardian angel.

Without hesitation, I leaned forward and kissed her. The instant my cold lips touched hers another electrifying spark ignited a broiling heat, and the monster in my chest growled.

I felt with excitement how her tongue burst into my mouth as I inhaled her scent; a cocktail of lust and yearning that boiled in my blood. Her lips were warm and silky soft, just like I had imagined, and their taste reminded me of the smell of fresh wildflowers during a smooth summer rain. My hands pulled her passionately to me, as if trying to crush her into my body.

If time could stand still, this was the perfect moment for it to happen. I didn't want our kiss to end. I wanted it to last for a lifetime.

She gently pulled away, panting, as she rested her forehead on mine, her eyes closed.

"You're not afraid?" she asked.

"Be not afraid of words spoken by an angel," I said, breathing in her scent.

Her confession and our kiss made me realize the reason for all of the feelings I had been having since our first meeting: I was absolutely in love with her.

We remained in complete silence with our eyes closed as we listened to each other's breathing. Our hands were still locked together when another one of her warm tears rolled down her cheek. I felt I had finally found a space of peace in this weary world, and I slowly opened my eyes when my breathing eventually slowed down.

"That's how Adam partook of the forbidden fruit," Caroline said.

She looked relieved, a euphoric smile on her lips. I could feel how she had relaxed, as if she had given up a heavy burden.

If she indeed was a forbidden pleasure, then I was ready to sin freely. I felt exhausted, in an intimate way. It was as though we had been entangled in each other for a very long time, and her revelation now felt like the crowning climax.

Her voice was serious as she said, "This will cause a lot of trouble."

"This is worth all possible trouble," I said, ignoring the worry on her face.

We both slowly leaned back in our chairs, our hands slowly unlocking; we knew we were safe together. Our surroundings started trickling back in, reminding us where we were. It had stopped snowing, and another group of people were sitting next to our table now. I felt wide-awake.

After another quiet moment of contemplation, she stood up and put her coat on.

"Come on, we have to go. It's time."

I protested instantly. "I'm not going home," I said, almost hysterical about her abrupt decision.

"I'm not taking you home," she replied and kept watching me with her glistening eyes.

I was confused.

"Time for what then?"

"Time to know the entire secret. I'm going to introduce you to my family. I can't let you go yet, not before I make sure that nothing wrong will happen."

Her words and the hint of concern in her beautiful voice took me completely by surprise. And then, the nervousness started sneaking up upon me. Were there even more revelations to come?

"Ready?"

Without knowing what to say, I threw on my coat and we headed out onto the snowy streets.

THE WORLD BEHIND

That was the day when everything changed in my life, and it changed because I accepted Caroline's incomprehensible confession that she was an angel, my own guardian angel. I had never thought life would confront me with such a remarkable situation, for I had always been a firm believer in facts and theories and her confession still seemed unreal. But it was the most reasonable explanation, since it most certainly accounted for all the previous happenings. And with it, it was as though she had soothed my mind and brought light back into my life. And remarkably, everything about her made sense to me now.

The streets of Belgrade were crowded with tourists who were popping up from shop to shop. Caroline waved down a cab with a tender movement of her hand, and we sat behind the driver, waiting patiently for the streetlight to turn green. He drove past the National Theatre and continued driving toward the eastern end of the city, to another quiet and rural-looking area I hadn't been to before.

The ride was quiet. Caroline seemed to be thinking about something very hard—I could see it in her face. After what seemed to be only 10 minutes, the driver pulled over to let us out and we found ourselves on a quiet lane with family houses and trees on each side.

"Everyone at home?" I asked nervously, breaking the silence as we walked past the first couple of houses. Everything seemed to be happening very fast and unexpectedly, as though someone were fast-forwarding time. Only yesterday I thought I was never going to see Caroline again, and here I was being taken to her home to meet her family. It was hard to believe.

"Mom and Dominic should be home," she said as we stopped in front of a huge house with massive windows, which appeared to be the largest one in the neighborhood. "I believe my father is still at work."

Caroline opened a small gate that led to the well-cared-for front garden. Statues greeted us from under two trees on the right. As we made our way to the front stairs, the freshly fallen snow felt crisp under my feet.

As we approached the front door, I grew very anxious. I wasn't sure if I was psychologically ready to meet the rest of her family. What if they disapproved of me? No matter what world I was going to find behind those walls, there was no way back.

Caroline gave me a pleasant look and opened the door.

The first thing I noticed was music. It was soothingly re-verberating from the back part of the house with a soft mix of different instruments, almost like a lullaby. A peaceful harmonic presence lingered in the house and was very much inviting.

"Mom's meditating," she said and closed the door behind us. She placed her keys on the shelf by the door and hung our coats on the rack.

I tensely asked, "You think it's a good idea to interrupt her?"

"We'll let her finish."

The entry hall featured a little fountain with small statues of angels, and the flowing water matched the harmony of the house and the music.

The melody was coming from behind a white sliding door, and I was impressed, because it felt as though the house was breathing flowing energy.

"Let's go upstairs," Caroline said, leading me to the glass staircase.

A pure crystal chandelier gave the whole entrance area a peaceful, if not luxurious, feeling, and I imagined that when it was touched by rays of sunlight, it would shine little particles of light throughout the room. Paintings had been neatly hung on the wall, many of them featuring landscapes, waterfalls and scenes of untouched nature.

Caroline saw my reaction.

"These are my parents' paintings—they made them together."

"They're beautiful."

I hadn't yet met her whole family, but it seemed to me that they had absorbed all the intelligence of the world.

"They use brushes. But Mom likes to use her fingers too. She says that way she feels more connected to the painting itself."

"I like them."

I had a closer look at one of them, imagining her mother's elegant fingers bringing color to the white paper.

"My parents are all about art," she continued as we reached the end of the stairs where we found ourselves facing a big window. The walls on this floor had been painted a light blue, and a hallway led slightly to the right.

The door at the end of the hallway was cracked, and the sun's rays were once again playing a warm game of lights in the opening. Caroline gently pushed the door, inviting me inside.

The room was huge, its walls shooting up to an immensely high ceiling.

"Welcome to my room."

A round bed had been placed in the middle of her room, surrounded by transparent silky curtains that hung from the ceiling. Her walls were covered with self-painted illustrations, and a walk-in closet formed part of the upper-left corner of the room. The right corner consisted of a shelf with an elegant mirror, under which combs and hair clips were neatly scattered. Her balcony door had been left open, inviting a cold breeze into the room that played gently with the soft curtains. It felt like being on a cloud.

She politely encouraged me to sit on the bed with a swift gesture of her hand.

"Can I offer you something to drink?"

I hadn't realized that she had loosened her hair. It looked perfect in the light breeze.

"I'm fine, thanks," I said nervously.

She sat next to me on the bed and pulled her hand through her hair. "There's no need to fear my family," she said in response to my puzzled expression. "I want you to know that."

"I will try," was all I said. She squeezed my hand and looked me in the eyes. And then, she gave me the simplest of pleasures: her smile.

"Come on, Mom's done," she said, leading me down the stairs before I could draw another breath.

"Mom?" she called, and the white sliding door opened with a quick jolt.

"Hi, dear."

Caroline's mother greeted her with a kiss on the forehead.

Not to my surprise, she was a very good-looking woman,

with dark-blond, long hair that reached to the middle of her back. Both her hair and eyes seemed to be glistening, as if they were radiating waves of light. Her skin color was a little lighter than Caroline's, and she had wonderful features, including perfect white teeth. Tight yoga pants revealed her long legs and convinced me she could easily pass as a perfectly skilled ballerina. She was so beautiful that she almost looked fragile. But there was one thing I was absolutely sure about: Every part of her being matched the perfect world of their home.

"Hello, Adam," she said, hugging me. "Nice to meet you. I was expecting your visit." The hug was unexpected. Her light warm arms bathed me in her warmth.

"Nice to meet you too, Mrs. Spes," I said, clearing my throat.

"Please, call me Elena."

She had a maternal quality I immediately liked.

"I'm going to get you two something to drink."

Elena disappeared into the room to the right of the entry door, and Caroline led me through the sliding door into the living room.

A huge glass table had been placed in the middle. Ceiling-to-floor windows were adorned with gold and silver curtains that matched a fluffy couch facing a big flat-screen TV on the wall. A fire was peacefully crackling in the fireplace, deepening the feeling of warmth throughout their home.

"Your place looks very…warm," I said.

Caroline smiled.

And then, my eyes caught sight of the most beautiful thing I had ever seen before: an altar table next to the balcony. Caroline saw that I was staring at it with my mouth wide open and encouraged me to take a step closer.

"I'm sorry," Elena said, standing in the doorway with a tray for afternoon tea. "I didn't want to interrupt." She smiled, placed the tray on the glass table, and floated out of the living room.

We turned back to the altar.

The altar wasn't the main attraction that had triggered my excitement. It was actually the four, long sturdy candles on it. The candles were white and almost transparent. Examining them, I had the feeling as if someone had actually lit a flame inside the wax so that the whole candle was shining in a mixture of gold light. A little golden flame was sitting with pride at the top of each candle, moving slightly in a tranquilizing way.

"They're beautiful," I said without taking my eyes away from them.

"Each one of them represents a member of our family," Caroline began explaining in her musical voice.

"The smallest of them stands for Lerato, my father," she said, pointing to the smallest candle.

"The engravings on the candles stand for our souls. In other words, they represent the meaning of our names and are the mirror of our heart."

I leaned closer to better examine the engraving on Lerato's candle.

It was so thin, as if someone had created it with a needle. No human hands could have made such a rare piece of wonderment. I could make out a man with wings holding a flute in his hands. His chest was bare, his hair curled down to his shoulders, and a smile decorated his face.

"*Song of my soul*—the meaning of Lerato's name," Caroline whispered with a smile. I instantly linked Lerato's musical voice to the meaning of his name.

I was in awe. This house alone was proof enough to me that living wonders existed.

The engraving on the next candle showed a winged woman. Her breasts were covered by her loose hair, and she was holding a burning candle in her right hand and a shining sun in her left. I didn't miss the warm smile on her face.

99

"*Light*—the meaning of Elena's name," Caroline said, and I saw Elena's beautiful golden eyes and glistening hair in my mind.

All of Caroline's fear about revealing her world to me seemed to be gone, and she presented the candles with much pleasure.

The next two candles were of equal height. I leaned forward to examine the engraving of the third one. It revealed a young man with a bare chest and two wings reaching out of his back. His lips were smiling and he was reaching up to a hand that was descending from the sky.

"*Belonging to God*—Dominic's name." His candle was quite beautiful as well, though it certainly would take me some time to find the link between the meaning of his name and his persona.

I already knew that the last candle was hers. My eyes flew to it with full attention and much excitement. Even the flame was holding a special unique spark.

The engraving showed a girl who was sitting on a stone at the shore of a sandy beach. Her hair covered most of her breasts, and the smooth breaking waves of the ocean touched her legs. Small fish were swimming around her feet. She was smiling, and her wings were spread wide, reaching far above her head and out to the horizon. I found this image the most appealing one. Caroline didn't need to explain the meaning of her name, for I had known and felt it from the moment I first met her.

"I like yours the best."

She blushed slightly, which made her cheeks look like cotton candy.

"We never blow them out. They don't only reflect our heart, but they also show how much time we have left."

I didn't understand and asked, "Time for what?"

"Time on Earth. Whenever an angel is born, a candle is being lit which will represent the meaning of their name and the warmth of their heart. The candle burns from the first breath of

100

the angel and goes out when they leave the world. Their height stands for the time we have left on Earth."

I was startled by how calmly she answered my question. She knew, I assumed, when she was going to die and wasn't anxious at all.

"How much time do you have left?" I asked tensely.

Her eyes gleamed.

"Plenty. Lerato's and Elena's candles have been burning for a little more than 40 years. You can hardly see the difference between Dominic's and mine. His has been burning for 20 years and mine for 21."

Hearing this, my worries ceased.

I was mesmerized by her explanations and truly believed I had entered a place where both heaven and earth existed at the same time. I was unable to move and found myself staring at the candles in astonishment.

"I want you to tell me more about yourself. About angels. How can it be possible for you to live among humans?"

She looked at me warmly and walked to the table where she handed me a cup of tea that I grabbed with skittish hands. I was nervous, and my brain was having a hard time dealing with Caroline's confessions about her world.

When she spoke, her voice was soft, as though she was being careful about how to best answer my question. "At the age of 21, each angel is assigned a protégé and is in charge of saving that human being's life. Every single day. No matter when, no matter how. The angel guides you through your life and shows you the path of light you're supposed to follow. Your angel is always ready to save you from death."

"Does everyone have a guardian angel?" I asked. I felt a tingling sensation in my body.

"Yes. Every single human being on this planet has a guardian angel. The only difference between other human beings and you is that they don't know who their guardian angel is," she answered while having a sip of tea.

My eyes flew to the altar where they lost their focus for a brief moment.

"What happens if an angel fails?" I couldn't help asking.

The answer came slowly, almost in a very elegant way. "The angel receives a punishment then," she said.

"A punishment?"

She nodded yes.

"I can't believe you have rules."

"No world could exist without rules," she reminded me and had another sip of tea.

I was tense as I asked, "But what exactly happens with an angel who fails to save the protégé's life?" I could feel my heart beating fast as my excitement grew with each of her answers.

"Those angels have to leave this world and go back to where they came from. Their candle is blown out, and they disappear without a trace. They have to begin everything again, and their souls leave their bodies to be reborn as children. That's the way it works."

"Why do they have to be reborn again?" I asked immediately, intrigued.

"Because of the rules. Angels are here to protect human beings. To save their lives, no matter how many times it's required. This is their only mission in life. And if an angel fails, that angel has to be reborn as a child again so that the world can forget them. The angel's soul leaves the body in order to be reborn in another form, another human body. But the angel's body dies."

I was frightened by her explanation.

"It's like a wheel. If your protégé dies, you have to die too."

My stomach twitched. I didn't like those rules. They seemed unreal, almost forced upon her perfect world. I couldn't help asking myself what would have happened if she had failed to save me the other day. Her potential death was a very unpleasant thought, as hurtful as death itself as far as I was concerned.

"That's unfair," I complained.

"It is not usual that the protégé dies before the guardian angel. The guardian angel always dies after the protégé."

We remained in silence for another brief instant while I rested my eyes on the fallen snow in the front garden. My heart rate had started accelerating the moment she began answering my questions and my hands were sweaty again.

"How did you find me on the lake?"

Her smile faded as she began to speak. "We, angels, work with our minds. Our minds work a hundred times faster than those of humans. We feel as one with our protégés, which makes it much easier for us when we heal them—easy because we know where they're feeling pain. And every time something bad happens, we just feel it. It's sort of like a premonition that we get, images that are forced upon us. The day you almost died I had one of those premonitions. I felt ice-cold water on my skin that numbed all my muscles. My mind guided me to you, to the lake. And I ran to save you."

"Angels are very fast. We run faster than humans, faster than cars and planes, because we move at the speed of light."

I didn't know what to say. She had told me so many things, things I had never thought possible, and yet, I had to find a way to start believing in them. The incomprehensible was now part of my life.

"What about wings?" I asked quickly. I didn't want to sound silly and sheepishly forced a smile on my face.

She looked amused.

"We don't have wings. I'm not saying they're a myth, but angels living on Earth don't have any. How could we expose ourselves to humans? We can't fly, though we can jump higher than humans and have the ability to rest in the air for a brief moment without falling right back down."

103

I felt woozy and closed my eyes for a second. Maybe she had been right, about the emotions and the brain damage. Maybe my brain couldn't handle all of it and was acting out accordingly. I had another sip of tea, allowing the warm liquid to sit on my tongue before swallowing it. I pressed my fingers around the cup until they turned white, and then released the pressure. The dizziness seemed to wear off as I listened to her steady breathing and the crackling of the wood in the fireplace.

"Are you okay?" she asked.

I could hear her sitting up straight in her chair, but I ignored her concern.

"Where have you been all the time?" I asked, opening my eyes slowly.

A mixture of apology and guilt was painted on her face.

"At home. And in class."

"But I haven't seen you for months," I protested.

"I wasn't allowed to show myself to you," she answered my question with a notable hint of apology in her voice. "We have the ability to make ourselves invisible to humans." I could feel she knew how unfair the whole situation was.

I felt miserable.

"You were going to class and didn't let me see you?"

"I'm sorry. I wasn't allowed to. Believe me."

I couldn't be angry with her, even if I wanted.

The sliding door opened slowly, and Elena entered.

"I'm sorry to interrupt, but Lerato is here and would like to talk to you two, if you've got a minute," she spoke in a light way and moved like a dancer to the glass table, where she put out another tray of tea and more glasses.

I quickly looked at Caroline's face, which eased my anxiety.

"Sure, let him join us," she said. Elena nodded politely and left the room for a brief moment.

"Is something wrong?" I asked Caroline quickly.

"Don't worry—everything is okay," she assured me with a smile on her face.

After a fraction of a second, Lerato appeared at the door. He looked very sturdy as he moved, like one of those people who never lose their temper. As he came closer, I could see how young he actually looked for being over 40.

"Hello, Adam, nice to see you again," he greeted with his deep voice.

He sat down on the other side of the table and took a sip of warm tea.

"Nice to see you too, Dr. Spes."

"Call me Lerato, you are part of the family now."

I was overwhelmed by how everything had happened so fast after Caroline's confession. My mind was still blurry, an ongoing whirlwind.

"I see Caroline has already told you a little about us," he added.

For a brief moment I was trying to figure out if he was angry with her for introducing me to their world, though I couldn't perceive any anger in his behavior. On the contrary, he seemed totally relaxed.

"She was showing me around," I said, my eyes darting toward the altar.

"That's very kind of her," he said and sipped his tea. "I see you like the altar."

"Lerato, there is no need to be worried that I will tell anyone what I've been told today," I tried to assure him, but he silenced me with a gesture of his hand.

"I know. I can feel it. There is no need for either of us to worry. It's just that I'm a little concerned about you two."

"Why?" I anxiously asked.

"You are Caroline's first protégé, and it simply happens that some angels need some extra dedication in the beginning," he explained.

Caroline fidgeted in her seat next to me.

"Dad, please."

I could see that she was uncomfortable being talked about by her father.

"I just want you two to be safe," he said with a concerned expression on his face while keeping his dark brown eyes locked on both of us.

"You know that *the Elders* are going to visit us soon because they know that he knows about us?" Lerato said directly to Caroline.

I was confused. "The Elders?" I asked, my eyes flashing to Caroline's face, where I found that noble frown again.

"You remember when I said that we had rules?" she asked in response to my question.

I nodded.

"The rules are from the Elders, the oldest existing community of angels. They have an overview of every angel's life and they see everything that the angels do. When they save their protégés lives, how they save them, and of course, when or if they fail. They visit angel families from time to time, especially families with angels who have recently been assigned their first protégé ever."

The concern deepened on Caroline's face as she made yet another unexpected confession. Their world was perfect, but very complex at the same time. These Elders seemed to be some otherworldly caped judges, which was, in the end, a somewhat unpleasant thought.

I looked at Lerato and asked, "And they want to pay you a visit?"

"I am sure that they will want to talk to you as well. You are part of a great secret. There is, however, no need for fear; they will only want to assure themselves that you won't tell anyone what you know."

My brain started to buzz. Some angelic judges were on their way to execute me. And my life could not have become more complicated.

"When are they coming?"

"I don't know, so I can't tell you," Lerato said, shaking his head no slowly. "The only thing I do know is that they will come soon."

I had a glance at Caroline's face.

"Don't worry," she said, calming me. "Everything is going to be alright."

I was in need of a timeout and was still thinking about the Elders when Elena appeared at the door.

"They won't harm you," she spoke in a soft voice and sat next to Lerato. "That's against their nature." It felt as though Elena's appearance had lightened up the room.

"Try not to worry," she added in her warm maternal way. "They are coming in peace to talk to you and let you know how important it is to keep our secret."

"I'm certain of this," she assured me after seeing the startled expression on my face. "I can feel it."

"Do you feel it too?" I couldn't help asking Caroline as well.

"Yes, I do, but they're definitely not coming today. We have some time, and I promise they won't do any harm to you."

Her soft hand squeezed mine, and I was relaxed by the warmth of her touch.

While we all remained in complete silence for a brief moment, I was silently being grateful that they approved of me.

I heard steps approaching from the stairs and Dominic entered the living room. Holding a guitar in his right hand, he was surprised when he saw me.

"Didn't know we had guests. I was wondering why it was so quiet in the house."

He was wearing a pair of gray sweatpants with a hoodie. He

gave me a quick look of apology, and for a moment, I thought he looked exactly like Lerato.

"You won't mind if I play?" he asked, gesturing to the guitar in his hand.

"No, go ahead," Elena said softly and smiled at him.

"Well then, see you."

He left the living room in a rush.

Elena's face looked warm.

"He's still having a hard time with us moving," she explained and rested her head on Lerato's shoulder.

I tried to be nice about him.

"I'm sorry."

"That's okay," she said.

Caroline cleared her throat and raised her head as she asked, "Mom, is it normal that a protégé sees the healing process while he is unconscious?"

Elena exchanged looks with Lerato. "Not to my knowledge. Why?" she asked, clearly surprised by Caroline's question. Lerato narrowed his eyes.

"Because Adam said he saw the healing process after the car accident," Caroline explained and waited for her parents' reaction.

Elena looked at Lerato. "That's news to me," she said. "It's not usual, though."

"What exactly did you see?" Lerato asked.

The muffled sound of Dominic's guitar sounded from upstairs as I recalled that scene.

"It all happened while I was unconscious. I thought I was dead, but then I saw Caroline. There was a lot of light—it was very blinding and I could hardly see anything. She appeared out of the light and gave me a kiss on my lips, and shortly afterwards I woke up in the hospital."

Caroline seemed tense all of a sudden.

"He saw everything."

"This shouldn't have happened," Lerato said with a concerned expression.

Elena studied me closely. "It's very rare," she whispered softly. I was confused by their reaction.

"Rare, but this could explain his feelings," Lerato noted.

"You mean the bond you told me about?" Caroline asked her father.

Lerato nodded yes.

"Maybe it happened when you kissed him while you were healing him. It certainly is not your fault that he saw you."

Caroline brushed her hand through her hair as her back stiffened.

"What bond?" I asked confused.

Elena gave me a warm compassionate smile.

"In order to save a person's life, we perform something that is called the illumination of the human heart and touch their soul and heart with love and warmth. And that's something we do with a kiss. Lerato thinks that you seeing the healing process is the reason for your strong feelings toward Caroline. And for hers toward you. He thinks that a bond was created, like a link between your hearts."

I realized only a moment after Elena said this that she had given me the answer to why I had been so attracted to Caroline. Her voice, her face, her warmth and the feeling in my chest—it all seemed to make sense, even though it sounded unbelievable.

"Do you really think this is possible?" Caroline asked her father.

"That's the best explanation I can think of," he said.

"I have heard of it once, but I never thought it could happen so easily, so simply, to be honest," Elena said, backing up Lerato's explanation.

In the midst of their unbelievable conversation, I was fascinated by the thought of this kind of bond.

"That's definitely one thing we can talk to the Elders about," Elena suggested.

Lerato nodded.

"Your mother is right. I think they should know that Adam saw the healing process. We should be as candid with them as possible."

"Are you sure we should let them know?" Caroline asked her mother, still unsure about their suggestion.

"I am," Elena said and smiled her warm smile.

"So am I," Lerato assured both of us.

Even though the thought of the Elders coming to talk to me soon was frightening, I was impressed at the same time. On the one hand, I hadn't had time to overthink things, since everything had happened so quickly after Caroline brought me home to meet her family, and on the other hand, the idea of our bond seemed too pleasant at the moment to be true. Something I had been waiting for so long had finally happened, though not in a way I would ever have imagined. But in a better one, of course.

A moment later, Elena stood up gracefully. "Worry is not good for the soul," she said, moving toward the door. "I'll bake some muffins."

She had very elegantly brought the conversation to an end, and I felt like I had awakened out of a trance as reality came trickling back in.

"I have to go home. My mother must be hysterical by now."

"That's completely fine," Elena said, coming back to the table to give me a hug. "I will see you soon."

"Thank you."

"I'll give her a hand with the muffins," Lerato announced. "Get home safely," he said on his way out the door.

I was silent while Caroline walked me to the entrance door.

"Are you worried?" she asked.

I didn't want to lie to her.

"I am."

I looked up at her immaculate face.

"I'm still not sure if I'm dreaming or if this is all real."

She stepped closer and gave me a tight hug. I automatically threw my arms around her and fervently pressed her against my body. The sleeping beast in my chest woke up all at once, and a wave of heat made my blood warm up in only a second. When she let go of me, I was almost panting.

"Does this help?" she asked.

My skin was hot and my knees felt like jelly. "I still have so much that I need to ask you," I said.

"We have all the time in the world," she assured me in her lovely voice and smiled.

"Promise you won't leave me again," I insisted.

"I won't," she said. "I promise."

I could see the truth in her eyes.

"When am I going to see you again?" I asked, already dreading the thought of leaving her.

"Soon," she mused.

"I love you," I whispered at last, allowing those words to be set free from within my chest.

She gently touched my cheek, and I inhaled her loving touch.

"I love you too."

I made my way through the front garden onto the street. Heaven could wait. I had found my sacred world here on Earth.

ANGEL OF DEATH

The restrictions of my logical mind were definitely challenged over the past couple of days, and thus, my basis for reality had completely changed.

I started looking at my current life situation like a personal challenge, a challenge to believe in more than just what human eyes can perceive.

Caroline's confession had changed me, and nothing was ever going to be the same. I started looking at her from a different point of view, and to my delight, everything about her seemed to make sense. Her elegantly brisk movements, her thoughts, her words—it all was explained because she was an angel.

I spent the following week at home working on a paper. May wouldn't let me out of her sight and was frantic whenever I tried to leave the apartment. She threatened to tape all the sharp edges on the furniture and doors, but luckily, she refrained from doing so after I convinced her that I had my clumsiness under control.

She became aware of the sudden shift in my mood. I told her I was just overly happy with our decision to move to Belgrade. I simply couldn't share any information about Caroline with her.

Only a couple of days after my visit to Caroline's home, I checked my email and was surprised to discover that she had written to me. She was willing to answer my questions further and had invited me over the following day.

I was happy that she kept her promise about answering all of my questions, and two days before Christmas, I decided to tell May about my plans to visit Caroline.

"It's the girl who helped me out of the lake with her brother. Remember that morning at the hospital? We're working on an important paper together."

I couldn't help adding the lie about the paper.

May looked at the ceiling as she thought about that dreadful night, but then relaxed.

"I do remember her. That girl looked very nice. I just want to make sure I'll get another chance to officially meet her."

She was teasing me.

"You will," I assured her, though I wasn't sure when that was going to happen, as I definitely couldn't share Caroline's secret with her.

Caroline greeted me with her warm smile. She seemed different, more relaxed.

"Hi," I said.

"Come on in," she said and closed the door. I was bathed by a wave of peace once inside. There was a nicely decorated Christmas tree now placed next to the fountain in the entrance area.

"Hello, Adam," Elena and Lerato said together, greeting me from the kitchen.

"Nice to see you both again."

They were each wearing an apron and looked amused.

"Just in time for some homemade cookies," Elena said as she handed us a plate with some kind of heavenly delight.

"You two better hurry up," Caroline told them politely.

Lerato raised his arms.

"She's throwing us out. Let's go before she starts throwing cookies at us."

He helped Elena loosen her apron.

"We'll see you later," Elena smiled.

"Lerato, do me a favor and get the flour out of her hair," Caroline said. She smiled after they went out the door.

She laughed, and my chest melted. "They're a mess," she said once we had found a soft spot on the couch.

"They're a lovely match."

"Rather a messy one. They met at the hospital."

"Elena works at the hospital too?"

She nodded. "She does—same department," she explained and rested her head on my shoulder. Her loose hair tickled my cheek. I tried not to move, afraid she might lean away. Her warmth made me feel ecstatic.

"Lerato wanted me to introduce you to him at the hospital. He wanted to see if there was any danger…if you'd be going around telling other people about us. But he approved."

She didn't move, but kept very still, as if giving me time to understand the precautions her family had to take.

"You have to know that every angel works someplace where they can help people. Elena and Lerato work in the maternity ward because that has a lot to do with life. Both with giving and *promoting* life. They say that there is nothing more beautiful than helping a mother give birth to her child, that this is their way of encouraging the growth of humanity. There are a lot of other angels who also work at the hospital, but there are also others who work in pharmacies, care homes, orphanages and, especially, kindergartens, as that is a place where they can take care of little children from a young age."

"That's not all. There are a broad range of angels incarnated as humans, such as self-help authors, dietitians and nutritionists, but also as directors of nonprofit and social service organizations. You can be sure that you'll find at least one angel in groups that promote human rights, fight global poverty and violence, and encourage peacekeeping among countries. Our higher purpose is to encourage and promote universal harmony."

Her musical voice had again put me into a state of trance, which deepened my feeling of inspiration and hope for the human race.

"This is uplifting," I said as I rested my eyes on the altar. "Were there any angels in the hospital you guys brought me to?" I asked without taking my gaze off the golden flames of the candles.

"Yes," she said in a soft voice. "I didn't see them, but I felt their presence."

"You felt their presence?"

"I did. Angels feel the presence of other angels around them. We might not always recognize them right away, but we certainly feel their companionship," she answered and grabbed a blanket from the side of the couch.

I allowed my fingers to lose themselves in her silky hair, and we remained in silence for a brief moment. The quiet crackling of the fire was whispering soothingly in the background.

"Caroline?"

"Hmh?"

"Why do you think I can remember your healing process?"

She lifted her head from my shoulder and gave me a quick comforting glance.

"This is a complex matter. As far as I know, it is not usual for a protégé to be aware of the healing process in any way. It's rare that you saw everything. Another possible reason it could have happened might be because I wasn't focused enough and somehow didn't block my thoughts from you."

She wore a soft expression on her stunning face.

"Whatever the trigger was I'm sure the Elders will know the answer."

Our moment together felt perfect, and I didn't want any scary thoughts about those Elders to invade my mind. I rested my eyes on the balcony; it was snowing again.

"Tell me about being invisible for others. How exactly do you do this?"

She gently squeezed my arm under the blanket.

"We have the ability to hide from humans. We do this by closing our heart and blocking our thoughts and feelings from them."

She spoke slowly, allowing my human brain to process her words.

The thought of any sort of blockage between the two of us felt suddenly very unfair.

"I'm not going to do it around you again—ever," she promised.

I pressed her closer to my body. For a moment it seemed irrational to me how just a couple of days before all I wanted was to talk to her, and now here I was, as close to her as I had ever been before.

"Do you get to choose your protégé?"

My questioning didn't bother her; on the contrary, she seemed very happy and relieved to have the opportunity to finally share it with a human being.

"It's not that easy. You can't choose your protégé. It's all up to the Elders who match you up with someone, though they put some effort in trying to find someone appropriate for everyone."

I started playing with her hair again.

"I'm one of the few young angels with a young protégé," she added.

"Is this bad?"

"Not at all," she said gently with her soothing voice. "Though it might bring some complications in the beginning, I definitely wouldn't consider it as something bad."

"You said that you were assigned a protégé at the age of 21. What happens to the humans before that age? Are they sort of *unprotected?*"

I made quotation marks with my fingers, emphasizing the last word.

Her voice was warm.

"Not really. Humans are assigned to angels at the age of 21 as that is the usual age for a personal guardian to be given a protégé. The Elders take care of all the humans before they receive their particular guardian angel. It just so happened that I was your first guardian angel, and you my first protégé."

We remained in complete silence for another moment while the muffled sound of Dominic's guitar echoed from upstairs. My thoughts drifted away; I was impressed and overwhelmed at the same time and needed to know as much about her as possible. The more time I spent with Caroline, and the more I knew about her, the more the thirst in my body seemed to be quenched.

"I was sort of freaked out when I dreamed about you a couple of months back. It involved a little girl who I followed through a school building. She was…dead."

Caroline sat up so she could look at me.

"I'm so sorry. You didn't dream this by yourself. I was trying to tell you who I was. What I do."

"Trying to tell me who you were?" I asked bewildered.

"Yes. We have the ability to influence the dreams of our protégés. That's another way we try to help them resolve many of their everyday problems. At the time of that dream, you were heartbroken, so I desperately tried to show you who I really was."

I needed a minute to take her apology in.

"You can influence my dreams?"

"I can. As a matter of fact, it's quite challenging in the beginning. I had never done it before, so it took me a while to get good at it. I have to focus on the message that I want to send, and then I have to create a link between your thoughts and my thoughts. Sort of like being on the same frequency."

"The dead girl...I used her to show you that I was a guide for the souls of the deceased," she revealed, speaking slowly.

I was startled, though finally the dream made complete sense.

"What a harsh way to tell me who you really are," I said.

She looked sorry.

"What about my other dream?"

"I was trying to make you see how complicated everything was by kindly asking you not to follow me. You clearly were having strong feelings toward me, which I couldn't reciprocate then. I really did intend to give you a pleasant dream, but I sort of lost the connection at the end and, consequently, I don't consider myself accountable for the way it ended."

"So you were brainwashing me," I complained sarcastically.

Her eyes looked apologetic.

"That's another way to describe my actions. I was desperately trying to show you the truth about me, at least in your dreams. I'm so sorry."

"Don't be. You did what you had to do."

"I also had strong feelings for you then."

She leaned closer, and I started playing with her hair again.

"The first time I ever physically saw you was in the cafeteria. Did you know...I mean...that I was there? You seemed pretty startled by something."

"I was told by the Elders you had moved to the White City, Belgrade. Both my parents and I thought it would be of great help if we all moved to Serbia as well. And so we did. I applied to the same university and even signed up for a couple of the same classes as you initially, only for the first couple of months. But things became intertwined and complicated. Shortly after your accident, I went to check up on you—I wanted to make sure you were alright—but I got scared when you started following me. I assumed you had recognized me."

The hint of concern reappeared on her forehead.

"That's why I hid myself in the restroom," she added apologetically, blushing.

The snow had stopped. The sun peaked out from behind the clouds, its rays touching the candles in a mesmerizing way.

I didn't want her to feel badly for her actions.

"I understand."

She sounded frustrated.

"I wish I could have told you from the beginning. It would have made everything much easier."

She seemed tense, almost uncomfortable.

"Shortly after I showed up in the same French class. I was trying to neutralize your thoughts and beliefs about having met me. Right after that class, I knew I had to do something, and that's when I started with the dreams. It felt very unfair to me to let you suffer in confusion."

"That Friday, in the kitchen, I showed up promising myself it would be the last time I checked up on you physically. I only did so because I believed you understood the dreams. But, of course, you were still under the impression that we had met before."

"I was scared after that incident and asked Dominic for some help, the way siblings do. I didn't want Elena and Lerato to know about you, though I had to tell them later on and they were very upset about it."

119

She squeezed my arm, and my heartbeat went wild as I recalled that day.

"Dominic and I were both very desperate to clear up how the dreams were influencing you, and we thought you would stop looking for me after his message."

I looked her straight in the eyes.

"I never stopped. I couldn't."

"Even if I had tried, I would have come back," she said and pressed her warm body closer to mine. "I wouldn't have been able to leave you."

Once again she had touched my soul and put me in a complete state of peace with her words. I took her hand gently, examining the smoothness of her skin.

"The cut," I said. "You don't bleed?"

I could feel her draw a deep breath.

"Angels don't," she said, confirming my doubts. "That's why you didn't see any blood that day."

"This serves to protect us from all kinds of injuries, and we are also immune to all diseases. This is solely for our protégés' good. So we can always be prepared, healthy and alert enough to save their lives at any moment."

The more she spoke, the closer I felt to her and the more captivated I was. The gray clouds had completely disappeared from the sky and the unobstructed sun was shining into the living room, adding yet more warmth to the space.

"Caroline?"

She squeezed my hand in response.

"Are we breaking some sort of rule with our feelings for each other?"

She sounded conflicted as she said, "Not just one. In fact, we are breaking all possible rules."

"We don't belong together?"

She lifted her head up from my shoulder and looked at me.

"We do. Forever. Don't ever question that."

I was relieved by her words and listened for a moment to the sound of Dominic's guitar. It was fluent and smooth, reminding me of flowing water.

"Have you ever heard of any kind of bond like ours?" I asked after some minutes of mutual silence.

"I haven't. All I know is that we formed an attachment when I was healing you after the car accident. We both have feelings of affection and trust, which is more than simply liking each other. Lerato thinks the trigger for this kind of bond might have been your awareness of the healing process, though he is not completely sure about this. On the other hand, neither he nor any of us can possibly explain why you would have been able to perceive the healing process in the first place."

I was also very curious to find out how this could have happened.

"Maybe there's something wrong with me," I said, more to myself than to her.

She responded almost immediately.

"There's nothing wrong with you. You're just different. No human being is ever supposed to be able to perceive our healing process. I have to learn to block my feelings from you when I'm healing you."

"I wasn't aware of any kind of healing from you after the accident on the lake though," I admitted in encouragement.

Her voice shifted. She was surprised.

"You didn't perceive anything that time?"

"I didn't. The first thing I remembered after going unconscious was waking up at the hospital."

"Maybe things are balancing out," she said with a pleased tone in her voice. I sincerely hoped they were indeed.

"I just don't know what you were doing on that lake," she said with a disapproving tone.

I was confused.

"Dominic told me to meet him there. I found a Post-it note from him in my locker that day telling me he wanted to meet me at the large square. He said it was very important and he asked me to come alone. And that's what I did, but neither Dominic nor you were there. I have actually been planning to call him out on that one."

Her back stiffened and she sat up. "His Post-it note?" she asked, frowning. "What are you talking about?"

I was even more confused. "He signed it with a *D*," I explained, noticing a mixture of confusion and anger on her face. "It was the same type of note he left me before, when he told me you were out of the country."

Her expression contorted.

"That's not possible; he would never do something like that. He never told me anything about leaving you a second note."

"It's okay. I was really lucky when you showed up and pulled me out of the water. His grip was strong."

Her beautiful face changed color.

"His grip!" she yelled and jumped off the couch abruptly, making me wince. She ran her hands through her hair several times, breathing fast.

"It's okay—I'll talk to him," I said, trying to calm her.

"No, it's not okay. He tried to kill you!"

I still didn't understand why she was overreacting.

"But he didn't. That's all that matters. It might have just been a bad joke of his."

I had never seen her that frantic.

"No, no! Not Dominic. *Him!* I can't believe how stupid I've been."

She clasped both of her hands to her face and ran to the foot of the stairs.

"Dominic!" she yelled.

I was both uneasy and confused at the same time. Her behavior was making me nervous.

"What are you talking about, Caroline?" I asked, grabbing her by the shoulder.

"No, you don't understand. This is a lot more complicated than I thought. We're in trouble, and you're in danger. Dominic!"

She was overly agitated, and her quick movements were making my head buzz.

Dominic appeared at the top of the stairs. "What's going on?" he responded.

"Did you ever leave a second Post-it note on Adam's locker?" Caroline asked, running halfway up the stairs. "Tell me, did you or did you not?"

His forehead wrinkled and his eyes narrowed.

"I didn't. Only the one that we both talked about."

"Call Mom and Dad—tell them they have to come home!" she yelled. "It's an emergency!"

He was down the stairs in a fraction of a second; immediately picking up the phone and calling.

"Caroline, please," I said, grabbing her hand.

"Don't you dare leave this house. This is a question of life and death," she said with tears in her eyes.

Feeling confused and totally lost, I hugged her, noticing the light had suddenly gone out of those beautiful eyes.

THE ELDERS

Hugging Caroline, I kept my eyes closed and inhaled her sweet scent. She wrapped her arms around me and I hugged her even tighter. Feeling the warmth of her body on mine relaxed me a little. She was shaking slightly as I brushed my hand through her hair.

"Caroline, please tell me what's going on," I begged, desperate to understand what was happening.

She released me slowly, a fearful expression on her delicate face. "He tried to kill you," she whispered. "Please understand this."

"Who is he?" I asked in confusion, my hands still on her waist.

"Your angel of death."

She became extremely tense. I tried to remain quiet. My head was still buzzing.

"What?"

"Your angel of death. I haven't told you yet. Every human

being has a guardian angel as well as an angel of death. This is the way life is balanced out on Earth, but it seems to me that yours tried to kill you at the lake," she spoke hastily, her eyes darting in all directions.

This latest revelation made my stomach clench.

"But isn't he supposed to do that?"

I tried to take this in, but my ego refused to believe what I had just heard. But now, I not only had enough faith in Caroline to believe her, I also clearly remembered feeling that grip around my ankle under the icy water.

"Yes, he is. But not in that way. He is playing against the rules."

I felt sick.

"Playing against the rules? Why does he want to kill me anyway?"

The thought of this made me very uneasy.

"I don't know. That's what I want to talk to Elena and Lerato about. The three of us will explain things further to you after we speak."

I felt lost, disoriented.

Dominic approached us from the living room. "I called and left a message. I believe they should be on their way soon."

He spoke in a calm way, but I knew he wasn't underestimating the danger we might be in.

"What exactly happened?" he asked.

I tried to explain. My mind felt cloudy.

"A second Post-it note appeared in my locker after you left the first one saying Caroline was out of country. She thinks it was from my angel of death."

"Though it was signed with a D just like the first one," I added. "That's what's confusing."

He seemed to think for a moment before saying, "If that's true, then it must have been a trap."

Caroline was frantic, her beautiful face darkened by a cloud of despair as she spoke.

"Do you know what this means? He must have been spying on us for quite some time now. How can we even be sure that he's not here with us right now in this very moment?"

The situation had unexpectedly become extremely tense and I was able to perceive the danger more clearly, almost as if all the previous events had just been fictitious.

"How can you be so sure that it really was his angel of death?" Dominic asked. "Do you feel his presence?"

Caroline remained silent for a moment, breathing fast.

"I don't," she said at last, her golden eyes narrowing to half-moons. Gasping, she ran her hands through her hair.

"Something's wrong. Something's not right. Something is telling me that it was him. There were also no human beings present that night."

"Since you don't feel his presence, we can't be sure it really was him," Dominic said reassuringly.

"But what if I simply just can't feel his presence?" she asked and paused in front of the fountain. "Or at least not yet?"

Dominic looked like Lerato as he spoke.

"The connection between the guardian angel and the angel of death is made when the protégé is assigned to us, right? If he was there, I think you would have felt his presence. At least I think so."

I could tell he was trying to be as helpful as possible, and the fact that he hadn't left the second Post-it note in my locker made me change my mind about him.

I was unable to say anything and I felt as though my blood had frozen as I listened to them analyzing my accident on the lake.

Dominic had a tone of urgency.

"Look, whatever or whoever was responsible for this, I'm

126

sure we will figure this out. Let's wait until Elena and Lerato get home before jumping to a conclusion."

I took Caroline's hand and we followed Dominic to the couch in silence. Only a fraction of a second later the door opened.

"We're here," Lerato said. His manner and Elena's had changed and become more aggressive than before. Elena's normally light features were darker and more mysterious. Lerato reminded me of a lion ready to pounce on its prey.

"What happened?" he asked with his sturdy voice as he removed Elena's coat. Both had snowflakes in their hair.

Caroline was off the couch in a flash, saying, "I think Adam's angel of death tried to kill him."

Elena and Lerato exchanged looks.

"Are you sure about this?" Elena asked.

"I am. At least I think so. I believe Adam's angel of death set a trap for him by leaving a Post-it note in his locker telling him to meet at the frozen lake. The note was signed with Dominic's initial, which made Adam believe Dominic had left it and wanted to meet him. Once the ice caved in on the lake's surface, Adam's angel of death grabbed him by the ankle and pulled him into the depths."

Caroline spoke very fast. Her words sounded like an indistinct buzzing to me, foreign almost. But the feeling of danger persisted.

"Did it feel like a human grip?" Lerato asked me.

"I believe so," I said drily, trying to remember.

Caroline's voice sounded worn as she said, "I didn't feel his presence though."

"So we don't know with any certainty then," Lerato said calmly. He and Elena sat down on the couch.

Caroline was sitting next to me. "But we also can't exclude his angel of death," she said, looking conflicted.

Elena frowned. "Can you sense something right now?"

Caroline closed her eyes for a moment and remained motionless. Her breathing slowed down and for a moment she looked as if she had turned into a ceramic doll.

"No. Nothing. Though I have a feeling that my assumptions are right. Even though I didn't feel his presence."

"Let's assume it indeed was him," Lerato said. "What reason would he have for trying to take Adam's life?"

Caroline ran her hands through her hair again, trying to think.

"None actually," she said abruptly. "I know it's not Adam's time to die. There is no reason for his angel of death to try to murder him," she said, giving me a quick glance.

"Another option could also be that Adam's angel of death is not obeying the rules," Elena said.

"What rules?" I managed to ask at last.

Lerato was calm.

"An angel of death is supposed to take your life in the sense of leading your soul toward the afterlife. From the moment a human being dies, the guardian angel is no longer in charge and is also not allowed to save the protégé's life anymore. The angel of death can be involved in your death in various ways, depending on your destiny. He or she will, in rare cases, lead you to circumstances that will make you miss seeing an oncoming car or train, or make you ignore warning signs. But they are definitely not allowed to actually physically touch you. Ever."

I kept staring at him in response while Caroline protectively held my hand.

"Can we talk to the Elders?" I asked, feeling intimidated by my life's current circumstances. The thought of talking with those judges was pleasant when compared with that of someone trying to kill me.

"It's not that simple; we can't just summon them for a casual meeting," Lerato spoke slowly. "They will want facts and proof, which we don't have."

"What if we take them to the lake?" Caroline asked.

Elena and Lerato exchanged another quick look. Sometimes, and in that moment in particular, I had the feeling that they were able to communicate with each other through their eyes and that no words were needed for them to understand each other.

"I doubt that would be successful," Lerato said after a quiet moment.

"They most likely won't find anything," Elena said. "But Lerato and I could go and have a look," she added hearteningly.

"I'll go with you," Caroline insisted.

My stomach clenched at the thought of them going back to the lake. I was panic-stricken.

"I don't want you in danger because of me."

A possible, sudden attack could severely injure, if not kill, all of them and make my entire universe collapse.

Lerato was composed as he said, "You are part of this family, and we will do anything to keep you safe."

Caroline still seemed to feel some danger. "So what do we do now?" she asked Lerato.

"We should sit tight for the time being. We can keep an eye on Adam to prevent a similar incident recurring. I don't feel any immediate threat at present."

"Wait?" Caroline said with a tone of complaint. "Dad, it's life and death." Even though she was aggravated, her face never lost its beauty.

"I am very much aware of that. What else can we do? We don't even know where Adam's angel of death is, what might have led him to these actions, and lastly, if it really was he who attacked Adam that night."

The atmosphere was tense, and the air felt electric on the back of my neck.

Caroline was stiff, as though in pain. "What if Adam is attacked again?" she asked.

"In that case, we will be here to confront whomever his attacker is," Lerato said. He was the only one courageous enough among them to take charge of the situation.

Nodding in agreement, Elena said, "I think this is the best we can do for now."

Caroline gave me another of her worried looks, her delicate eyes piercing me. She thought for a long moment. I could clearly see what a hard time she was having not protesting her parents' decision. If she was convinced it had been my angel of death who was behind the attack at the lake that night, shouldn't we do something?

Her soft lips parted and she looked ready to rebel. Her forehead wrinkled and her light eyes caressed mine with a sadness. When she finally spoke, she still sounded conflicted, but a little calmer—to my relief.

"We'll wait."

I just nodded in agreement, unable to speak. In the end, I would do whatever they wanted, as it had been my angel of death who set a trap for me and then grabbed my ankle, dragging me down into the icy lake that night; he had almost killed me once already.

"I suggest that I drive you home now. We want all our bases covered. If your angel of death has indeed been following us, he might then assume that you are with Caroline and under our protection. I will also make sure to secure your apartment when we get there."

Lerato caught me off guard. I wasn't expecting this. I didn't feel ready to leave yet, even though he already had his coat on. As much as I wanted to stay there and indulge in the security I felt in their home, I couldn't disagree with what he just said, even if that meant feeling unsafe for a while.

I nodded in silence and grabbed my coat while all of us walked to the front door.

Standing next to me, Elena smiled warmly and said, "You are cordially invited to our Christmas dinner tomorrow night."

"I will make sure to be here," I managed to say. At least I had a reason to come back—if I was ever going to make it back alive at all, that is.

Caroline hugged me good-bye. "We'll be fine, I promise," she said, though her face showed some indecision about this.

I hugged her to me, harder than ever before, and inhaled her warmth. "I will see you tomorrow," I told her. And reluctantly letting her go, I followed Lerato out into the cold December evening.

When I was back at home, I made my way to the bathroom to take a shower. I turned the hot water all the way up, put my face directly under the showerhead, and let the downpour slowly relax my tense muscles. The possibility of suffering another injury made me very anxious and I tried to calm myself down with the thought of Caroline's family watching over me.

But as hard as I tried, I couldn't stop thinking about what Caroline had said—though in the end, she had agreed to follow her parents' plan. Maybe because she knew there was no more danger in store for me? Or at least not for the time being? I was conflicted, but she had let me go, which she wouldn't have done if she had felt my angel of death's presence, I thought.

Slowly, unwillingly, I realized how unprepared I was for something like that to happen to me. To be killed by my angel of death had never been a way I had imagined dying. But I was mostly unprepared because of Caroline. If something happened to me, then she would suffer as a consequence.

Would we be able to find a way out of this if her concerns turned out to be valid? And if so, what would we do—or was my angel of death already lurking outside just waiting for me? At that thought, I turned the hot water up to the max and held my face under its steamy stream until my cheeks burned. At least that prevented me from further overanalyzing the current danger.

When I emerged, May was in the living room watching TV, her laptop on the coffee table.

"Hi, Mom," I said as casually as possible.

It was getting dark outside and the little red and green lights from the Christmas tree she had put up while I was in the hospital were throwing colorful shadows onto the walls.

"Hi there. How did it go?"

I remembered I had told her I was working on a paper with Caroline.

"It went pretty well."

"How's your lab partner?" she asked mockingly.

I laughed.

"I'm studying linguistics, not chemistry or biology."

May laughed too. I realized we hadn't talked like this since we moved to Belgrade.

"I apologize," she said with a smirk on her face. "How is your linguistics partner?"

"She's good. We got a lot done today."

Yeah, a lot of otherworldly talking actually.

"That's good. I'm glad you get to spend some time with someone."

May had always been very caring; she had always been there for me, in good and in bad times.

"Talking about friends, her family invited me over for dinner tomorrow night. Do you mind if I go?"

I didn't want her to spend Christmas all by herself.

She looked cheerful though.

"Of course not. That's very kind of them. You should go and have some fun. I will call up Ana—from my high school re-union—and invite her to do something in the city."

A nicely wrapped box under the Christmas tree caught my attention and reminded me that I had some last-minute Christmas shopping to do.

As I retired, I closed my windows and drew the curtains before turning off the lights, and then made sure our door was properly locked.

On Christmas Day I woke up earlier than usual. I rubbed my eyes and sat up in bed, double-checking that I was still alive. I looked around to make sure that nothing indicated someone had tried to break in, and when I strained my ears, I could only hear silence.

I got out of bed and drew the curtains aside. It was snowing, again, and Belgrade indeed was living up to its international reputation of being the *White City* in the most literal way possible.

It was no surprise that my windows wouldn't open when I tried to crack them, and that was proof enough for me that Lerato had kept his word.

I was sick of the snow and the cold—though both were very unimportant, even silly, to complain about given the fact that someone was trying to kill me. I stared at the snowflakes for a moment, trying to think of a reason why someone was trying to take my life; and as hard as I tried, I could not come up with a plausible explanation. I had always been good to others, but was that just another limited human thought? I was dealing with otherworldly experiences, and thus couldn't expect to find an answer for something that I didn't understand.

For a brief moment, I thought about karma. Maybe this was payback for something I had done in the past or in a previous life? Suddenly I felt desperate; I wasn't ready to leave this life. But who is ever ready to die? I felt as though I had so much more to accomplish, so much more to do in life, and the possibility of dying felt very unfair.

My death would always be linked to Caroline's death, and I couldn't let that happen. I knew that human beings could plan their lives, but they definitely couldn't plan their destinies. And if my destiny was to die, then I promised myself once I got to heaven I would escape, come back and run away with Caroline. I'd crack the sky open just to be with her.

I realized how overwhelmed I actually was only after I got to *Knez Mihailova*. Firstly, I needed to be finished with my shopping before dinnertime, and secondly, I had no clue what to give angels as a present.

I decided to look for Caroline's gift first, since hers would definitely take the most time. All I knew was that I wanted it to be something unique and beautiful—which only ended up causing me more anxiety.

I feverishly entered several bookshops and clothing stores without success. Finding her gift turned out to be much harder than I had originally thought and I decided to focus on other presents instead, hoping this might lead me to the right one for Caroline.

I chose to focus on May's present next and I knew I had found it when I spotted a store window with the sign: Book Your Weekend Getaway Here!

I entered and looked for a special winter offer that I knew May would enjoy. She had been talking about how she wanted to spend some time in the mountains, and Zlatibor seemed like the perfect choice. Without hesitation, I booked the second week after New Year's for her and had the sales associate wrap the voucher in a nice envelope.

Time was passing quickly, and the snow picked up, muffling the usual noise and worsening my vision. I was glad though, since I would not be an easy-to-spot target for my murderer, or at least I hoped so.

I entered a bookshop and was glad when I found a guitar book for Dominic. Half of the book consisted of blank pages where he could write down music notes for his own compositions. It was simple and, above all, it encouraged art, so I was sure he would like it.

Further down the historical street, a banner caught my attention: Belgrade Art Fair, January 2 to February 10.

I made my way to the information desk and was relieved when I walked away with two tickets for Elena and Lerato.

Noon was approaching and I still hadn't found anything for Caroline. I had passed several jewelry stores, but I didn't think she was into rings and necklaces. In fact, I had never even seen her wear either.

Desperate and half-frozen, I entered a renowned flower shop called *Jelena* and checked out some of its special floral arrangements. I was on my way out when a golden rose on a stand by the door caught my attention. The sign read:

Create your own and unique everlasting present: a white rose delicately covered in pure gold that stands for everlasting love is a true gift of luxury with a deeply personal touch.

This was it, the perfect present for Caroline, and I was happy to have found it finally.

It took almost an hour to have it created for her, and when it was ready, I was amazed by the beauty it radiated. It was covered in shining gold and inscribed with a single word: *forever.*

Content with my purchases, I made my way home through the thick snow.

I placed May's present under the Christmas tree and waited until she was done showering. The table was already set for the two of us, with plates, champagne glasses and May's homemade Christmas cake. My father's sister was married to a Catholic, so we had a family tradition of celebrating both the Catholic Christmas on December 25 and the Orthodox Christmas on January 7.

"Merry Christmas," May said.

"Merry Christmas to you, too."

"You got everything you needed?" she asked, stepping into the kitchen.

"I did, though it was quite the challenge," I said, taking a seat at the table. May had always been a good cook and never afraid to try out new recipes.

We started with her Christmas soup, which was always different and tasty. This year her invention was a broth of mixed vegetables, thin pieces of pasta and chicken.

"I love your soup, Mom," I said with praise.

She looked pleased.

"Do you think I added too much kale?"

"Not at all. I like it a lot just the way it is."

"I thought it would be nice to add some more greens. Wait until you see the entrée." She disappeared into the kitchen and returned holding a warm tray in her right hand and a kitchen towel in her left.

"It's Christmas ham with raspberry mustard. It came out pretty good. I found the recipe on Google."

Throwing the kitchen towel dramatically over her shoulder, she pronounced the *e* at the end of Google.

I couldn't help laughing.

"Where did you find the recipe?"

"I found it on...are you mocking me?"

She pretended to be insulted.

"Me? No way. Why would you say that? Let's try it. It looks delicious."

I burst out in loud laughter when the kitchen towel fell onto her plate.

"I'll clean it later," she said in her silliest voice. "Let's eat."

The meat was tender, the aftertaste a mix of sweet and sour. The cabbage salad had been nicely prepared and went well with the ham.

Half an hour later, we finished the meal with chocolate croissants and clinked glasses.

"There's something under the tree for you," I said.

She excitedly got up and grabbed my envelope with a small box from under the Christmas tree.

"You did not! This is so generous of you."

"You deserve it, Mom."

"I'm so excited," she said, clapping her hands like a child. "This is for you," she said as she handed me a small box with a new smartphone inside.

"This is exactly what I need. Thank you so much."

I was glad to finally have a new phone, as I hadn't used my old one since the accident on the lake.

"I'm very happy you like it," she said pleased, as I helped her clean up the table.

The rest of the afternoon drifted by in a slow, relaxed way. I zapped through TV channels while May did her hair and pulled dress after dress out of her closet.

"Shoes!" I heard her exclaim from her room. "How am I going to wear heels in this slush?"

"Maybe you should go barefoot," I said, teasing and making her laugh.

In her latest email, Caroline had told me to be there at eight, so I started getting ready around seven-thirty. I had just put on my black tuxedo when May came into my room to show me her dress.

"You look beautiful, Mom," I said. She was wearing a red gown that curled elegantly down her body.

"Thank you. I like your outfit too."

And with that flattering remark, she left for her evening out.

Cold, I rang the doorbell at Caroline's house 20 minutes later.

137

It was still snowing and the streets were empty, with the usual peaceful silence of Christmas Day. The door opened, and Caroline greeted me.

I paused.

She gave me a perfect smile, her lips curving somewhere between seductive and extraterrestrial beauty. She was wearing a beautiful white dress, the front revealing her knees and the silky back cascaded down until it almost touched her feet. White high-heel sandals showed off her delicate bare feet. She had curled her hair and wore it down, and its tips moved gently in the breeze. She had contoured her cheeks slightly, making them look like fluffy clouds. Her small, rounded nose was perfectly centered under a pair of unfairly beautiful eyes. The sleeping monster in my chest inhaled her scent and woke up. The feeling was violent, almost like an aphrodisiac.

"Hi," I said with awe and gave her a kiss on her warm lips.

"Merry Christmas," she said, closing the door behind us. "Come on in."

The interior of the house had changed. There were a million little candles that illuminated every single step along the entire staircase. The chandelier's white, but muffled, light created a feeling of warmth and safety. The lights of the Christmas tree had been lit too, and looked like little floating stars. The sound of soft instrumental music was coming from the living room.

"Everything looks beautiful," I said, placing my presents under the tree.

"It is," she said, taking my hand gently. "Because you're here."

The living room door slid open and Elena, Lerato and Dominic greeted me, all with a beautiful warm smile on their faces. They were all dressed in white and it occurred to me how much they looked like waves of light. It truly seemed as though the Heavens had overflowed and sent their small, but perfect, empire of angels to Earth.

Elena was the first to give me a hug. "Merry Christmas," she said. Her warm arms felt nice on my back, and her curly hair tickled my face.

"Merry Christmas to you, too."

"Come on in, we've been waiting for you," she said warmly.

"Merry Christmas, Adam, and welcome," Lerato said, giving me a fatherly hug. Dominic gave me an approving look while we shook hands.

As they stepped aside, I could see that the living room had also changed completely. The huge glass table had been moved to the middle of the room and was perfectly decorated with symbols of love and peace: little glass Christmas trees, wine and champagne glasses, tiny branches from the Christmas tree, colored glass balls and golden cutlery. The whole floor was covered with white rose petals, and they looked like snow under our feet. A soft fire was crackling in the fireplace, and the altar had been moved further into the room, its candles shining in such charming way that I could feel a heavenly vibration in the air.

"The house and the decorations are really captivating," I said, almost intimidated by their beauty. I took a seat next to Caroline, and Lerato filled up our glasses with champagne.

Elena beamed at me with a perfect smile.

"Thank you. We really put a lot of love into them. Especially for special events like Christmas."

She was sitting across the table, next to Lerato.

"Cheers, and Merry Christmas," Lerato said, raising his glass and offering a toast that we all reciprocated.

"Thank you so much for inviting me," I said.

"Of course, it is our pleasure," Elena said in her warm maternal voice. She had another sip of champagne and leaned over the table toward me.

"Truth be told, we are not really supposed to socialize with human beings," she added and winked at me.

Before I was even able to respond, Lerato said, "Let's not spoil the evening, but rather spoil ourselves." He politely took the glass of champagne out of her hand, placed it on the table in front of her and offered her his hand.

"Shall we?"

"We will be right back," Elena said smiling. She took Lerato's hand and they both graciously left the living room.

"They're both excited to have you over for dinner," Dominic said and poured himself some more champagne.

I was excited too, though Elena's words had already affected me. "I'm pleased to be here, but I don't want you all in trouble because of me," I responded.

"Are we causing any harm to anyone by innocently sharing this moment together?" Caroline asked and grabbed my hand under the table.

She had fiercely locked her eyes on mine, and I stared back at her while she intertwined her warm fingers with mine. She had spoken so subtly and wholeheartedly, her sweet words sounding like whispers of wonder. I didn't say anything, but remained motionless while I tried to absorb her being with my eyes. Her exceptionally flawless skin was shining in the muffled light, her hair curled elegantly down her soft silky cheeks, her delicate eyes rested on mine with the most beautiful golden light shining from them, and her smooth dress slowly followed the movements of her breath. The music in the background reached its peak simultaneously, making her appear like a beautiful melody to me. Her soft rose lips slowly curved into an almost invisible, but impeccable, smile.

"This is *escudella*," Elena said from the door. She was walking next to Lerato, who was carrying a steaming bowl in his hands. He placed it in the middle of the table, and Elena grabbed a golden ladle and started serving us.

"*Escudella* means "bowl," and it is usually served for Christmas in Catalonia. This year I used slightly more chicken and beef than last year, and then added chickpeas and turnips for the first time ever. Actually, Lerato was the one who convinced me."

She neatly filled our plates.

This stew-soup had a unique rustic taste, its appetizing flavors dissolving slowly in my mouth and leaving a pleasant aftertaste.

"It's delicious," I said.

"Thank you," Elena responded with her warm smile, pushing back a strand of curls from her forehead with an elegant movement of her head. I had never seen her with curly hair, and that night it looked even shinier than before.

Lerato seemed amused. "Have I ever convinced her to do something bad?" he asked Caroline and Dominic with a smirk forming on his face.

"Never," was Dominic's response, as he helped himself to some more *escudella*.

"Actually, you have," Caroline said sarcastically. "That one time you convinced her to help you make some mint-chocolate garlic ice cream."

Dominic made a face. Lerato grinned and waved with his spoon.

"Come on, that's not a fair one. Garlic is healthy, and it wasn't that bad."

"And that's why you ended up eating it all by yourself," Elena said with a smile, teasing him.

We all laughed, and a mutual silence followed. A soothing song had just ended, and for a brief moment, all I could hear was the clinking of golden spoons until the next instrumental piece filled the air.

"So you recently moved to Belgrade with your mother?" Lerato asked, the first one to break the silence. His eyes glimmered in the candlelight.

"Yes, we did. She just recently started a position at the national bank. We sold our house in Switzerland, so I think this is something permanent."

The soup had pleasantly warmed my stomach.

"That's very lovely of her to move for your studies," Elena acknowledged.

"She's very supportive."

"Support is best indeed when provided by our parents," Lerato noted in a friendly manner. "I apologize for almost forgetting to ask how your day has been so far—did you have any trouble?"

A warm pinch shot down my spine as he said this. I knew what he meant.

"None, everything has been pretty normal. Thank you for securing our apartment."

"Absolutely. We will keep it secured until we have talked to the Elders," he said in his firm voice.

"I've tried to sense his angel of death a couple of times, but without success," Caroline added.

"Which still doesn't mean that any of us is exposed to danger," Elena said in response to Caroline's concern.

Lerato was off his chair before we could discuss the matter further. "Which reminds me that we should continue spoiling ourselves," he interjected with another smile. Elena was also up, helping him collect our soup bowls. Then they disappeared into the kitchen again.

"Sometimes I feel like we're the adults and they're the children," Dominic said, absentmindedly fixing his tie.

"They're only totally quiet when they paint," Caroline said with a smile on her face.

For an instant I wondered how Elena and Lerato had met and how long they had been together—their relationship truly seemed one of complete harmony.

"Cannelloni with mushrooms," Elena announced proudly

from the door as she approached the table with Lerato by her side.

"These are filled with mixed vegetables, and these with seafood," Lerato said, inviting us to eat with a gesture of his hand. "Another one of my inspirations."

They had rolled the cannelloni extremely tight, and although I didn't like mushrooms, the taste was surprisingly good.

"I've never had this before," I said. "I should have my mother try out this recipe."

Elena beamed at me. "I'm glad you like it," she said. "Though I have to admit Lerato was the maestro."

Lerato nudged her with his elbow.

"To which I have to say that my cannelloni can never be as good as yours. The way you can cut the mushrooms so small always amazes me."

He then turned to me, saying, "And yes, it is a very simple recipe that I'm sure your mother can master with ease."

Another moment of silence followed as we indulged ourselves in the cannelloni. Each of their presences was uplifting, and I had the feeling that normality was part of my life again. They had let me into their world, which felt so perfect that night that I hoped to stay there forever.

"We will be right back again," Elena said and touched her lips with her napkin.

It felt like three seconds later when they reappeared. "Here we have *poularde ballotine* with candied tomatoes," Elena cheered.

"We worked on this one together," Lerato said, placing the tray in the middle of the table.

"I'm pretty happy about the creamy consistency of the sauce," Elena admitted and cut the *ballotines* into thick slices while Dominic chuckled.

The poultry was very tender, layered with a mixture of fried peppers and garlic. Lerato poured us all some wine, and a conversation about my life in Switzerland followed.

"How was your life in Spain?" I then asked. I was eager to know as much about them as possible.

"Great and busy," Lerato said while having a sip of wine.

"We lived in the center of Madrid and worked many more hours than we work here," Elena said, pushing another strand of hair from her forehead.

"We had planned to go back by the end of this year actually," she added. "Although we will stay here until we have talked to the Elders."

I was uneasy at that thought and asked, "You're planning on going back?"

"We are, indeed," Elena said.

"It won't be anytime soon though," Caroline said. Her voice was calming and eased my panic. She leaned her head against my shoulder. The thought of her leaving was making me sick.

Lerato dabbed his lips with his napkin and said, "You can always come visit—especially during the summer when we go to our summer house."

"You have a summer house?"

"We do. It's in a mountain region in Montenegro, hidden in a national park called Durmitor. Nature there is endlessly fascinating throughout the year."

Elena smiled dreamily, saying, "The house is surrounded by fir trees, and sometimes you can hear nature breathe there."

I wondered, briefly, how they had managed to own a house in a national park, but then reminded myself that everything was possible for them. No matter how unfair it seemed to me.

When we finished with the *poularde ballotine*, Elena and Lerato disappeared again, only to reappear with chocolate parfait this time.

"There's always room for dessert," Dominic said, rubbing his hands together.

"This is actually Caroline's creation," Elena said while Caroline gave me one of her beautiful silent looks.

I got drowsy after we finished dessert, and I had to lean back in my chair. Our glasses were empty. I was amazed by how the amount of food and alcohol we had consumed didn't have any effect on Caroline and her family at all. My eyes flew to the altar and then to the balcony. It was dark outside, and fluffy white flakes were falling breezily to the ground. It wasn't until that moment that I realized I had completely lost track of time.

Elena lit some more candles and suggested we move to the couch in the back of the room.

"We can't leave this bottle open," Lerato said. "This needs to be finished." He filled up our glasses with the remaining wine and added some wood to the fire. He then joined us on the couch, sitting down next to Elena and wrapping his hand around hers. Dominic grabbed his guitar from upstairs and played quietly for us, and we remained quiet for a long time. I was contemplating how his fingers briskly touched the chords and released a soothing melody. While he played, my thoughts drifted away and I reminded myself of my circumstances, wondering how long I would be able to run away and hide from my angel of death until he finally killed me. He probably had it all planned out already.

"Did you go back to the lake?" I couldn't help asking, as that question was suddenly burning within my mind.

Dominic stopped playing and four pairs of eyes looked at me. Lerato sat up and exchanged a quick glance with Elena.

"We did," he said, "the three of us." His eyes darted from Elena to Caroline.

"We didn't find anything," Caroline said. "Though Lerato thinks that there has been some sort of *action*," she added in response to my questioning look.

"Action?" I asked, curious what she meant.

Lerato looked at me patiently, narrowed his eyes and said,

145

"Yes, I have the feeling that the energetic field has somehow been disturbed."

"Meaning my angel of death was there?" I asked, still confused.

"We aren't excluding that anymore," Elena said with concern and crossed her legs.

Lerato kept his eyes on the red liquid in his glass while he spoke.

"All I'm saying is that electric charges have been moved in that part of the city. Our senses allow us to navigate using the Earth's own magnetic field, which has been slightly disorganized in that area. The reading you would get on a magnetic compass there would be incorrect."

I was both disconcerted and speechless at the same time. My mouth was dry, and I felt unwillingly tense.

"Does that mean that something otherworldly must have happened there?" I demanded.

"Yes, we agree on that," Caroline said.

"Could the presence of an angel of death cause such a reaction?" I inquired further.

Lerato shook his head in denial and said, "Not necessarily, for it is not proven that angels of death interfere with the surroundings when they're present."

"And that's why there may be another explanation as well," Elena added.

"Could that be enough proof for the Elders though?" I asked everyone.

Lerato raised his shoulders slightly, saying, "It most likely will be, though I'm sure that by the time they get here those sub-atomic particles will have gone back to normal."

I felt defeated.

"We will explicitly explain what we discovered when they come here," Elena said, trying to encourage me in her kind, maternal way.

Caroline sensed my mood and tried to comfort me with her words.

"Nothing is set in stone, and we definitely will find out what happened that night. Maybe my assumption was wrong from the very beginning."

I remained quiet and hoped secretly that it was indeed wrong.

"Do angels of death live among human beings like you do?" I wondered aloud after a short pause.

"Yes and no," Elena said.

"Since the relationship between the guardian angel and the angel of death is kept at a distance, we like to refer to angels of death as living in an alternate reality. Their work is always parallel to that of their corresponding guardian angel, but, of course, never the same."

"That's why the ability to set up a form of communication between the two of us is very rare and requires exceptional skills," Lerato added.

I had grown even more desperate and looked at Caroline, hoping I would find the answer written on her beautiful face.

"I'll keep trying," she said, with an apologetic expression in her eyes.

"Don't, please. If I think back, I'm not even sure if the grip was human or if some seaweed had tangled around my foot."

Her voice was insistent, though her face remained marvelously calm.

"I *need* to find out what happened. Why would the energetic field have been changed exactly at the time you were there?"

"Maybe that happened way before I showed up," I responded, knowing this didn't sound convincing.

Her eyes were piercing.

"Then what about the Post-it note in your locker? It must have definitely been left by someone who is involved in your life to some extent."

147

"I can't think of anyone who might have possibly seen me when I left my note," Dominic said from the left side of the couch. He was still holding his guitar on his lap and was slowly moving his glass of wine in circles so that the red liquid spun around.

"Which leads us back to my statement that your angel of death must have been following you," Caroline spoke directly to me.

Lerato sat closer to the edge of the couch.

"We will make sure to find out who is behind this. We've found out more than we had expected."

Caroline's back relaxed and she sat back on the couch with her golden eyes still locked on mine. "I just don't want anything bad to happen," she said quietly.

"Nothing bad is going to happen," Elena said, trying to ease her worries. "You're not alone."

Lerato inclined his head toward us and said, "We're here to help."

I was grateful for all they were doing to keep me safe. In fact, it wasn't like there was a choice. I *needed* to stay safe so nothing terrible would happen to Caroline.

Elena rose graciously and walked to the media cabinet in the corner of the room to select another soothing playlist while Lerato spoke.

"I have, however, come up with some thoughts regarding your ability to perceive the healing process and would like to share these, if you don't mind."

While he gave me a moment to respond, he brought his glass to his lips and kept his eyes focused on me. His statement had completely taken my attention away from the lake and I could feel excitement growing inside of me again. I was eager to hear what he had found out and have at least some sort of idea what was wrong with me.

"I'd love to hear your thoughts."

He leaned forward and rested his elbows on his knees as he said, "I've considered a wide range of theories, both from the scientific and medical points of view, and have narrowed them down." His dominant, but peaceful voice had gathered all the attention in the room.

"It is possible, but not certain, that your perception might be linked to various parts of your body," he continued.

"First, I have thought about your central nervous system, the major parts of which are the brain and spinal cord. I thought of the possibility that some information, such as the answer to your ability to perceive your healing process, might have been stored in your spinal nerves. However, the reason for your actual ability to perceive this is unknown to me, and might even be congenital."

His explanation whipped up a whole lot of questions inside my mind. My case, in the end, seemed to be a very complex matter after all.

"Is there any way to activate or trigger those cells in my back?" I asked, puzzled.

"Not that I know of," he answered with confidence. "The attempt to read such embedded information would require an intervention that reaches beyond human understanding."

I could feel how my ears turned red as I started to feel defeated again. "You're saying some sort of surgery will be necessary?" I asked.

"Yes. The protocol for which I know nothing about."

I gave Caroline a crushed look while I mentally crossed that possibility off the list. She had wrinkled her smooth forehead and was giving me a disapproving look. I had no desire anyway to voluntarily go under the knife just to find out if there might be some readable information in some of my cells.

"I don't really have a liking for cuts and needles," I said. A firm smile appeared on Lerato's face in response.

149

"I very much understand. I don't think we would have wanted that for you either."

"I have also thought about your cerebral cortex," he continued after a quiet interval.

I gave him a questioning look, while Caroline supportively reached for my hand.

"It plays a significant part in a human being's perceptual awareness and consciousness," he added informatively.

"Is there something wrong with my perception?" I asked.

"There's nothing wrong with it, but it's different," Elena said, her heartfelt words once more comforting me.

"Each and every human cell is completely different and unique at birth. Yours might have developed differently. Expanded. More advanced."

"Yours are indeed different—I can feel it," Caroline said. "I know I blocked my thoughts when I was healing you, but you perceived the healing process anyway."

I was perplexed by their scientific explanations. I had, quite frankly, never felt different, always considering myself an average human being.

Intimidated, I said, "I've never thought about it that way."

Lerato took another sip of wine and said, "A simple, but comprehensible, explanation of your case could very much be that your mental process operates at a faster speed than the average human's."

I sat still for a brief moment and listened to the crackling of the fire while I thought about his latest explanation.

"Do you know if there's a way to control it?" I asked tensely. All of a sudden I felt a desperate urge to be normal, with just an average sense capacity.

Lerato smiled at my human words and kept his glimmering eyes focused on the flickering fire.

"Trying to control the mind is never an easy thing to attempt. I believe that the trigger of your faster mental process might not even be something that is under your conscious control. It most likely only happens under a very high level of stress, discomfort or fear."

"Such as the accident," I said, catching up with his theory.

"Correct. The release of adrenaline in such a moment would play another key role."

"Like a chemical reaction," I said more to myself than to them.

"Yes, if you want to put it that way. The entire human body is nothing more than reactions and interactions of cells and hormones."

If his theory about my fast mental process was correct, then I wasn't worried. Nor was I freaked out. I was rather more in a limbo state about judging it.

"Please keep in mind that these are just speculations on my part, and that they aren't meant to be taken too seriously," Lerato said after seeing my perturbed expression. I moved in my seat and forced a smile onto my face.

"I understand."

"Not all of the possibilities I've mentioned are necessarily true. Your cardiac plexus could also be related to your different perception."

Lerato's voice was stern. I was alarmed by how much he had attempted to analyze me.

I was getting exceedingly confused by the medical terms he was throwing around, though at the same time I was still slightly relieved to hear that not all of them were linked to my mental ability.

"Those nerves and vessels are located at the base of the human heart. I don't think of their physical state as being changed or different, but rather of your heart's frequency that changed them. Any frequency expressed by the heart is immeasurably stronger than any other expressed solely by the brain."

He continued to speak in his strong, dominant voice. Lerato's fingers were rigidly holding his glass of wine, his hair was precisely combed to the side, and his full lips pronounced every syllable in a sophisticated manner while he moved his eyes slowly from Caroline to me.

"Every emotion has a frequency. And here, again, I think that the interaction of cortisol and fear under stress releases drastically intense heart frequencies from your body that might allow you to see the healing process," he concluded at last.

I flexed my jaw. His theories sounded overwhelming, and he seemed to have an endless supply of them piled up in the corner of his brilliant mind.

"Seeing the healing process doesn't bother me at all, though the fact that we don't know why I'm able to see the process makes me uneasy. It always comes down to something being wrong with me."

Caroline squeezed my hand.

"There's absolutely nothing wrong with you. In fact, the only thing wrong about you is that you think there's actually something wrong with you."

Piercing me with her golden eyes, she looked at me with her most intense expression and pursed her soft lips.

"By *different* we never meant *disadvantaged,*" Elena told me serenely.

I silently appreciated their efforts to make me feel better about myself. My stubborn mind was giving me a hard time though.

"We firmly agree," Lerato said. "Thinking of yourself as wrong is wrong in the first place." He certainly had a very deft ability to call me out on inaccurate thinking.

I sighed and asked, "Which one of your theories do you think is the most likely to be true?"

"Frankly, I think all of them are equally possible," he said, a smile returning to his face. "In fact, I have also thought about energy channels and chakras—two of them in particular."

Elena smiled encouragingly at me, and Dominic moved in his seat. I had almost forgotten he was still there.

"Maybe two of these chakras are stimulated more than any other energy points in your body. The first chakra that came to my mind is called the *sahasrara*. It is located at the crown of the head and represents pure consciousness. It is connected to the central nervous system, and its characteristic deals with the mental action of the entire consciousness."

He circled his hand above his head.

"I don't meditate," I said, confused.

"There is no need to always mediate in order to stimulate and activate chakras. Some of them might just naturally be more active than others. The other chakra I thought about is called the *anahata*, also referred to as the heart chakra. It is located in the chest and deals with emotions. I believe these two chakras could have played an important part as well during your perception of the healing process."

I stared at him with a blank expression.

"I don't think the answer is necessarily to be found in something physical," Caroline said, taking my hand in hers. "We have to widen our range of thought and consider spiritual possibilities as well."

"Which basically leaves us with limitless possibilities," I said. They all smiled warmly in response.

"Limitless has always been better than limited," Lerato said, lifting his glass for a toast.

I could never be tired of or resistant to their seemingly endless ability to counter my hopelessness.

153

"However, since we can only live this night once, I think we should get our hands on the presents," Lerato happily announced, a smile stretching across his face.

"I second that!" Elena said, out of her seat on the couch in a flash. Her sudden movement made me realize how perfect this moment of celebration was and I followed her to the Christmas tree and grabbed my presents.

Presents in hand, everyone had already gathered around the table when I gave Elena the envelope with the tickets to the art fair.

"These are for you and Lerato," I said nervously. Elena's fine fingers elegantly brushed over the envelope as she flipped it open.

"Lerato, look!" she said joyfully as she waved with the tickets in the air.

"Thank you so much," she said, giving me one of her warm hugs.

Lerato held the tickets up in the air and said, "This is very kind of you."

"We should inquire about exhibiting our paintings there. What do you think, Elena?"

He wrapped his arms around her waist. She was beaming.

"Of course we will. Why do you think we got the tickets in the first place?"

I was relieved that they had liked their present.

I handed Dominic his package, saying, "This is for you." He opened it carefully, and after viewing the contents, wore an expression of thanks on his face.

"Thanks, this is exactly what I needed," he said, skimming through the pages of the book. Elena and Lerato giggled in the background, still talking about their future exhibit.

Dominic handed me a small organza bag.

"And this is yours. It's a malachite stone bracelet. Malachite represents the greenery of nature. It is said to heal both on physical and emotional levels, assisting the wearer in coping with life's ever-changing situations while at the same time promoting spiritual growth."

I contemplated the perfectly round-shaped stones. Each of them was of the same shade of green, but at the same time their lines and design differed.

"It's amazing," I said as I slipped the bracelet on my wrist. "Thank you so much."

"Don't forget this one," Lerato said, as he handed me a square package wrapped in blue paper from him and Elena. I opened it to find one of their own paintings with the image of a couple kissing in a garden surrounded by a variety of flowers, lush trees and rose bushes. I noticed the artistic brushstrokes where they had brought the canvas to life. Their inscription consisted of three words: *forever in bloom.*

"I like it, really," I said. It was amazing how much of their personality they had put into the painting.

"We're happy you like it," Lerato said.

"This is for you, Caroline," I said, handing the rose to her. She gave me a heartwarming smile as she gently took the tube with the rose out of my hands, making sure her fingers touched mine. As she tilted her head down to guide the rose out of its box, her curly hair appealingly fell, draping both sides of her face.

The lights of the room magnificently reflected off the golden surface of the flower, and in her hands, it looked like a key to a perfectly happy life.

"This is incredibly beautiful," she said, tracing her delicate fingers across the leaves.

"How majestic and peculiar it looks at the same time," Elena said as she and Lerato came closer to contemplate the rose.

Elena carefully took the rose from Caroline, as she proclaimed, "Outstanding invention."

"Outstanding as Christmas itself," Lerato added. Content, he grabbed another bottle of wine, saying, "Let's have some more." Elena and Dominic handed him their glasses.

Caroline placed the rose on the table, took my hand and said, "I'd like to give you my present." She took in my expression for a moment. "I've thought of something that will always make you remember me," she continued, as I slowly lifted my eyes to meet hers. Because the sight of the filtered sunlight in her eyes always gave me a sweet feeling of satisfaction, I intentionally delayed looking into them until the very last moment to prolong my bliss.

I intertwined my fingers with hers and said, "You're all I need."

She showed me her soft smile. "It's my wish," she said. She walked me toward the living room door, and we turned to look at her family. Lerato was lifting his glass for a toast.

I decided not to resist at all and allowed her to guide me completely.

"There's a saying: *Save the Best for Last,*" she said teasingly as she guided me up the stairs, with an almost undetectable smile in the right corner of her rosy lips.

I smiled back, happy to be alone with her again. Her mischievous behavior added a tempting kind of electricity to the air as we reached the top of the stairs.

The second floor was completely dark except for a beam of muffled light coming from behind the door to her room, which had been left ajar. It was cold inside, as the balcony door had been left open, allowing a cold breeze in that moved through her curtains like silky hands reaching for our yearning hearts.

Once inside, she briefly let go of my hand and gracefully slipped off her high heels. I allowed my eyes to lose themselves in the vast ocean of silky skin that covered her bare feet and to drown in her beauty, while she encouraged me to do the same. Any other day I might have felt weird taking off my shoes in a dark, cold room, but that night was different, because when you love someone, all the silly things you do together make sense. With a soft smile covering her face, she gently grabbed my hand and took me to the balcony, her safe place, where the sky was about to become the only witness to how she, once more, changed my life. After that night, I would never look at love in the same way.

The night was cold and the fallen snow under my bare feet awakened my senses. The winter sky was sending down small flakes, which made a crispy sound as they landed on my cheeks and ears. As we paused in the middle of the balcony, she turned around to face me and pulled me close, until there was no longer any empty space between our bodies. I took a deep breath, addictively inhaling her warmth.

"Cold?" she asked.

"Feels like fire and snow," I said breathing fast, trying to best describe the sensation my body was experiencing.

She smiled and wrapped her warm arms around my back; I put mine around her waist, pressed her soft, tender body against mine, and tilted my head down to rest my forehead on hers, keeping my eyes shut.

"This bond that we feel is unlimited like the sky itself," I said.

"We each contain a seed of the other," she said, her voice filled with compassion. "Alone, we're different, but we'll always come together as part of a mutual whole." A mutual whole— that's exactly how I felt when I was with her: complete.

"I'd like to let you know what it feels like to hold the sky," she murmured.

I remained silent as I traced my hand along her perfect spine. As I was hoping for us to get lost together somewhere outside of time, a mellifluous orchestral song started playing in the living room, its invisible melody embracing both of us. It was a song as captivating as the splendor in her eyes, as soft as her flawless skin, as delicate as her cheeks, as inviting as her lips, and as beautiful as her very being. It was our song.

We began moving slowly, following the flow of the music.

My heart was racing as I said, "I hear you in this song."

She remained silent as I peeked through my eyes to steal another glance at her face. She had her eyes closed, her soft eyelids resting peacefully as a steady breath emanated from her curved lips.

My thoughts drifted away as I tried to decipher her silence, which made her feel distant yet so close at the same time. I comforted myself with the fact that I was with her; that we were alone together, and I pressed her even closer to me, as if to become one with her. As we kept moving, I could feel how an alluring storm of emotions washed over me, feeling like rain falling from the heavens.

In that moment, she made complete sense to me. I understood why when we first met, she never reciprocated any of my emotions, never looked at me the same way I looked at her. But now, after knowing her secret, I had no doubt she had done all of that because she cared about me. From the moment our bond was created and her soul met mine, she, too, was made a slave to our love. And that is when I understood that love is a bond, a fragile promise that two hearts make.

"Step on my feet," she asked quietly.

We stopped moving as I hesitated for a brief moment and then, slowly, placed my feet on hers. Warm electric currents shot up my spine by the touch of her warm, soft feet, and she locked her hands behind my back. I was afraid of breaking her ribs as I pressed her even harder against my body. We remained in silence, motionless, as we both listened to our song. I had completely given myself over to her; she was the leader tonight. The fire in my chest was back, boiling up and erupting.

At first, I almost didn't realize that something different was happening. I could feel how the wind had picked up, blowing snowflakes into my face and through my hair. A sudden, peculiar, feeling in my stomach made me open my eyes and realize that we were floating in the air.

This startled me, and my fingers dug into the soft flesh of her back. My throbbing heart was in my throat. My hands began to sweat as we rose to the height of the roof. I sheepishly looked up at the sky and was astonished to find glittering sprinkles of stars spread everywhere throughout it. I looked down on Belgrade sleeping in an ocean of Christmas lights and then up to meet Caroline's teary eyes.

She was returning my gaze with a smile. I pressed my forehead on hers as I enjoyed this once in a lifetime gift. Floating in the air with her felt freeing, as though none of the earthly rules or boundaries applied to us. I felt free to live with her and to love her as my own guardian angel.

I kept my eyes locked on hers during our gentle descent, and as soon as our feet touched the snowy balcony, we embraced for a long time. Neither of us had the slightest intention of letting go.

"You're not my fantasy," I whispered, out of breath. "You are my reality." I had no reason to believe in the unseen, for I had seen the unbelievable. I gave her a long kiss on the lips. I didn't try to analyze or think about what had happened. I knew I would fail at trying to understand her, and suddenly I was glad I would actually never fully get to comprehend who she was; for I feared that if I did, the magic might be gone.

"I love you," she said.

Moments later, in mutual silence, we made our way back into her room and slipped on our shoes. I was surprised that my feet weren't cold at all and was in awe by what had happened.

She held my hand as we made our way downstairs, but paused suddenly halfway down.

"Are you okay?" I asked, my hands moving around her waist.

Her face was white. "They're coming," she said.

"Who's coming?" I asked, confused. Our floating put me in

a state of mind I had never been in before, almost as if I were tipsy.

"The Elders," she said icily. "Let's go down."

"Mom, Dad," Caroline said as we reached the living room door.

Elena, Lerato and Dominic were all on their feet. It looked as though they had been waiting for us—they had definitely felt it too.

"We know," Elena said.

None of them looked frightened, though I could sense a notable amount of nervousness in the air.

"Let's greet our guests," Lerato said, placing his glass on the table. "Good manners are important." He was the least stressed one among us.

I felt lost, and my head was spinning as I searched Caroline's face for some kind of comfort.

"I know this might sound crazy, but try to remain calm," she said tersely and paused for a second as though she was thinking of what to say next. "Think of the point that we want to discuss with them."

"What if it doesn't work?"

I could hear how her breath almost stopped.

"It will, hopefully. We've only got one shot."

ENTELECHIA SPIRITUS

In his uniquely sophisticated way, Lerato led us through the front door into the garden. My heart was throbbing in my ears and my mouth felt dry and sticky all of a sudden. I didn't know what to expect. I was not quite sure where to keep my eyes focused. I had definitely left my comfort zone and the bubble of safety I felt with Caroline and her family. This sudden visit of the Elders snuck up on me and hit me quite hard in the aftermath of too much wine and champagne combined with the humanly impossible act of floating in the air.

I tilted my head toward the sky and took a deep breath, inhaling the cold, snowy air and appreciating for a short moment just how normal the sensation of melting snowflakes felt on my skin. It caused a sparkling sensation, and seemed to freeze my worries away. I sighed silently and contemplated how my outbreath emanated in the form of a milky cloud. I realized how the thought of the word *normal* felt strange, and it was in that very moment when complete homesickness overcame me.

I felt lost and grabbed Caroline's hand as I tried to compose myself. Lerato and Elena were standing a few steps in front of us, hand in hand, and I could hear Dominic's nervous breathing behind me. My sense awareness was coming back, and I could feel the icy coldness sneaking under my skin as my whole body began to tremble. Caroline noticed my nervousness and tightened her grip on my hand.

Lerato looked up and we did the same, though I was still wondering how the Elders would arrive. My question was answered only a brief moment later when he pointed at the sky.

"There," he said. "They are approaching."

At first I didn't see anything peculiar as the snow hindered my sight, but then I did see something, and I was sure it was them.

I could clearly see two shooting stars among the snowflakes that were not shooting across, but rather down, from the heavens. They sped up as they descended and looked like little particles of meteoroids. I narrowed my eyes and could make out colorful traces of gold and silver, which lingered in the air behind them for only a fraction of a second. Any other person who might have seen this celestial spectacle that night might have described the happening as a Christmas phenomenon, and I silently hoped I could have been one of them.

We all took a step back toward the house, and I expected a big impact. The wind picked up slightly, and the two shooting stars fell to the ground in the darkness behind two trees in the garden with a soft, almost inaudible thud. I held my breath while we waited for them to appear.

Time seemed to stand still. My eyes focused on the darkness, I swallowed and wet my dry throat. I could see how the low-hanging branches of the trees were moving slightly, followed by an indistinct whisper.

Then, silence. I stole a quick glance at Caroline's deep eyes, through which she was promising that we would be alright.

Finally, the Elders stepped out and I watched in utmost astonishment.

Two angels were walking in our direction.

A man and a woman.

They both looked ageless, of course, and not like anyone I had ever seen before. Her perfect oval face had a smooth jawline that ran into a small, round chin. Her nose rose into an immaculate forehead, and she had curly, plush brown hair, which reached down to her elbows. She was wearing a white velvet dress that left her arms bare, accentuated her enticing body, and ended just a little above her knees.

The other Elder, a male, looked very muscular and sturdy. His facial features were short and edgy; his jawline was appealingly masculine. He had a big forehead and light-brown eyebrows. A curly strand of his brown hair fell above his right eye. He was wearing a simple white shirt and light pants, of the same velvet as the female Elder, highlighting the contours of his athletic chest.

Both of them had deep blue eyes and were barefoot. They also had huge wings that stuck out from behind their backs, generously feathered and reaching far below their waistlines. A marvelous ring of light was floating above each of their heads. And as they moved toward us in a confident way without making a single sound, I realized they weren't leaving any footprints in the snow.

"*Acceptus*," Lerato said politely and took a step toward them.

"Good evening, relatives," the female said, with a singing, but compelling, voice that conveyed a strong character, wisdom and power.

"Our apologies for interrupting your family gathering," she said, her piercing eyes scanning all of us.

Elena smiled, but still sounded nervous, as she said, "You are very welcome in our family."

"We thank you for your kindness," the woman added with a slight appreciative nod of her head.

She was standing a few steps in front of the male Elder, and he seemed not to have any intention of interrupting her. I wondered if they were of different ranks, in which case she was unmistakably the higher of the two.

"I am Vivienne and this is Janus," she said. "We felt it was time for our first visit." She approached Caroline and me, her eyes piercing both of us.

"You must be Adam," Vivienne said. "We are pleased to meet the one-who-knows."

I tried to suppress my nervousness as I said, "I am pleased to meet you, too." I was surprised by their gentleness and the fact that they were everything that I hadn't expected them to be, and I reminded myself to let go of any expectations.

Vivienne was now standing only an inch away from me, and I could feel the warmth her body radiated. She looked quite intimidating from close up, and I had the strange sensation of a stream of currents running through her body making her appear like a vivid, holographic dream.

"Caroline, good evening to you, too—the angel who is never afraid to spread her wings to save a life," Vivienne said directly to Caroline. I could feel Caroline's grip soften in my hand.

"Thank for your kind words," Caroline politely said in her sweet voice. "Welcome to my family." I could feel how her back was still stiff, though she was unquestionably more relaxed than before their arrival, which I hoped was a good sign.

"Let us seek shelter from human eyes inside of your home," Vivienne requested, speaking to all of us now. "We have many matters to talk about."

Lerato gestured toward the front door, saying, "But of course, after you." We followed them into the house, Caroline and I at the end of the group. I waited for her to close the door and couldn't help but try to read her pristine face. She answered my gaze with hers, showing me a loving expression and easing my worries. I took her hand and a deep breath, and we joined everyone in the living room.

"You have a very keen eye for detail and a skill for blending in with the humans," Vivienne said, noting the decor while her piercing eyes took in the room.

"Thank you," Elena said, relieved. "Can we offer you anything to drink?"

"We are all set," was Vivienne's short answer. With a brisk wave of her hand, she indicated for us to have a seat at the table. We did so immediately, and I made sure to sit next to Caroline. Janus took a seat at the other end of the table, where he sat very still, looking like a statue. Lerato offered Vivienne a chair, but she declined it with another wave of her hand, walking from one end of the table to the other with her arms crossed in front of her chest before pausing and looking at us.

"I am certain that we all know the reason for our gathering on this night," she said in a powerful voice.

"It is known that we descend to Earth to visit those of our future generation who have recently been assigned their first protégés. Caroline has proven herself very loyal to her duty and has planted many seeds of promise along the way. Those shall be taken care of very well until they are ripe, and this, I promise you, will require pain and sacrifice. Challenge will not be lacking in any aspect of your life, but it is the most valuable blessing that has been cast upon you. Challenge a young woman once and she will learn how to conquer the world."

The sound of her words hung in the air even after she finished speaking.

We weren't expecting this sudden proclamation from her. I could feel how Caroline's hand trembled faintly in my grip and how she released the tension in her back with a soft sigh from her lips. Elena and Lerato were smiling warmly, each with a satisfied and relieved expression on their flawless faces, while Dominic leaned back in his chair stiffly, his eyes moving from Vivienne to Caroline.

Caroline paused slightly before saying, "I appreciate your kind, encouraging words." Full of love, her eyes locked on mine for a brief second and I answered her gaze with mine in a promise that she would never walk alone on the winding road of her life.

"Those are words composed by the future I can see in your candle," Vivienne said. "I have left the door of your future ajar for you and I shall not share any more information."

She had given us a glimpse of Caroline's future without being asked, and I was astonished by her ability to see it through Caroline's candle alone.

Vivienne stopped pacing and looked at me.

"A future that will partially be drawn by your protégé and will always depend on his decision whether or not to reveal his knowledge about us to a human soul."

I held my breath, though I answered her gaze and ignored the impulse to look away out of fear.

"You are involved in a great secret of the universe, and we have to assure ourselves that you will never, under any circumstances, reveal this knowledge. You have no choice. You must quieten your tongue, but temptations will arise and you will have to resist. However, if you fail, you will be punished with the proper consequences."

She had spoken like a true leader, a warrior who knew how to bring order into any possible situation. She had gotten my full attention with her powerful voice from the moment she started speaking, and it was absolutely clear to me that she was not to be messed around with.

I swallowed, and blinked a few times to wet my itchy eyes. I had no intention of even thinking about revealing their existence to anyone.

"I promise, I will never tell anyone of what I know," I said, making sure to make eye contact with both her and Janus. He was still sitting in his chair, unmoving, but I was sure he absorbed every single one of our spoken words.

"We shall rest assured," she said with great seriousness, locked her hands behind her back and resumed walking back and forth again. When she walked past the fireplace, I realized that she didn't cast a shadow.

"Tell us about the first time you saw Caroline," she said after a quiet moment.

I cleared my throat and sat up in my chair.

"It happened only an instant after a car hit me. I was unconscious and thought I was dreaming. It felt strange, but as though everything was very realistic at the same time. I remember lying on the pavement and being surrounded by a white light when Caroline appeared out of a spark, knelt down next to me and gave me a kiss, after which I woke up at the hospital. I might not have even remembered the healing process if I hadn't seen her at my university campus shortly after this happened."

Even though my mind was racing, I tried to recall all possible details of our first meeting.

"I firmly believe that a bond was created," Lerato said with a serious expression. Vivienne's head turned in his direction, her halo following the movement smoothly.

"We have discussed that possibility as well, because it is not common for humans to perceive the healing process at all. A human heart is never weaker than when it's at the precipice of life and death."

"Your hearts are linked, bonded. It is no coincidence that you recognized Caroline when you physically saw her. Your affection toward each other serves as a sole proof of this bond," she said serenely. I squeezed Caroline's hand, and Elena gave us a loving smile. I was pleased by the fact that our hearts were linked and would do everything possible to keep it that way.

My heart jumped, and the sleeping monster in my chest released a contented sigh of love.

"It is more than a slight concern that this bond has potential for growth. If it develops, it will deepen your feelings for each other and can make you experience the same exact feelings simultaneously to an unimaginably intense degree. This ultimately might make Caroline become vulnerable as a guardian angel and lead to unfulfilled duties and failure on her part," Vivienne explained, with a slight nod in our direction. She unfolded her arms and started walking again.

"How is this possible?" Caroline asked.

"You seeing and remembering the healing process caused unexpected reactions on both the physical and psychological levels. We all know that love is the most powerful healing ingredient. Love is the fundamental elixir for treating any imaginable wound, visible or invisible. It is an unpredictable power that connects on all levels."

"Have you heard of this ever happening before?" I asked.

"I have. However, the one and only last similar happening dates back more than 50 years ago."

I was somehow relieved to hear that I wasn't the only human being who had ever witnessed the healing process, though I didn't know how that would be of any great help to Caroline and me.

"But why me?" I couldn't help asking. "Where does this ability to see the healing process come from?" My mind longed for more of an explanation.

Vivienne stopped walking for a moment, folded her arms in front of her chest again and looked at me with her head tilted slightly to the right.

"*Memini etiam quae nolo; oblivisci non possum quae volo,*" Janus said. I had almost forgotten he was there, and it was the first time since their arrival that he moved in his chair. His feathered wings fluttered slightly above his head as he moved his shoulders and his eyes looked around the table. He gave us a patient look.

"I remember what I don't want to, and I cannot forget what I want to," he translated, placing his hands on the table.

"The ability has been with you ever since your birth. You see what others don't, for the world reveals things to you that are kept away from others. This is a phenomenon that gives you the seeing eyes and makes you to what we call clairvoyant."

His voice had a subtle ability of sneaking into my mind, leaving me confused and impressed at the same time. Caroline squeezed my hand in response to what Janus had said, and Elena and Lerato kept their eyes on me with noticeably delighted expressions on their faces.

I suddenly felt defeated and said, "I'm afraid I don't really understand."

Janus nodded patiently and folded his hands.

"By clairvoyance we mean the ability to perceive information that is sensed with consciousness. You perceive information about events, such as the healing process, not available to the normal human senses, in the form of a vision. It can also be referred to as extrasensory perception."

He paused, allowing my mind to absorb his words.

I remained quiet while I thought about his explanation. In other words, he had told me that I was experiencing a way of being psychic and my self-defense mechanism allowed a longing for normality to overcome me. Maybe I should have never been told this, but then again that wouldn't have changed anything. He said it had always been with me.

My eyes searched Elena and Lerato for an answer. "This is all new to me," I said. They both looked happy about what Janus revealed, and their expressions reminded me not to be harsh with myself.

"You can see it as a biological gift," Janus said in response to my puzzled expression.

I nervously said, "No one in my family is clairvoyant."

"Clairvoyance is unexplainable; it never follows a pattern and can be of great help if one learns how to use it in his favor," he calmly said.

"We like to refer to this phenomenon as your entelechy, which shall, once discussed, help you to better understand your potential," Vivienne said.

"Under entelechy we understand the capacity of something to have a goal in itself," Janus began to explain. My confusion was written all over my face.

"It is the complete understanding, the final and perfect form of some prospective function."

I could see Lerato nod in understanding while Elena kept smiling. Caroline's face seemed to have brightened too.

My confused expression hadn't escaped Janus' eagle eyes.

"For example, an angel is a form of entelechy for a human being, since the angel has reached his perfected form."

I pondered his words in silence. My mind felt foggy.

"It represents the tenure of perfect skills that are available at any time, as those are the property of that specific individual," Janus explained further. "In conclusion, the angel's entelechy is the ability to fly."

I was having a hard time putting the scattered pieces of this puzzle together in order to understand what he was saying.

"It is inside of you," he added.

"The reason we are informing you about this serves solely to develop your understanding of your own entelechy. Your entelechy is seeing the healing process of your guardian angel, as you appear to evolve from the established basic cosmological patterns. It is as if your soul was touched by an invisible current of energy, and we assume that you have been born with this ability."

And there it was, the long-awaited answer to my burning question about where all of it had come from. I felt relieved, confused and irritated at the same time, as I had expected something simpler, something more human; but instead I received a truth about myself I had never expected to hear. I had to learn how to accept that this ability had been inside of me all the time.

I turned my head to face Caroline. Her lips stretched into a small smile; for an instant she looked exhausted, but then the expression in her eyes promised peace in my life, and I knew I should be at ease with the Elders' revelation. I traced my fingers across her soft knuckles, feeling more connected to her than ever. My entelechy was a power I had within that allowed me to see her at moments I wasn't supposed to, and I promised myself that night I'd learn how to use it to make myself see into her heart.

"Thank you," I said, tired.

Vivienne was still standing a few steps away from the table with her perfect hair majestically sitting on her shoulders and her blue eyes moved from Caroline to me. Janus hadn't moved at all, his hands were still folded on the surface of the table, and he nodded in acknowledgment.

"Your entelechy will develop," Vivienne added. "Seek help from your guardian angel, as it is her duty to comfort your aching human soul."

"I will make sure to always do that," I immediately said.

"We shall be witnesses of your actions," Vivienne said in response and started walking again up and down along the table.

"But we cannot depart until we have discussed the behavior of your *hostes hostium*."

Elena and Caroline shuddered at these words, Dominic sat back in his chair, and Lerato narrowed his eyes.

"The enemy," Janus translated for me.

171

I could feel how the atmosphere changed suddenly and I froze in my seat. I knew whom she was talking about: the one who had tried to kill me, the one because of whom Caroline could have failed as a guardian angel.

Vivienne's voice was cold as she said, "Your angel of death has a very stubborn mind."

Lerato leaned his weight on the table as he heard these words.

"He tried to take Adam's life twice," Caroline said very quickly, with a worried expression wrinkling her forehead. "During his second attempt, he even used his bare hands to pull Adam down into the depths of a frozen lake."

"We are aware of his actions," Vivienne responded.

"We went back to the place of the accident, and I discovered a sudden change in the energetic field," Lerato interjected.

Vivienne turned to face him and said, "That location is precisely where we've come from." She looked toward the windows. "We cannot rely on assumptions and decided to search that area ourselves for proof of what actually happened to Adam, especially since no human beings will be going to the lake tonight," she continued.

"The change in the energetic field and its subatomic particles at the exact time of the accident and the sudden disappearance of your angel of death offer obvious indications that he is not following his duties."

"Disappearance?" Caroline asked, moving forward in her seat. "What do you mean?" She exchanged a quick look with her parents. I knew something was wrong.

"Can't you locate him?" Elena asked concerned.

Janus spoke, his eyebrows moving.

"We've tried, but we can't find him. This is inexplicable, since we are able to locate every single angel on this planet. He has made himself a target of our attention, but we don't know where he is. All we know is that he is hiding, and he is doing it very well."

Caroline ran her hands through her hair, something she did more frequently when she was nervous. Elena shook her head slightly in confusion, and Lerato formed his hands into fists.

If the Elders couldn't locate my angel of death, then who could? I had proof enough now that things were beyond messed up, and I needed to figure out a way to keep Caroline safe. My angel of death was probably playing a game with all of us and was waiting for the right moment to attack me again. I was scared for the first time in the presence of Caroline and her family.

"There must be a way to find him," Lerato said, pressing them. "He can't just disappear without leaving a trace."

Vivienne almost cut him off.

"And we will find that way. We've searched the lake and its surroundings. Nothing indicates that he is hiding in that area, and we are going to extend our search globally."

Her voice became cold again, as she said, "We are being confronted with something entirely new."

"In what way is this new?" Lerato asked, serious.

We all looked toward Vivienne for an answer. She kept walking up and down and moving her wings, her halo gently following the movements of her head.

"The angels today are different from those of a decade ago. We have observed changes and developments in many aspects of their functions, such as increased speed and strength. This ability to hide from us makes us realize some of their skills we've been unaware of."

She stopped in front of the altar and looked at the candles from left to right.

I was concerned by her confession about the ways the new angels were developing, as I had longed for shelter and security from her and Janus. I grew suddenly nervous at the realization of how intensified the situation had become, both in their world and mine. Elena looked sad as she drew her hand to her mouth.

"Is he using the new abilities to make himself invisible?" Lerato asked. His eyes were firmly locked on Vivienne, and he looked extremely serious.

Vivienne nodded yes.

"It's possible. If he has indeed developed skills that help him hide from us, then we will develop skills to make him visible. We will keep looking for him in other countries, and we have several guardian angels involved in our search for him. Wherever he is, we will find him, and he will pay for the consequences of his actions."

Caroline's eyes locked on mine as she fastened her grip on my hand. I knew very well that we both were in danger until they found him. I released a silent sigh and reminded myself that I had already had my fair share of accidents and hospital visits. The last thing I wanted to do was to play hide-and-seek with my angel of death.

I rubbed my temples. "Do you know why he wants to kill me?" I asked, feeling tired.

Vivienne stopped walking and turned to face me.

"No, we don't. His behavior is still a riddle to us. However, we firmly believe that he has a strong motive, since he has never before shown such behavior while carrying out his duties. Your time has not come yet to leave this world, and Caroline must be very careful not to lose your soul and cause imbalance upon the universe."

With piercing eyes, she continued to warn us.

"Your angel of death is hiding; he is running away. But you, Adam, should not do the same. You cannot become the hero of your own destiny if you let fear seep into your heart, for fear does not exist where there is courage. I shall not speak of the cruelty that lies hidden in the darkness. Know that your angel of death answers to the name of Corbett and his soul holds the meaning of a black raven."

The sound of her voice made my stomach clench. I felt sick all of a sudden, and I opened my mouth to breathe more deeply. My angel of death had a name, a meaning and a motive for killing me. I felt trapped and suddenly wanted the conversation to end.

"What if he attacks Adam again?" Caroline asked with concern. I glanced at her face quickly and saw that she was scared.

"We are here to help, but first we have to find him," Janus said, his deep voice echoing in my mind.

"*Contra legem,*" Vivienne said. "*Against the law,* in your human tongue. It seems as if he's calling for war. There is no excuse for breaking the regulations in this way."

"How do you take the life of an angel of death?" I asked desperately. We needed to be prepared; there was no time to take any risks.

Caroline turned to face me, surprised by my question. I gazed deeply into her eyes and saw that she was sorry her first assumptions had turned out to be right.

Vivienne stopped in front of the fireplace; only her dark silhouette was visible.

"To kill an angel of death one has to rip out his heart, crush it, and then burn it. There is no other way to kill him."

My heartbeat accelerated, and my headache sharpened. Lerato didn't seem startled at all by Vivienne's words, while Elena and Caroline looked equally concerned. Dominic's eyes were focused downward on the table.

"Is there anything in particular that we have to pay attention to?" Lerato asked, breaking the silence.

Vivienne moved away from the fireplace and was bathed in light.

"Make sure to always stay together whenever possible, and Adam shouldn't stay out alone after sunset. Note anything unfamiliar, and let us know if you sense a potential attack."

We remained in complete silence for well over a minute. Ler-

175

ato had put his arm around Elena, Dominic's gaze was lost somewhere outside in the dark night, and Caroline rested her head on my shoulder. My head was buzzing, I tried to keep my breath even to prevent myself from having a panic attack. I allowed all this information to trickle into my mind, as my eyes sought out the candles on the altar. They were soothing, very comforting somehow.

"We shall depart now," Vivienne announced.

Janus nodded and silently got off his chair. I felt tired and worn out all of a sudden, eager to fall asleep and forget about my life for a few hours.

"May peace be with you," Janus said.

"The same to you," Lerato said, opening the front door for them. The cold air from outside felt good on my hot skin.

Vivienne paused in the doorway and turned around to face me with her piercing blue eyes.

"We have left you a book as a gift under the Christmas tree. Read the story and study its six lessons. This book will serve as a medium of communication for us. Be sure to keep it in a safe place."

"I promise I won't let it out of my sight," I assured her. I turned to look at the Christmas tree and saw there was indeed a small golden package for me.

"Thank you," I said, turning back to the door, but the Elders were already gone.

HISTORIA MAGISTRA VITAE

"I can't believe it," Elena said.

I felt the effects of the Elders' unexpected visit as I made my way back to the living room. I felt excruciatingly exhausted and threw myself onto the couch next to the fireplace and closed my eyes for a moment.

Elena's and Lerato's voices sounded as if they were underwater. My hands were slightly shaking, and I slowly moved my legs to make their jelly-like feeling go away. The insides of my stomach felt weird, sort of empty, and I inhaled through my mouth in order to help the nausea. I had been told that my angel of death was playing a sick game with us and appeared to want to take my life at any cost; Caroline's future and its challenges had been foretold; and I had met winged angels. I was allowed to freak out to some extent and took a human moment to rub my throbbing temples. I felt a desperate urge to sink into the softness of the couch and linger in its darkness until my life went back to normal.

I felt Caroline's warmth as she sat next to me and rested her head on my shoulder. *Stop whining,* I told myself and opened my eyes.

Lerato was still sitting next to Elena at the table, having an indistinct conversation with both words and looks. A glass of champagne pressed to his lips, Dominic was at the other end of the table, trying not to look startled by what he had heard.

"I don't want you to worry too much," I said. Elena and Lerato stopped talking and looked at me.

Elena looked concerned as she said, "I've never heard of such behavior before." She paused and looked at Lerato. "Very unusual behavior after all," she added. "I don't understand why or how Adam's angel of death is hiding."

"There's got to be a reason for his behavior," Dominic speculated.

Lerato bravely tried to make us feel better.

"Of course there is a reason, and we will make sure to find out what it is. The patterns of his actions are very peculiar and not at all common for an angel of death. I firmly believe that he knows that the Elders are aware of what he has done, and that is precisely the reason for his disappearance. We can flip things around and say that he isn't hiding so that he can attack Adam, but rather to avoid the consequences awaiting him once he's found."

I appreciated his effort.

"Maybe he is trying to tell us something," I suggested.

Caroline was off the couch in a heartbeat.

"Tell us what? That he is all about taking your life? It just doesn't add up. I hoped the Elders would know more about him."

I followed her to the table.

"What if this is only a test from the Elders to see how you would deal with such a situation?" I conjectured.

Elena wrinkled her forehead, Lerato shook his head no, and Caroline pursed her soft lips.

Lerato wrapped his hand around Elena's.

"That's not possible. It would be against the Elders' nature. They are the ones bringing order to both the human and angelic worlds."

"He's right," Elena said, her maternal expression directed to me. She still looked the same as before dinner; her hair was still impeccably curled and appeared lighter than before, and her dress fitted her body perfectly. The only difference was the concern that showed in her flawless face.

I had done everything possible to convince them that my angel of death wasn't behind the strange accidents that had befallen me, but now I had to face reality.

"What could their new skills be?" I asked.

Lerato answered instantly.

"Many, to be honest with you. It can be anything from speed to sharply developed senses. Those are just two that immediately come to my mind."

"Adam's angel of death is missing and the Elders are not able to find him," Caroline said tensely. "There must be something more to it than just speed or sensing." She seemed to be trying hard to find out where Corbett was.

"The fact is that he is not gone," Lerato said abruptly. "He might just not be revealing himself to us."

Caroline doubtfully asked, "You really think he is invisible?"

"Now that I think about it, I actually do," Lerato said and scratched his chin. "It might even make more sense and correlate with our discovery."

We all gave him a questioning look, and he explained with a patient expression.

"Invisibility is perceived in a wide range of forms, though I can think of two in particular. It is most likely possible that he is camouflaging himself as something that he is not to make himself appear invisible to our eyes."

"But is it even possible for him to use camouflage the same way animals do?" Caroline asked.

"At this point it might be," Lerato said diplomatically. "He could step in front of any object that he pleases, such as a tree trunk, and adopt its coloration."

I was growing nervous about his theory, because that meant that Corbett could have been among us for a longer period of time than I had thought.

"If he indeed was among us, wouldn't you feel his presence?" I asked Caroline. She looked nervous and irritated at the same time.

"I think I would," she said and gave me an unsure look with her delicate eyes.

"Not necessarily," Lerato interjected. "By using camouflage he might completely block himself away from us, and that's why I believe not even the Elders have been able to locate him. It's as if he were on another frequency."

Pulling her hands through her hair Caroline groaned and said, "He could be anywhere!"

"Indeed, though I don't believe he would dare to attack Adam one more time," Lerato said, trying to ease her worries. Caroline tilted her head sideways to look at me, and it took a lot of effort for me to remain calm and keep my head up. My eyes were itchy, and my body longed for sleep.

Lerato continued.

"He might also be using a form of transparency. He most likely could have developed a skill that makes him neither absorb nor reflect light, allowing it to pass through him."

I remained silent for a good moment and listened to the

sound of the crackling fire in order to give my human brain another very much needed minute. Lerato's theories sounded accurate and intimidating, and while I hoped that he was wrong, the fact that his assumptions about my perception of Caroline's healing process were close to what the Elders had revealed made me feel very little hope.

"How can angels of death just adopt new skills?" Elena wondered. "That doesn't sound right."

Lerato looked at her thoughtfully.

"We can't assume anything, since nothing has been proven yet. It could be possible that they have used their consciousness to expand their minds, which they could have done through special training. Their minds already operate differently than ours; we don't know what they are capable of."

"You're saying that as long as Adam's angel of death is invisible, no one can know where he is?" Caroline demanded. From the tone in her voice I knew that she was agitated.

"That would make sense, especially since he was not visible in the electromagnetic spectrum the night we went back to the lake," Lerato answered swiftly.

Sighing, Caroline said, "I can't believe it is so simple for him to be invisible to me."

"He will eventually have a reason to reveal himself, sooner or later," I said, trying to be helpful.

"He most definitely will reveal himself at the moment of his next planned attack," Caroline responded, her eyes gleaming in the firelight.

"We have to make sure to be alert at all times," Lerato said with a calm gesture of his hands. Caroline pressed her back against the chair. She intertwined her fingers with mine, and I enjoyed her gentle touch.

"Maybe," Lerato said and narrowed his eyes, "the one who could see where Corbett is hiding is you, Adam."

I was taken by surprise by his statement and stared back at him with a puzzled expression on my face. Caroline leaned forward in her seat.

"I could?" I asked, doubtful.

He nodded yes.

"You already see what is not revealed to any human being. Your entelechy could possibly even allow you to sense your angel of death."

I exchanged a perplexed look with Caroline while her family looked at me. Feeling how Lerato's proposal added a hint of crisp electricity to the air, I thought about his theory. It would have never occurred to me to use my entelechy to sense Corbett. I didn't even know how to use it, because I had always used it unconsciously.

"Maybe this is just a very early stage of clairvoyance," I said in dilemma.

Lerato's lips twitched into a smile.

"I encourage you to think differently. You have, as you know, used it once before, if not several times. You can use your entelechy in your favor. I will be more than happy to help you practice it."

"I'll do whatever it takes to help," Caroline said hearteningly from my side, giving me a loving smile. I could see that she was pleased with Lerato's idea, and for a moment, I felt claustrophobic as I realized that I actually didn't have another choice. Refusing to try to find out where Corbett was could end up badly for all of us, and I couldn't live with that thought.

"I will try," I finally said, still unsure. "I just don't know how or what to focus on."

"Let me do some research on this," Lerato said. "There is no need to rush. Clairvoyance needs to be approached with respect, as any lack of preparedness might result in unpleasant and overwhelming experiences."

"I understand," I said and sank lower in my chair to rest my head. A heavy tiredness had completely snuck up upon me.

Lerato played another soothing song while Elena started taking the dishes to the kitchen.

"I think it's time for me to leave," I said, prying myself from my chair and following her. She was loading the dishes in the dishwasher and turned around to face me, her maternal smile playing with the features of her flawless face.

"Of course you're not leaving. It would be a very risky thing to do. It's already too late to leave, and you'll stay here for the night. Lerato will drive you home first thing tomorrow."

I wasn't happy with her offer. "Mom might send out the cops to look for me if I don't show up soon," I said a bit sarcastically. She smiled.

"I'm sure she will know you're fine if you let her know you're going to stay here overnight," she said, switching the dishwasher on.

I felt bad, as I didn't want to impose on them any further. I especially didn't want them to feel forced to look after me in case Corbett decided to attack me again while I was with them.

"Elena is right," Lerato said, coming in from the living room and putting the champagne glasses in the sink. I forced an appreciative smile onto my face, remembering that my life was linked to Caroline's. It would had been selfish to insist on leaving, no matter how uncomfortable I felt.

"I'll stay."

"Perfect," Lerato said, looking satisfied. I grabbed my phone from my pocket and sent a message to May letting her know I wouldn't be back until the next day.

Caroline joined us in the kitchen, and we helped Elena clean up. I felt drowsy and wondered silently how much alcohol angels could drink, for none of them showed the slightest sign of tipsiness.

Elena beamed at me and said, "Dominic will give you an extra pair of his pajamas, and I'll put a fresh towel and toothbrush in the bathroom for you."

"Thank you," I said, appreciating her efforts to make me feel at home.

"It is our pleasure," she said as she hugged both of us good night.

I felt that the longest day of my life was coming to an end as I leaned against the sink after Elena left. It felt good being alone with Caroline; the special sense of security and understanding she gave me helped calm my racing mind.

"Thank you for staying," she said and rested her head on my shoulder. The softness of her curly hair on my cheek felt soothing. I put my arm around her waist and closed my eyes, enjoying this moment together.

"I don't want to be the reason for your future challenges," I said. She remained quiet, and I listened to her steady breathing.

Her voice was warm as she raised her head and looked into my eyes.

"This extraordinary time that we spend on Earth and call life is a gift of love and is supposed to bring both happiness and pain. My destiny was written on my candle the moment I was born and says that I will love you forever."

The sight of her face in the dimmed light was beautiful. Her hair was neatly resting on both sides of her face while her soft lips stretched into one of her loving smiles. I leaned my head down and kissed her silky forehead, euphorically inhaling her warmth.

"You need some rest," she said gently. She took me by the hand and we made our way upstairs. I paused and stepped toward the Christmas tree to pick up the Elders' package. It was light and its neat golden wrapping caused a tickling sensation in my fingers.

"Do you mind if we open it tomorrow?" I asked drowsily on our way upstairs.

"Not at all," she said, opening the door to her room.

A nice breeze ruffled our hair and moved the silky curtains in a tranquilizing way as I sat on the edge of her bed.

"I'll go change and get ready for bed," she said on her way out. "Dominic should have a pair of his pajamas ready for you."

I stared after her for a good while and played with the gift in my hands. I was curious what the book would look like and couldn't think of how the Elders could communicate with me through it. I would surely know soon enough, I thought, placing it on the night table, and made my way to Dominic's room.

"Come in," I heard him say from inside after I knocked on his door.

I wrapped my hand around the door handle and hesitantly entered his room. It was smaller than Caroline's but had been arranged comfortably. He was sitting on his bed with his back against the wall, his face hidden behind a book under a small reading lamp. The walls of his room were painted the same shade of blue as the hallway, and his bed sheets matched. A small wooden table with books placed according to their sizes was neatly pushed against the wall to our right.

"Elena said I could have a spare pair of your pajamas," I said.

He stopped reading, lowered the book and pointed with his head to a chair tucked under the table.

"Sure. They're right there. Hope they fit."

I pulled the chair out and grabbed his pajamas.

"Thanks."

"No problem."

I awkwardly made my way to the door. I felt uncomfortable and guilty being alone with him, especially after having wrongfully accused him of being behind my accident on the lake.

"What do children refer to as things they find captivating but cannot understand?" he asked abruptly. I paused with my grip on the door handle.

"I'm not sure I know," I said, wondering what he was getting at.

"They refer to it as magic," he answered, his eyes focused on mine. He pointed to his guitar at the foot of his bed with another gesture of his head.

"If I told a child that this was a magical guitar and that it would play the most beautiful sounds when I told it to, he would believe me. Wouldn't he?"

"He would," I said puzzled.

"Children are innocent and believe wholeheartedly. What do you think makes magic possible in their lives?"

I stared at him for a while, trying to clear my foggy mind.

"I don't know."

He seemed to speak through his eyes.

"It's their belief system. It's all about how strong you believe in yourself. You've got something that hardly anyone has. If you believe in yourself, you will be able to achieve great things. You've got the *numen* inside of you, look closely and you'll see."

His conversation had completely astonished me. He proved once more that he was eager to be of assistance to Caroline and me.

"I will do my best. Thanks for your help."

His face was serious.

"My intention was never to offend you. I'm very protective of Caroline and desperate to help."

"That makes two of us."

I tightened my grip on the door handle and kept my eyes focused on his while he gave me another of his somber looks.

"Good night," he said and hid his face behind his book again.

I made my way downstairs to the bathroom, where I splashed my face with cold water. I grabbed the fresh towel Elena had left for me and pressed it against my eyes, trying to block out my surroundings for a moment. The soft fabric of the towel felt good against my hot skin as I breathed through my mouth. The pressure against my eyes made me see spinning circles of light, and I lowered the towel and stared into the mirror for a good while.

I wondered where my life would have taken me if I had never seen Caroline the day of the accident, and I simply couldn't imagine it without her. Despite the sudden changes in my life since I had met her, I was glad to admit to myself that I was content with my life. As long as I was with her.

"They fit," Caroline said when I went back in her room. She was alluringly brushing her hair and sitting on the edge of the bed, wearing only a silky nightgown over her perfect body.

I sat down next to her.

"You can sleep next to me," she said in a serious tone. "That's where I can keep you the safest right now." I could feel my heart jump, and I silently thought that being in mortal danger maybe wasn't so bad after all. The sparks in my chest were back.

"I appreciate it," I said and laughed at my silly thought.

The warmth her body radiated as she rested her head on my chest seemed to ease away all my fatigue and worries. Her soft hair tickled my nose, and we remained in complete silence while I moved my hand up and down her shoulder. Her gentle presence and her warm heart made me realize how completely overcome I was with her.

"What is a *numen?*" I asked, curious. She looked at me.

"It's a term usually used by sociologists to represent a magical power inhabiting an object."

I remained silent as I thought about Dominic's words of wisdom and the way he had tried to make me believe in myself. My entelechy had been with me since my birth and suppressing it would mean suppressing who I was. I promised myself I would do everything possible to find out where Corbett was.

Caroline's peaceful breathing sounded like a lullaby composed in love just for me. I was still awake after she fell asleep and enjoyed the fact that our hearts were linked.

I thought about something that I never considered before: *How was I ever going to measure up to her previous relationships?* Suddenly, I realized I was thinking about insecurities I wasn't even aware of before lying next to her.

Why didn't she have any biological and social expectations from me? Maybe she did, secretly, I wondered, but refrained from bringing them up. I sighed and traced my hand down her spine. Her body seemed perfect—too perfect next to mine. What if she was too experienced, in the most intimate sense? Would I ever be able to fulfill her?

But then my thoughts shifted from insecurity to comfort as I thought about our unique bond, something I had never shared with anyone before. We were connected, linked, and she felt the same way. She wouldn't lie to me, of that I was completely sure. My mind eased as I realized there was no competition. Simply because no one else could ever live up to our special connection.

That was the night when I learned that being close to someone only physically could never create a strong and lasting bond. Only when two souls emerge from deep within two yearning hearts and silently exchange vows, each one taking a part of his and her life and handing it to the other; only then is a true eternal bond created.

When I opened my eyes the next morning, Caroline was still resting her head on my chest. I blinked a few times and allowed my eyes to wander throughout her room. The sun was shining brightly through her windows, and the silky curtains were peacefully moving in the breeze. I realized how energized and completely rested I felt. I moved slightly, trying not to wake her up.

"How do you feel?" she asked.

"Bad for waking you up," I said. She lifted her head from

my chest and smiled a perfect morning smile in response, amused.

"I was awake way before you were."

"Then why didn't you wake me up?" I teased.

"I'm not supposed to interrupt your dreams," she said, still smiling. "You needed some rest, remember?"

I leaned forward and placed a kiss on her forehead.

"Do you mind if we open your present?"

She rolled to the side and supported her upper body with her arm on the pillow while her hair fell to the side.

I had almost forgotten about my gift from the Elders, and grabbed it from the night table.

"Wait," she said. "Let's open it in the library."

I paused and asked, "Where?"

"In Lerato's library. I'll show you."

She took my hand and walked me down the hallway to the first door on the right.

His library was immense, much bigger than I would had expected from the outside. Thick curtains were neatly tied to the lower corners of the windows, and small pieces of dust reflected the filtering sunlight. Caroline closed the door behind me as I approached a wooden table in the middle of the room where an open book rested, along with a glass of water and Lerato's notes.

It almost felt as if we had entered another century, one in which people still relied on books and cared for them with much affection. The bookshelves reached from floor to ceiling. Some had wheels and could be rolled aside to reveal yet another packed set of shelves behind them. A couple of books were piled up and placed on a wooden ladder that was attached to the front row of the shelves, and I could clearly picture Lerato placing them there for future reference during one of his research sessions. I was amazed by how sophisticated and perfect the library looked, and how much it expressed his nature.

"Welcome to Lerato's world."

"This is amazing."

I was in awe and stepped closer to one of the shelves.

Caroline's amusement brightened her face.

"He likes to read and finds pleasure in conducting his studies in here late at night. Some books that he keeps on top of the shelves have been passed on to him by previous generations. He doesn't have a favorite book—he says that he likes them all equally. 'There's no such thing as a useless book,' he likes to say, 'but only the wrong book at the inappropriate moment. Seek advice in the books you pick according to your circumstances and you'll always choose the right one.'"

She walked behind me, her fingers brushing over the spines of the books.

I was utterly consumed by Lerato's world and imagined him climbing the ladder in search of advice and grabbing a specific book with his polished hands.

"*In Harmonia Progressio,*" I practiced my Latin, reading the title of a worn-out book.

"Which means *Progress in Harmony,*" Caroline translated. "It was written by Adriel Candidus—one of the most influential angel writers of her time."

"What do you mean 'angel writer'?" I asked, raising my eyebrows at her. "I didn't know angels had their own books."

"Of course we have angel writers," she said, smiling at me. "It's just that their books are not accessible to human beings; they're written strictly for our own community."

I was being introduced to yet another secret from the angelic world that other humans didn't know about, and I enjoyed the privilege Caroline was bestowing upon me.

"This is...fascinating," I said and inhaled the scent of the books.

"*Lapsus Memoriae,*" I read another title out loud.

She glanced at me sideways, still smiling. "That means *Slip of Memory*, and it was written by Cassius Diutinus."

"*Cassius* means *box*, and *Diutinus* means *lasting a long time*. He chose his last name after he had suffered from amnesia. I find his story very fascinating. According to the tale, he recovered his memories by creating a small white glass box in which he could store his memories and access them whenever he pleased. This way he wouldn't completely lose his slipping memories. But his book is very complicated to read, since due to his illness, he writes in a way that's hard to comprehend. He does reveal how to use the box, but forgets to mention where he hid it. Many of our scientists have been looking for it without success, and there have even been some conspiracy theories associated with his invention, as no one knows where it is."

I was voluntarily drowning in her world as she revealed these details in her sweet voice.

"Do you believe in his invention?" I asked.

"Absolutely. He's done some miraculous work with this book."

I stared at *Lapsus Memoriae* briefly, put it back on the shelf and grabbed another book.

"*Magno cum Gaudio.*"

"*With Great Joy*, by Lelia Persolvo," she translated.

"This is sort of a self-help book. She emphasizes how we can live with great joy and reminds us that everything in this world is connected. She states numerous times how our thoughts are more important than we think they are. Her last name means *to explain* or *to unloosen*. She writes without sparing a single word, as you can see from the 900-page tome you're holding in your hands."

I could see that Caroline was entertained by sharing stories of her world as she followed me to another bookshelf across the room where a red leather book caught my attention.

"*Mirabile Visu,*" I read.

"That means *Wonderful to See,* and it was written by Marcus Secundus. Actually, this book has a sequel called *Mirabile Dictu,* which means *Wonderful to Tell.* Marcus Secundus was a doctor during many wars between human beings on Earth, and he describes in these books how beautiful it was to witness the healing process of his human patients."

I silently appreciated the existence of the angels among humans and came to realize how much we actually had to attribute to them. Angels were allowed to live among humans for some reason, and I was convinced that it definitely served our betterment.

I climbed the ladder and grabbed a blue book. "*The Problems of Humanity,* by Alice Bailey," I said aloud. "Her name doesn't sound Latin."

Caroline smiled lovingly.

"It's not. She was a human theosophist who wrote on a wide range of subjects. The title reveals what this book is about. In it, she talks about economic imbalance, disease and poverty as well as underprivileged countries, among other issues. Lerato likes to refer to this book during his studies of the human race, human thought processes and the political aspects of human life."

I took her hand and walked over to the table. We sat down, and I saw that Lerato had scribbled some notes on the edges of the pages of the book in front of us.

"As you see, Lerato focuses on both the human and angelic worlds. He likes to keep his knowledge universal and balanced."

I looked around.

"I'm more than impressed. This looks like a perfectly designed world where not a single piece of the puzzle is missing."

She beamed with amusement, and a strand of hair fell in front of her eyes.

"We're not supposed to share our world with human beings.

The moment I met you was the moment I let you inside of my soul. This is your world as much as it is mine."

I leaned closer to her, brushed the strand of hair behind her ear and gave her a long kiss on the forehead.

"You are my world," I said, looking deeply into her golden eyes.

"What is *your* favorite book?" I asked, curious. The details about her world seemed to provoke an unusual desire in me.

She tilted her upper body toward me and gave me a loving look.

"It's called *Unitas Humanus* and was written by Regina Volatilis. The literal translation is *Human Unity,* and it has gained a tremendous amount of followers from those of all ages. I admire Regina Volatilis a lot as a person; she is an incredibly influential woman, who lost her mother just before she published this book. She strongly believes in universal salvation and has created a way to unite humanity. She has also provided a very clear resolution to life-threatening problems, such as wars, discrimination, poverty, child abuse and their institutionalization. In fact, her theory is very precise. It's intended to provide a sense of relief and complete understanding for every human soul. One of her aspirations is to make humans color-blind when they meet others, for this would completely eliminate racism and inequality."

"She has presented her studies to the Elders and asked for permission to be active in the human world and to practice her theory by revealing herself to the world by being at several places at the same time. The Elders have denied her request though, as humans are not ready yet for such a drastic positive change. I admire her courage for stepping up, allowing her voice to be heard and for believing in the human race, for that is truly where the Earth needs improvement. It is unfortunate how parts of humanity believe in corruption, wars and domination."

"Though her request was denied, she was given the *Ordo Mens*

193

Divinus, the Order of the Divine Mind, the highest order angels can receive from the Elders. She was the seventh and last angel of this century to receive this honor."

I saw her golden eyes light up with every word she spoke and felt the pride she took in Volatilis's ideas and accomplishments. Once again, I fell more deeply in love with her and her entire world.

"The world needs more angels like her," I said.

"I absolutely agree," she said compassionately. "Let's open your present."

The electric tingling sensation in my fingers awakened as I slowly tore the golden wrapping paper open. The book was thin and light, decorated with a delicate violet and white cover. It was inscribed with the words *Entelechia Spiritus,* and the letters popped out against their background.

"Let's see what it says," Caroline said encouragingly. She grabbed my other hand as I flipped the cover page open. The first page was blank and my excitement grew as I turned the page one more time.

"*Historia Magistra Vitae,*" I said, reading the title. Although I didn't understand the meaning of the text, I could feel the excitement growing inside of me, along with a racing heart and sweaty hands. I cleared my throat and began to read the short poem that was written in elegant old-fashioned letters.

"*Magistra vitae,* it is too complicated what you are asking from me in this moment. For every life lesson is sweltering like venom in me."

Without giving much thought to the introductory poem, I began reading:

"1958, Great Britain, London -
This is the year when Severino was assigned his first protégée, Godeva,
whose parents were poor farmers. Severino made a habit of influencing her

dreams in order to help her overcome the misery and suffering her destiny had cast upon her. It occurred, later the same year, that he started to visit her by night after desperately witnessing no betterment of her situation. He did not reveal himself to her physically, but could not resist the temptation to influence her dreams more intensively after which he allowed her to dream of him.

The influence and effect his dreams had on Godeva were unpleasant, as her human heart was bound to his by seeing him, which made her desperate, as she started to long for him physically. Severino, aware of what he had done, decided to reveal himself to her by pretending to be a human being. He sought work at her parents' farm, and they both were blinded by their feelings and decided they belonged together in body and soul.

One day, shortly after he began working at the farm, he confessed that he was her guardian angel and revealed to her the secrets of our existence. The course of their lives changed forever after she expressed her desire to become an angel.

Severino then remembered his duties as a guardian angel and explained that her wish went against all laws and could not be fulfilled under any circumstances. Not willing to accept no for an answer, Godeva then expressed another human desire that following spring: to create a family with Severino. He again refused her human caprice with great effort, until she finally gave up this idea with an aching heart. But not for long.

The following month she insisted on being transformed into a white one, after which an overwhelmed Severino distanced himself from her for a while. Godeva suffered from a great depression and decided to force the transformation process upon him. She knew that she first had to die, and so committed suicide by drinking venom.

The sight of his dead lover caused Severino unbearable pain, and he did the forbidden: He touched her dead heart and called her back to life. Godeva became an angel—but not the one he had expected to create. She became an angel of destruction—a dark one.

The transformation had changed Godeva completely, and Severino witnessed how she not only lost control over her human body and feelings but *also tried to murder both of them. She died of a hatred that ate her crippled human soul.*

'Amor et melle et felle est fecundissimus,' were the last words that she spoke. The Elders burned her heart, and Severino paid the price for his actions: He had to live for the rest of that life as a human being.

Here ends the story about the love between Severino and Godeva. May you never encounter such a love in your life."

Caroline still had her hand wrapped around mine after I had finished, and neither of us moved. We allowed our hearts to absorb the story. The profound effect this short-but-intense tale had on us was visible on our faces.

"What a way to tell a love story," Caroline sighed as she slowly ran her hand through her hair.

I drew a deep breath. The words of the story were imprinted on my mind. Overwhelming and stirring emotions spread throughout my body, and I was sure that the Elders had put their point across in a singularly effective way.

"What does Godeva's last sentence mean?" I asked, pointing to the Latin words. I was startled, if not quite grieved, as I began to draw the parallels between Godeva's love for Severino and my love for Caroline.

"'*Amor et melle et felle est fecundissimus*', means that love is rich with both honey and venom," she explained. "Regret," she added and locked her eyes with mine for a brief moment.

"I am sure that these words were spoken by the human part of Godeva before she died. By honey she refers to the richness of the good things she could have had with Severino, and she mentions venom in reference to how she had chosen to leave the world. In other words, she realized that love is always composed of both happiness and sacrifice. I feel so bad for her; it's as if I could feel her pain."

Caroline turned her head away from the book.

I was conflicted, desperate even.

"I don't understand why they didn't give her human soul another chance. She was lost and depressed, and her only wish was to be with him. That seems like a contradiction."

I felt nauseous.

Caroline looked back at me and held my hand.

"What the Elders want to say with this story is that everyone has to think first about the consequences of their actions. When Godeva was dying, she instantly regretted everything she had done. But regret, unfortunately, can't change the past. Rather, it teaches us a lesson. Try to look at it from another point of view. *Historia Magistra Vitae* is a Latin expression that means *History is life's teacher*. It refers to the idea that the study of the past should serve as a lesson for the future, and I am more than convinced that the Elders have a strong reason for gifting you with this story. They are showing us which mistakes to avoid."

I sighed as I stared into her warm eyes for a while. I felt the neurons whirl in my brain, and horrified, I started to understand the message of the story.

I squeezed her hand and said, "I would never force you to transform me."

"I know," she said, looking sad. "I trust you wholeheartedly."

I flipped the page and saw the following words in the same elegant old-fashioned font: *I hereby know that the six lessons in this story are:*

The rest of the book was blank.

"Look!" she said, speaking quickly and pointing at the text. "That's exactly what I thought. Everything is about lessons, and we need to find six."

It took me a second to catch up. "It's pretty obvious that we're not allowed to force the transformation process," I said, underlining the words with my index finger.

"Absolutely," Caroline said in agreement. "Never."

Her eyes skimmed the page with immense speed. Then she looked up, locking her eyes on mine, and spoke softly in response to my startled expression.

"He wasn't allowed to confess that he was her guardian angel. Our circumstances are different. Sooner or later you would have found out through your entelechy."

Her words were soothing, and I returned her gaze with understanding.

"The child…," she continued. "…humans and angels aren't allowed to have children."

This time she lowered her eyes to avoid mine. I drew another breath and allowed my lungs to expand, hoping that would ease the pain in my chest. I gently placed my fingers on her chin and lifted her head to look at me.

"It's all about sacrifice, isn't it? I'll even sacrifice my life just so I can be with you."

A moment of mutual silence followed as she looked profoundly into my eyes. Sometimes I had the feeling that she used her eyes to look inside of me and touch my soul.

She spoke quietly with teary eyes.

"He healed her after she committed suicide. Suicide is a sad, painful personal way to leave the world and cannot be stopped by us. The dead cannot…mustn't be called back to life…."

My heart ached at her words. Her thoughts about such a possible outcome of our future made my stomach contract. I hugged her tightly and promised wordlessly that I would always live for her.

"We should write the lessons down," she said softly and handed me one of Lerato's pens. I flipped the page and winced in amazement; the first five lessons we had named appeared on the paper and I traced my fingers across the writing as if to prove they were real.

Caroline looked delighted, and the tension that had been

steadily building in her body vanished. "Now we know how it works," she said.

I stared at the words and finally understood the communication process with the Elders.

"But there's still one that's missing," she noted.

"Maybe the way he influenced her dreams?" I speculated, and we both stared at the page waiting for the words to appear.

I rewound the story in my brain.

"What about the poem? He fulfilled her wish even though what she was asking was too complicated. Maybe if he had fulfilled her desire at a later time or under different circumstances it would have been different."

"They want us to read between the lines," Caroline said and scratched her forehead, her golden eyes narrowing to tiny slits. "A guardian angel is never allowed to forget their duties."

Caroline stared at the words for a long time. "He shouldn't have sought work on her parents' premises," she finally said. "His approach to helping her wasn't strategic enough." We proceeded to name several lessons, though no words appeared on the page.

"There's got to be another link to the missing lesson," she exclaimed anxiously after half an hour of pondering. "It's just not an obvious one."

The movement of the rays of sunlight up the walls reminded me of the amount of time we had spent in Lerato's library. Caroline suggested taking a break and then we could resume our brainstorming session over the single missing lesson later.

"What an impressive story," Lerato said after we showed him the book.

"And very emotional," Elena added, leaning over so she could have a better look at the book in his hands.

Caroline, Lerato, Elena and I sat around the glass table to discuss the story in detail. Lerato gestured warningly with his knife.

"The Elders are aware that our world has been exposed to a human soul—you—and want to make sure that you value and understand the consequences that can easily be created if you are not cautious enough."

"As if we weren't cautious enough already," Caroline said, sighing. "There could have been another way to teach us about a potential outcome."

"We've tried for over an hour," I said, feeling defeated and helping myself to another slice of toast.

Elena reached for the book and hid her face behind it. "Let me have another look," she said.

"Maybe he should have never exposed himself to her," Elena said in her caring voice. "There are lots of other ways he could have helped her."

"We've tried that already," Caroline interjected as Elena flipped the page.

"Let me see," Lerato said.

"Lerato, dear, you're staining the pages with butter," Elena scolded him affectionately as she handed him the book.

"I'm not; don't you worry," he replied. He grabbed a napkin from the side of the table, and I suppressed a chuckle.

"It might be possible that he was supposed to take her life after he turned her into an angel of destruction," Lerato speculated.

Elena stopped chewing and widened her eyes at him. "That does not fit into a love story," she said in a serious tone.

"Maybe Dad is right, Mom," Caroline said and leaned forward in her seat. "It is the guardian angel's duty to eliminate all existing evil, right?" she asked as she exchanged looks with her parents.

"That is a reasonable explanation," Lerato said and flipped the page, but nothing happened.

"Don't be disappointed," he said encouragingly, putting the book aside. "You will find the remaining lesson when the time is right." Caroline grabbed my hand from under the table and gave me a promising look.

"And don't forget that we will always be here to help," Elena said, beaming at us from across the table.

I chewed slowly on my toast and allowed my eyes to rest on the candles in the back of the room. Their sacred flames moved peacefully and reminded me how much they represented the calmness of these angels when facing stressful situations.

"Good morning," Dominic said, stepping into the living room and joining us at the table with a bush of hair standing up on the back of his head.

"Morning sleepyhead," Elena said as she poured some juice for him.

He spread some butter on a piece of toast and said, "I almost missed the morning's excitement."

"I'm not really sure if we should call it excitement or frustration," Caroline said, pointing to the book next to Lerato.

Dominic opened the book and flipped through a couple of pages before putting it down. "He definitely believed in her love," he stated. "Never question love, did you try that?"

Caroline grabbed the book and flipped the page. Nothing happened.

"It must be something profound that's not immediately obvious," Lerato said, reassuringly. "We can't use our brains to think this one through; we should use our hearts instead."

"I got it!" Dominic exclaimed after a moment of silence. "Maybe this Severino should have given her a gift card for plastic surgery. That's what they're all about, isn't it?"

Lerato was the first one of us who couldn't suppress his laughter, and Caroline and I loudly joined in. Elena gently shook her head no and pretended to wipe her lips with a napkin, though I knew she was hiding a smile. A lovely one at that.

Both Elena and Lerato insisted on having me over for lunch

later, in addition to conducting further research on Corbett and the missing lesson. I declined politely at the thought of a hysterical May waiting for me at home.

Leaving Caroline felt unpleasant, as that was the longest we had ever spent together.

"I will see you at school," she said in my ear as I hugged her good-bye.

"That sounds like an eternity away," I said, unwilling to leave.

"I love you," I said finally, placed a kiss on her lips, and made my way out into the sunny day with Lerato, and headed for home.

INDECISION

I woke up in my bed on Saturday, New Year's Day, and rubbed the sleep out of my eyes. I had spent the last couple of days with May, not because she had insisted, but because both Caroline and I thought it was a good precaution.

At first May was teasing me about my new relationship and kept asking when I would invite Caroline over so she could finally, and officially, get to spend time with her. I was proud of myself when I came up with a quick lie about a big family reunion Caroline was having. I couldn't risk the chance of exposing May to the kind of danger I was in and was always tense when she left the apartment. Though Caroline had assured me that May had a guardian angel who was looking after her and that there was no need to worry about May on top of everything else, I knew Caroline well enough to clearly recognize the worry that snuck into her voice.

New Year's Eve with May was fun, and I was overly relieved when she said she wasn't eager to go out to a public party in the city. We stayed in that night, and the thought of the secret security system Lerato had installed enormously helped me relax and enjoy the evening. We made it our own special event. May opened a bottle of wine, served some homemade pastries and turned the TV all the way up for the countdown to midnight. My life felt normal again for the first night in a long time, even though Caroline was missing.

I stayed up late many nights thinking about the missing lesson, even though neither Vivienne nor Janus had mentioned a due date. Both Caroline and I were anxious to find that missing piece and couldn't help trying out whatever ideas popped into our minds. We rethought the story from Severino's point of view, looking at the key sentences that best described his actions; tried them out, and then did the same with Godeva. Much to our disappointment, nothing worked.

The story from the Elders was turning out to be an unpleasant chore, and though each session usually ended up giving me a slight headache, I was more than willing to accept the challenge from the angelic realm.

May almost caught me talking to myself and waving my hands once in the bathroom and I quickly had to come up with another lie about having to practice for a presentation the following week. Every time I thought something reasonable had occurred to me, I grabbed a piece of paper to note my thoughts down and then waited for May to leave the apartment, so I could actually *tell* the book about it. I felt more than silly doing this, though I reminded myself that I was doing it for both Caroline and myself. After confessing that she was my guardian angel, I felt nothing could startle me anymore. We all fall in love sometime, and when we do, we stop questioning life and start thinking with a heart of foolish courage.

My life had a new beginning from the moment I met Caroline. Her tender heart made a soul sacrifice and promised to be there for me beyond forever. Some days I thought I knew what it felt like to share my life with an angel, but then I reminded myself that we had only just began our journey of undying love.

I spent the following snowy Sunday locked up in my room editing and rewriting a paper that was due the first day after break. When I complained to Caroline about the headache the essay was giving me, she offered to help. She emailed it back with all her edits in 20 minutes.

"Hi," her beautiful voice said through the phone. She had made it a habit to call and check in on me.

"How are you?" I asked.

"I'm good," she said with amusement. "Except that your paper made me feel dizzy."

"You were the one to offer your help," I said, smiling into the phone.

"My help, yes, but I didn't say I was going to rewrite your whole paper," she said teasingly.

I laughed and said, "Alright, I'll give you my grade and will tell the professor that it was your work."

"Listen, the reason I'm calling is because of the story. I thought that maybe Severino should have contacted the Elders immediately after turning Godeva into an angel of destruction, and they should have manifested the consequences right away. Try that."

My hand reached under my pillow to grab the book even before she had finished speaking. I mumbled the thought quietly in front of me and waited for the words to appear on the page with the other answers, but nothing happened. I shut the book with annoyance and buried it back under my pillow.

"Nothing."

"That's impossible!" she exclaimed. "The story is full of

echoes of passion, but we just simply seem unable to see the final lesson."

"We will find it sooner or later," I said encouragingly. "Maybe once I know how to use my entelechy consciously, it will reveal the final answer."

I could almost sense her back stiffening as she said, "I don't want you to be overwhelmed."

"I won't. Lerato said that he's going do some research on how I can use my entelechy more efficiently, and once I know how to do this, I will use it to both find Corbett and solve the last lesson."

"I feel so useless," Caroline said, sighing. "I wish I could help."

"Your existence alone is help enough," I said, feeling her loving smile.

"How was New Year's Eve?" I asked, trying to change the topic.

"It was brilliant. We had a lot of fun, and Lerato surprised us with fireworks in the garden—but you were missed."

"I wish I could have been there with you. But I can hardly wait to see you tomorrow."

"Promise that you'll be alright and come straight to campus."

"It's not like I have another choice," I said teasingly.

"I'll be alright, I promise. Our windows don't open, and the doors lock automatically. That should do."

"I love you."

"Love you too."

I printed out my paper and joined May for dinner. She was excited about her upcoming trip the following Saturday and was making a list of winter clothes to pack. When I reminded her about the spa on the lower level of her hotel, she was overwhelmed but made plans to go swimsuit shopping the next day.

It was six-thirty when the sound of my alarm tore me from my dreams. I knew I was going to miss being able to sleep in during the coming semester. I groaned, got out of bed, started my usual morning routine, and had some breakfast in the kitchen before cautiously making my way to the bus stop.

It was as if time had stood still on campus. While my life had changed drastically over the break, everything at school was business as usual. I silently contemplated my surroundings and wished I could be one of the other students resuming just a normal university life.

For once I was glad when I spotted Teo in the main building and was relieved to have someone take my thoughts off Corbett's threat, even if for a brief moment. He was wrapped in a thick winter jacket, his ears and nose red from the cold.

"How have you been?" I asked.

"I've been good, though I already miss the Mexican weather," he said, protesting the cold and rubbing his hands. Because his face was suntanned, his green eyes stood out more strongly than before.

"Look who's coming," he said, rolling his eyes.

"Hi, guys. I was looking for you."

It was Natasha. She was wearing a gray hat, with her uncombed hair peeping out, and had her jeans tucked into black boots and her sleeves pulled down to cover her hands. She was hopping from foot to foot smiling at both of us and showcasing her yellow teeth.

"Hi, Natasha," I said. Teo made a face behind her back.

"Did you have a good start to the new year?" I asked, hoping she would be as brief as possible.

"I did," she said gushingly. "It was really nice to see my boyfriend."

"And what about you two?"

"I stayed here, but Teo did some exotic stuff, didn't you? He's all eager to tell you about it and I'll catch up with you two later."

I spotted Caroline at the door. Teo poked me in my ribs with his elbow, clearly not happy to be left alone with the babbling Natasha.

"You didn't have to leave them," Caroline said when I approached her. "Everything is alright?" she asked on our way down the hallway. She seemed tense.

I held her hand in mine. "Now it is," I said.

Her soft lips formed a half-smile.

"You're silly. You didn't notice anything strange?"

We reached the conference room on the second floor and dropped off our papers.

"Nothing."

She turned her head in all directions, as though making sure that Corbett wasn't around.

"We have to be very cautious. Corbett could attack whenever he wants. I mean it."

She frowned, and for a moment, her golden eyes revealed the full weight of her concern. Ever since the Elders had left, she had been tense and somehow different. And I was nauseous thinking about living my life playing hide-and-seek with my angel of death, who was a threat to both of us.

"You worry too much," I told her warmly. "I'll take care, I promise."

"I want to be around you while you're on campus," she said. It didn't come across as an offer, but rather an order.

"That's not necessary," I tried to complain. "The last place I think he would attack me would be somewhere public like campus."

"You can't know that. He might even be listening to our conversation right now. I can't let him get close to you one more time; remember that he tried to kill you and almost succeeded. We have to be alert, please."

She was waiting for me to say something.

"I won't be able to forgive myself if I fail one more time. If he took you away from me, that would completely destroy my existence."

We paused in front of the door, and I looked into her golden eyes with a silent promise that we would find a way out of our current danger.

"I will always be right here," I promised and gave her a tight hug.

"Remember to notice everything strange, such as the movements or behavior of others. Don't talk to strangers, and don't let anyone convince you to leave campus with them."

She insisted on walking me to Spanish and was giving me this loving speech about safeguarding my well-being as we walked down the hallway.

"That's my strategy of taking precautions," she added. I was about to complain, but she gently hushed me and sent me into the classroom. I hurried to a free seat next to Teo, who wanted me to fill him in about my relationship with Caroline. I stuck to the basics, of course, and was relieved when Ms. Arrigoberta silenced the class.

Time seems to fly by when you're in constant danger. Most of my classes intensified this semester, to make life more complicated, and I caught myself asking Ms. Arrigoberta several times for further explanations about different grammatical structures.

When the bell rang for Spanish to end, I found Caroline waiting for me just outside of the classroom.

"Any news?" she asked as we walked to French class.

"Nothing," I said.

Mr. Auberson began the class with an unannounced exam and made us all sit a seat apart.

Even lunch period resembled an extended tutoring class, and

many students already had their textbooks open on the tables in anticipation of the upcoming exam season.

This was the first time that Caroline, Dominic, Teo, Natasha and I sat together during lunch. Natasha, as usual, rambled on about her private life, while Caroline sat up in her chair and scanned the cafeteria, her eyes moving frantically from face to face.

"What books are we looking for exactly?" I asked.

Caroline and I went to the library after lunch, as the following class had been canceled, to find an appropriate book in the Latin section that might possibly lead us to a solution for the sixth lesson. I kept suggesting that with the aid of Lerato's help I could try to sense the final lesson with my entelechy, but she insisted on looking for an answer wherever we could, even if it was in a common library among regular books.

"What about Lerato's library?" I asked.

She was reading some worn-out titles while I walked behind her and played with her hair.

"He's already doing some research," she said and grabbed a thick leather-bound book. "No, this won't do," she groaned.

"I'm trying to focus," she said gently. "You could take this book and put it away for me while I check the lower shelves."

I took the book out of her hands and placed it on the closest shelf and blocked her way. We were surrounded by huge shelves that reached far above our heads, and no one could see us.

She teased me with her eyes and said, "That's not the right shelf."

"I'm starting to become overwhelmed," I admitted. "What if we're not supposed to find the lessons all at once? I can't remember the Elders mentioning a due date."

She gave me a loving expression and gently took my hand.

"Maybe that's precisely why they didn't tell us how quickly we have to find it. They might want to see how much time we devote to it voluntarily, without any pressure."

"As if we weren't dealing with enough right now," I said.

"Come on, there's only one lesson to go, and I'm sure we'll find it," she said, reassuringly.

"When there seems to be no way out, the only thing we can do is be the heroes in our own hearts," she added. I allowed myself to get lost in her eyes for a moment, placed a kiss on her lips and put the book back on the proper shelf.

On Tuesday morning, Caroline caught up with me at the bus stop in front of campus. I had to promise her, involuntarily, that I was going to meet her there each morning, while Dominic went ahead of us and checked out the campus for any potential danger.

"Anything?" I asked on our way to the main building.

"Nothing. We should be fine. We've been here for two hours and haven't seen anything suspicious. I did some sensory exercises last night, just in case."

"Two hours? Caroline, that's a lot."

"We're fine, and this is for your safety. We've discussed this already; it's just for the time being. Elena and Lerato are alert, too."

Her eyes were piercing as she walked me to class. I didn't complain further and left her in front of the classroom with a worried expression on her sublime face. Teo realized that I wasn't up for much talking and I was glad when he remained quiet for the rest of the class, as I surely didn't know what lie I was going to come up with to cover up what was really going on.

The snow had finally ceased that day, but that didn't greatly improve my mood, as the sky was a mixture of gray and black clouds that muffled the sun. In the afternoon, when the clouds opened up and seemed to be spilling waterfalls of rain down on us, I asked Mr. Slipper during English for permission to go to the restroom, where I splashed cold water on my face to keep myself from falling asleep. It seemed to help, and it eased my growing headache.

"We're still good," Dominic said in my ear as he joined us at lunch. It took me a lot of effort to focus on my food. Caroline was sitting so close to me I could almost feel her tense body stiffening and relaxing as she breathed. Teo pretended he hadn't noticed our strange behavior, and Natasha went on about her dog that had thrown up in the bathroom that morning.

"We'll wait for you after class," Caroline announced after lunch on our way to German.

Her tension started to increase my own nervousness. "Try to relax," I said, shaking her arm softly.

"I'll do my best," she promised and pushed me inside. Teo gave me an apologetic look as the seat next to him had already been taken, and I made my way to a free seat next to a row of windows in the back of the classroom.

With a mixture of tiredness, growing paranoia and boredom, I was feeling dizzy and didn't know if Mr. Rosenberg's class was exhausting or just more complicated than the previous semester. He announced three exams, drily discussed theories of German grammar, and then had us write a paper for the rest of the class.

The paper was a pain in the neck. This was the fifth class of the day. My body was exhausted, and it took a lot of effort to keep my mind coherent. I closed my eyes for a moment and absentmindedly started counting the seconds of the ticking clock to refocus on my writing, which surprisingly calmed my racing thoughts. I was already halfway through the paper when the ticking sounds became uneven. This made me glance at the clock above Mr. Rosenberg's desk, and confused, I lowered my head back to my paper, convinced that my mind was playing tricks on me. A short moment later, just when I was ready to hand in my paper, the uneven ticking caught my attention again. This time it sounded louder than before, but I seemed to be the only one hearing it. I rubbed my eyes and inhaled through my mouth when I heard the uneven ticking begin again—but this time the sounds were coming from my left. I turned my head toward them and winced.

A black raven was sitting outside the window and was pecking his beak against it, as if trying to break the glass. He stopped pecking and opened his crooked beak as far as possible to release a hissing sound, and I leaned as far back in my seat as possible. He was bigger than any raven I had ever seen before, with wings larger than my palms; his crooked beak was pointy, as sharp as the tip of a knife; and he widened his monstrous pitch-black eyes at me.

The sight of this crippled, ugly creature had paralyzed me, and it took me a good while to realize what was actually happening. I could feel my heart throbbing in my throat. Both of my hands began to sweat, and my stomach made a sick noise. I frantically remembered Vivienne's words the night she had talked about the meaning of *his* name. And then, very unexpectedly, the answer came to me in a blink: The raven could only be Corbett— there was absolutely no doubt.

I sunk lower in my chair, while images flashed in front of my eyes, scarily accurate. I suddenly understood the way he was blocking himself from Caroline. My angel of death was here, and the only barrier between life and death was the window between the two of us.

With a final look at the black beast, I jumped out of my seat, threw my paper on Mr. Rosenberg's desk and rushed out of the classroom. Once in the hallway, I gasped for air and clasped my hands to my face.

Think, I told myself, and started walking up and down. I was extremely hot all of a sudden and could feel droplets of sweat forming on my forehead.

I bit my lower lip and tried to figure out what to do. I had been the one who was telling Caroline that she was exaggerating, and it was also I who had assumed that Corbett would never attack me in public. A cold shiver ran down my spine at the thought that I had unquestionably underestimated the danger I had been exposed to the entire time. I narrowed all my racing thoughts down to one: What should we do next?

"Come on," I mumbled as I ran down the hallway, unsure if I should hide in the library or cafeteria and winced at the sound of the bell that announced the end of class. Only seconds later the hallway was flooded with students, and I silently hoped that Corbett would have a hard time finding me among the crowd.

Caroline, come on, please, I begged in my thoughts, hoping she would hear me calling. I was desperately relieved when she came running in my direction.

"What happened?"

"He's here!" I said quickly. "Corbett is here. I saw him in front of my classroom window in the shape of a black raven." She frowned.

"This is impossible!" she exclaimed and instantaneously grabbed my hand. "I didn't feel his presence at all." She looked down the hallway.

"Maybe that's precisely the reason you could never sense him," I said, tense. "What are we going to do now?" I asked, frightened. I could see the fear painted all over her face.

"Hide?" I urged her impatiently, as the surge of the crowd pushed us down the hallway.

"Go home?" I tugged on her hand.

She closed her eyes for a moment and mumbled something I couldn't understand.

"No, not alone. Maybe this is exactly what he's trying to make us do. We'll go to our next two classes, and then we'll wait for Dominic and all go home together. It's easier to move within the crowd. I've just notified Dominic, so he's aware of this."

She spoke so fast I could only catch every other word she said. I was still paralyzed and frightened, so I didn't make any effort to complain. Corbett had decided to attack me in public after all, and that meant we were exposed to danger at all times. Anywhere.

We made our way to text analysis in complete silence, hand in hand, and were both relieved at the sight of the crowded auditorium, though Caroline still kept turning her head from left to right. The first hour seemed to pass in a blink. She jumped up from her seat twice and made me wince each time, though I was thankful when she apologized about both being false alarms. Caroline forbade me to talk to anyone during the short five-minute break.

She had spotted where Dominic was sitting and was exchanging hasty, inaudible words with him across the auditorium. Her facial expressions changed from a mixture of sadness and confusion to anger and desperation.

"He's going to wait outside of the auditorium for us," she said with an uneven breath after phonetics had started.

She ran her hands through her silky hair. "Shape-shifter? I don't get it!"

"Maybe I'm wrong?" I asked, and suddenly wished I really was.

She frowned, and her forehead creased.

"You're not. This makes complete sense to me now. I just never thought that an angel of death would be able to take the form of an animal. As long as he's not in his usual physical state, I won't be able to sense him."

I failed to provide further words of encouragement and didn't say anything. I felt as though I was underwater and couldn't hear everything clearly, and was trying to sort the sound by danger. I couldn't help noticing the big windows that looked to me like nothing else but the eyes of evil itself. Darkness had already fallen, worsening the visibility outside, but my eyes still kept looking at the sky for my destroyer. What if he wasn't outside anymore, but had already taken the form of one of the students and was just a couple of seats away from me?

"Your books," Caroline said, interrupting my thoughts. I winced at the sound of her words and gave her a blank expression.

"The bell is going to ring soon," she said, gesturing with her head at the books in front of me. It took me a while to understand, but once I did, I hastily shoved the books into my bag.

She kept her eyes on the door on the other side of the room.

"Ten seconds, and then you'll give me your hand and will walk right by my side. Avoid making eye contact with anyone in here, don't turn back if someone says your name, and do not let go of my hand under any circumstances."

Her voice was so low that I could hardly hear her. I had never seen her like this, and to be honest, it was scary. My heart ached at the realization that she was fighting with all of her being for something that could result in pain and loss.

I felt as though I was trapped in one of those bad dreams where you can't escape from the danger; no matter how hard you try, your feet just won't carry you any further. My pulse was making drumming sounds in my ears, while the layer of sweat appeared on my forehead again. I was too frightened to say anything. I took Caroline's hand.

"Three seconds," she said, fastening a grip of steel around my hand. Then, the bell announced the end of class.

The other students instantaneously got up and surged toward the door. Caroline pulled me up swiftly, and we made our way toward the door where Dominic was waiting for us. I stumbled down the stairs, bumping into some students who cursed at me, but Caroline just kept pulling me through the crowd. I kept my eyes on my feet, frightened that Corbett might spot me among the other faces.

"Over here!" Dominic called. "Hurry up, in here," he said and held a door open for us that led down a set of dark stairs. Caroline fastened her grip even tighter as we ran downstairs through the darkness. I smelled gas.

I was out of breath when we reached the foot of the stairs and was glad when we paused for a moment. Both Caroline and Dominic froze, their eyes were moving from ceiling to floor and then from left to right.

"We're good," Dominic whispered and waved us on with a quick gesture of his hand. "Try to walk next to the wall."

I was disoriented from their fast movements. "Where are we?"

"The garage, in the basement," Dominic said, keeping his voice low as we walked among parked cars. "We can't use the main exit."

"This way we'll end up on the other side of the building and gain some time in case your angel of death has decided to wait for you."

I realized that I was trembling and was desperately in need of words of encouragement. I looked at Caroline, who was walking on my right and wearing a determined expression.

We paused abruptly behind a black Range Rover, as Dominic laid out our route.

"It's all about timing now. The door at the other end of the garage will lead us to the parking lot behind building C. We'll have to cross a short field and then we'll be at the bus stop."

"We're almost there," Caroline said after she saw the expression on my face.

We waited for some people to get into their cars, and when they drove through the automatic door, we stepped out from behind our shelter and ran across the garage. Dominic cracked the door open only an inch, peeked outside and then held it open for us. Once I was outside, my eyes darted up to the sky in search of a moving black spot.

"We're still good," Caroline said as we ran across the frozen field and finally reached the bus stop. "Stand in the crowd," she ordered. Dominic kept walking up and down the sidewalk until the bus came. We hopped on and made our way into the middle of the standing passengers.

I stared at Caroline and Dominic; everything had happened too fast for my brain to process.

"Nothing," Dominic said after a while. I could almost feel how tense their bodies were as all of their senses listened and focused on every single movement during the ride. Caroline still had her hand wrapped tightly around mine when we got off some 15 minutes later.

"Don't walk under the street lights," she warned me.

We moved further away from the sidewalk into the darkness. I was out of breath and completely exhausted when we finally reached my apartment.

Caroline was so serious she almost looked sinister. She didn't take her eyes off me.

"I want you to go upstairs right now. Always check who's in front of the door before opening and don't you dare leave without me."

I was frantic and asked, "What about you two?"

"We'll be fine. Just go! Remember, he's after you and not after us. I'll pick you up tomorrow."

I didn't look back once as I ran up the stairs. I stumbled into the apartment, pressed my weight against the door and waited to hear the lock click shut. I blinked a few times until my eyes adjusted to the dim light, alertly listening for any strange sounds. I slowly allowed my body to sink down onto my bed, where I stayed for a good while until I stopped trembling.

My racing heart was about to split my chest wide open. I finally sat up and switched the lights on. I hastily looked around, trying to make out anything different, though it didn't look like anyone had tried to break in. I threw my weight forward, stumbled toward the windows and made sure they were still locked. It had started raining outside; the sky was flashing a dark purple, and the sound of the falling raindrops against my windows only added to my anxiety. I drew the curtains closed and rested my weight against my wardrobe, still breathing through my mouth.

My body was shaking uncontrollably as I dropped to the floor and tried to focus my mind. I felt paralyzed and as though the energy had been sucked out of my limbs. I rubbed my temples and tried once more to figure out why Corbett wanted to kill me, without any success. Vivienne had clearly said my time hadn't come yet, so why was he after me? Before meeting Caroline, I wouldn't have minded if he attacked me and took my life, but surrender was out of the question now. Giving up would mean giving up on Caroline, and that was the last thing I would ever do.

I winced at the sound of my cell phone.

"Call me if anything happens. We're home, and Lerato and Elena are figuring things out. I'll pick you up tomorrow. Love you."

Caroline spoke very fast and hung up before I could even confess how frightened I was. I wished I could have been with her that night instead. I stayed on the floor until my body stopped quivering. *We are still fine, and that's all that matters,* I told myself, feeling the awareness of my surroundings start trickling in again.

May was home now, and the sound of her in the kitchen and the TV in the living room helped to further calm my senses. I made my way to the bathroom to have a hot shower, trying to wash the fear away with steaming water.

"You're back," she said when I joined her in the kitchen.

"Let me help you, Mom," I said, needing to be busy with my hands. I didn't want her to realize that something was wrong. The hot shower had eased my trembling, and I slowly grabbed two soup bowls and set the table.

"You think three swimsuits are going to be enough?" May asked me halfway through dinner. She had pulled her hair back in a bun and looked fluffy in her cotton robe.

I smiled tiredly and said, "It's just a weekend, Mom."

She smiled back at me, still not realizing that something was wrong.

"I know. I looked up the hotel on the Internet, and it seems pretty fancy. I need to make sure I blend in with the ambience."

I laughed and finished with my soup faster than usual.

I helped her with the dishes afterward and lingered in the living room for a while, taking any opportunity to procrastinate about going to sleep. Soon enough though, complete exhaustion washed over me and I was forced to wish her good night. I felt silly when I left the night lamp on, but that was the only way I could get myself to fall asleep. And luckily, it worked.

It was a scary night during which I had several bad dreams, one of them about being followed by a black raven. It was a foggy gloomy evening, and I was running across the parking lot on campus screaming Caroline's name, though for some reason she couldn't hear me. Corbett didn't physically attack me, though he kept flying above my head until I raced to the door of the main building only to realize that it was locked. I pressed my back against it and covered my face with my bare hands as I saw the black spot in the sky descending with immense speed toward me.

The next instant I woke up weary, sitting up straight and checking the windows to make sure he wasn't actually there. I silently wished for dawn to finally break and was relieved when I fell back asleep.

The second time I woke up was because thunder so loud shook my bed, causing me to jump out of it, followed by the endless sound of heavy raindrops against my windows. I picked up my sheets from the floor, rubbed my eyes and checked the time. It was just a little before six-thirty, when the sound of my alarm would likely make me jump out of bed yet another time. I switched off the night lamp and tried to get five more minutes of sleep. But before I could close my eyes, another purple flash lit up my room. I sat up, blinked and froze on the spot.

I rubbed my eyes just to make sure they hadn't played a game with me, though I was pretty much convinced I had seen the silhouette of a raven in front of my window through the curtains. With my senses numbed and my body still unable to move, I grabbed my phone with great effort and managed to call Caroline's number.

"He's here," I said before she had a chance to speak.

"Dammit! Stay inside. I'm coming to pick you up."

I got out of bed and cursed when my alarm went off. I felt sick and headed to the bathroom to splash cold water on my face, threw on some warm clothes, and froze again when I heard someone knocking on the door. I paused for an instant and slowly approached the door with determined precaution. *If he attacks now, I'm lost,* I told myself, and looked through the peephole. My heart leapt when I saw Caroline's face on the other side.

"How did you…"

"Let me in first," she said, slipping through the open gap so fast I couldn't even blink and closing the door with a rapid movement of her hand.

Only after she gave me a hug did I realize that she was completely soaked. Her hair was sticking to her face, and water kept dripping down her unbuttoned raincoat. The light in her golden eyes seemed dimmed, and her face appeared porcelain as drops ran down her silky forehead.

"Are you okay? Where is he? I ran as fast as I could. That was too close."

I shushed her tears with a tight hug.

"I'm okay. Nothing happened. He was in front of my window."

She buried her face in the shallow of my shoulder. "This has to stop," she said. "It's literally freaking me out."

I kept hugging her tightly until she stopped shaking.

"We'll find a way out of this," I said, hoping against hope. "Let me get you a towel so you can dry your hair."

"Lerato and Dominic should already be downstairs in the car waiting for us," she said as she dried her hair. "We're taking you to class."

"What if he comes back and hurts my mother?" I asked. The thought of leaving May behind unprotected made me uneasy.

Caroline seemed to think for a moment. "He won't," she said. "Honestly, he could have already done that if he had wanted to. He's clearly only after you, and I won't let you out of my sight until we know the reason for his actions." I hoped she was right, grabbed my backpack from my room, and we made our way downstairs in silence.

"Good morning," Lerato said. Dominic was sitting in the passenger seat next to him, and it took me a good moment until I could speak.

"Morning," I finally said, and sat between them, as close to the middle of the car as possible.

"I heard you had some trouble," Lerato said and looked at me through the rearview mirror. He was driving fast and we made it to the highway within seconds.

"Shape-shifter!" Caroline exclaimed with annoyance. "We've figured out his new skill—what's the point with him still using it?"

"Simply because it makes it easier for him to follow Adam," Lerato answered. "None of my research led me to the possibility of him developing the skill to metamorphose himself."

I fidgeted. "What does that mean for us?" I asked.

He kept his eyes on the road as he spoke.

"It means that there are no existing writings or studies that can inform us about his abilities simply because no one might have experienced them before. There are decades worth of studies recorded on the development of the skills of an angel's body; however, if we cannot find any written explanation of this newly occurring shift, that means it has never happened in history before."

He looked back at me for a split second and said, "An unknown skill needs to be treated with respect, especially if possessed by an enemy."

I sighed and felt more defeated than ever before—though I was glad that Lerato was stating things the way they were, rather than telling us stories to cover up what was actually happening, just to try to make us feel better.

"Should we talk to the Elders?" I asked. Lerato made a sharp left and looked back at me for a brief moment.

"I think they might already be aware of what's happening, though they haven't decided to take any action yet."

"Well, we're pretty much running out of ideas about what to do," Caroline said, staring at the roof of the car.

Lerato's voice never changed. In fact, it still sounded calm when he said, "All we can do is focus on staying safe until justice prevails."

None of us said anything, though we all knew that was going to be a challenge.

Everything changed drastically from that moment forward. After that, we began following a precise set of plans, and I was introduced to a system of safety. This time, I had no intention of either complaining about or refusing the help Caroline's family was voluntarily offering.

Caroline picked me up every morning and took me to school, and then back home when classes were over. Once on campus I wasn't allowed to leave her side—she would even walk me to the restroom.

Even lunch was intense. She refused to eat and insisted that we sit alone at a table in the back of the cafeteria so she could keep an eye on the people around us. She told me that metamorphosis was worse than any other imaginable skill Corbett could have developed, for that meant we never knew *whom* we were hiding from. How do you win a fight when you don't know who or *what* your enemy is?

"They're going through a hard time right now," I lied to Teo after he called me out on my strange behavior one afternoon. It was more than obvious that he had started questioning our sanity, and I told myself I better make a habit of lying to people for the time being. He nodded in understanding and walked alone to his next class, which made me feel bad. And even though Teo was always looking for a way to rid himself of Natasha's company, I would have been more than glad if she were the one following me instead of Corbett.

"It just doesn't feel like my regular life anymore," I complained to Caroline on our way out of the cafeteria.

Her eyes bore a promising sparkle as she said, "It's going to be over soon and we'll both be able to resume our lives again."

Lerato was able to change his schedule at the hospital and always waited for us in the car after classes, and he usually drove me home in silence. He mentioned briefly that he and his family had discussed several ways of keeping me safe in the coming days, though he refused to be specific about anything and spoke in riddles whenever I tried to get more detailed information from him. He explained that he wasn't sure whether Corbett was able to hear our conversations or not.

I felt as though I was only passively involved in my life, living in constant fear, and hoping that whatever happened that Caroline would be the one to walk away safely at the end.

"We will decide what to do further tomorrow after classes," Lerato said as he picked me up on a cold Thursday morning, two days after Corbett's appearance as the raven. We decided to continue with our classes at the university, though we weren't sure how much longer that would be possible. Everything that could eventually expose me to an attack by Corbett was put on the back burner, though sadly that involved *all* of my everyday activities.

The days seemed to drag on forever as we followed our secret security system. I still wasn't allowed to sit near the windows in any classroom and always had to wait for Caroline or Dominic to pick me up before I walked down the hallways. The only silver lining so far was the fact that I aced the paper we handed in after winter break, and upon hearing this, Caroline lightened up and started teasing me about how none of it was my work.

"I owe you," I told her after I found out.

"The only thing I want is a promise that you'll make it safe and sound through all of this," she said on our way through the garage to the parking lot. We decided to keep using that exit, as according to her, it was still the safest.

I gazed at her, promising myself that I would always give her a reason to have a spark of hope in her eyes.

Friday morning was the same as all the previous ones, except that I woke up with an unbearable headache, which I tried to hide, unsuccessfully. Caroline was already waiting for me at the front door and walked me to the car in a rush.

Lerato looked calm and took everything in stride. He kept his hands firmly on the wheel.

"We'll leave the hospital earlier tonight. Make sure you take a cab since we won't be able to pick you up. But we'll be waiting for you."

It was a cold morning, and a thin layer of fog had descended to the streets of Belgrade and had drastically worsened the visibility.

I couldn't keep my thoughts straight during my classes and was nervous about that evening. I had tried to convince myself several times that I wasn't frightened, though the more I did, the more I felt trapped.

"You're tense," Caroline said when I spilled some of my soda during lunch.

I sighed and rubbed my head. I still had a headache. "I can't help it," I said.

To my great relief, the afternoon turned out to be pleasant. I tried really hard to focus in my classes and perceived every word more intensively. I even took some notes and wasn't bothered at all when a yawning Natasha started copying my phonetics homework.

Caroline took my hand when our last class was dismissed and said, "Let's go."

"Where's Dominic?" I asked.

"He's already left, just to make sure we have a green light."

We made our way through the garage in a rush and waved down a cab away from campus. Before we got inside, Caroline stepped in front of the door, tuned in with her eyes closed, and then gave us the okay to take this cab.

Elena opened their front door, saying, "Come on in." She had her hair tied in a ponytail and wore blue yoga pants with a white sweater. While she was giving me a prolonged hug, I mentally absorbed as much of her maternal aura as possible.

"Could you two help me spread some *Moneos* around the house?" she asked, still standing at the door and handing us a pair of big purple candles.

"Let me get some more," she added. "I'll be right back."

"Help her do what exactly?" I was confused and decided to own my right as a human to ask Caroline my question.

She gave me a loving smile and waved one of the candles in front of my face.

"We call this candle a *Moneo*. They're Lerato's invention and are similar to those human smoke and carbon monoxide detectors, with the slight difference that they don't detect fire but rather movements and vibrations on *other* frequencies. Once they do, they light up like a torch and cast a flame that scares the intruder and warns the victim. It's safe to be exposed to them as a human being, and they're hardly distinguishable from regular candles. Lerato wants us to place them around the house to make sure Corbett doesn't try to come inside."

I was startled, alert even. The fact that we were asked to set up the *Moneos* only pointed out once more how worrying the situation was. Caroline's family wasn't excluding the possibility of further attacks, and I made sure my candles were stuck firmly in the ground around the house.

"I appreciate your help," Elena said as she rejoined us. "Lerato just got back. Let's go inside."

We found Lerato and Dominic sitting at the table in the living room. Instrumental music was playing in the background, the fire was crackling softly, and I felt safe again.

"Just in time for some garlic green tea," Lerato said with a smirk stretched across his face.

Elena smiled and said, "I've known you long enough to know when you're being truthful and can tell right away when you're teasing."

"You spoiled my timing," Lerato complained politely as he helped her fill our cups. Elena nudged him gently with her elbow. Sweet laughter filled the room, and I realized once more how their affection made me feel as if I had entered my own special place of healing.

The next second though, Lerato became serious. "Are you sure no one followed you?" he asked both Caroline and me.

"I made sure we were alone," Caroline said. "I did some sensory tests on our way here."

Lerato nodded in acknowledgment and pressed his cup to his lips.

"We have to find a way to keep you safe," Elena said. My stomach contracted at her words, and I looked at the balcony, contemplating the *Moneos* for a pleasant moment.

"Elena and I have come up with some ideas, though before we take any actions, I would like to help you use your clairvoyance," Lerato said serenely. I looked at him and he returned my gaze with confidence.

"Caroline, please."

Caroline rose from her seat and came back with her golden rose. Lerato explained what he had in mind while Caroline, Dominic and Elena stood before me.

"One of them will be holding this rose behind her or his back, and you will use your intuition to determine who has it. This should be easy since you already have a connection to the missing object. Please close your eyes now."

He caught me off guard with this experiment, but I did as he asked. I sat quietly for a moment, pressing my fingers into the chair and feeling my heartbeat accelerate as I listened to their swift movements in front of me.

"Open your eyes—and feel free to stand up," Lerato said. I looked at Caroline, Dominic and Elena with their hands behind their backs.

"Take a step closer and try to relax. Focus on your breathing."

Once again I did as I was asked and opened my mouth so I could breathe better. The three angels in front of me were all wearing serious expressions, and I was suddenly nervous about figuring out where Caroline's rose was.

Lerato broke the silence by asking, "Right now, without overthinking it, do you have a sense of where the rose might be?" I looked from left to right, as though actually trying to see through their bodies.

"I don't," I said nervously.

"Very good, that is completely okay," he said soothingly. "Can you tell me what could possibly prevent you from seeing where Corbett is?"

I chewed on the inside of my cheek as I grew more nervous

and tried to think of a reasonable explanation about why I wasn't able to use my clairvoyance on demand. The thought of failure snuck into my mind and forced grotesque pictures of its aftermath to flash in front of my inner eyes.

"I'm...afraid," I admitted and rubbed my head.

"Very good. One important aspect is to let go of any fear of seeing the future. He who wants to know can never fear seeing even unpleasant things. Trust in what you do see."

I focused on Caroline's face and tried to even out my breath. She answered my gaze with a serious expression, which made it even harder to read her. Elena and Dominic both had softened their focus, and it seemed to me as if all three of them tried to block any of their feelings or thoughts from me. I blinked a few times, slightly intimidated by their stares, and moved my toes to prevent further devastating thoughts from running through my mind. Lerato was so close to me that I could feel his breath on my neck, which added enormously to my nervousness.

Think, come on, I told myself, and tried to pull myself together. I had done it before, though only unconsciously, but there had to be a way to trigger that part of my mind.

I closed my eyes this time, and I tried to make myself nervous on purpose with the thought of Corbett lingering outside of the house and waiting for me to leave. I could feel how my hands began to sweat and my breathing accelerated at the thought of this scene.

"Time will not always be in your favor," Lerato whispered.

I started stepping from foot to foot, and I forced myself to think of losing both Caroline and May. Loss was all that I feared, wasn't it? I would be left alone with nothing but my aching soul, and Corbett would finally get to have a devil's feast.

"Time," Lerato said, pressing me.

Think of the rose, I told myself. I had discovered this power within the moment I had seen Caroline for the first time; I knew it was inside of me. The car accident had triggered a domino effect within my body. I couldn't allow myself to fail, not at the moment when I most needed to be there for those who would sacrifice their lives for mine.

"Time."

"Elena!" I shouted suddenly, moved by an invisible current that shot down my spine. I held my breath for a moment as I stared at all of them, both surprised and confused about how I had even made myself speak.

Elena and Dominic kept their eyes focused on me. Caroline smiled with relief, while Elena, very elegantly, revealed the rose she had been hiding behind her back.

Lerato squeezed my shoulder and said, "Excellent."

"I knew you could do it," Caroline said as she gave me a hug. I absorbed her warmth, and it gently calmed my racing heart.

"Let's keep it up and try one more time," Lerato said. "Do you mind?"

I continued hugging Caroline for another moment and sighed in exhaustion, but I was eager to try again. I was positive that before the end of the evening, Lerato would manage to find the trigger for my clairvoyance.

I nodded at him and sat down, closing my eyes again. I was encouraged to look up only a brief second later. Lerato had placed the rose on the table in front of me.

"As you can see, I am raising the stakes, and now you won't be looking for an object, but instead for someone who is very close to you. I have asked Caroline to step into a room of her choice and will ask you to use your clairvoyance to tell me where she is."

I immediately felt panicked and pressured, so I stood up.

"Trust the process," Lerato said optimistically. Elena smiled warmly at me.

I spun around in circle and narrowed my eyes as I tried again to force frightening images into my inner vision.

I thought it would be easy at first, but the more I tried, the harder and more complicated it seemed. The thought of Caroline missing had ruffled my mind and I couldn't get a cohesive picture of where she was. *Our hearts are linked,* I reminded myself, squinting and trying to see whatever came into my mind.

I mentally pictured myself walking through the house, up the stairs and down the hallway to her room. That felt cold, somehow neutral, and I decided to make my way to Lerato's library. I paused among books and looked around, though the picture was very indistinct and the lights appeared to be switched off. I hurriedly ran to Dominic's room, mentally calling her name, though no answer came. His room was empty and I made my way to the bathroom and then down to the kitchen. *Caroline, come on I need you,* I begged her in my mind, hoping for some kind of sign from her. I felt some drops of sweat appear on my forehead as I started panting.

"Time," Lerato's voice clung in my mind.

"Your library…I'm not sure!" I opened my eyes. Lerato was still standing by my side, and Elena and Dominic were each giving me a promising look.

I felt complete desperation and a feeling of failure wash over me as Caroline stepped out from behind the curtains in the living room. I put my hands on my head and sighed out loud. She was in the same room, only steps away, and I had failed to feel that. I was devastated.

She took my hands and said, "You did great." I avoided her eyes.

"I'm sorry," I said, beaten. I felt a huge sense of disappointment about failing to intuit where Caroline was. I had failed to find the person I loved the most.

"Don't apologize," she said softly. "You were brilliant."

"I failed to sense where you were. How can this be something great?"

She squeezed my hands.

"Your acts of courage were stronger than your doubts. That's all that matters."

"We're basically living off borrowed time. This is not our time Caroline, it's Corbett's. It's his because we've only got as much as he's given us, and I don't think there's much left. There's no time for me to fail you!"

Only after I finished speaking, did I realize that they were all standing around me. I had raised my voice at Caroline out of despair and immediately felt badly about it. She stepped closer and gave me a comforting hug until my breathing was under control.

"The reason we're all here tonight is to figure a way to keep you safe," she said in her soothing voice. I glanced sheepishly at her family through her hair and wished I could disappear in its comfortable darkness until things went back to normal.

Instead we all sat down at the table together, while Elena went into the kitchen and brought us more tea.

"What options do we have?" I asked. "Have you tried talking any further with the Elders?"

Ever calm, Lerato was the first to speak.

"We haven't asked for their help, though they have sent down the mist in order to keep you safe. This way we can't look up and Corbett can't look down. This is their way of helping us for the time being since they don't like to interfere with the human dimension for a prolonged period of time."

I looked at the windows and felt my body relax at the sight of the thick mist lingering above the street. With the knowledge that the Elders were providing some sort of help, I let myself be at ease.

Elena spoke next.

"Lerato and I have thought about two ways to keep you safe. We could try to deceive Corbett by telling everyone that you are out of country. But we would keep you here in our house instead until we find out any further information about how to track him down."

I allowed the liquid warmth of the tea to sit on my tongue before swallowing it and looked at Caroline in search of her opinion about this.

"Do you think this will work?" she asked.

"We would gain more time with this option," Lerato responded. "Adam would stay in our house and wouldn't be allowed to leave until we confront Corbett."

Caroline said with dissatisfaction, "It'll be like jail for him."

"Just for a while," Elena added, sipping her tea.

"What do you think?" Caroline asked me.

I sat up in my chair and mulled this over. On one hand, I would definitely feel trapped; but on the other, their house had always made me feel safe since it seemed immune to any imaginable intruder.

"I wouldn't mind," I said, exhausted. "Whatever you think is safest." I knew well enough that this was not the time to be picky.

"I'm not sure," Caroline said. "Are there any other options?"

"Grandparents," Elena said as she lowered her teacup.

The soothing music stopped playing for a second, and I listened to the crackling of the fire.

"I'm not sure about that option either, Mom," Caroline said, leaning forward in her seat and running her hand through her hair. "I think it would be better just to keep him here."

Her face pale, Caroline said, "If that was the right option, I think I would be more certain about it. I don't like the idea of Adam being away from me."

I remained silent, though I felt the same as Caroline about being away from her.

"Not all the options would mean being separated," Lerato added, looking at us from across the table. "You could go with Adam somewhere, though that could be precisely what Corbett might be assuming you would do."

I could feel how my brain cells contracted at the thought of being separated from Caroline. Even though staying together was more dangerous for both of us, it still made me feel the safest.

"What if Caroline takes Adam to my sister's?" Elena asked. Lerato scratched his chin and he conversed with Elena wordlessly.

Her eyes focused on the ceiling, Caroline began to think this over. "I don't know why I'm having such a hard time with this," she confessed. "I'm not sure about Buenos Aires."

Lerato responded calmly, "You would be far away from here, and Corbett would need to search the entire globe before he found you there. And that would definitely give us some more time to come up with a solution for all of this."

For a moment, it seemed as though his voice matched the vibration of the music. And his ability to speak with great calmness even in such an intense situation continued to amaze me.

"I know, though it still doesn't convince me," Caroline said, sighing and looking at me. I looked into her eyes and held her hand under the table.

"Where else could we go?" I asked.

Caroline looked at the dark windows in deep thought.

"Switzerland?" I asked after a while. Lerato leaned forward in his seat and responded, "I don't think that would be safe, since it would be easy for Corbett to find you there because you resided there for so long."

"The question is: How long can we hide wherever we go?" Caroline exclaimed and started walking around the table. "Corbett's been playing with us for quite a while now, and I still have no clue about what he's plotted so far."

The desperation in her voice freaked me out. We needed a place to hide right away, not even a day from now. I leaned back in my chair and forced myself to think. I was already nervous and under stress, two things that seemed to trigger my clairvoyance in a positive way, so I decided to go for it.

Come on, just one more time, I told myself, as I mentally sharpened my senses and forced myself to think of a reasonable solution. I suddenly felt the mental urge to go back in time and, surprisingly, saw myself as a little boy. Children believe with innocence, Dominic had said, and I squinted my eyes to keep this image focused.

I observed my younger self and mentally asked where I would had gone to hide at the age of three. At that time, we still lived in our old house further away from the center of a small city, and I remembered how much I liked to play hide-and-seek with May. I saw myself hiding behind a big tree and recalled how much I liked the forest when I was a boy. And then, a second later, I opened my eyes, feeling wide-awake.

"The forest!" I yelled, impelled by some invisible current in my body. "Didn't you say you had a summer house somewhere in the forest? Why don't we hide there?"

I was as surprised by these words as they were. Caroline and Elena stared at me with their eyes wide open, Lerato was on his feet in a blink, and Dominic's hand froze in midair. After a brief moment of silence, everyone began to unfreeze.

"That's it!" Caroline said with excitement and pulled me out of my chair. "It feels right."

"Are you sure?" Elena asked cautiously, exchanging a series of looks with Lerato.

"It feels right to me," Caroline said quickly, strands of her hair dancing on her shoulders as she moved her hands. "No one has ever seen that house, and it's well hidden. We can stay there until we figure out how to confront Corbett and don't have to hide anymore."

"Lerato, what do you think?" Elena asked.

He was still thinking about my suggestion and kept his eyes focused on something behind us. He pressed his lips together slightly and tilted his head sideways as he said, "I am happy to say this might indeed work. Both fear and pressure promote your clairvoyance; it's turning out to be a very precise process after all."

"It will work," Dominic said. "They'll be safe there."

Caroline took my hand and gave me a promising look.

"I think it's a safe idea," Lerato said, fixing his eyes on Caroline. "If you think this is the right choice, then you have my blessing."

Caroline looked content for the first time since the conversation started. "When should we go?" she asked.

"As soon as possible," Lerato said, surprising me with his quick decision. "It would be best if you left tomorrow night after sunset."

"But Lerato, you know that we can't leave the hospital until Tuesday," Elena interjected. Lerato started thinking again, but stayed calm.

"I know. But I am positive that everything will work out in our favor. As soon as we leave the hospital on Tuesday, we can catch up with them and bring them home safely. There's no need to worry."

"So be it," Elena said, standing up and still looking concerned. "Let us not lose a single instant then. I'm going to start organizing some stuff for your trip."

A lot of things were said, thought and decided that night without me even being fully aware of them. Everything seemed to happen in a rush; plans were made and words spoken faster than a human ear could perceive them. Caroline was euphoric about the way I had come up with this idea. Elena ran up and down the stairs with a checklist that she had written in the blink of an eye. We briefly discussed whether to have Dominic go with us, though it was ultimately decided that it would be best if he stayed at home. The less buzz we created about our departure, the less suspicious Corbett might become.

"And what do I tell my mother?" I asked Caroline in the car on my way home. I hadn't yet come up with a reasonable lie to tell May.

"Tell her that we invited you to Montenegro to celebrate my parents' thirtieth anniversary," she said, her eyes reflecting the flickering streetlights outside.

I didn't say anything. I felt bad for lying to May so many times already, even though I told myself that it was the best way to keep her safe. The farther away I was from May, the safer she was. And I was happy with that thought. The headache returned, and I rubbed my temples and rested my head on the seat while Caroline held my hand.

Lerato drove through the mist very quickly, and once more, this brought home to me how serious our situation had become. I closed my eyes, my mind racing, and we all were silent until Lerato turned off the engine in front of my apartment building.

"Elena and I decided that to ensure your safety we will come and pick you up tomorrow morning and you will spend the day at our house until it's time to go to the airport," Lerato said. He waited until I was inside to drive off.

I walked up the stairs slowly, aware of the lump in my throat. It felt strange to have to run away from home without knowing when I would be coming back again.

My hand on the door handle, I knew there was no way back now. I had already dragged Caroline too far into the mess Corbett had caused in my life. It's said that making a decision always involves giving up something, and if ever required, I knew I would always give up my own life for Caroline or May.

I took a deep breath and opened the door.

The lights in the hallway were switched off, but May wasn't asleep. I found her in the living room watching a movie with subtitles. She was wearing a soft bathrobe and pink slippers, and had her feet on the coffee table. I sat down next to her and gave her a hug.

"This guy robbed a bank, and now the *Phoebe* is after him," she said without taking her eyes off the screen.

Her silliness made my heart ache with love, and I blinked some tears away. *Phoebe* was the way May pronounced the English word *FBI*.

"Mom, I've decided to prolong my vacation," I blurted out without taking a breath. "I'm going away with Caroline and her family to Montenegro, where her parents are going to be celebrating their thirtieth wedding anniversary." I was glad that the lights were dimmed since I couldn't stop blinking.

She gave me her full attention now.

"What about classes?"

"There's no problem. The university's policy allows students to ask for two weeks off during the semester."

I was surprised how quickly I had come up with that lie.

May kept looking at me questioningly. I was relieved when her expression finally softened. She had never had a problem with any of my decisions.

"It's a big family gathering, and many of Caroline's relatives are going to be there."

I was still blinking uncontrollably. I wished I could tell her the truth: that for some unknown reason my angel of death had been stalking me for months and was about to attack me again at any moment. I didn't say this, of course, and made myself feel less guilty by reminding myself that lying to her was the best way to keep her safe.

"That's quite an honor you've been invited, isn't it? I just want you to be happy, and if you feel like going, you should. Just make sure you don't fall behind at school."

For a split second, I wished she had said no. It felt as though I was saying good-bye to her.

"When are you leaving?"

"Tomorrow night," I said and then lied further. "They have already gotten the tickets."

"I'm leaving pretty early in the morning—you might still be

238

asleep," she said. Then I remembered that she was going to Zlatibor the next morning and felt my eyes itch at the thought of how much of a good-bye this actually was. Both of us were going away, May to have fun and me to run away from death. Could I have unconsciously known through my entelechy when I had purchased that ticket for her that I would be running away at the same time? Whatever made me buy her that gift for Christmas, it certainly turned out to be the perfect time for us to be apart.

"I need to go start getting my stuff ready," I said, trying to end the conversation. "I'm tired."

"I love you," she said, giving me one of her warm smiles. "Take care of yourself."

"I love you too, Mom," I said and left the living room in a rush.

Once in my room, I grabbed my backpack from under my bed and tried to figure out what to pack. When you don't know if you'll ever come back home, what do you take with you? Clothes and money both have no value against death the way a loving heart does, for that is truly where memory lives.

I rubbed my aching head as I rummaged through my clothes and other belongings. Caroline had advised me to take very little, only what I needed. I packed and unpacked my backpack twice. I was nervous and frightened at the thought of not knowing how we would confront Corbett if he showed up. What if he already knew about our plan?

And suddenly, everything seemed so useless. Not a single piece of clothing I had stuffed in my bag would help us stop him. We had to be brave enough to stand up against his evilness with the weapon of our bonded hearts. And then I promised myself I would fight for our love at all costs.

I sat on my bed and drew a loud breath. The Elders' book caught my eyes. I grabbed it, flipped through some pages, threw it unthinkingly into my backpack, and switched off the lights.

INVISIBLE

I woke up the following day wishing that everything had been a dream. I slowly opened my sticky eyes and blinked a few times until my vision came into focus. The fact that I still had a head-ache reminded me that everything was real. Remembering every-thing that happened the previous day made me aware of an anx-ious pressure in my chest, and recalling our decision to leave the country made me feel sick.

I knew there was no turning back now. Both Caroline and I had mutually agreed on seeking shelter from Corbett at her family's summer house in Montenegro, and I silently hoped for a peaceful resolution, in which neither one of us would be forced to choose between everything and nothing.

I found myself staring at the ceiling in procrastination, un-willing to leave my retreat from reality. Actually, Caroline and I were about to *hide* and *run away* from my angel of death, even though that was the opposite of what Vivienne had encouraged us to do. But what were we supposed to do when running away was the only remaining safe option left?

I finally got out of bed and took a long shower. I was glad May had already left, as having to say good-bye to her again would only have made it harder for me to leave. I took a last look at the apartment. The sofa still had a slight indent from where she sat last night, and her coffee mug left light-brown stains on the unopened mail and her travel checklist was on the coffee table. I picked up the list she wrote with so much excitement a few days before and traced my fingers along the smooth lines that connected the words, silently grateful that she was safe and far away from even imagining what I was going through. That thought calmed my racing mind, and I loaded her mug into the dishwasher, grabbed my backpack from my room and closed the door behind me, pausing to hear the *click* that indicated it locked behind me.

"Morning," Caroline said, greeting me with a warm kiss as I got into the car.

"How are you today?" Lerato asked me as he merged onto the highway. I was already used to the choreography of Caroline and Lerato picking me up each morning.

"Good, I guess," I said and remained quiet for the rest of the ride. Caroline wrapped her arm around my shoulder, and after a while, my headache was completely gone. Our silent trip felt unusually short, and Lerato turned off the engine as he parked in the garage.

Elena and Dominic were already waiting for us in the living room; the table had been set for breakfast, though no one really seemed in the mood to eat.

"The coffee is still hot, and I've got some tea steeping in the kitchen," Elena said as she gestured for me to take the seat next to the fireplace. "I'll go get the eggs and toast." I smiled dryly as I sank into the chair next to Caroline and looked at the *Moneos* in the front garden. The day seemed peaceful, almost completely normal.

"I've composed two letters, one for each of you, and will have Dominic drop them off at the university on Monday," Lerato said, placing two envelopes on the table. "There should be no problem with you both missing classes for up to two weeks."

I stopped peeling the egg in my hands. "Two weeks?" I asked. "Do you really think we will be gone for that long?"

"If it takes us that long to figure out what to do next, then yes," Lerato said matter-of-factly, completely relaxed.

"There's still absolutely no way to find out where Corbett is?" I asked him, feeling frustrated.

"We will try to talk to the Elders to see if there might be a way of tracking him now. I have studied his behavior and realized that the change in the energetic field makes sense because shape-shifting changes not only parts of your body but also sub-atomic particles in your surroundings. This confirms once again that he was actually there the night of your accident on the lake and shape-shifted after Caroline and Dominic showed up."

I washed my eggs down with a sip of coffee and asked, "How will this help us track him down?"

Lerato looked up from his plate, pressed his napkin to his lips and said, "If we track the trail of places where subatomic particles can be observed changing, we will at least know what direction he is moving in."

"We need to be sure not to run anywhere near that when that kind of change is happening," Caroline interjected.

Lerato looked at her patiently.

"We cannot and probably will not have to once we consult the Elders. I marked the area of the lake on a map and went back there last night. Everything is back to normal in that area now, and I was not able to sense any further changes nearby, which confirms that the campus is indeed the last place where he applied this new ability. I have thought about different patterns, such as hidden symbols or embedded information, which may, unintentionally, yet possibly reveal the sequence of locations where he has exercised this new shape-shifting power."

Caroline groaned and ran a hand through her hair. Elena then spoke up maternally.

"At present, we know that Corbett is still out there in the form of a raven. But this should not stop us from sticking to our plan. Your flight leaves at eleven-twenty. After you land in Montenegro, you will then go on by bus to a resort at the border of the national park. From there, you will need to hike the rest of the way to our house. Entrants need a permit to enter the park, but since you won't actually be checking in at the resort, we took care of that in advance."

This all sounded positive, and I tried to suppress my anxiety by focusing on the steady touch of Caroline's hand.

The rest of the morning was slow and uneventful. We were all tense, which was exhausting and did not help my recurring headache at all. I was glad to have something to divert my mind from thoughts of potentially bad outcomes of our trip when Lerato asked if I was up for another sensory practice with him in the library. I nodded yes and wearily followed him up the stairs. He had asked the others to stay downstairs, explaining that this time I was going to practice focusing on finding some*one*—not some*thing:* Corbett.

"Have a seat," he said.

He dimmed the lights in the library, drew the curtains and lit a candle on the table in front of me.

"The closest I can bring you to Corbett is this map," he said, handing me a map of Belgrade on which he had highlighted the place of Corbett's last appearance in yellow and marked it with a small *x*.

"Feel free to start engaging your intuition anytime," he said with a polished movement of his hands. I looked up at him and awkwardly rested my hands on the map. He locked his eyes on mine as he spoke.

"The idea is to trigger your entelechy with all possible physical and cerebral elements. My voice will trigger your sense of hearing, the candle flame your senses of smell and taste, and the map your senses of touch and sight. However, keep in mind that you have one more sense, the sixth sense, which only you can activate as it is deeply imprinted inside of your soul. Combine all of your five senses and you will enter the state of clairvoyance."

I nodded yes in response and tried not to look overwhelmed by his explanation and the setting.

"Focus on the flame in front of you."

I did as he said and rested my eyes on the unmoving yellow liquid light in the center of the candle. It took me some time to calm my racing mind, and in a long moment of silence, I had the feeling that the flame started to expand. The longer I focused my eyes on it, the bigger it seemed to grow. It was peaceful, yet I could still perceive slight movements as I pierced the golden warmth with my eyes, trying to make out images in it. I followed a drop of wax that ran smoothly down its thin body only to merge with its base on a small plate. I took a deep breath and inhaled the smell of the hot wax, the flame flickering slightly, and leaned back in my chair, as Lerato spoke from behind my back.

"Now, press your hands firmly on the map and feel the outlines of the city under your palms. Imagine a form of vibration within those, feel the sensation of a current flowing up through your fingers, and be open to receive remote information. Hold that current within your fingers and slowly drop all barriers, allowing it to flow up your arms and into your chest, where you feel it filling up your heart and then overflowing into your mind. And there you will encounter all the answers you need to find

Corbett. You have the power; you are in complete control of your mind."

I narrowed my eyes, and the flame flickered again.

"Don't forget to breathe. Allow the current to flow through your entire body as you inhale the scent of your surroundings. Feel how this current flows inside of you, and then exhale steadily." I could feel how Lerato's eloquent voice had completely relaxed my body, and I kept imagining the current running in my blood.

"Narrow your vision to the center of the flame," he directed. I could hear him move behind my back.

"I will be saying words to which I want you to respond whatever comes to your mind. It needs to be your first impulse; don't think about what you are going to say. It doesn't need to make sense to you at all. You're doing excellently. Maintain your focus, trust the process and be open."

At one point, his voice sounded like liquid words. I noticed another flicker of the candle and squinted my eyes a little more.

"Earth," he said after a moment of silence.

"Sky," I said and blinked to prevent myself from thinking.

"Summer."

"Winter."

"Sunshine."

"Don't think about it."

"Snow," I said.

"Wood."

"Branches."

"Continent."

"Europe."

"Nature."

"Nature," he repeated.

"City."

"South."

"North."

245

"Imagine that Corbett is now after your mother. Caroline is gone, and you're alone. There's nowhere you can go, nowhere you can hide. You're lost and he's coming for you. His tiny claws will pierce your flesh as death comes for you. What does it feel like to scream for help and not to be heard? Fight your enemy with your mind, for that is your strongest weapon!"

My hands curled into fists, and in the next second, a series of images flashed in my mind...big and small buildings, naked treetops, pointy branches, worms, snowflakes, soil, pebbles...and then a draft of air hit my face.

"It's over," someone said from a distance.

"You're safe; it's over," the voice said again. I felt a firm grip on my left shoulder and my eyes popped wide open.

My hands were still curled in fists. A piece of the map was scrunched on the table, and the candle had lost its flame.

"Good. Here, have a sip," Lerato said, his firm arm handing me a glass of water. I reached for it with shaky hands and poured its contents down my throat, though some of it ran down my chin.

"Breathe," he said, pressing his hands on my shoulders. He then drew the curtains open. The sun was blindingly strong, and my hands shot up to cover my eyes. For a moment I listened to his footsteps. He walked away from the desk and came back closer to me. And then I heard him pouring more water into the glass. A second later I felt him sitting on the edge of the table and heard him silently scribbling with a pen. It took me a moment to realize what had happened. I kept my hands over my eyes, as the comforting darkness helped to ease my racing heartbeat.

"I'm not sure I know what just happened," I said.

"You did well," he said. I lowered my hands, and he was still scribbling something quickly in blue ink on a notepad.

"I don't understand."

"But I do," he said and lifted his head to look at me. He was

246

smiling contentedly, and he politely gestured to the full glass of water in front of me.

"Nothing in what I said makes sense," I said between gulps.

"I must congratulate you," he said, still smiling. "It does completely." He showed me what he had written down. I stared at it for a while, looking from the paper to his face, and then shook my head in confusion.

"Apologies, I wrote too fast," he said, chuckling, and stood up. "The answers you gave me make complete sense." He started walking up and down.

"Do we know where Corbett is?" I asked. I felt confused and tried to remember what I had said.

"We don't have an exact location, but we know where he is headed," he said.

"Once you let down all your barriers and entered into a clairvoyant state, I asked you a series of questions to which you provided precise answers."

"And you think they made sense?" I asked, still feeling dazed.

"They did. From what you said, we know that he is in a snowy region on the European continent. He is still in the form of a raven, somewhere in a city. And he is moving northward."

I stared at him for a while as I allowed his words to form a cohesive picture in my mind.

I felt doubtful and asked, "How can we rely on what I said though?"

"I will answer this with a question. What did you *see?* Not before, but after you had closed your eyes?"

He locked his piercing eyes on mine.

I tried to recall the pictures in my mind.

"Fragments…pictures…flashing…worms…branches… snow…wind…for a moment I thought I was there…and a moment later I was back."

"And this is precisely the proof that we indeed can rely on

your words, for you have seen those images with the eyes of your soul, with your inner, clairvoyant, eyes. Paths of the present and the future meet when the sight and the words are aligned, and this is what you have just proved."

I held my breath as I thought about what he had said. If this was true, then Corbett was moving in the opposite direction, and that meant we were still safe. I emptied the glass of water one more time and leaned back in my chair. I felt exhausted, though that seemed to wear off.

"Is this even…"

"Possible?" he interjected, finishing my question.

"It is. You have done very well. I expected vague answers, although your state of clairvoyance seems pretty advanced to me. Believe in yourself and you will never fail."

He squeezed my shoulder. "I am sure the others will be eager to hear about your discovery," he said cheerily and held the door open for me. By the time we reached the foot of the stairs, I no longer felt tired.

Caroline jumped up off the couch when she saw us. Elena and Dominic were comparing her checklist with the contents of a brown backpack on the chair next to them.

"How did it go?" Caroline asked.

"Well," I said. "I saw some things, so that's good."

"Some good things," Lerato added as we joined them.

"We always believed in you," Elena said, smiling warmly as her hair fell to one side.

"What did you see?" Caroline said, nudging me with delight.

"Corbett is headed north, away from here. That's good for us. But he is still somewhere on the European continent, in the form of a raven."

Caroline's hand found mine under the table, and she leaned back in her seat with a relieved expression on her stunning face. "I'm so glad he's headed that way," she said.

"Were you able to see his exact location?" Elena asked, exchanging concerned looks with Lerato.

"No. All I could see is that he is still somewhere in a city."

"I am so proud of you," Elena said, still smiling warmly. "Let us hope he stays away from you until we find out how to track him down. I have packed a stash of emergency supplies for you two. We want all the bases covered."

"We will come and join you first thing on Tuesday," Lerato declared thoughtfully.

"And then we will take you home," Elena added. "Safe and sound." I felt I knew her well enough by now to know that she had spoken from a place of deep faith.

The afternoon seemed to drag on. Elena and Lerato went up and down the stairs with more of Elena's checklists. Dominic had grabbed his guitar and was playing quietly in the corner of the living room, while Caroline and I sat silently in front of the fireplace.

"Promise that whatever happens on this trip you will always come home to me," she said gently. "I will take you out of the darkness and above the clouds."

"I always will."

I knew I couldn't fail her. I couldn't fail the person who was fighting to free me from death.

It was dark outside when we made our way downstairs to the garage. Lerato had already put our bags in the trunk and had the engine running, ready to go.

"I love you both," Elena said, wrapping her warm arms around my back and giving me a long hug. "I'll see you on Tuesday," she added, blinking away a wave of tears.

"Take care," Dominic said and held the door open for me. In the warmth of the car, I rested my head on the back of the seat, breathing through my mouth and feeling nauseous.

The sound of the engine muffled their voices outside, though

249

I could easily guess what they were discussing: the possibility of us not coming back. Ever.

Caroline got in and sat next to me. Her eyes were glassy as she smiled at me.

"I just want you to be happy," I whispered and reached for her hand. "You deserve it."

"I don't deserve happiness more than you or anyone else in this world. No matter what happens, we'll stay together."

Lerato got in, fastened his seat belt and headed toward the airport. The ride there seemed short. He was driving very fast, and none of us was eager to start a conversation. The night was cold, and the air felt gray and empty. We checked our bags, and Lerato hastily walked us to the security entrance.

"I want you to go straight to your gate," he said. "Stay together and be safe." I looked back after we had gone through security, but he wasn't there anymore.

"Stop saying good-bye with your eyes, please," Caroline said once we had found a seat in the waiting area. I looked up at her sleepily, tucked a strand of hair behind her ear and gave her a soft smile.

We were silent as we boarded the plane. I was glad when we sat down—Caroline took the window seat. I tried to stop myself from thinking by contemplating the other passengers. There were a lot of children, a few couples, and the rest consisted of elderly people who looked excited about their trips.

I fell asleep immediately, but then woke up the moment we took off. The flight was uncomfortable, and even though it was actually short, it seemed to drag on for hours. My temples started throbbing and the annoying headache returned again. I tried to suppress it by making myself fall asleep, though this failed when my head fell forward every time I closed my eyes. Caroline sat completely still next to me, looking like a statue, her eyes scanning the pages of a magazine.

When we landed, I felt like all my energy had been drained out of my body, and my headache intensified. To my relief, it was a little warmer in Montenegro, and Caroline held my hand firmly as we moved through the crowd.

"Ground transportation," she mumbled and spun around in circle.

I squinted my itchy eyes at a sign nearby and said, "Right down there."

We connected to our bus at the airport, along with a couple of other tourists. It was a two-hour ride. The driver made stops along the way, dropping groups of two to three at each stop until we were the last ones on the bus. Caroline closed her eyes multiple times and tried to sense Corbett. I was relieved every time she opened them and gave me a reassuring look, though I wasn't certain if that meant we were completely safe. The driver drove through towns and then past rural landscapes on unlit roads through dense forests. After two hours, we stopped near the border of the national park. I could see a nice-looking resort in the distance up a hill between huge fir trees.

"Thank you," Caroline said to the driver. "You can drop us off here."

After we got off, she tugged softly on my arm and said, "Come on, we're not there yet."

It was pitch dark outside, the only light coming from the resort. There were trees as far as my eyes could see. When I flinched at the sound of an owl somewhere in the forest, Caroline threw herself in front of me in a split second.

"Put your backpack on," she said. "We have to hike the rest of the way." She looked around to make sure we were still alone. The night was humid, but cool, and we started walking toward the resort.

"Give me your hand and do not let go of me," she commanded me.

As soon as I reached for her hand, she intertwined her fingers with mine and gripped me tightly. As we walked toward the resort, the closer we got the more I could feel an invisible warmth tingling up my right arm all the way to my head. It felt like warm sprinkles of water on my face flowed out the tips of my hair and then slowly ran down my chest, heart, hips and legs until the tingling finally reached my toes. This feeling was new to me, a perception of an otherworldly sweetness that persisted in my body long after I knew what was happening. I felt as if I was being touched by invisible hands, almost like an imperceptible embrace, that made me feel safe in the midst of the wilderness. I felt as though happiness and joy were overflowing my body in that moment, and this experience seemed to contradict the reality of the situation we were in.

"Just keep walking," Caroline whispered.

We walked past the resort, into the darkness behind it down a marked walkway and under a ramp with a stop sign. Then the night completely swallowed us. The walking became climbing, but I wasn't exhausted, not even after we clambered up a steep hill, continuing in silence. The trees were scattered at first and then turned into a dark, misty forest dense with leaves that seemed like a never-ending labyrinth. I inhaled the scent of the forest and felt totally safe. No words of explanation were needed between Caroline and me. Her grip had made us both invisible, and not even the night could find us.

I lost all sense of time, and the only thing that mattered to me was that Caroline and I were together. We climbed over rocks and hills and among thick tree trunks.

Thriving forests and glacial lakes glittered in the gorges in the moonlight, and the scenery was dramatically beautiful—too perfect for a place to be hiding from death. The snowy landscape changed after every few feet, and we found ourselves hiking through rocky peaks and alpine meadows and along the ridges of canyons.

Corbett wasn't the only predator Caroline had made us invisible from. We had to stop and freeze as we waited for a large brown bear to sniff its way away from us. And a while later, just as we were passing a cave, a pack of hunting wolves almost made me fall into a lake. Caroline gave me a look promising that if we remained still, none of the animals could sense our presence.

Miles later, after we had reached another dense forest, Caroline finally pointed into the distance. I narrowed my eyes in search of our place of shelter and saw it in the darkness. The silhouette of a barely visible wooden house was embedded between trees in the densest part of the forest in a place that looked inaccessible to humans. Massive branches and leaves from the trees almost covered the entire house, camouflaging it in a way that made it appear like there was nothing else behind or around them, even close-up.

We stopped in front of the door, moving some fallen branches and shoveling the snow out of the way. This done, Caroline grabbed some *Moneos* out of her bag.

"Let's do this first," she said and we arranged and lit them on the ice-covered soil around the house.

"Come on inside," she said.

I followed her into the safe obscurity of the house. I felt confident that if someone had been watching us, it would look as if we were just moving further down into the depths of the forest.

She locked the door, and we paused for a moment. I couldn't hear the wind anymore, and I no longer felt cold. A sweet scent was hanging in the air.

"Hold on," she said and lit a candle on the wall. "We shouldn't switch the lights on, at least not for the first night. Let's use these instead." She started lighting more candles along the walls.

As the light spread and cast shadows on the walls, I could see a short hallway leading to a living room. I walked into the middle of it to familiarize myself with our shelter while Caroline was lighting more candles throughout the house.

A thick, soft rug covered the wooden floor, and the furniture had been protected by throw cloths. This house felt like a piece of Caroline I hadn't yet had the chance to get to know, and despite our circumstances, I felt a special kind of curiosity about it that only she could elicit from me.

Surprisingly warm, the living room was inviting, and I walked around to have a look at the photographs in the candlelight. The first one showed a younger Dominic, probably before the age of ten, opening his birthday presents in the same room. The next picture, a big square one in a golden frame, had been neatly hung above the fireplace in a place of honor and showed a smiling Elena and Lerato the moment they had become one during their wedding ceremony. The picture had a special spark in it and appeared golden even in the dimmed light. They were both dressed in white; Elena was holding flowers and Lerato's arms were wrapped around her waist. The image was timeless and warm; it would never get old. For a moment I thought they were moving in it—it was that alive.

The rest of the photographs showed people I didn't know, but believed to belong to Caroline's family. One of them depicted a little girl wearing a white worn-out morning gown. It was probably taken during the summertime because she was standing barefoot in a water fountain in front of a house that looked like a hospital. She was smiling wearily, and her body posture said she was anything but happy. The inscription on the bottom read *June 1911*.

"It might be a little dusty in here," Caroline said from the back of the room. She had lit a fire in the fireplace and was giving me an apologetic look.

"I'm sorry," she said and dropped her shoulders. "This is all we've got." I touched her chin gently to make her look up at me. Her face looked marvelous in the darkness, almost sphinxlike, with the shadows and the fire making her eyes look like two emeralds delicately designed to enrapture the onlooker.

"Don't be silly," I said, pressing her against my body. "It's perfect, I like it."

"I've got some food for us," she said in a soft, almost guilty, voice. "We should have some dinner and then make ourselves comfortable here."

We brought our heavy backpacks upstairs to her room, which was spacious and had a nice view of the endless pine forest. A glass door led to a balcony that connected all three of the bedrooms upstairs.

"I like it here, really," I said again.

She opened the curtains dreamily.

"It's a nice place to hang out. Wait until I bring you here during the summer. We usually stay awake all night long and just listen to the sounds of nature. It's beyond beautiful."

We had dinner in silence around a wooden table downstairs in the living room, and I gratefully appreciated Elena's cooking skills as I scooped the rest of her Spanish rice out of my container. At moments I felt as if I were on vacation, but couldn't pretend that I didn't feel the ominous presence of danger in the air. Caroline had drawn all the curtains in the house closed, and I wasn't allowed to step close to any of the windows or doors as she said we had to continue with our precautionary behavior.

After we finished eating, Caroline said, "Let's get ready for bed." She took my hand, and we went upstairs to grab some bedding. Once we were back in the living room, we put it down on the couch.

"I'm sorry for making you escape with me," she said.

I shushed her with a kiss on the forehead.

"It's not your fault. There's nothing you should be sorry for. It's my angel of death who made us run away. What can I say?"

"Don't ever blame yourself for this," I said and hit her gently with one of the pillows as she was unfolding a blanket. She dropped it on the floor, caught by surprise.

"You did not just hit me with that pillow?" she exclaimed, her finger in front of my nose.

"I absolutely didn't," I responded, hitting her again.

She grabbed another pillow from the couch. "You better run now," she warned.

I hit her again, this time on her head, which messed up her ponytail. She stumbled softly to the side, laughing, and tried to tidy up her hair.

"You don't know whom you're messing with," she said, ready to come after me.

She laughed, and with a smooth, rapid movement jumped over the furniture and landed right in front of me. This happened so fast that it completely rattled me and messed with my brain, but in a lovely way.

"Cheater!" I howled, and before I could move, she started hitting me with her pillow.

"Look who's talking now," she giggled heartwarmingly and chased me around the room. I was laughing so hard I couldn't run away, and I stumbled in front of the fireplace. She was right behind me, still hitting me with her pillow until it tore and little feathers burst out like soft fireworks. When we realized what had happened, we both started laughing even harder, and she sank to the floor next to me and we curled into balls. I was laughing so hard I was crying when she made funny faces and made a strange hissing sound from having caught a feather with her tongue.

"You just had…"

My words were drowned by more laughter.

"It's tickling," she coughed as we rolled on the floor in the softness of the white feathers. We kept laughing until we kissed, and then remained quiet, her head on my chest, allowing the silence to speak for itself.

"Do you mind if we sleep on the floor next to the fire?" she asked.

"I don't," I said, allowing my hand to get lost in her silky hair. Her eyes looked like golden liquid in the firelight.

"I used to sleep on this rug next to the fire when I was little. Especially during the wintertime. The fire makes me feel safe."

"Let me change and get us another pillow since we can't use this one," I said as we both got off the floor.

"I'll go get more blankets," she said, walking away with a trace of white feathers falling out of her hair.

I made my way upstairs to the bathroom and tried to wash away my recurring headache with cold water. I didn't want to bother Caroline with it; it seemed like the least important thing to worry about given our circumstances. As I was fishing my pajamas out of my backpack in the darkness, I felt the pointy edge of the Elders' book poking my fingers and I unthinkingly took it downstairs with me.

Caroline had blown out some of the candles in the living room and was lying on a layer of soft blankets in front of the fire.

"I think this will do," she said as I snuck under the blanket and she rested her head on my chest. She was so pleasantly warm it almost made me feel as if I was actually stepping into the fire, without any burning pain. I closed my eyes for a moment and inhaled her warmth, which soothed my headache.

"You can't stop thinking about it," she said, seeing the book. I shifted my weight to the side to look at her.

"I guess I can't."

We both kept staring at the book for a while, its shades of purple and white pleasingly flowing into each other in the firelight. I flipped it open and ran my fingers over the words of the story as Caroline spoke softly.

"When love makes you commit mistakes, that's when you know how strong it is. She loved him too much to know that she was asking something dreadful from him. The same way he loved her too much to know that he was doing something forbidden when he turned her into an angel. This story is proof that such love exists and we should embrace our world."

I looked into her eyes as she spoke, and it appeared to me as if she was made out of water and fire in that moment. Her soft lips moved gracefully as they released words that opened the eyes of my heart; her cheeks looked rosy, and her bare arms seemed pale, yet irresistibly appealing.

"Janus and Vivienne have reason enough for giving you this book."

I sighed and confessed, "I feel completely useless for not being able to find out what the missing lesson is."

She looked up at me with a soft expression.

"Don't. Believe in the timing. Maybe we can't know yet just because we're not ready enough."

"They must be thinking the same thing," I said, looking at the ceiling. Caroline lifted her head up from my chest and smiled a silly smile.

"They're not. I know that."

I was skeptical.

"How can you be so sure? I'm convinced they're going to show up one day soon and tell us that our time is up."

"They would've already given us a time limit, but they chose not to. Our main focus is to find a way to keep you safe. My family has heard a lot about Vivienne and Janus throughout the years, and we know their *modus operandi*. They're patient, unlike many others, and highly respected among the community of the Elders."

"How long have they existed? The Elders?" I was suddenly curious to know more about them.

"No one knows exactly. We were taught at a young age that they were estimated to have founded their community in the twelfth century. However, no one really knows if this is accurate. All we know is that they're the most powerful angel community that has ever existed."

"Vivienne and Janus are that old?"

"They're not. The community of the Elders was founded by four angels. Their full names are Riothamus Pirus, Stasius Quercus, Proserpina Ficus and Viatrix Picea to be exact. They were descendants of the Latins."

"The Latins?"

"Their tribe was one of the first inhabitants of the city of Rome. For many years the Elders lived and operated from Rome, but then moved their community to a place in the spiritual world. No one knows where it is as it is not in solid form."

"What makes them so powerful though?"

"They're sort of our supreme court. All of their rules are based on self-fulfilling prophecies, which makes their community an invincible empire, as all of their regulations are unbreakable. Their law is self-fulfilling in the literal sense."

"What does that mean?"

I was already alarmed by their existence and felt human just asking that.

"Once they give an order, their strong set of beliefs and behavior make it become true. This is exactly what makes them invulnerable—the combination of them holding their thoughts in their sharp minds with their actions doesn't allow any outcome to differ from the intended result."

I noted a glimmer of respect in her eyes as she spoke.

"Who exactly are the Elders? Is it just Vivienne and Janus?"

Her story about them had intrigued me, though I learned quickly that they were to be treated with great respect.

"No. They're like a family. There's thirteen of them, to be specific."

She moved her head slightly and her hair tickled my chin.

"Interesting. Isn't thirteen an unfortunate number?"

She lifted her head from my chest and gave me a soft, understanding smile.

"That's a classical human superstition," she said. I was intimidated by how her world seemed much more complicated than I originally thought it was. A pinching pain shot through my temples, and I wasn't sure if it was the recurring headache or if it was due to the amount of otherworldly information my brain was processing. I moved slowly and turned my head away from the fire so she wouldn't see the tears in my eyes.

"They are in charge of everyone in my world," she continued.

"Even the angels of death?" I asked, turning my head back to look at her.

"Even them."

A short silence followed during which my thoughts drifted away somewhere between angels and human beings, and I rested my eyes on the fire burning next to us. The flames appeared peaceful, very inviting, and I understood why Caroline liked to sleep next to them.

"Who lights the angels' candles?" I asked, inspired by the fire. Caroline seemed entertained by my questions.

"The Guardians of the Earth."

I wrinkled my forehead questioningly.

"The Guardians of the Earth are regular human beings who live on Earth among us. The only difference between them and other humans is that they're strongly connected to the angels' world. They are by far the most loyal souls and would never reveal their purpose or anything that they know about us to other human beings. We refer to them as the *chosen ones* since they're hand selected by the Elders, who usually, but not always, choose elderly people whom you would never think of as connected to something greater than what your normal senses can perceive about them. A Guardian of the Earth could be your neighbor or the lady from the rest home."

I was fascinated that her world wasn't actually far away from mine. It had always been within grasp, though I would have never known it if she hadn't taught me how to see with the eyes of my heart.

"Are there any more people among us who work for the Elders?" I asked captivated.

"I'm sure there must be more of their faithful followers that I've never heard of. No one knows everything about the Elders and their entire community."

"How many of their communities do you know of?"

"I know about three communities that the Elders are in charge of. You can picture it like an organizational chart, if you'd like."

She paused to make sure I was keeping up.

"The first community is mine, the guardian angels, who are in charge of their human protégés. The second community consists of the angels of death, who are in charge of the souls of the deceased. And the third community is comprised of the Guardians of the Earth, who light the angels' candles."

I traced my fingers up and down her delicate arm as I thought in silence about all the details she had shared about her perfect world. Her words sounded like my own song, a song without words that only I was able to hear, and just looking into her eyes, I felt a warm quiver run down my entire body.

"What are those candles made of?" I asked, recalling their bright light in my mind.

"They're made of liquid souls," she said and paused again. She always knew when I needed another mental timeout due to my human limitations.

"The Guardians of the Earth breathe light into the candles, and each time they do so, they sacrifice a part of their own soul that detaches from their body giving life to the candle. This is a very powerful but painful process. It is not an easy path because giving up a part of your own soul to give someone else life is the purest form of sacrifice. The light inside the candles is the light of life and cannot be put out by anyone else but the Guardians of the Earth. They also do the carvings."

"Do…they…die?"

Her expression saddened and she looked thoughtful.

"They don't. However, you can only imagine how painful their task is. Each one can only light as many candles as they have been destined to."

"Do you ever get to meet your Guardian of the Earth?"

"I don't. Their task is an invisible silence that is echoed in each life they make possible."

I knew that even if the fire wasn't next to us, I would still see the spark of compassion in her eyes.

"The moment you saved me was the moment you lit up my life," I said as I locked my fingers with hers and held her hand tightly. "A part of your soul will always be within me." She responded to my grip, resting her soft fingertips on my knuckles, and for a long time we didn't say anything as we allowed the silence to be the witness of our wordless affection.

I sighed, remembering, and asked, "What happens to the candles of the angels who fail?"

"Their light goes out, and the Guardians of the Earth take their candle away."

"And what exactly happens when a protégé dies?"

"If it's not a protégé's time to die, then his or her guardian angel has to die, too. However, the rules are different when it *is* a protégé's destined time to die."

She paused and waited for me to react.

"How are they different?" I prompted.

"When a protégé's time has come to leave the Earth, his or her guardian angel accompanies their soul to the angel of death who is assigned to take care of them beyond that. Have you ever heard of people saying they see a white light as they are passing away?"

I nodded.

"That's the one and only time a human being actually gets to face his or her guardian angel. The white light is a guardian angel waiting for their soul."

"I will never be afraid of death now that I know I will always see you again," I said. This knowledge gave me a pleasant way to think about death, and I comforted myself with the thought that, in case things went badly with my angel of death and I wasn't able to return home, I would at least get to see Caroline one more time.

She wasn't pleased with my words. "Don't be afraid, not because you'll see me again, but because I'll never let you die," she promised and leaned back on my chest.

I had a million questions in my mind and hesitated before formulating the next one. "Would you be assigned a new protégé if I did die though?" I asked.

I felt her body shudder. "I would," she said quickly. "Only if it was your time to go though."

"How do you know when your protégé's time to die has come?" I couldn't help asking further.

She was focused on something in the distance.

"We simply don't feel the urgent need to save a protégé in that moment, our power becomes immune against death then, and we can't do anything else but to wait for the protégé's soul to be set free from his or her body."

I hesitantly asked my next question: "Have you ever known anyone who failed to save a protégé?"

"I have. Lerato's brother. We almost never talk about it unless Dad brings it up."

Even though her eyes were filled with sorrow, Caroline's face was still beautiful in the firelight. I could feel my body stiffen, and I was surprised by the revelation that her uncle had failed as a guardian angel.

263

"I'm sorry."

"Don't worry," she said. "It's okay."

"Is he still…alive?"

"He is. He didn't die because he was a young, new guardian angel at the time and that eased his case before the Elders. As you already know, new guardian angels need a great deal of dedication when they start out."

She paused again before continuing.

"His protégée was an elderly woman in her late sixties. She lived in Romania and was often violently abused by her husband until one day she cut her wrists to free herself from the suffering in her marriage. My uncle ran to her side immediately and healed her—saved her life. He thought that was the right thing to do, but it wasn't. He was supposed to watch her die."

"But that's not fair," I said with grief.

"It's not. But we can't do anything once a human being decides to take his or her own life. It's beyond our control, and we can't—aren't allowed—to stop it."

"Aren't you *supposed* to save them?" I asked in anger. "What if they're not aware of what they're doing?" I was offended by the unfairness of this rule.

She looked up at me in agony, her face immaculate.

"We are. But each person can only live as long as fate allows. I know this sounds cruel, but we can't help with everything. Don't you think I wish we could heal cancer and other incurable diseases? We can only help to a certain extent."

"She's still alive though?" I couldn't help asking.

"She's not. She passed away soon after from complications."

"That's the reason my uncle isn't an angel anymore. We treat him normally though, but hardly ever talk about this. He lives a human life and has a lovely wife. He says that the loss of one person is an open wound to be filled by someone else. He's starting to forget the part of his life when he was an angel, though we share moments with him to make him remember through memories."

Her voice was barely a whisper now. The story about Lerato's brother had moved something inside of me, and I suddenly wished I could meet him one day, talk to the man who gave up the right to be a guardian angel for doing something he believed was right. What a sad story to be told by an angel.

"Being a guardian angel can also be interesting and fun at times," Caroline said trying to shift our mood, the glimmer back in her eyes.

"Elena's protégée, for instance, is a middle-aged woman who fights for animal rights worldwide. Elena says she's never seen that many wild animals in her life before."

Fascinated, I asked, "So she's been on one of those wildlife trips in Africa?"

"Not only one. Wait until I have her tell you about her trip to the Amazon in South America. She kept talking about it for weeks afterward, until we all literally believed we were hearing the sounds of jungle animals in our house."

Caroline laughed musically, and my heart skipped a beat.

"Has Elena also saved animals?"

"We can only help animals in human ways. Not because they're worth less than humans—animals also have a spiritual essence. However, they can only be helped by those who both help and endanger them the most: human beings."

"Your family is great. I've never known anyone who has contributed so much to the world."

She smiled warmly at me, and I allowed my hand to get lost in her soft hair. Knowing about her family's duties made me feel worthless at moments. I knew she would never want me to compare myself to her—I guess that was just another one of my human weaknesses.

I decided to probe: "How do you become an angel?"

"You have to be born as one," she answered in a soft voice. "There's no other way."

I never told her about my silly idea of somehow qualifying as an angel due to my entelechy, and I would absolutely never force such a process, though deep down I held the vision of the two of us living in total equality, with no complications or differences at all.

I fell silent as I enjoyed her warmth on my body. The fire had relaxed me, the next moment I was hot, and before I realized that my chest felt as though it was burning, I allowed my arm to freely glide down her spine.

The sensation was electric, my senses felt awake, and my heart throbbed in my throat. She noticed the stiffness of my body and looked up at me, and before she could say anything, I leaned forward and gave her a kiss. Her lips felt silky and plump, and her back was warm from the flames. Slowly, very hesitantly, always afraid she would run away, I reached under her shirt. I stopped moving my hand, waiting for her permission, and then traced my fingers up her delicate backbone.

Her skin was sensual, smooth and fine. I sighed at the way it felt and closed my eyes as I pressed her against my body. The heat was uncontrollable, as I stroked her hair with my other hand, less tentatively now. I opened my eyes, just long enough to make sure hers were closed, and continued inhaling her scent with each breath.

My pulse was thudding, any sense of danger had vanished and was replaced by my irrepressible feelings. The thirst in my chest swelled up, and as I reached the straps of her bra with my hand on her back, the fire in my chest boiled up and burst into fireworks.

The next moment I moved on top of her. We continued kissing as I passionately pressed her against me, as if trying to get under her skin. My other hand was still lost in her hair, and her moist, hot skin burned my body.

266

I unhooked her bra, and within a split second and without effort, she immediately rolled out from under me and leaned away. My eyes popped open, and I gasped, disoriented. My pajamas were soaking wet with steamy sweat, and I slowly, gradually, allowed my lust to fade.

Panting, Caroline looked as though she had been running, and she stared at me in shock. Her hair was standing out all around her marvelous face. One of her hands was gently, but very firmly, pushing me away. She still seemed to be analyzing what had happened, and without taking her eyes from mine, she pulled the blanket up to the top of her chest.

"I'm sorry," I said, breathless. My body felt electric.

"No, I am," she said, her eyes wide.

Moments passed by before she dared to move. She slowly disentangled herself from me but stayed right next to me on her back. I was still frozen and tried to apologize by being still, as if doing so could atone for my actions.

In the silence, I could hear her catch her breath, and finally my pulse slowed down. I swallowed, and it occurred to me that neither of us had been prepared for such an intense physical reaction.

"I didn't expect..." I managed to say.

She kept her eyes on the ceiling. "Neither did I." When she finally looked at me, she was sad. "We're not supposed to. We have to resist."

Right, as if that was ever going to be easy after that experience. I felt morbid.

"I shouldn't have started."

"I shouldn't have let it happen. I thought it would be easier to stop, to withstand..."

I cautiously leaned closer to her and slowly brushed the hair out of her face.

"We can't let this come between us. We have to be careful. I wish...I could change the rules."

She sighed and pulled the blanket closer to her bosom. Placing a finger on her rosy lips, I said, "I promise I'll never let anything pull us apart." I wrapped my arms around her and pressed her tightly to my body.

I woke up the next day before Caroline. When dawn peeked through the curtains, she looked like a soft unopened flower that taught me what it feels like to sleep on angel wings. I stayed on the floor with her head still on my chest, as my headache had come back and made me feel drowsy. It was colder in the house; the flames of the fire had disappeared and left behind a layer of glowing ashes.

There was not much to do that Sunday, and we spent the day in the living room after having some eggs and toast for breakfast. It was raining, and a milky layer of fog had swallowed the entire forest outside, turning everything into different shades of gray. Caroline wouldn't let me out of her sight. The wind picked up and howled through the cracks of the windows and doors, and after a few hours, I grew paranoid and thought the falling rain against the house sounded like tiny claws and beaks striking the walls.

"I'd call Elena and tell them that we're okay if there was any cell service here," she said later that afternoon while drying her hair after a shower. "Though that doesn't matter that much; she and Lerato already know we've arrived safely."

We walked around the house pointing our cell phones at the ceiling, trying to find reception. After the rain stopped, I managed to send a message to May, who texted back asking about the anniversary celebration and sent a selfie of her in a spa with a green mask on her face. I told her I was fine, and then lied, saying that we were getting ready for the party the next morning and that I was glad to be meeting Caroline's relatives. I was happy that May was fine, far away from me and having a good time, which she absolutely deserved.

After dinner I couldn't stand the headache anymore and unwillingly told Caroline about it. She wasn't happy about it either and eased my discomfort by gently pressing her soft lips on my forehead.

Monday wasn't much different than the previous day, except that the rain had been replaced by snow. I greatly anticipated Elena's and Lerato's arrival on Tuesday, though Caroline said they still hadn't found a way to locate Corbett. I offered to try to sense him, but she wouldn't let me. She was concerned about my recurring headache and didn't want me to drain my energy. I ended up feeling even worse.

We went through the Elders' book for hours, but grew frustrated after none of our ideas worked for the sixth lesson, finally and completely running out of solutions. We even consulted some of Lerato's books upstairs that were part of his extended library, but that didn't help either.

"I wish I could find a way to finally stop it," she said, making me look up from a book. "Your headache."

"It's not your fault. I must not be taking our circumstances well. Your presence alone heals my life."

I reached for her hands.

"We'll be out of here soon, I promise," she said gently and walked to the fireplace to add more wood to the fire.

In the evening, when all the light outside had disappeared, we sat by the fire, the Elders' book on my lap. I had convinced her to let me try to sense the remaining lesson, and I thought this might, in some odd way, lead us to where Corbett was. Since I couldn't control what I wanted to see, I hoped to randomly crack the door to that knowledge open once I was in my clairvoyant state.

"Stop if the headache worsens," Caroline said with concern, sitting next to me.

I stared into her emerald eyes for a long time and then placed my flat palms on the pages of the book and closed my eyes. I imagined how I pressed my eyelids into the sockets of my eyes until I started seeing spinning silver circles and held that image until those circles turned into liquid white light. I then pressed my hands tighter on the pages of the book, imagining how the words flowed up my arms all the way up to my brain. I clenched my jaw as I recalled Lerato's guiding voice in my head and inhaled the scent of the fire next to me.

Go back in time, I told myself, and I kept moving through the whiteness until I found myself in the same living room Caroline and I were in. I looked around slowly, but the house seemed completely empty. The curtains were drawn open, and warm sunlight was entering through the windows. I was confused by that image and took a step closer to one of the chairs and sat down. The house gave me a feeling of melancholy and it washed over me as I contemplated the emptiness of the space I found myself in.

"Where are Severino and Godeva?" I heard myself ask in the silence.

My question was answered by a sudden painful cry from outside, and I mentally ran to the closest window to peek outside. There they were.

The landscape had changed completely; I wasn't looking at the crowns of fir trees and I knew right away that the painful cry had come from Godeva.

I was looking at her parents' farm from a distance. She and Severino were walking toward a massive gate. He was several steps in front of her, and she was falling behind him, hindered by a long gown that she was trying to hold up with one of her hands. When he reached the gate to her farm, she caught up with him and threw her arms around his neck, begging him not to leave. He hugged her briefly and then hurriedly walked through the gate. Godeva cried out in more pain and sank to the dusty ground, burying her face in her hands. I opened the window, ready to jump out and make him go back to her.

"Come back!" I heard myself yell at him. "Don't go!" The image turned indistinct, and my head hit against something solid. "You're safe!" Caroline's voice said. I opened my eyes.

I had fallen to the side, and she pressed her hands on my body while I frantically blinked several times.

"He's gone," I kept saying. "Caroline, he's gone." She helped me sit up and squeezed my hands.

"Who's gone? What did you see?"

"Severino. He wasn't supposed to leave her. She's in pain. The first time he left caused her to suffer from depression. I saw it. I was there. She's in pain."

Caroline held me against her soft body until my breathing came back to normal. "It's okay," she said. "You're with me now." Her warmth was relaxing, and coming back to reality, I remembered what had happened. I hadn't intended at all to trigger such an intense experience, and I looked at her remorsefully.

"I can't control it. I don't know why this happened."

She slowly released me and said, "Your entelechy grows or is intensified by your surroundings."

"Here," she said, handing me a glass of water.

"It's as if I felt her pain," I said after a short pause. Caroline ran her hand through her hair and looked at me anxiously.

"I never knew it could be this strong," she said. "Maybe we acted too quickly and should have taken some precautions."

"Whatever it was, it was a much stronger experience than when I worked with Lerato," I said and emptied the glass of water.

"Better?"

"Yes. I just don't understand why he walked away from her, from their problems. He should have taken responsibility."

"That might be it," she said. "At the end that was the trigger for Godeva's later actions."

I stared at the Elders' book, drew a deep breath and hesitantly took it in my hands.

"Severino should have never walked away. He should have taken responsibility," I said and nervously flipped the page.

I was convinced I had *seen* the missing lesson and grew impatient when no words appeared. We both kept our eyes fixed on the page for a long time, and I felt the urge to tear out the pages and throw them into the fire. I could feel Caroline's hand on my shoulder as she tried to silently comfort me. I lowered my head and sighed in despair.

"I don't understand! What's the point in making me see something that doesn't even have anything to do with the missing lesson?"

Her voice was calming.

"It most likely does have a meaning. We just must read between the lines."

"I'm tired, Caroline. This has gone too far for me. I'm overwhelmed. Look at us: We're hiding from my angel of death far away from our homes with no idea what's going to happen next. I feel like a huge failure."

"Don't, please."

"I can't help it. Why do I even have this clairvoyance if I can't use it when I need it the most?"

"You're shaking," she said. "Stop." Alarmed, she threw her arms around me. I stopped talking and surrendered into her warm embrace. I was suddenly cold, and the headache was back.

"I don't know what's going to happen either, but we must believe in ourselves. We'll find a way out of this. You need some rest."

I enjoyed the safety of her hug for another moment and then made my way upstairs to get ready for bed. When I came back downstairs, she was already lying down next to the fire. I silently snuck under the blankets next to her. I stayed awake long after she had fallen asleep, and it occurred to me that perhaps that vision had only been a reflection of my inner fear of Caroline actually leaving me. I turned on my side and wrapped my arm around her waist, though it was unusually cold that night, no matter how close I held my body to hers. I focused on the whisper of the flames and Caroline's warmth, and finally fell asleep. That night I had another oddly vivid dream.

As I was sleeping, I was aware of how my blood pressure rose and my muscles tightened, along with a feeling of hopelessness and complete desperation. I was lost somewhere in time and found myself in a dark forest with trees standing densely next to each other. Above my head, their crowns intertwined to create a never-ending green cage.

It was dawn, and the first rays of sun had just touched the tips of the trees around me. It wasn't snowing, and I wasn't cold as I realized that I was barefoot. The leafy soil felt soft under my feet, and the forest was unusually silent; the only sound I could hear was the crackling of tiny branches and leaves under my toes. I turned around several times to determine where I was, though that didn't help me orient myself.

Caroline wasn't anywhere to be seen, but nevertheless, I stayed calm and decided to keep walking further into the endless forest. I could hear the sound of a waterfall in the near distance and decided to walk toward it. After climbing a steep hill, I came to a narrow river. Its water was clear, and I followed its bank as the sound of the waterfall came closer. I ended up in a beautiful clearing, where I could see the sky for the first time.

It was a mixture of dark colors; some rain clouds were approaching in the far distance. I still wasn't bothered by my surroundings and reached the waterfall with little effort, only to be agitated by something about it. I cautiously stepped closer to the bank and looked down into the crashing waters, which were pitch black.

That's when I became nervous and realized that the entire river was actually black. I impulsively turned around to walk away from the water when an excruciating pain suddenly shot through my head. I sank to the soil, my hands at my temples. My eyes started welling up with tears. I made myself stand back up, and when I was back on my feet, I found myself facing a man dressed all in black.

Still as a marble statue, he was standing only a few steps away from me, unmoving, his eyes resting patiently on me. His skin was slightly gray, and his hair and small eyes were brown, almost black. He had small, evenly shaped eyebrows, and I had the feeling that I had somehow met him before; something about him was unusually familiar to me. I looked at him and he looked right back at me, piercing me with his small eyes, the way predators did with their prey before attacking. My gut was telling me to walk away, that I was in danger, but against my own will, I was fascinated by his appearance and couldn't leave.

He looked like an angel dressed in black, and I realized that I couldn't speak when I asked him where we were. The sound of thunder made me look up at that sky, and when I looked back down, he was gone. I grew more nervous than before and started to walk back but was caught in a downpour. I started running but fell several times. Then I realized that was just another of those dreams where you can't run away from danger. Another loud rumble of thunder shook the trees around me, the soil under my feet cracked open, and I fell into its humid darkness.

I gasped and opened my eyes, rubbing my incredibly aching head. My heart was thumping so loudly that for a moment I thought it would wake up Caroline, who to my surprise turned out to be still asleep. I was drenched in my own sweat and felt dizzy and sick at the same time. I kept rubbing my head, this time with my knuckles. When I somehow managed to stand up, I held on to the closest chair and then sat down to prevent myself from collapsing. The thought of waking up Caroline felt wrong, though I knew that more was wrong, and it was bothering me.

Another wave of nausea hit me, and I felt the urge to head upstairs to the balcony, even though I wasn't allowed to leave the house. It took a lot of effort to move, and I climbed up the stairs on my hands and knees. Once I reached the top, I sank to the floor and rested my heavy head on the cold wooden floor, hoping that would ease the pain. I crawled to Caroline's room, and once the door to the balcony gave in under my weight, I let my body slump on the snowy marble.

It was drizzling now, and I allowed the soft drops of slush to tickle my face. The first rays of dawn were painting the sky a rosy orange. I hoped Elena and Lerato would be here soon and would take care of my pain. I opened my mouth, breathing in the drizzle, but no matter what I tried, the pain still persisted. My head was buzzing, and I was having problems with my balance.

I had a hard time pulling myself up on the handrail. My stomach contracted, and my mouth opened as the contents of my stomach gushed out over the edge of the balcony. The taste was sour and burned my nose, and I shut my eyes as the headache intensified. I hit my face with my knuckles to stop the sound of the voices I heard whispering in my head. I was frightened, and thought about going to get Caroline, but felt I shouldn't wake her up. I had already dragged her too deeply into the mess I had caused, and I told myself I must have just caught the flu.

The muffled voices in my head grew louder as I made my way downstairs. *I need to leave the house,* I told myself, feeling this was the only right thing to do. I would just go for a quick walk and then I'd hopefully feel better and come back. Caroline didn't need to know I was leaving.

I put on my bathrobe, grabbed a flashlight, tiptoed to the front door and opened it softly. I was relieved to be outside at last.

I breathed in the morning air and made my way through the forest without thinking. The snow was freezing my toes, but it was as though my feet were obediently carrying me away from the house. I had to—it would make the pain go away—and so I kept walking further and further away from the house.

The morning air was cold and felt good on my burning skin. After all, this was the right thing to do, to walk and ease my pain. There was no time to be scared of anything.

When I tried to go back, it was as if my senses had gone haywire and were doing the opposite of what I wanted. The whispering of the voices in my head grew louder with each step I took. I kept walking until I found myself running—running away from myself, my thoughts and my life. Was I committing the same mistake Severino did by walking away from Caroline?

I pressed my back against a thick tree trunk and dropped down into the snow as my headache began to feel as if someone was stabbing me in the same spot on my head over and over again. I rested there for a while and waited for the voices to quiet down. First, they completely went silent. Then they came back even louder, this time more distinct, and I was able to make out two words that kept ringing in my head: *Rara avis.*

I screamed out in pain, hitting my head with the flashlight, but the voice, a creepy mixture of whisper and bitter laughter, grew louder and more painful.

Rara avis.

Rara avis.

At that instant the pain had become so unbearable I thought I was going to pass out, and I started hitting my head with the flashlight until I felt my warm, rusty blood running down my nose.

Rara avis.

"Stop! Stop it!" I screamed, crying out of desperation with my fingers digging into the soil. I got up on my feet with weak knees, wanting to walk back to the house only to find myself lost in a maze among the immense trees.

"Breathe," I said out loud and clasped my hands to my throat.

276

To my relief, the dizziness wore off and the pain stopped for a fraction of a second, long enough for me to realize what I had done. And then a single thought hit me like a bolt of lightning from above: *Caroline!*

I had to go back to her as fast as possible, something was going on with me, and I wasn't supposed to be walking around in the woods alone by myself. Panic-stricken, I tried to make out where I had come from. I spotted some broken low-hanging branches to my right and tried to run.

I winced every time the higher branches cracked above my head when the lower ones hit my face, but I felt awake again, as if all my senses had come back to life. Fear overcame me as I tried to find my way back to Caroline, my safe shelter, and I regretted having left her, though I couldn't remember having done this deliberately on purpose. I quickened my pace, but then the voice in my head came back again.

Rara avis.

I covered both of my ears with my hands, but the shrill sound of the voice seemed to painfully pierce my mind. I froze on the spot when I heard the caw of a raven—a scratchy, icy, gurgling sound that chilled the blood in my veins.

I realized this was not just any raven, and instantly everything made sense to me. He was there. My angel of death was alone with me in the woods and was about to kill me if I didn't manage to find my way back to Caroline.

I tried to run as fast as I could. I brushed against trees and fell down over and over again, leaving a trail of blood in the snow. The flashlight slipped out of my hand, and I left it behind. Time was of the essence now, and time was running out. If Corbett killed me, Caroline would have to die too. I couldn't let that happen. I was running back to her, as I always would, and I was ready to fight for our love with my life.

The wind howled in my ears, and everything rushed past me

in hazy, indistinct images as I fought my way through the forest with my arms out in front, trying to protect my face. I heard the raven's caw again, this time it was closer. Branches sliced my face open as I ran even faster. The wind picked up, and a black fuzzy cloud rushed past me. The pain came back, slicing and sharp, and I became aware of an open wound on my head. I was bleeding. The raven began attacking me from above.

I quickened my pace, but he was there again, coming at my left side. Somehow I made a sharp right and he missed me, which only angered and provoked him even more. He caught up with me, this time leaving a wound on my right knee with his sharply chiseled claw.

I made another left and descended the hill that I climbed up before, but Corbett was faster and gaining on me. He kept diving down and attacking me from all sides, and he seemed to be on my left and my right at the same time. I felt more useless as I stumbled through the leaves and branches with my hands waving above my head to fend him off. I randomly hit him, and my arm numbed out for a moment. Now, he was even more upset and enraged. That's when he cawed loudly at me, flying out of the dense forest ahead and struck me forcefully right in the middle of my chest, knocking all the wind out of me. The immediate impact threw me vigorously back on the ground with a piercing pain that felt like ravaging fire ants under my skin.

Rara avis.

Ignoring the pain and rushing blood flowing from my wounds, I managed to stand up and crawl over the thick trunks and gnarly, long roots of the trees.

"Caroline!" I screamed, desperate for her to hear me.

Rara avis.

Rara avis.

"Caroline, I'm here!" I cried out with all of my might. It was getting brighter, and the sun started coming out through the low, heavy clouds. It was mid-morning by the time I reached the house. My face was matted and covered in a warm paste of sticky blood, and it took all the strength I had left to push open the door.

"Caroline!" I screamed.

In a fraction of a second she was there, her face completely ashen.

She gasped, "What happened? Where were you?"

As she touched all of my bleeding wounds one by one, each of them healed. Instantly.

I pulled back. "He's here. He's right here!" I screamed but was interrupted by the voice in my head.

Rara avis.

Rara avis.

Rara avis.

"Stop. Caroline, tell him to stop, please!" I yelled. When she stepped closer toward me, my hands shot up, hurling involuntarily and I hit her so hard in the chest that she soared across the living room and crashed into a bookshelf on the other side.

"I want to die," I begged, running upstairs. "Tell him to stop!"

I was shocked by the force of the violent blow when I struck her. *She's probably hurt,* I thought. *I should go back to her.* But my body seemed to have a will of its own. I wasn't able to fight against it. No matter how hard I tried, I couldn't. I wanted to stop, go back and apologize, but my feet kept going, further and further, carrying me to the balcony. That was it, everything was lost now. I couldn't stop anything. We were both going to die, and it was my fault.

I forcefully slammed the door closed, but Caroline was right there, right behind me.

"Listen to my voice!" she yelled through the glass door. "This is not you." I froze on the spot, unable to move, facing the edge of the balcony.

"Listen to my voice!"

I tried to look at her, but sank down on my knees—the headache had come back so intensely this time my nose started bleeding. She collapsed and crumbled right to the floor as well, and then she cried out, wailing in pain.

I could hear her fighting with all her might; fighting against something I couldn't see. I struggled to stand up, to chase away whatever was crippling and paralyzing her, but her desperate cries sounded so very far away.

Go.

The voice was back. Even though I fought against it, I still got up and felt a sharp, stabbing pain in my chest. It felt like a cry from the very depths of my soul because now I didn't have any strength; now I couldn't change anything that was going on. I managed to look back at Caroline; she was still curled up on the floor, her face as I'd never seen it before, a face overcome with pain and agony.

Go.

The throbbing ache in my head built to excruciating pain. It was a blinding pain; a point now where I could no longer see anything clearly.

Go. And do not look back.

I took another step forward.

"No!" Caroline screamed. She was begging and pleading, "Don't, please Adam. Don't!" But she still sounded faint, miles away. It sounded as though she was underwater. Even though I wanted to stop, I absolutely could not. I couldn't stop moving, just as the voice commanded me. I felt trapped, imprisoned in some kind of a trance. There was too much pain in my heart. And now, I only wished I could die a fast death.

"Listen to me!" she cried, over and over again, banging and banging her hands against the glass.

I couldn't resist; I had to follow the voice. I took another two steps forward and reached the handrail.

"Don't listen to him!" was all I heard from inside the house, but my body ignored all of her warnings. I reached out for the handrail with both of my hands.

Die on three.

I cried out from what I was seeing; I was watching my body obey what it was commanded to do. Through tears of pain and desperation, I heaved one of my legs over the handrail. The headache was unbearable, and insufferable now.

"He wants you to kill yourself. You know I can't stop the process. Be strong. Only you can do this. Come back to me, please!"

No matter what she said, it was already too late for me. I felt completely beyond the point of help and now I could only witness my own suicide.

I heaved my other foot over the handrail and found myself sitting on the ledge. I placed one foot after the other on the very edge of the balcony and turned around to face the house. Caroline, my lost hero, was still on the floor, her angelic face tear-stained as she begged with her eyes for me to turn back, to come back to her. But I had to follow the voice, and do as I was told.

One.

I closed my eyes.

Pictures of May flashed through my mind, cloudy moments of happiness and echoes of time that hurt as I held her warm image during these final seconds of my life.

Two.

I took a quick breath, probably one of the very last ones I would ever take before leaving the Earth. I cried, feeling sorry for what was to come for Caroline. I couldn't save her, I couldn't save us, and that was the greatest pain that hurt me the most. I would let go in a moment, would see her one last time, and that was enough—it was all that I needed in that moment to embrace death.

Three.

"Don't do it! He's standing right in front of you!"

This time Caroline's voice penetrated my heart, and suddenly, instantly, I was wide-awake.

I opened my eyes. There he was. My angel of death was standing only steps away from me. His skin was the same as in my dream. His eyes pierced me in the coldest way possible, and he smiled bitterly.

It took only half a second for his fist to shoot through the handrail and punch me in the stomach. Caroline's painful scream was drowned by the sound of smashing wood, and the next thing I knew I was flying through the air.

Everything was rushing past at such an immense speed that I lost any sense of orientation. My body hit a fir tree, the impact causing several of my ribs to break immediately, and I dropped down into the depths of the forest. I couldn't move, I was paralyzed.

Through tears of pain I could see how he landed softly in front of my disfigured body. He looked happy and content that he had finally gotten his victim this time. He stepped closer to me and turned my head with his foot so I could look him directly in the eye.

"I've been waiting a very long time for this," he hissed. He rolled up his sleeves, drew his right arm back and slammed it forward with inhuman speed.

I held my breath.

His fist hit my chest and his sharp fingers lacerated my flesh, as he dug his hand deeper until his fingers reached my heart, wrapping around it like a spider's legs. I screamed out in pain as he started crushing my heart. Bloody tears ran down my cheeks and images of Caroline's candle losing its light flashed through my mind as Corbett's predator-like hand quickly and ruthlessly dealt the final deathblow.

Warm blood gushed out of my wound, and my eyes slowly rolled back as I manically gasped for air. And then, I died.

THE HEARTBEAT STOPS

Death is always peaceful when you know who you're dying for. Pain doesn't matter; colors, lights and any kind of feeling fade away, what only remains is the love in our hearts. Violence can take everything away from us—our life, our body—but not our love, since it is not physical matter. Love persists; it never dies, because of its omnipotent spiritual power and significance. It can't be grasped or held on to since it doesn't exist in solid form, though we can still express it with our physical forms through affection. And taught well by Caroline, I realized only after I died that love is precisely about the heart, the physical and the soul— the spiritual—being in harmony.

Killed by my worst enemy, I had died for Caroline, and I would die another thousand deaths, sacrifice my life, just to see her one more time and return to our love. Every time an angel fails and falls, a dream dies; but their sacrifice was a choice from the heart. Realizing this after my death, I held on to the essence of that thought, and my pain became joy, and joy turned into pure happiness when I embraced death as a possibility for being reunited with Caroline. In the end, that was all that mattered.

Once I accepted that, the process felt like flowing music that played on without end, and I felt my soul disconnect from my body to make its way into Caroline's embrace on a gentle breeze.

Dying felt ephemeral, and the ground my feet now touched felt solid, even though it seemed as if I were walking on clouds. A white door materialized in front of me. As I stepped closer, it swung open, with no sound, and I walked through it to find myself in a hospital.

I had gone back in time. The colors of everything around me appeared washed out, though a sense of peace hung in the air. I kept walking down a long hallway that led to a round desk with a middle-aged lady sitting behind it.

I paused for a second and looked at her from the distance. I was afraid she might notice me since I didn't know her role in the afterlife. *She must know where Caroline is,* I told myself, but I still kept watching her in silence, although something about her seemed odd.

Her eyes were focused on an old computer screen. She hadn't completely buttoned the white doctor's gown she had on, revealing a shirt underneath. My eyes followed the draft of air that was playing with her hair, and I spotted a small fan that she had taped next to the monitor. I decided it must be summer, and I observed the way she twisted her neck to both sides for the fan to cool her. She was clicking her tongue, and her upper body seemed to shake slightly. She crossed her legs under the table and was swinging one of them back and forth in anticipation of her awaited break. Consumed by her administrative work, she seemed normal, and yet there was something peculiar about her. With her eyes still on the screen, she suddenly answered the phone in front of her and started to talk. And that's when I knew what was odd: I couldn't hear anything that she was saying.

Puzzled, I stepped into the middle of the room and took a closer look at my surroundings. There were other people there too, old and young, and while I assumed they were all conversing as well, I couldn't hear any of their words either. It was as though I had stepped back in time and was part of an old muted movie.

A door to my right was pushed open, silently, and I moved to the side as a doctor and some other hospital personnel ran past me while speedily wheeling a bed with a patient on it. My eyes followed them until they disappeared behind the emergency room door, and even though I was startled, I remained calm, as I felt sure Caroline was there somewhere. I just needed to find my way to her.

Another door was pushed open and a pregnant woman in labor stepped out in the hallway supported by her husband and some other family members, probably looking for the nurses. Breathing through her mouth, the woman was in pain, and the future father looked both nervous and happy at the same time. I couldn't hear their happy, supportive conversation, but nevertheless decided to follow them. On the way down the hallway I tried to remember if Caroline had ever mentioned that she would meet me at the hospital, a place where each end is a new beginning. But my thoughts felt silky, sort of cloudy, and I was distracted by two nurses who appeared to help the young mother onto a bed, allowing only her husband to stay with her.

Even though they were rushing, I could still keep up with them. Everything appeared in slow motion, and no one seemed to notice my presence. We rushed down long corridors and past rooms with glass walls. I looked away for a fraction of a second and saw that one of the rooms was where they kept the newborn babies. I stepped closer to the glass and peeked inside.

All rolled up in blankets, the little babies were in tiny beds that had been lined up along the wall and filled the room, forming three sections. There was some space between each of them for the nurses to move and watch over their soft bodies. There were two figures bent over a bed in the middle of the center row. The air felt unusually electric, and without thinking, I decided to join them.

I reached for the door handle, but my hand passed right through and I only grabbed the empty air. I had forgotten—I was dead. I stepped through the door as if it was made of water and looked down the row of the babies' beds. Some of the newborns were asleep, some were awake, and a few were crying, though I still couldn't hear anything. Still in awe of my journey and drawn inexplicably to the two figures, I walked through the beds as if they weren't there, to have a closer look at those two people.

They turned out to be two elderly women, who looked like anything but two nurses, though their appearances were soothing. At first they seemed to be about the same age, and one was taller than the other. The taller one was skinny and looked fragile at the same time. Her hair was short, curly and gray, and her facial features revealed drooping eyelids and laugh lines. One of her leathery hands was resting on a cane. The other woman was smaller, round and statuesque. Her hair was short and curly, too, but was reddish, almost a dark ginger. She had laugh lines, too, though upon closer observance appeared younger than her companion. She was patting pearls of sweat from her forehead with a tissue, and moving a sandalwood fan with her other hand up and down in front of her face.

I cautiously stepped closer to them. I wasn't sure if they would notice me, and I was astonished that I was able to hear what they were saying.

"You know that one day the dark forces will know his secret and he will be in mortal danger," the one with reddish hair said.

Her voice sounded lovely, though she stuttered with concern. She closed her fan for a moment and rested her hand on her chest above her heart as her eyes filled with tears.

Her friend sighed and looked around the room to make sure they were still alone.

"It is our fault," she said weeping and reached out to stroke the baby's head.

The baby, a boy, was deeply asleep and seemed not to notice the stranger's gentle touch. His tiny head turned to the side and his little tongue peeked out of his minute mouth between two plump cheeks.

"His destiny is…" the gray-haired woman said, stopping herself from finishing her sentence and resting her leathery hand on her mouth to suppress a sigh.

Her companion also sighed and started fanning herself again. "I know well enough what the child's destiny is," she said. And then she stood lost in thought. "Our mistake almost took an innocent life," she added eventually and wiped her forehead with a crumbling tissue.

"It's a miracle he's still alive," the taller lady said, taking a step closer to the sleeping boy with her cane. "He could have been only a day old."

"Do the others know?"

"Only a few," the smaller one said, patting her upper lip with the tissue. "And those who do are afraid to speak about it."

Her companion almost dropped her cane as she said, "We will have to take care of him."

"We don't know to what extent this will affect his life and body. If he lives to survive his eleventh year, I think the danger will be avoided," the one with the reddish hair said with concern. Her fragile friend shook her head in disagreement.

"We cannot rely on hope. We have to protect him."

They both remained in silence as they sorrowfully contemplated the sleeping baby. I was in awe of what was happening and stepped out of the way as they held their hands above the bed with their eyes closed.

"*Resolvo erratum mortifier,*" the woman with the reddish hair said in a humming voice.

"*Fatum incolumis in aeternum,*" the taller one hummed in the same singing voice.

Nothing really happened after they said those strange words or when they held hands afterward in complete silence.

I was curious about what they wanted to protect the baby from. And why was I there? Was I supposed to help them in some way? I tried to grab the closest one by her shoulders but my hand just reached through her.

"May no one on this Earth ever know about your secret," she said as they let go of each other's hands. With one last look at the baby they turned toward me and made their way out of the nursery. When they unexpectedly walked through me, I closed my eyes for a fraction of a second, and when I opened them again, I was blinded by the sun.

I blinked and looked around, confused. I wasn't at the hospital anymore. The two women had disappeared, as had all the babies and the baby boy they were visiting.

I was somewhere outside. It was a warm day, and the sun was shining through fluffy clouds and warming the pavement under my bare feet. My surroundings seemed to be more colorful, and I contemplated the juicy green leaves on the treetops nearby.

The warm concrete under my feet felt unusually soft. I started walking into the greenery, guided by some instinctive current from within. I found myself on a meadow, in what seemed like a park, and was determined to cross it when I spotted a woman and a little girl coming in my direction. The girl was about three years old and was dressed nicely. The woman, her mother, was pushing a stroller with some toys in it. They seemed happy, perhaps on their way home after a day of playing. I waved at the little girl, but neither one of them seemed to notice me. I turned around after they walked past me and noticed that I couldn't hear anything again, even though I had clearly seen both of them laughing and talking. I was back in a silent movie, and everything continued to move in slow motion.

Fascinated by how the grass felt under my feet, I kept walking, feeling sure I was closer to Caroline than before. The place I found myself in looked somewhat familiar, as if I had already been there before. On my way along the grass, I came across a couple of families having picnics on blankets and other people who were peacefully lying on the grass, their faces turned up toward the sun. Some of the children were playing hide-and-seek, while others were running around among the blankets and picnic baskets.

No one noticed my presence, and I continued walking through the scenery as if everything was made of clouds and smoke. I was sure that under other circumstances I would have been bothered by my invisibility, but instead I was fascinated by how it felt. And I connected that sensation to how Caroline had made me feel in the forest the night we hiked to her country house—which ultimately turned out to be the place of my death.

I walked past a fountain where children were jumping in and out, and splashing water at their parents. A feeling of sadness overcame me, and I had the irresistible desire to join them, but I told myself to resist every temptation until I found my way to Caroline.

I came upon a huge slide where kids were sliding down and being caught and scooped up by their parents at the bottom. I contemplated the happiness of the scene at the slide and questioned again why I was being shown these things. A very rare calmness that persisted in my spiritual being prevented me from growing anxious by trying to decipher the meaning of this journey. I was convinced I needed to find Caroline, and I walked away in search of her, my savior.

The playground started to look even more familiar when I made my way out of it and spotted a little boy playing with a ball in the near distance. His mother was lying on a blanket in the shade, wearing sunglasses and reading a book in her lap. As I reached the gate, the two women sitting next to it caught my attention. They were the same two elderly ladies I had seen at the hospital, and once again, I could clearly hear only what they were saying.

As I approached them, they stopped talking and remained silent for a while, focusing on the boy playing with the ball on the other side of the gate. No one seemed to notice their presence either, as sigh after sigh escaped from their wrinkled mouths.

"It's growing," the woman with the cane said, looking sorrowful. Her friend only nodded slightly in response. They both looked very concerned about something.

"It is indeed. And it is our responsibility to make sure that no one is able to know his secret."

I assumed that I had travelled forward in time since the boy was clearly older and they still hadn't found a way to resolve the problem about his secret. Their conversation seemed intriguing, and I wanted to ask if I could be of some help or if they knew where Caroline was, but they didn't notice me at all.

"Is there a way to undo it?" the taller woman asked, breaking the silence. "They will go after him one day."

Her friend blinked some tears away.

"It's too late now. It will continue to grow as he does. In a couple of years from now, he will turn eleven, and we shall see if he survives."

They stopped talking when the boy's ball landed in front of the gate, only two steps away from them, and looked at him with teary eyes.

The boy came up to the gate, grabbed his ball and turned his head in our direction, as though he had heard the two women talking before. As I watched his small eyes pierce the emptiness where they sat, my mouth popped wide open, and I was petrified. He briskly ran back to where he had been playing before, and the two women sighed.

"Did he see us?" the shorter one asked, staring at the boy.

"He didn't," the gray-haired lady said weakly. "But he senses our presence."

I too stared at the boy, but in astonishment, unable to move, because I knew who he was. That boy was me at the age of three. I was positive. And now it suddenly made sense why the playground felt familiar. But what was the secret and danger that the two strangers were talking about? What was I involved in, and who would come after me? My feeling of peace vanished, and I turned to the two women to confront them.

"Wait!" I yelled. "Wait for me!" I hadn't noticed until then that they had made their way out of the park. I started running, desperate to catch up with them and to make them tell me what was going on with my younger self. But I wasn't able to keep up with their fast pace.

Was I really dead, or somehow still alive? Did they know that Corbett was going to come after me and take my life, and had they been trying to prevent that from happening since I was born? I felt that I deserved to know what was going on and ran even faster. They made a right on the other side of the street, and I was only a few steps away from them now.

"Please! I need to talk to you!" I yelled on my way across the street. But I was taken by surprise by a truck that drove right through me, and I closed my eyes.

I spun around and opened my eyes again. The scene had shifted. The playground, my three-year-old self and the two ladies were nowhere to be seen now. I blinked a few times to get used to the dimmer light and realized that I was in an apartment building at the foot of a staircase. The hallway behind me was empty, and I could see a rainy day outside the glass front door. It was quiet, and the only thing I could hear was the sound of raindrops falling against the door. Everything looked slightly familiar.

"Hello?" I asked, but didn't get a response. I walked to the door and tried to open it, but all my hand grabbed was empty air. I was still dead.

Confused by the sudden scene changes, I still kept going and walked through the door. Outside the streets were empty. It was a stormy afternoon, and the sky was a mixture of gray and black. Strong winds were moving through the treetops in a mysterious way. And even though I was standing in the rain, I didn't get wet; my clothes stayed completely dry. I looked around hoping to find Caroline, but I didn't see her anywhere nearby and grew slightly uneasy about the fact that I had already failed to find her in the two previous places.

The wind swung a mailbox lid open. It was freely flapping back and forth in the storm, and I had a sudden urge to close it. I knew why the building looked familiar to me when I saw May's maiden name on the lid as I shut it. This had once been our mailbox, and we used to live here when I was a child. Since my guardian angel was supposed to always be near me, was Caroline there waiting for me to find her?

Without thinking, I made my way back into the apartment building through the glass door and paused at the foot of the stairs. Third floor, I remembered. We moved away from here when I was six.

I wondered, yet again, when this flashback trip would be over so I could finally reach Caroline. Why was I seeing my past if I was already dead? Everything seemed like a riddle with no reasonable answer to any of my questions, and I grew nervous when my bare feet touched the first couple of steps. Going back in time and contemplating my childhood again felt peculiar, and I walked up the stairs very slowly as I tried to take in every small detail of the building since Caroline might not be here in a physical state herself. I needed to be able to recognize her in any possible detail so we could be together again.

When I reached the third floor, I recognized the doormat in front of the apartment where we used to live. It had a creamy yellow background, and each letter of the word *welcome* was a different color. I took a step closer to the door and leaned my ear on it to see if I could hear anything inside. I hesitated, took a deep breath and walked through it.

A wave of memories flowed through me as I found myself inside our old apartment. May's coat was hanging on the hanger next to the door, and a child's shoes were scattered in the tiny hallway. I paused, lost in emotion, and allowed my surroundings to affect me. I noticed that I could hear the sound of the TV and moved into the living room, step after step into my past. A feeling of innocent warmth overcame me, as I smelled the scent of May's croissants baking. The TV was playing Tom and Jerry, my favorite show as a child. I stopped in the doorway and watched Tom failing to catch Jerry. A small plate with a half-finished bun was on the table.

I nervously cleared my throat and said, "Anyone here?" No one responded.

I slowly stepped into the kitchen and felt my soul soften. Mom was peacefully lost in thought as she rolled her special croissant dough that she had made ever since I can remember. It was always a special treat. She filled each croissant with chocolate, and I contemplated her movements from only steps away. I was glad I had the possibility to see her again, to say good-bye, even though it was only a silent farewell.

"Mom?" I asked, but she didn't hear me.

I had the desire to step closer, give her a tight hug and tell her that I was sorry for leaving her, for failing at life since she was now alone and had no one else to take care of her. I stepped closer with the deep hope that she might notice my presence and inhaled the scent of her warm pastry. When I reached out to try to touch her, the doorbell rang and she looked up. I stepped back as she left her unfinished croissants on the baking tray, washed her hands and made her way to the door. I made sure she didn't step through me, as I didn't want to miss this moment of my childhood.

When she took longer than I had expected to come back, I stepped into the hallway and recognized the voices on the other side of the door. It was the two elderly women I had seen in the two earlier scenes, and I hastily approached them so I could eavesdrop on their conversation.

"Miss, we are two new nannies at the local kindergarten and would like to offer our services should you need some extra help," the one with the reddish hair said, subtly trying to peek into the apartment.

May seemed confused and politely shook her head no. I was startled that May had met these two ladies and had never told me anything about them. And I wondered if they had ever appeared again later in my life. Could May possibly know anything about the secret I heard them talking about?

"We can also look after your son when you're at home," the taller lady insisted. "Every single mom always needs a little extra help from time to time."

May looked nervous and said, "I appreciate your offer very much, but I don't think I can afford a nanny right now." She had never been good at saying no to polite people.

"It's free of charge," the smaller of the two said, insisting one more time. But May kept nodding no with a slight movement of her head. She seemed confused, though, and I couldn't tell if she was suspicious of the intention of the two strangers in front of her or not.

"I will certainly let you know if I ever need help," May said. "Have a lovely day." And she closed the door on them.

I was bewildered that they hadn't told May about the danger her son was in, and I stepped through the front door without thinking, ready to get some answers from them finally.

They were both wearing long robes that reached to their ankles.

The shorter lady had her face buried in her hands as she asked, "What are we going to do now?"

"I don't know," the other said desperately. "It seems to me that we've tried everything."

"Can you hear me?" I asked loudly. "I need to talk to you!" But neither of them noticed me. I tried to touch them several times, but my hand only passed through them.

"Impossible! There must be something that we can still do."

The taller lady's face looked so sad that her eyes seemed to droop down to the middle of her cheeks.

"The one and only thing we can do is hope that the forces of good will keep him alive."

They lingered in silence in front of the apartment door before making their way down the stairs in defeat.

"Wait! You can't go!" I yelled desperately. But I was forced to close my eyes for a short instant when a door on the second floor was pushed open through me as I was following the ladies downstairs.

The scene shifted again, and I found myself somewhere unfamiliar, surrounded by dark shades of light. Everything had disappeared now, and it took some effort to figure out where I was. I turned around several times, but couldn't make out anything but a dim light as far as my eyes could see. I felt the anxiety growing inside of me as I realized that I was again nowhere near Caroline, and then the feeling of being followed by someone washed over my being. I ran into the darkness in front of me, and it felt as though I were running through a black tunnel. I was relieved when I spotted the white light not too far away. *She must be there,* I told myself. *That must be the entrance to my afterlife. I'm almost there.*

As I ran, pictures of my younger self and the voices of the two elderly ladies echoed and flashed all around me. *I can't fail now,* I thought, *not one more time.* I finally reached the white light. The otherworldly brightness, pleasantness and warmth was coming from a huge mirror that was standing at the end of the dark tunnel.

The mirror appeared silky, as if made of water, and looked almost transparent. I slowly took a step closer to it and was confounded when I saw my own reflection in it.

I looked at my being, my soul, and realized how pale I was. The face I saw in the mirror was sad and defeated, yearning for a reunion with Caroline. I stared at myself in both pain and anger, and as I took another step closer to the mirror, I noticed a bloody hole in my chest: ripped flesh and cracked bones torn open to reveal a dead heart. For a moment, I could almost feel Corbett's cold fingers stabbing into the wound again.

I shuddered and stepped through the mirror, the only way forward on my journey to find Caroline, and found myself in a forest surrounded by thick fir trees. The soil still felt soft under my bare feet as I walked up a small hill. I knew immediately which forest I was in. This was not just any forest, it was the one I had died in, and I looked around in all possible directions for Caroline. I didn't worry about Corbett. I was already dead, and he was no longer a threat to me. But I still needed to find the missing piece of my puzzle, Caroline, my warrior and victor; for she had won the battle on the day of the car accident when she saved my life the first time and allowed me to see inside her heart.

"Caroline?" I asked the silent forest in grief.

Even though their summerhouse was only steps away, it still appeared miles further at the same time. She needed to hear me; I had to make her notice me.

I made my way through the trees only to be slowed down by an inordinate drowsiness that numbed every single one of my remaining feelings; and completely exhausted, I sank down into the white snow. With every last bit of energy I had left, I crawled several more inches and managed to lie on my back, my eyes scanning the sky through the firs' branches, until I was completely paralyzed and unable to move anymore at all.

I tried to speak, but my voice failed, and it occurred to me that maybe I had to die one more time for all of it to be really over. This time I hoped it would be painless. I winced and my face contorted as excruciating pain shot from the wound in my chest through my vanishing self, and I was left with no other choice but to die another painful death. This time I knew Caroline wouldn't come and save me, since I had failed to find her in my journey through the past.

Tears of desperation filled my eyes as the pain grew more intense, and just when I thought I was about to close my eyes forever and disappear into endless darkness, I heard the steps approaching. I assumed it was my angel of death coming for my soul, and I smiled tiredly, ready to greet him.

Instead, I squinted when a bright, marvelous face appeared above me. It was *my* guardian angel: My Caroline.

She was dressed completely in white. Her hair was loose, and when she bent down over me, it tickled my numb cheeks. Her ethereal beauty instantly numbed my pain as she radiated streams of healing currents that promised a peaceful ending at last. A delicate halo was floating above her head and bathed me in eternal light. And her two celestially feathered wings opened wide, revealing her pure and majestic being.

"We can't stop the world," she spoke gently and knelt next to me. I had only seen her cry a few times, but whenever she did, I could see the stars shining in her eyes.

"I'm glad you found your way back to me. I never doubted you would."

She smiled wearily and reached for my hand. Her warmth felt comforting.

"Remember how we met for the first time?" she asked with tears in her eyes. "This is how we meet again."

Her eyes were intense.

"Can we try one more time without pain, here and now?" I asked weakly as she pressed my hand to her lips. "Please?"

Now the light was blinding.

"Tell me how I can live again," I begged. "I can't go yet; I don't want to let go."

The light grew even stronger.

She ran a warm finger down my forehead.

"I'm here to take you back home with me. To the place where you belong."

A tear made its way down her cheek.

"Don't be afraid—there's no fear in love," she said softly; her voice fading, as though from a distance.

I closed my eyes. I was drifting away.

"Can you keep a secret?" my guardian angel asked. Something tickled my face, and I realized I was being kissed by a white, pure rose.

I leaned into the all-consuming light.

I fell into a sea of tranquility as warmth and love rushed throughout my whole body. She was breathing the essence of life into me, and I knew it was time to heal. I felt how her love—my morphine—spread like a drug, rapidly and uncontrollably through my entire body, calling every one of my dead cells back to life again. I was being given more time, another chance, a reunion, and I longed for more of her sweet elixir of life.

When this current reached my wound, I could feel it begin to completely heal. My ribs grew back into position, and my veins tingled and mended back together as fresh blood was pumped into them. It was both warm and sweet at the same time, and I gave myself entirely to it and welcomed love's return. And then, a sweet electrifying moment later, I could hear my own heartbeat start. Hot and comfortable, the fire in my chest was coming back, as sure and sweet as her voice. Her love was dissolving the world around us; she was drugging me, making me her devotee and teaching me how to fly. And I knew in that instant that love always heals, without exception. I was being reborn, called back to life, as she took me home on her wings.

She, Caroline, my guardian angel, was saving me.

Again.

I gasped and opened my eyes. Silence.

I was staring at a wooden ceiling; my body had been placed on a soft couch. My surroundings were warm; the safe and sheltered feeling of being home overcame me. I blinked several times, took a deep breath and exhaled. Something was different. I felt totally healed, absolutely alive.

"I knew you would come back!"

Caroline hugged me tightly. My arms automatically flew back around her, and I euphorically pressed her against me, this time almost violently, as though fully claiming her as mine. She was here, I had found her, and that was all that mattered to me in that moment. Dead, or alive, all I wanted was to be with her. I breathed in her sweet scent as I hugged her tight, frantically checking her for any wounds. She looked pale and weak, but relief was written on her face.

"When love finds you, you want to make sure it doesn't slip out of your hands ever again," I said and traced my fingers along her soft lips. Her tired eyes locked on mine as we enjoyed this moment together, heart to heart.

"Have some water," a familiar voice said.

Caroline moved to the side, and I could see Elena and Lerato standing next to the couch. They both looked concerned. Elena's eyes looked like two round crystals, watery and transparent, and her hair was down, looking slightly untidy around her fragile face. Lerato's arms were crossed in front of his chest, and for the very first time since I had met him, he looked worried. With a wrinkled forehead, he looked from Caroline to me.

I reached for the glass in Elena's hands and emptied it in a blink. When I gave it back to her, she threw her arms around me and gave me a long hug.

From the way they looked, I knew that they hadn't come the way they originally planned. They had clearly come in a hurry to face not only the prospect of my death, but also that of their daughter.

And then I panicked.

"Corbett! Where is he? He's out there, he was running after me!"

"We're safe. He's not going to attack us again."

Caroline's heavy arms reached out for my hands weakly and gently pulling me toward her.

He is gone, again, I thought as I opened my fists and sat down, breathing fast.

"How do you feel?" Lerato asked, kneeling in front of the couch.

I sat up and said, "I think I'm okay." The dizziness was gone, and so was all the previous pain in my body.

He smiled fully and pressed a cold, wet towel on Caroline's forehead that Elena handed to him.

It took me a second to react. "Is something wrong?" I asked, turning to face Caroline who sank down next to me on the couch.

"Don't worry," she said wearily. "I'll be fine." She closed her eyes, letting the wet cotton towel soothe her.

"Lerato, she's pale," I said anxiously.

"She replaced a lot of the blood that you lost during Corbett's attack," he said calmly, without to take his eyes off of her. "It will take her body some time to replenish it."

"Blood...when?" I asked alarmed. "Why would she do that?" My shaky fingers touched her tender face.

"This is a normal process for us. We are able to change our blood type in such a situation and perform a transfusion without medical assistance. She'll recover quickly. Her body is strong."

"She changed her blood type for me?"

I reached for her hand. She squeezed it back in response.

"She did."

I was heartbroken and felt sad about what she had to go through to save my life.

"Why didn't she wait for the two of you to arrive or call the ambulance?"

"She did the right thing. If she had done either, you would have died."

"We made our way here as fast as we could once she notified us about what happened," Elena added, walking over to the couch. "We encouraged her to act quickly. There was no time for hesitation." Elena's hair glistened in the morning light.

I realized that Caroline had almost given up her own life to save mine. She was leaning her head slightly back on the upper edge of the sofa, and as I looked at her face more closely, I could see that it wasn't as pale as before. A drop of cold water from the towel ran down her throat.

"She didn't think about herself," I said, more to myself than to them.

"It's against our nature to think about ourselves when it comes down to saving the lives of our protégés," Lerato said, slowly removing the towel from Caroline's forehead.

I squeezed her hand to let her know I loved her, and when she pressed mine back, more strongly this time, I was relieved. She opened her eyes and gave me a weary smile.

"She is out of danger and will recover soon," a voice said from the doorway.

Vivienne and Janus were standing behind us, both looking like unfairly attractive, recently risen archangels.

Their sudden appearance left me speechless for a moment. I looked at Lerato for assurance, and with a slight nod of his head, his calm expression somehow let me know that they had already been here with us for a while.

Vivienne spoke first in her powerful voice as they both stepped into the room.

"When virtue almost takes an angel's life, that is when her light will shine the strongest. That is when she has learned the true meaning of sacrifice and will, without doubt, be rewarded with the strength to stand up stronger again."

Elena released a sigh of relief, and Lerato's expression softened. I was still startled by their unexpected visit, but I was glad when Caroline found the strength to sit up on the couch, almost effortlessly, as though Vivienne's words alone had instantly healed her on the spot.

"Great courage is what we welcome," Vivienne continued, her eyes piercing. "We will always boldly punish our enemies."

Caroline's soft cheeks turned rosy. She reached for my hand and moved closer to me. Seconds later she looked almost completely recovered.

Vivienne moved her wings.

"We have been summoned on this day as a result of the unlawful actions of your angel of death. We don't have a lot of time,

302

as our presence is required back in our community. We believe that the reason behind Corbett's behavior lies within you, Adam. We need you to tell us what you remember. Be advised though that any false statements you make can be held against you."

Vivienne started walking up and down, while Janus stood as still as a statue.

I fidgeted in my seat, suddenly nervous, trying to think of how to put into words what I actually remembered before I had died. Her statement that I somehow knew the trigger for Corbett's actions confused me. I first recalled the headache, then running away from the house and Caroline against my own will.

"There were whispers in my head, shrill and painful…and I did what I was told. I tried to fight it, to break the trance I was in, but it was too strong for me. I don't know why I behaved the way I did."

I gave Caroline an apologetic look.

"Were there any previous symptoms beforehand?" Vivienne asked and paused in front of the window.

"Your headache," Caroline said. Vivienne's head turned in her direction and her deep blue eyes locked on Caroline's in an intimidating way.

"Were you able to perform healing?"

Caroline said nervously, "I was, although it wore off within a couple of hours each time, and then I would have to do it again."

"The patterns of his behavior indicate that he must have been planning the way he took control of your body for a long time," Vivienne noted and started walking up and down again.

"You think he took control of my body?" I asked anxiously.

"*Actus me invito factus, non est meus actus,*" Janus said, answering my question. He slowly made his way to the front of the couch, moving his wings slightly up and down while his halo followed his head in glorious precision. He looked exactly the same as he did when I met him the first time: strong, edgy and sharp.

303

"The act done by me against my will is not my act," he translated before I could even ask what it meant.

"You are not to blame for your actions since it was your angel of death who acted through your body."

I grew more nervous and tense at the thought of Corbett taking control of me so easily.

"What happened to you is beyond any reason and explanation," Lerato said when he saw my startled expression.

"How could he do that?" I asked and looked at each of them for an answer, my gaze settling on Caroline last.

Vivienne responded quickly, "*Absolutum dominium.*" She stepped next to Janus, her ageless face looking cold and beautiful at the same time.

Janus flexed his muscular jaws.

"He took complete control of your human body, and thus was able to have you execute what he had already planned out: your suicide."

A shiver ran down my spine.

"You're saying I was possessed by Corbett?"

"Unfortunately, to some extent, yes," Janus answered, folding his hands.

Suddenly, all of my actions made sense to me, including walking alone into the forest, trying to hurt Caroline and trying to take my own life. I turned to Caroline, defeat written all over my face.

In agony, I pressed my lips on the back of her hand. Her eyes were tender, filled with compassion.

Her voice was faint as she said, "I had trouble breaking the trance."

Vivienne tilted her head sideways, as if trying to actually pierce through Caroline with her eyes.

"He has taken his skills to a completely new level of intensity. No one should be able to interfere with the connection between a guardian angel and her protégé."

"He is able to metamorphose himself and take control of a human body," Lerato said authoritatively. "How did he develop such skills, and most importantly, how can we find what the source of them is?" I knew he was keen enough to study Corbett's behavior for safety purposes, and I could sense the intense dislike he felt for Corbett, though he would never express that in words.

Vivienne's face grew even colder.

"Those are questions that we cannot answer now. We don't have enough information yet. We are planning to investigate him and all of the angels of death, as we do not permit such doings."

I could feel how agitated she was that Corbett was involved in something that they knew nothing about.

"But all the Elders agree that Corbett has acted against the law and shall receive his deserved punishment."

"I don't understand," Caroline said, disturbed. "If he knew his actions were not lawful, why did he even try to take Adam's life?"

"We do not know yet, but will not fail to find out," Vivienne responded.

"Is he just killing for pleasure?" I asked. Everyone stared at me grimly.

Vivienne narrowed her eyes.

"We will take this into consideration as well. And rest assured that our investigation will eventually get to the bottom of things and provide answers about Corbett's motives."

"He went for my heart," I said nervously, flinching at the memory of Corbett's cold fingers slicing up my chest.

"He almost completely…smashed it," Caroline said, remembering as well and frowning.

Vivienne crossed her arms in front of her chest.

"He might have known about your bond with Adam and wanted to destroy it. This kind of bond between a guardian angel and her protégé is unusual, and this might have irritated him for some reason."

"Why would it bother Corbett that much?" Caroline asked sadly. "We can't be blamed for our bond."

"A loving heart is death's strongest fear," Vivienne stated, giving us a possible answer for Corbett's brutality. "Some perceive your unique bond as a threat, and they will continue to do as it grows stronger."

I was still having a hard time finding a reasonable human explanation about why Corbett would punish us for something that was completely out of our control. Elena exchanged a silent look with Lerato.

"The time will come when your bond will be safest when kept a secret," Vivienne warned us, a blank expression on her immaculate face. I moved uncomfortably in my seat, hoping that since she had no candle to look at in that moment her prediction would never come to pass. I wondered if Vivienne had known this when she had looked at Caroline's candle the first time we met. And if so, why had she waited until now to share this information?

Caroline and I looked at each other for a moment. She was still a little tired, and I promised her through my eyes that I would love her forever, no matter what happened.

"How could he have known about our bond though?" I wondered aloud.

This time it was Janus who answered my question.

"We assume that once he took control of your body he also had control of your mind. And once he had access to your mind, it was simple enough for him to know more than you would ever want him to."

I felt conflicted, almost ashamed about having been an easy target.

"He obviously knew that Caroline couldn't stop me from

committing suicide, but what would he have gotten from my death?"

"This remains a riddle until we know more," Vivienne assertively answered. "Our investigation has already started." Slightly relieved, I exhaled through my mouth. I knew Corbett wouldn't dare try to attack us in their presence.

"It felt as if he had completely snuck into my head," I said, making myself remember what had happened in the forest. "At first I only heard indistinct whispers, but then that turned into a steady voice that told my body what to do."

"*Rara avis*—that's what I kept hearing," I added. All of their eyes were locked on me.

Lerato wrinkled his forehead and translated: "Rare bird."

"Which justifies his appearance as a raven," Elena added.

"That's not the first time I saw him in the form of a raven. This also happened a couple of days ago during class."

I shuddered at the memory, but things were starting to make sense to my human brain.

"He knew that talking to you in your head was the only way to separate you from Caroline," Vivienne noted. Her long legs appeared shiny as she walked in front of the fireplace.

"I felt Adam's pain," Caroline confessed in anguish. Elena widened her eyes, and Lerato scratched his chin questioningly.

"What do you mean you felt my pain?" I asked in alarm.

"We don't feel the same amount of pain that you do. But, this time was much stronger. The moment he snuck into your head and broke our bond I realized something was terribly wrong. And when he went for your heart, I couldn't move anymore because I felt all of your pain."

If Caroline had felt my pain to the extent she just described, then we weren't safe from future attacks—and that wasn't good at all.

"This is because you have been connected," Janus said.

"How can this be possible?" I asked, feeling a sense of horror in my stomach. "We won't be able to get past this point if she feels my pain to such an extent."

"This won't change. Your hearts have been connected from the moment you first consciously perceived Caroline's healing process. This confirms that your bond is growing and gaining strength with each passing day."

I was glad he was talking slowly, giving my human brain time to digest an amount of information I was having a hard time dealing with. I felt defeated and worried at the same time. A wave of desperation washed over me. What do you do when the dearest thing to you is also the most dangerous—and the most fragile? If our bond, innocent and unbreakable, could be the reason for our death one day, then what were we supposed to do?

"We can't always just hope for a good outcome and give in to whatever is happening to us," Caroline said, full of agony. I looked into her eyes; they were deep and sorrowful. As it was for me; the only thing she wished was for us to be able to embrace our bond without any danger.

"The bond between two hearts that become one is strongest as the souls merge, and in your case, it simultaneously represents a threat. However, you might be able to change this with time," Janus said.

Puzzled, Caroline asked, "What do you mean?"

Janus took one step to the left and made a perfect gesture with his hands.

"By controlling it. There must be a way to learn how to block Adam's pain from affecting you. Guardian angels are not supposed to feel so much intensity of their protégés' pain."

A brief silence followed, during which I exchanged looks with Caroline and the other angels. Lerato did not seem to be affected in a negative way by what he heard—he usually saw the silver lining in every obstacle. Elena was mumbling something

I couldn't understand; her face looked even more delicate than before. Vivienne's oval face was blank, yet represented the most perfect form of supernatural beauty. And Janus had turned completely to stone; the only part of him moving were his tiny blue eyes.

"I am more than ready to conduct some research and study beneficial techniques that will best serve such situations," Lerato said, allowing a small smile to appear on his lips.

I appreciated his words of encouragement. I knew Caroline was hoping that through his guidance our bond would stop being a threat to us.

"We highly recommend this for preventing future attacks," Vivienne said in her commanding voice. "Attacks are always unpredictable, except the ones from Corbett from this moment onward. I now ask you to rise."

Elena, Lerato and Caroline were on their feet within the blink of an eye, all with a serious expression, and I followed them hesitantly. I was confused by Vivienne's request, though I was too nervous to ask for an explanation. Vivienne made a majestic gesture toward the door with her wings and walked out, as if floating, chin up and chest out. Janus followed behind Caroline and me.

"Don't worry," Caroline said. She only looked up at me for a split second and kept her head lowered.

When I walked outside with Caroline she reached for my hand. The morning was cool, the day felt fresh and crisp, and we walked around the house in silence. I shuddered at the sight of the scattered pieces of the balcony's handrail in the snow.

Vivienne stopped only a few steps ahead of us and focused her piercing eyes on something behind a massive fir tree, the branches of which seemed to have been chopped off. We stepped closer, and I almost fell backward.

Corbett's body was pressed against the trunk some inches

309

above the ground. His hands were tied together above his head by an invisible string, and his face was distorted in pain, his lips pressed tightly together. He couldn't speak and seemed to be in a daze; he was only able to move his black eyes. I took a step back, and Caroline fastened her grip around my hand. Elena and Lerato stayed close to us.

With her back to Corbett, Vivienne said, "We found him not too far away from here, trying to escape."

I flinched when Corbett's body suddenly fell to the ground. Purple blood covered his face, and he groaned, twisting on his side in pain. His hands convulsed behind his curved back. The icy expression on Vivienne's face revealed that she had invisibly punched Corbett with the power of her mind.

Corbett seemed not to have any intention of trying to run away. I felt certain he knew there was no escape from the angels of justice. For a brief moment, his sinister eyes found mine, and I looked death right in the eyes, trying to understand Corbett's relentless commitment to breaking our innocent bond. But I failed to comprehend it, since death and hatred speak a language too dark to be understood in the presence of angels.

Vivienne started walking around him.

"You can either defend your actions or you can remain quiet," she spoke directly to him. He began to whimper. His nose had sunken into his skull and he continued bleeding.

He remained quiet, and when he locked his pitch-black eyes on mine, he narrowed them to tiny cat-like slits and released a hissing sound that made me leap back another step. In that moment I wanted nothing more than for him to receive his deserved punishment and his right to be an angel of death to be taken away once and for all.

Vivienne kept circling him like a snake about to strike her victim. I watched her face become as cold as ice, until she almost appeared as diabolical as Corbett.

She came to a stop, resting one of her hands on her head just under her halo and placing the other one on her jaw while her powerful eyes scrutinized Corbett in deadly silence.

"Look away," Caroline whispered before I even knew what was about to happen. But it was too late.

"*Diripio*," Vivienne said, brutally twisting her neck to the side. The sound of breaking bones could be heard, and Corbett's head thrust back, his little black eyes opening wide. Even though Vivienne's head would have been disconnected from her body if she were human, she appeared not to have suffered any damage. Instead of breaking her own neck, she had actually broken Corbett's. I tried not to vomit as I caught a glimpse of the worm-like blood vessels that were still keeping his head attached to his body.

"His heart, Janus," Vivienne commanded, her head returning to its normal position.

Caroline tugged on my hand, indicating that we should turn away.

"Let's go," she said. We rushed back toward the house with Elena and Lerato in total silence.

I was shocked and felt wobbly as I had thought that Corbett's punishment would have been losing the right to live his life as an angel of death. I covered my nose when I smelled burning flesh.

Everything happened quickly once we were back inside the house. Elena immediately rushed upstairs and helped us get our belongings together.

"We are leaving," she said in a shaky voice. Her eyes were shiny and she kept her head lowered in respect and fear of the Elders' presence and power. Lerato remained quiet, though I could sense how uncomfortable he was as well. He helped us make sure all windows were properly locked and the furniture was covered again.

I couldn't speak, and my mouth felt dry. I mimed their movements to prevent myself from collapsing on my way up the stairs.

I felt disoriented and sick. We packed our bags, and as I took a last look through Caroline's windows, I noticed that the balcony's handrail was completely repaired and looked as if nothing had ever happened. Then we pulled all the blinds down.

We met Vivienne and Janus outside, waiting for us. They looked like two sculptures dressed in white. Vivienne spoke commandingly.

"Our law requires us to reevaluate your life, Adam, since your current situation is not permitted and can cause inequity in the universe. Your life will be forever changed. We will see you again very soon, but we shall now depart."

"Your guidance is greatly appreciated," Lerato said. Janus gave us a patient look, and in a heartbeat they disappeared into the thick forest.

We made our way back to the resort at the edge of the national park in silence. Even though my steps felt heavy, I was relieved when we reached the resort area in what seemed like only a minute. We hurried into a jeep that Lerato rented at the resort, and I felt completely exhausted.

"We're going home, and everything will be alright," Caroline said, sitting next to me, holding my hand. "What happened is already in the past, and I will never let this happen to you again."

As I held her hand, I closed my eyes and appreciated the blackness that I found there. It felt safe and soft, and it numbed my weary thoughts.

Lerato started the engine.

SHARING AURAS

What is love?

That question was burning in my mind on our way back to the airport.

Lerato drove quickly. The vast landscapes of nature, cars, buildings and people whizzed past, flashing in segments of blurred colors. I weakly opened my eyes from time to time, not wanting to contemplate them but to assure myself that Caroline was still by my side. She was, and I was happy about that, allowing myself to feel all emotions and not trying to force myself to be brave.

I didn't need to be brave; I simply wasn't. But Caroline was. She had proved that she was strong enough to call me back from the dead, to breathe life into me. She had almost sacrificed her own life for mine, so I could be reborn.

I was told several times that my time hadn't yet come to die, and I knew that I still had a mission to fulfill on Earth. Whatever my purpose was, I was going to spend the rest of my life with Caroline.

Forcing open my heavy eyelids, I searched for her eyes, and when I found them, I had the answer to my question.

Love is sacrifice, a voluntary offering of the heart. And Caroline was living proof of that, my living proof.

Later, when Caroline gently shook me by my shoulders, I slowly opened my eyes. We were at the airport. I had fallen asleep during the ride and taken a much-needed rest. I shook out my numb legs and we made our way through the crowd to the check-in desk. Lerato and Elena had arranged to have our tickets waiting there, and I was glad that everything was organized. No longer in a rush, we boarded the plane in silence and flew home together.

It was an unusually warm winter night when we landed at Belgrade's *Nikola Tesla* airport that Tuesday. I still remember how good the crisp breeze felt on my skin, refreshing and welcoming. Breathing here was different, too. The air felt lighter and as though it provided a sense of clarity. I filled my lungs until my chest hurt.

Lerato's car was parked on the lower level right by the elevators. As I sat down on the backseat, I felt a noticeable relief. Lerato was back to normal; all the worry and agony was gone from his face, and when I caught his eyes in the rearview mirror, he gave me one of his polished smiles.

Elena's shoulders were relaxed; it seemed as if she had left a good amount of fear and concern behind her. As Lerato exited the airport, she quickly looked back and gave me a motherly smile. Her hair was glistening from the streetlights, or so I thought, and her fragile hand held Lerato's during the entire ride back.

Ready to fight for our eternal love beyond forever, Caroline, my heroine and my reason for being alive, looked like a white rose with perfect silky-smooth and delicate petals.

When Lerato pulled over to park in front of my apartment, I grew hysterical. I wasn't ready to be parted from them; it felt too soon.

"This is not what we agreed on," I protested.

Lerato gave me an apologetic look and got out with Elena to grab my bag from the trunk, leaving me and Caroline inside.

"You need to rest, please," Caroline said, nudging me out.

"No one needs to know that I'm back yet," I objected. "I can stay at your place."

She gave me a beautiful smile.

"We're done hiding. It's time to embrace our new reality. Our safe reality."

I played with her hand and said, "I don't know if I'm ready to leave you now, especially after what happened."

"I'll be right here if you need me," she promised.

"I need you every second of my life," I said.

"What if I promise that you'll see me tomorrow in class?"

This was tempting, and I knew I was overreacting, though I had reason enough for doing so.

She pressed her rosy lips on mine and I responded to her kiss almost automatically, making sure it lasted for a satisfying moment.

"I'm seeing you first thing tomorrow," I said.

"I love you."

"I love you too," I said and stumbled out weakly into the night.

Elena wrapped her soothing arms around me and said, "Take care, please."

"Thank you. Really."

I looked at her and Lerato with deep gratitude, and could feel their protective eyes on my back until I disappeared behind the front door.

I made my way upstairs with immense relief. My feet felt light, and the steps felt soft. I was excited to see May again. She wasn't going to be alone now, and I thought that maybe I *was* brave. In the end, I had come back from where only few had returned, with the help of Caroline, of course. But still, I had made it back for some reason, maybe because Caroline was the last person I saw in the dream sequence I had after Corbett killed me, and that was a very satisfying thought.

"Mom?" I called as I opened the door.

The apartment was warm. It felt safe, and the smell of May's cooking was heartwarming.

"You're back early!" she said, hopping up from the couch to give me a hug in her bare feet.

I embraced her—and this moment together. I looked at her closely. She was still silly, still herself.

Her hair was pulled up under a damp towel, and she was wearing her soft cotton bathrobe. I caught her in the middle of giving herself a mani-pedi, and she was wearing floppy toe dividers.

"We came back early, and I thought I'd make it a surprise," I said. As she jumped up and down, her towel loosened. She kept her fingers spread as wide apart as possible so the fresh nail polish wouldn't get on the towel, and motioned for me to remove it.

"That's so sweet of you. Come on, put your stuff down. I want to hear all about your trip, and then I want to show you some pictures from mine. Let's make ourselves comfortable. Oh, and I've got some croissants in the oven."

She rambled on. As I watched her, I realized how much I had missed her and all her silliness.

I could have lost all of this, actually more than just her—I could have lost everything.

"Chocolate?"

"Yes, yes. Come on, I can't wait to hear all the details. Oh no, I need to do my left hand again. Did I get some of the polish on my forehead?"

She was hysterical in such a funny way, and I was happy to be back with her. I owed her so much. Could I have asked for a more pleasant outcome than a messy May and chocolate croissants?

I'll take this as a sign, I said to myself as I dropped my bag in my room.

It looked the same as when I had left it, warm and slightly disorganized, and I couldn't resist the temptation to try to open my windows. When they flung open, I was ecstatic and had no intention of closing them again for the rest of the night.

I had a long, hot shower and spent the rest of the evening with May, who had to redo her nails at least three more times. She was glad to hear about what we did in Montenegro, all invented, of course. I explained that the reason we came back earlier was because we finished everything more quickly than we had anticipated and decided to return sooner, so we wouldn't miss any more classes.

I told her Caroline's family had hired a professional photographer, and it would take a while until we had some shots to share.

"Let me see your photos," I said, quickly changing the subject. She then showed me her pictures, if I can call them that. She was cut off in most of them.

"They're not bad at all," she said, laughing, as she swiped from one to the next on her phone. "Actually, they're artistic."

They certainly were: hotel slippers that she wanted to show me; a half-finished piece of strawberry cake that she only remembered to shoot once she was halfway through eating it; May sitting on a spa chair, though the light was so dim that only her eyes were visible. The rest were random snaps of the inside of her bag that her phone had accidentally taken when she forgot to hit the lock button.

Yes, May is artistic in her very own way, and I wouldn't change her for any other mother. Ever.

She was innocently pleased with my made-up story, and though the itching desire to ask her about the two elderly women from the past burned on my tongue, I held back. I didn't want to bring it up before I could consult with Caroline's family.

I needed to tell them as soon as possible. The knowledge that someone, or something, might potentially be coming after me one day soon was making me nervous. I needed to know, for my own sake, and decided to share this with them sometime over the next few days.

For a moment my thoughts were contradictory. I had survived my eleventh year and Corbett was dead, so why make a big deal about it? It had happened in the past, so that meant it wouldn't affect my current life situation anymore, right?

Could there be more to it than I wanted to think possible? And, hypothetically, if so, was there still some sort of danger or threat that persisted and needed to be taken care of? I shuddered at the thought of it.

I looked into my ghostly reflection in the windows of my bedroom and paused for a moment.

Was I ready to go through hell again if anyone tried to break my bond with Caroline one more time?

Of course I am, I told myself at first, though after I switched off the lights I felt safe enough in the darkness to admit that I wasn't. In fact, I would never be.

Wednesday morning started off with two alarms: the physically annoying beeping machine on the night table next to my bed and a mental, stabbing one in my brain. Disoriented, I sat up straight and looked around trying to figure out where I was.

The dim morning light, the warmth of my sheets and the ticking of the clock in the hallway helped my senses register that I was home, in a safe place, far away from the forest that had been haunting me in my dreams.

A little lightheaded, I got out of bed and started my day with a bowl of cereal and a lot of cold milk to wash away the scratchy feeling in my throat.

I had awakened from a nightmare, short but intense, and my mouth had popped wide open as I was gasping for air during the dream.

Corbett was there in the form of a raven and was trying to get me. I couldn't find Caroline. I ran through the thick forest until, at one point, I encountered the two elderly ladies I saw after I had died.

I found them by a bonfire in a misty part of the forest where the branches were too thick to allow any sunlight to reach the soil. They were sitting on a fallen tree trunk covered in moss, and their eyes were focused on the dancing flames in front of them.

Their gazes were blank, depressed and full of pain. As I came closer, I noticed that the younger one was holding the same infant they had been looking at in the hospital.

"The boy is dead," the older one cried, hiding her face behind her wrinkly hands.

"The boy is dead," the younger one repeated with a shaky voice, looking down at the dead little body in her arms. "The evil is too strong."

The sound of my alarm woke me up just at the moment when she stepped toward the fire and threw the boy into its flames.

As I sat by myself in the kitchen, I tried to sort out my thoughts.

First, Corbett was gone and couldn't be a threat to me ever again, and second, I had seen the two ladies only in some astral state and wasn't even sure if they existed in real life. Even if Corbett had made some plans—and it was clear he had—those had been thwarted by the Elders, so there was absolutely no chance anything bad could happen.

I decided not to give much further thought to this. I couldn't let my post-traumatic dreams consume me. I kept drinking more milk until the itchy feeling in my throat caused by the deadly flames in my nightmare had dissolved.

My thoughts were better when I got on the bus. The ride to school felt short and surprisingly pleasant, knowing I was shortly going to encounter Caroline's marvelous touch. When I got off, I inhaled the cold morning air and made my way to Spanish with anticipation. We were back, and there was no reason to allow anything to come between Caroline and myself ever again. We could resume our lives—together.

Teo approached me when he saw me by the lockers, and asked about my absence.

"They did not!" he said when I told him the same lie I told May. "That's amazing."

He told me he was glad I was finally back. He had a hard time with his roommate when I was gone, and had to move out into his own room in the dorm. He kept asking for more details about my trip, and I filled him in a bit more, though only about the *safe* part of the story.

I was entertained when he started complaining about Natasha's behavior during lunch, and I couldn't suppress a chuckle when she showed up near the lockers and he rolled his eyes at her.

"Good morning, you guys!" she said, smiling and showing her yellow teeth.

"You've been gone for quite some time. You've got to tell *us* about your trip, and then I'll tell you guys about my weekend with Ben. You don't know how much fun he is. He's here in the country visiting. We've all got to get together for drinks and have some fun. You'll love him; he's such a people person."

"Absolutely," I said, laughing.

She wiped her nose with her sleeve, gave us a thumbs-up and walked away.

I was euphoric before French and ran down the hallway in eagerness.

"I'm ready for my French lesson," I said, pulling Caroline's chair closer to mine.

She smiled, and I placed my lips on hers. She had curled her hair and wore a light blue coat and boots that reached up to her knees. Her legs were crossed in a perfect angle—as if anything could ever be anything but perfect about her. She gently reminded me about our surroundings with a soft push of her hand on my chest.

"A kiss is the only way I ever want to stop you from smiling," I said, sinking back in my chair. She gave me her fairy smile and lowered her eyes to her folded hands on the table.

Too late. I had already caught the tell-tale glimpse of a frown on her forehead.

"What's wrong?" I asked cautiously.

Her eyes were deep; the light in them only barely visible. "Can you come over on Friday?" she asked.

I panicked and responded, "Is everything okay?"

"Nothing to worry about," she said tensely. "At least not for now."

"He's back?" I asked anxiously, my ears turning hot.

"He's not."

"Is it the Elders?"

Her voice was smooth, almost careful, when she answered.

"We just need to share some thoughts. There's no reason to panic."

Mr. Auberson silenced the class and asked us to open our books. I immediately forgot the page number he said—I was that distracted already.

Irritated, I flung my book open to the wrong page, of course, and refrained from bothering Caroline with any more questions. There was no need to anyway, because I knew she had lied when she said there was no reason to worry. So much for resuming our lives as though nothing had happened.

I ended up pushing my pasta around my plate during lunch while Natasha was completely consumed by her own babbling. It didn't bother me after a while, and I was able to block it out until it sounded like a smooth on-going hum in the background. Caroline kept looking at me apologetically. I asked her several more times to tell me what was going on, but she kept insisting that we had to wait.

Thursday morning was better. I could only vaguely remember my dreams from the previous night. I sorted out my thoughts during breakfast, a new habit I suddenly developed, and decided to share my after-death dreamlike vision with Caroline's family when I saw them the next day. The timing felt right, and I would be at her place anyway, so I couldn't find any reason to procrastinate about this.

Text analysis was nothing but a blurry, dim cloud of words projected by the professor at the far end of the tunnel that my surroundings turned into, and it took a lot of effort to stay focused. Four more exams were announced in my other classes that day for the upcoming exam season, which didn't improve my mood at all.

I went to the library with Caroline after class, and we looked for some books to use as reference for our studies. I wasn't even in the slightest mood to work and couldn't keep up with her. She was never tired, never confused about any classes, and always made it all seem so easy. She also never needed to study for any exams; though she told me she did, as an attempt to blend in more with the other students.

She walked from shelf to shelf, restlessly, and her golden eyes moved from book to book while the soft tips of her fingers brushed against their dusty spines. I walked behind her and played with her hair, hoping I could distract her just long enough to tell me what was on her mind. After several failed attempts, I grabbed a thick book and pressed my hand between its pages.

"This book is trying to eat my hand. I need your help."

She looked at me lovingly, her hand on the spine of a book on the shelf in front of her.

"If you don't put it back, I'll give it permission to eat you."

I got away with a kiss, though that was all, as she gracefully insisted on continuing with our studies.

On Friday, I awoke way before my alarm went off. I lingered in bed, wide awake, and thought about my meeting with Caroline's family that evening after school.

Had the Elders requested a reunion with me, and was she hesitant to tell me this since she knew how nervous they made me?

I sighed.

Friday was a day that so many people looked forward to. *Why can't I look forward to it with just as much anticipation?* I asked myself. I could, though that meant ignoring all the worry and persistent questions in my mind, and I knew I needed to get my thoughts straight or I'd literally go crazy for sure.

The day was cold, gray and gloomy. I was noticing how eagerly I was awaiting the warmth of spring when I met Caroline and Dominic by the bus stop only 15 minutes later. Unfairly, they seemed completely unbothered by the cold as they walked me to class.

Dominic was glad we were back and told me how hard it had been for him to stay home and not be able to help us after what had happened in the forest. He said he actually made it as far as the border of Montenegro to help us, but Lerato caught up with him and convinced him to go back home, insisting there was nothing he could do to help us after Corbett's attack.

Dominic went on about how he would have chased Corbett down and made him suffer until the Elders arrived. Caroline in-

323

terrupted and said there was no reason for him to prove his brav-
ery, as she knew how much he cared. I had never heard him speak
like that; it just didn't match his calm appearance. At the same
time, I hoped he would never have a reason to prove how brave
he really was. For when death comes after you, there's not much
time to think, that much I already knew.

Classes seemed long and intense that day. I ate lunch quickly, hoping that would somehow fast-forward the remaining time
until classes were over. When we finally left campus, I was upset
with myself. I had grown nervous and tried to suppress it by evening out my breath.

I held Caroline's hand on our way through their front garden
and she looked at me intensely; her eyes were calm and bright,
which was promising, I hoped. Her shoulders were relaxed; her
movements were brisk, but still smooth and natural; and her skin
reflected the purity of the snow around us. I was sure she would
have prepared me if we were meeting the Elders, but I peeked
sheepishly into her house when she opened the door.

The Christmas tree in the entry hall had been replaced by
pots of flowers. The handrail on the staircase was lit up, and the
crystal chandelier was bathing us in a warm light, giving me a
much-needed feeling of safety and shelter. The little fountain
filled the space with sprinkling whispers of dancing water. And I
inhaled the sweet scent of fresh pastry.

"Welcome back," Elena said, greeting me warmly as she
stepped out of the kitchen with Lerato.

They were both wearing aprons and had rolled their shirt-
sleeves up to their elbows. Her arms instantly wrapped around
me, and I inhaled her warmth as I surrendered myself into her
otherworldly embrace.

Her motherly hug was the most special physical sensation I
looked forward to. Her beauty made her look fragile under the
light of the chandelier, but her hug was anything but weak. It was

neither too strong, nor was it too soft. The way she threw her arms around me was art in physical form, graceful and light, just as one would expect from her slender figure. When her hair fell into my face, blocking all the light, I felt as if I had fallen into a pile of soft, freshly washed linen.

"How do you feel?" Lerato asked.

"Normal," I said, and they smiled.

"That is always nice to hear."

"Go on into the living room," Elena said encouragingly as they headed back toward the kitchen. "We'll join you soon."

I sat down next to Caroline on the couch in the living room, which also exuded a feeling of warmth. A quiet fire was burning in the fireplace, and my nervousness wore off a bit as I spotted five place settings on the dining table. Still dazed by Elena's hug, I was glad to realize that they weren't expecting anyone else.

I looked at the altar in the back of the room and contemplated the streams of light it was emanating. The captivating candles looked majestic, and their flames seemed to stand still, as if they weren't flickering at all. As I now had more knowledge about how they were created, they looked slightly different to me than before. The light—the angels' souls—inside the wax was peaceful, and I felt I could stare at their eternal flames for a very long time, knowing firsthand how each of these four beings embodied the pure beauty of sacrifice.

"There's cinnamon, Ferrero and honey ones on this tray," Elena said as she placed a tray full of cookies in the middle of the dining table. "Be careful, the filling might still be hot." Lerato was right behind her with cups and freshly brewed tea.

Caroline and I joined them at the table. I had one of each kind of cookie and thought about how unfair it was that they were able to incorporate art into whatever their hands touched.

Lerato sat down across from Elena and slowly filled our cups with the steaming tea. My stomach made a noise, luckily not loud enough for them to hear—or maybe they did, but they politely refrained from saying anything to avoid embarrassing me, the only human being present. I was eager to hear why they had invited me over tonight.

I looked over at Caroline and she instantly and warmly responded to my gaze. When a smile appeared on her lips, I knew that whatever the reason for our meeting, it couldn't be that bad.

"We all know that what happened in the forest has changed many aspects of your life," Lerato said in response to my thoughts.

I chewed slowly on my cookie. The tea was so hot it burned my tongue immediately.

"What do you mean?" I asked. "What changes exactly?" There were a million thoughts running through my mind and I was struggling to phrase a coherent question.

Lerato stayed calm and took his time responding, perhaps as a way of letting me know that we were fine after all. "Imbalance," he finally said, placing the tea pot back on the table as if it was made out of plastic and not fine china.

"Not having an angel of death is simply not possible," Elena added as she saw the expression on my face.

I felt tense, because I didn't know what they were getting at.

"What do we do now, and what does that mean for us?"

A short silence followed, during which only the crackling of the fire could be heard.

"The Elders will call for a meeting as soon as they decide on something," Caroline said with a conflicted expression on her face.

"Decide on *something?*" I asked, hearing the agony in my voice.

"There won't be any drastic changes," she said, trying to ease my mind. "I'm pretty positive about that."

I wrapped my hand around the hot teacup in front of me; I needed a physical distraction.

"Define drastic changes," I demanded.

"They might ask us to move away to avoid physical contact between you as my protégé and me as your guardian angel."

I played with the teacup and said, "I don't like that."

"Neither do we," Elena said.

"However, it is much better to know the worst that can happen is that we might be forced to move away from each other," Lerato added. "That's still better than having an angel of death who is a constant threat both to you and Caroline."

I stared at him for a moment, trying to shift his words from one side of my brain to the other.

"The most important thing is that you both are safe now," he reminded us.

I protested, "Do we have to go along with whatever their decision turns out to be?"

Four pairs of eyes looked at me almost instantly, and I knew how to interpret their looks and silence.

The situation felt unfair.

"We both hardly survived. Why should anyone rule our lives now?"

Elena tilted her head to the side as if letting me know that she felt the same way. Lerato kept looking at me with his most diplomatic expression.

"They're not," Caroline said. "It's just their rules." She looked as desperate as I felt, but since she was an angel, she had to follow their laws.

"I'm human. Maybe none of their rules apply to me."

"I am obliged to remind you that you are part of this as much as any of us," Lerato said.

Caroline squeezed my hand under the table and I looked her into her soothing eyes. They looked like two glorious moonflowers, open and ever-blooming, and the sight of them eased my irritation against my own will. She had shifted her hair to one side of her face and looked like a porcelain doll, immaculate and irresistible, an angelic vision in flesh and bones.

"Can we talk to them?" I asked more calmly.

"They are already holding their three-day balance meeting," Lerato said. "They will share the results with us as soon as they have made a decision."

"They've already started?" I asked nervously.

Lerato nodded yes.

"When did they start?"

"Today," he said, taking a sip from his teacup while keeping eye contact with me.

"I won't accept another guardian angel."

I took a sip of my now warm tea, pressing the liquid against my teeth with my tongue before swallowing.

"The change of a guardian angel only happens under one condition: failure," Elena said comfortingly with her warm voice.

Hearing this, I could feel my racing senses slow down. I traced a finger along the edge of Caroline's hand all the way up to her perfectly shaped fingertip, where her skin was soft.

"As long as their decision doesn't involve *moving us apart*," I uttered.

Lerato smiled confidently and said, "Be assured that this will not happen."

Doubtful, I asked, "Do we have proof of that?"

Caroline's musical voice enlightened us.

"We don't need proof. Don't you think they would have already done that if they wanted to? Our bond has resulted in affection beyond comprehension, without any negative intention from either of us, and there's no law allowing one angel to pass judgment on and make decisions about another angel's love. Not even the Elders. The only exception is if knowledge of the angelic realm were in danger of being exposed to human beings.

But you have something inside that convinces the Elders that you won't share your knowledge about us with anyone. Taking an angel's love away and prohibiting it is like breaking an angel's wings."

I absorbed what Caroline said. Her words felt like soothing water seeping into my mind, washing away my toxic thoughts and the fear of being separated from her.

"Feelings cannot be controlled, and therefore, should never be suppressed," Lerato said. "Your inner bond will never be broken; the only thing that could happen would be for your physical contact to be modified in some way."

I was finally calm again. I exhaled in relief as I silently contemplated everything that had been said so far. Lerato refilled all of our cups with more tea.

Caroline and I were safe together, and I promised myself I would use my entelechy, whenever I ever had to, to prevent anyone or anything from coming between us.

"Can't they just decide on something as simple as giving me another angel of death, so that things can go back to normal?"

"We assume this is what is most likely going to happen," Lerato said.

"It simply takes time; the Elders have their own way and pace in taking care of these kinds of issues," Elena added.

For a moment everything was quiet. I listened to the sound of the fire and felt my muscles relax.

Elena rested her palms on the table and said, "There is one more thing that has been brought to our attention, and we think you should know about it as well." I stopped chewing and looked at her nervously.

"We have been told that Corbett has a wife," Lerato said cautiously.

Alarmed, I could feel a chill run down my back and my heart started racing, a pulse shooting like a hot wave into my stomach.

I nibbled on a cookie, squeezing the honey from the center

and chewing slowly on the sticky creaminess, to give my brain some time to process this new information.

"Do you think Corbett's wife might be my new angel of death?" I asked tensely and swallowed. The cookie stuck in my throat.

"Not at all," Caroline said almost immediately.

My mouth was dry as I asked, "In what way does that affect us and our circumstances though?"

"A wife who loses her husband is surely not happy about it," Lerato said calmly.

My heart skipped a beat. "She's coming after us!" I exclaimed, leaping up off of the chair.

Caroline's soothing hands grabbed my arm instantly.

"She's not."

I panicked.

"She must know though, about me. What if she wants to take revenge on us?"

Lerato gestured calmly and said, "We don't know anything about her or what she wants to do yet, but that seems unlikely since she would know that the Elders were the ones who killed Corbett under law, not us."

Elena elaborated on this.

"The reason we are sharing this piece of information is for preventative purposes. Corbett's wife will be under observation by the Elders. We assume they will interrogate her to find out if she knew about his actions. Unfortunately, we cannot exclude the idea of her not being involved in Corbett's plans to attack you. Of course, the worst outcome would be if they had indeed planned all this together since his actions have already raised so many questions. While she doesn't live in this country, we should be prepared for all possibilities."

I felt devastated and looked for comforting shelter in Caroline's golden eyes.

Why is it, I asked myself, *that when we had just overcome a mortal threat, another danger had to arise?* I could feel my ears turning red.

"The Elders should have questioned Corbett and forced him to tell us the reason for his actions, rather than just killing him." Lerato's voice sounded serious as he spoke.

"Sometimes it's better not to ask questions of something evil, but instead to destroy it immediately. Uncertainty—the unknown—in the end, leads to the feeling of being threatened, and that is the reason the Elders killed Corbett right away. We have no knowledge about how he developed his skills of metamorphosis and also know nothing about the source of them."

I weighed Lerato's words carefully, though I couldn't—didn't—want to understand why the Elders killed Corbett so quickly. If they had waited to question him first, then they could have prevented the danger we were now facing.

Lerato continued.

"I have started researching about unknown skills and how to trigger their development. I am concerned about my assumptions so far that Corbett knew about ancient techniques of how to unfold skills infused by the literal meaning of his symbolic name of the raven, which might be why and how he was able to shapeshift into a raven. If my studies ultimately confirm these assumptions, this will mean that the angels have reached a turning point in our history. I hope this turns out not to be the case, because it will mean that forces are ruling the angelic realm that none of us are able to control."

Lerato's forehead wrinkled and his eyes narrowed, his gaze lost in the darkness of the night outside. None of us spoke for a while. I could feel the electricity in the air and was having trouble breathing.

Far away from being calm, I was annoyed, and I asked myself a series of fundamental questions. *Had Corbett been feeding on some dangerous force or source for his powers, and had he passed that skill on to his*

331

wife? And if so, did she or would she ever have more power than the Elders, who were the strongest community of angels?

I felt uncomfortable in my own skin and hoped Lerato's assumptions would be disproved.

"Right before he took control of my body and made me go out into the woods by myself, I dreamed about him," I said, breaking the silence. They all looked at me questioningly.

"In that dream I saw myself walk to the exact same place in the forest where I saw him for the first time in physical form. It's as though that dream was a trigger for my later behavior."

Caroline turned her head and looked at me. Elena narrowed her eyes, and Dominic changed his posture.

"A premonition in the form of a dream," Lerato said, scratching his chin. He exchanged a quick look with Elena.

"Your entelechy is most certainly also a power that can keep you safe. That dream was your entelechy talking to you, a built-in self-defense mechanism warning you about what was about to happen."

My eyes looked sorrowfully at Caroline, realizing that if I had known how to interpret that dream, how to understand it, I would have been able to prevent everything that happened afterward.

I reached for her soft hand and said, "I didn't know."

Her face softened and she gave me a comforting look.

"Don't be sorry, please. Even if you had told me about that dream, I wouldn't have known this either. There's nothing you could have done to stop what happened."

Understanding now what I could have prevented, I urgently wanted her to understand how sorry I was.

"If I had woken you up and told you what I had seen, then maybe we could have prevented everything that happened with Corbett at your summerhouse."

"Entelechy takes time to be understood," Elena said, trying

to make me feel better about myself. "Your circumstances were so frightening they threw you off track."

"I could have prevented my own death," I insisted.

"That's what I'm here for," Caroline reminded me gently.

Lerato gave her an encouraging nod and went to the kitchen to steep a fresh pot of tea.

"There's something else I've got to share as well," I said nervously, folding my hands in front me on the table.

I could feel all their eyes piercing me. Caroline moved so close to me that I felt her breath on my skin.

"After Corbett took my life, I had a very vivid dream. A couple of them, actually. One especially right after his attack."

Lerato had returned with a new pot of tea, and he exchanged a quick look with Elena.

"We are eager to hear about it," Caroline said, running a hand through her hair.

"I found myself in a hospital, back in the nineties. The experience was like being in a silent slow-motion movie. I could walk through doors and people—I assume I was experiencing myself as my spiritual essence. I ended up in a room full of newborn babies, where I encountered two elderly women who were hovering over a little boy. I hadn't been able to hear anything else anyone was saying, but I could hear them clearly when they spoke."

I paused briefly to take in all the angels' patient reactions.

"They were saying that the baby boy was in mortal danger and that some dark forces knew about his secret. They vaguely mentioned something about the child's destiny, and I believe they performed some kind of incantation to protect him."

Caroline and her family seemed surprised by my dream, and they appeared to have turned to stone. No one moved, even slightly.

"The newborn boy was me. I realized this later when I traveled forward in time and saw a series of other scenes from my childhood that they also appeared in. I can't remember those two ladies from my childhood at all, though I have been asking myself if they could have possibly known about Corbett back then."

Everyone unfroze at the same time. I felt uneasy.

"You are wondering about its interpretation, I assume?" Lerato asked, leaning forward on the table.

"Yes. But what I'm wondering about more is the potential danger they said I was in. One of them said that their mistake almost took my life and that there's more people who know about my supposed secret. I'm confused about what I witnessed—and why I was allowed to know this."

Caroline muttered something to herself so quickly I couldn't understand what she said. Lerato seemed to be thinking hard as he looked from his hands to the windows. He finally spoke confidently.

"What an entirely bizarre experience. First, without a doubt, the source of your vision was your entelechy, as it already allows you to see experiences beyond the understanding of your logical mind. I do not understand yet what the potential danger is that those two women were talking about. But if you are sure the boy was you, then I am convinced that the answer to all of your questions, including what the danger is and where your entelechy comes from, can be found within yourself and not anywhere else."

Caroline moved in her seat anxiously and asked Lerato, "Do you think those two ladies knew about Corbett from the day Adam was born?"

"Possibly. We have to find out exactly what they were talking about."

I could feel how tense Caroline had become. "I don't like this at all," she said, her back stiffening. "We need to find out what the danger is immediately, if not sooner."

I filled them in further.

"There's more. In the second dream, I was on a playground and ran into the two ladies again. This time they were sitting on a bench at the edge of a park contemplating a little boy—me at the age of three—playing with a ball. I've tried, but I can't remember that day of my life. One of the ladies said that the boy couldn't see them, but felt their presence. Later in their conversation, they said that if I survived until age eleven, they thought the danger might wear off with time. Just before that, one of them said that *something was growing,* but she never revealed what she meant by that."

I could see that Caroline was annoyed. She sighed and asked, "You don't remember anything of that from your childhood?"

"I don't. The only one who might is my mother, because in a later dream in this series, I saw the elderly ladies talking to her. I'm not sure if I should ask Mom about it though."

"I don't think you should consult your mother about any of this," Lerato said. "At least until we figure out the meaning of what you saw in this dream sequence."

I took that as a cue to continue my story.

"The secret, whatever it is, must be important because the elderly ladies said it was their responsibility to make sure that no one found out about it. They talked about undoing *something.* One of them made it sound as if it was their fault that I was in danger."

"Have you ever had any potentially fatal accidents in the past?" Elena asked.

"Not as far as I can remember. I can't recall what happened when I was 11 very clearly, but none of what I heard them talking about ever happened before I moved to Belgrade late last summer."

"So, what could these dreams mean?" Caroline asked all of us.

"We need to analyze everything properly. However, we can immediately assume that your entelechy has been with you from day one of your life," Lerato said, taking another sip of tea.

"Whatever those two elderly ladies did to you, they didn't want anyone else to know about it and they tried to undo it. I am not concerned that they ever represented any threat; on the contrary, they seemed eager to keep you alive."

I felt conflicted.

"What if none of that actually happened to me and was simply a dream I had after I had died?"

"A soul on its way to the afterlife enters a space where reality exists in a life review," Lerato responded in his scientific manner. "Those events are as real as anything else that has happened in your life."

"In the next dream in the series, I was at our old apartment, the place we moved from when I was six. The same two elderly ladies knocked on our front door. When my mother answered it, they pretended to be nannies at the local kindergarten and offered to take care of me when she needed extra help. Mom turned them down, and I followed them out into the hallway. They said that they had done everything they could to save me. One of them added that the only thing they could do from that point on was to hope that the forces of good would keep me alive."

"Did they mention any names?" Elena asked abruptly.

"No."

Caroline's hand took mine under the table, her eyes darkened by anguish. She said, "I don't understand why I get to feel Adam's pain, but I didn't get to see any of these afterlife visions with him."

"Bonds are complex, and sometimes can't be explained at all," Elena said comfortingly. "Perhaps if you had participated in his dream sequence, you would have been distracted from the process of healing Adam and bringing him back to life."

Caroline sighed and apologized to me with her eyes. Still, she knew what Elena said was true.

"That's exactly when I saw Caroline again. When she was

healing me this time, I experienced and perceived the healing process more intensely than ever before."

Caroline's delicate eyes still looked sad, and I had an urgent desire to run away with her somewhere far away, to a place where none of our current challenges could find us.

"So how do we find the answer to why I saw all of that? It doesn't make sense for me to witness something that happened in my life when I can't remember any of it from my own memory at all."

Lerato scratched his chin and rested his elbows on the edge of the table. "You don't remember; that is true," he said. "But you have something that can *make* you remember." He paused for a moment, as though to give me time to think about what he had said.

"It is safe to say now that your entelechy has been within you for your entire life and will, without doubt, grow. Maybe even to the extent where one day you might be able to see past and future events."

I admitted to myself I had hoped he would come up with something more simple, rather than telling me I had to use my entelechy to find out all the answers on my own. I felt trapped between my past and future, and felt all alone. Of course, I wasn't physically. But I was now realizing that only I would be able to find out the meaning of those key events in my life from the dream sequence; no one else could do that for me.

Lerato interrupted my racing mind and brought me back to reality.

"Sometimes we are too distracted by looking for answers outside ourselves, instead of looking into our own souls. You already see what others don't, so do not doubt in yourself. Spirit understands what the mind is never able to understand. Coincidences are very rare; in fact, I have never encountered one in my own life."

The wrinkles on Lerato's forehead had vanished, and a smile

appeared on his lips. His words were calming and promising at the same time, though they didn't fully ease my anxiety.

"Then, in the end, I suppose Corbett's attack was never a coincidence," I said.

Looking up from his teacup quickly, Lerato responded, "It wasn't."

I still felt uneasy.

"Something isn't right, though. Things just don't add up. Why would Corbett want me to commit suicide?"

"He knew I couldn't stop you from doing that," Caroline said with a trace of sadness in her voice.

"I know. But *why* though? Why did he want me dead in the first place anyway? Don't you see: He must have known something that none of us do."

I grew more frustrated with each word I uttered and was beyond desperate to resolve the riddle Corbett had left us with.

"He has been following me for a long time. Who knows how long he was planning his attacks. He could have even been in the same room as us many times, without anyone of us realizing it. He spied on us, left a note with Dominic's signature in my locker, tried to kill me on the lake, and then followed me and Caroline all the way to Montenegro, despite the protective mist the Elders had sent down. He knew me inside and out; he knew exactly how to track me. There must be more to his actions than some sick addiction to ultraviolence and my destruction."

I realized I was losing my temper when Caroline threw her arms around me and hugged me tightly to her.

I fell silent. I felt how I softly fell into a place of peace in her embrace as she brought me back to myself.

"We understand your concerns," Elena said, breaking the silence.

I looked at Elena's fragile face. Her eyes revealed how much she wanted to help us out of the current situation.

Lerato spoke slowly through his folded hands under his chin.

"We can't decide alone about what to do next; it is in the Elders' hands now. We will hear from them soon and will know if they have gotten more information about Corbett's wife. Let's wait to hear what they have to tell us, then take things from there. Maybe what they share with us will provide some kind of clue about the two elderly ladies from your dreams in the afterlife— and that might lead us to the answers to the rest of your questions. We can't do much right now, although we can focus on teaching you how to block your mind from intruders."

He spoke to me like a father.

"Your mind is your own complex weapon against any imaginable threat and should not be made accessible to anyone else but you. Corbett knew how to enter it, and we shall practice how to avoid ever letting that happen again. I will conduct some research into techniques that will let you know when someone is trying to access your mind. And then we will teach you how to completely block anyone from invading your consciousness."

His voice was sharper than usual, his authoritativeness always had an unexplainable ability to bring my mind back into focus. My breathing slowed down, the tension in my muscles released, and the lump in my throat dissolved.

"The same for Caroline. I will do some research into how she can block herself from feeling your pain to such an extent that she's then unable to heal you."

Feeling overwhelmed, I asked, "That all sounds great, but where do we start?"

Lerato smiled. His ability to lighten our moods with each of his perfectly articulated words was awe-inspiring.

"We already have. Each ending opens the door to new possibilities. We are a great team and are able to move mountains when we work together. Do not put your life on hold right now just because something bad has happened, as there is an answer for everything. The worst has already happened, and both you and Caroline were strong enough to find a way to survive it. You both defeated death, something that not many have done. This proves how unbreakable your bond is. Let's shift our focus from worrying about what could happen next to moving forward one step at a time, and appreciating each and every step as we do. You are both safe and alive. Should we ask for anything more than that right now?"

In a surprisingly peaceful state of mind, I remained quiet and allowed Lerato's words to sink into me. Elena smiled warmly, and Caroline held my hand.

Lerato was right. In the end, I felt he had spoken with his heart. We were alive, together, and that was what mattered the most. I took a moment to silently appreciate Caroline's existence and the fact that I was simply able to sit next to her.

By the time Elena got up to add more wood to the fire, I felt certain that Lerato had used one of his subtle techniques on us, one that had brought peace into our minds.

Corbett's attack and actions had come quickly into our lives and left us with many unanswered questions. But I had found another missing piece of the puzzle that evening, one that I wouldn't have discovered without Lerato's brilliant words of encouragement: the knowledge that my time with Caroline wasn't over yet, that nothing was lost and that there was going to be another day for me. With Caroline.

Lerato had taught me about the power of choice. I could choose to worry about the unknown and embitter the remaining time I had been given to live with those fears, or I could choose to live fully in the moment. I looked at Caroline, and without hesitation, chose the latter. The remainder of my life was a gift—I had died and shouldn't even be here now—and I didn't want to spend the rest of my life worrying about things.

Elena, the subtle and most fragile angel of the family, found the perfect way to end the conversation by asking me to stay for dinner. Lerato took her hand, and they went into the kitchen, looking like a victorious king and queen who had just conquered the world.

I had almost forgotten Dominic was there; he had been so quiet. He got up, went to grab his guitar from upstairs, and stood next to the fire and played one of his sweet compositions, filling the house with harmony.

A vision of beauty, Caroline took me by the hand and led me upstairs to her room and my most favorite place in the entire house: her balcony. The silky curtains welcomed our return.

The night was late. It was remarkable how time passed by so quickly when I was with her. I didn't even feel the cold at all as we stood on the balcony, crisp snow under our feet.

"Hi," I whispered.

She placed her arms on my shoulders and whispered back, "Hi."

We started moving back and forth as if dancing to inaudible music, staring into each other's eyes for the longest time. My heartbeat was louder than the sound of the wind rushing through the flapping curtains.

"How are you?" I asked.

"Depends on how you are," she said gently, keeping her eyes on mine.

I ran my finger along her lips.

"I've never been better."

She exhaled through her mouth. Her skin was warm, and its scent refreshing.

"Then I'm good as well."

I smiled and leaned forward to kiss her. Then I pressed her to me as tightly as possible, locked in an embrace. Her eyelashes felt like butterfly wings on my cheeks.

"I'm sorry," I said in her ear.

She loosened the hug and looked at me, asking, "What are you apologizing for?"

"For almost taking your life."

The starlight gleamed in her eyes. "Never apologize for something that was out of your control," she reminded me gently.

"What now?" I asked.

"What do you mean, what now?" she asked sadly.

I sighed.

"What happens next? Where do you and I stand?"

Her eyes had an intense look in them.

"I don't want to be a negative influence in your life. I'm involved in some kind of a danger. Which means you're automatically in danger as well because of our bond. If you need—or want—to move away, then I'll be fine with that. I'll come see you as often as possible, or you can come see me. I just want you to know that I'll be fine with whatever you decide."

"You're silly. You'll never be in my way. And I'm not moving away from you. I need you as much as you need me."

Her words alone healed me. I hugged her again, this time tighter, and enjoyed how her warmth felt like liquid love against my skin.

She said softly, "I simply don't see any reason why we should stay away from each other."

"I just wish things were easier right now. There are so many things swirling around in my brain, and I can't stop thinking about them. So many loose ends: the Elders' decision, my new angel of death, us, the future…"

I looked up at the starry night.

"Nobody said it was going to be easy," she responded, comforting me. "We have to fight for what we want." I looked at her absurdly beautiful face. She knew how to breathe hope into me with only her voice.

"Before you healed me in the forest, I saw you in your pure angelic form," I said.

Her eyes brightened in surprise.

"Your entelechy is advanced and is growing uncontrollably fast."

"I have never seen anything more beautiful. If I had died then and that had been the last thing I ever saw, it would have been a very peaceful death indeed."

"I was calling your soul back to me."

"When I was experiencing the afterlife dream sequence, I felt I was getting closer to you every time I traveled forward in time and my surroundings changed. Tell me what exactly happened... when I died..."

She locked her hands behind my back and took her time before answering. I knew it was painful for her to talk about it, and I felt badly asking her to, but I needed to know in order to resolve what happened and put it out of my mind.

"The moment Corbett reached for your heart I was able to block myself from feeling your pain. I don't know how I did it—everything happened so fast—and I went after him."

Her voice was weak, and her eyes had turned glassy.

"He was surprised when he saw that he could no longer use his power against me, and I was able to fight him off for as long as I needed to heal you. Lerato, Elena and the Elders showed up shortly after that and found him on the other side of the forest."

"But something seemed odd. He looked like he was in pain."

"You're strong."

She shook her head.

"No, it wasn't me. Right before I reached you, I could see his hand inside your chest, but his arm seemed to be cramping."

I remembered his fast slicing movements and shuddered.

"Do you have any idea what it was?"

"No. It was unexplainable. He could have killed you, but something prevented him from doing that before I attacked him.

He seemed scared. But he definitely had enough time to take your life, of that I am sure."

Yet another riddle that Corbett had left behind for us to unravel making my temples throb.

"Maybe your entelechy was defending you and acting as your own personal shield."

I thought about this suggestion for a moment. I was surprised to learn that there was something else that kept him from finishing me off before Caroline intervened.

Feeling confused, I said, "I'm not even sure anymore what theory to believe in or hold as possible."

We stopped dancing, and I contemplated how the wind played with her silky hair.

"Your entelechy is a gift from within and will always serve you. Even if I fail you."

My stomach contracted at the thought of her ever failing us. I promised myself that if one day she indeed was destined to fail, I would use my entelechy to save both of us and bring her back to me.

"I thought I had lost you," she said, blinking a few times. "It was unbearable."

"You didn't," I said, holding her tight. "You never will."

I could feel her tears falling on my shoulders and running down my back.

"It's okay," I said. "We're safe now."

I could feel her body stiffen slightly, and she took a deep breath. I moved back softly from our embrace to look at her. The tears made her eyes look like two setting moons in the sky over the ocean.

"What is it?" I asked.

"When we came back from our summerhouse in Durmitor's national park, I did some research on my own. I couldn't—I refused—to understand the reasoning behind why I would not be allowed to heal you. I could never have accepted you really dying then…if I had lost you because of something that wasn't caused by your own doing."

"I came across a book in Lerato's library and read about an ancient technique that is called *sharing auras* that enables angels to call human beings back to life, but in an angelic body instead of a human one."

She looked up at the starry sky, and something warm shot through my stomach.

"I had never heard about this technique before. The only thing I knew was that the aura is an energized, fluid part of the soul, and I thought that if I shared mine with yours, I might perhaps be able to change you."

I swallowed and wet my throat.

"So I thought that since you hadn't died by suicide, because Corbett was controlling you, the process wouldn't have been forced and you might have turned out to be a good angel, instead of a bad one."

"Is there a way to still do it?" I asked. I could feel my heart in my throat.

She started crying and shook her head no.

"Don't cry, please."

"At the same time, I'm glad I didn't know about that technique before he tried to kill you in the forest. What if I had turned you into something dark, such as a bad angel? I couldn't have lived with that burden for the rest of my life."

Her tears made her look more fragile than ever.

"You know what, why change yourself when you're perfect just the way you are right now? Why run the risk of trying to bring you closer to me, when we're the closest we've ever been?"

I could feel my eyes start to water. I took her delicate hands into mine.

"Your blood runs in my veins—what else could I want? How much closer could I possibly ever want to get to you?"

My voice was weak, and the lump in my throat had returned.

"Maybe your life, the way you knew it—it would all have completely changed. I don't even know if the Elders would have approved of *sharing auras*. What if I turned out to be the danger to you after all?"

I wiped her glittery tears from her soft cheeks with a shaking finger.

"I asked Lerato and Elena to let me be the one to tell you about this. I *needed* to. I can't and don't want to keep this knowledge—this possibility—from you. I'll always be candid with you."

"Then why are you crying?" I asked gently. "Nothing bad happened." My voice was still weak, and a million questions were running through my mind.

"I'm sad and conflicted. We could have been equal, with no differences. I'm sad that I came across this knowledge only after Corbett's most recent attack."

Her love and unselfishness had once more touched my heart, and at a loss for words, I gave her a long hug.

She was shaking slightly, and I tried to let her know through my touch that I wasn't upset at all by her *late* discovery. I never would be. I was fine with the way things had turned out. Of course, it would have made everything a lot easier, but why should we worry about a missed opportunity that we weren't even sure would have worked?

"Would you ever try it?" I asked cautiously. "I'm only curious in case I should ever die again."

I could still feel her tears rolling down my back when she spoke, still holding me tight.

"When I saw you on the ground in the forest, with your ribs broken, your head cracked open, your face bloodied, and your heart almost ripped out...I admit...I wished in that moment I could have changed you. I wanted nothing more than to heal you, to make you whole again. My answer is yes. Should you ever die again in a similarly painful way, yes, I will risk everything to make you what I am."

I took her head between both of my hands and spoke honestly, gazing into her eyes.

"I am completely fine with that. Do you want to know why? Because that is the most loving, unselfish and best promise anyone has ever made to me. I am utterly devoted to you, and I want you to know this means forever."

I leaned down, pressing my lips to hers. Her rosy lips were soft and wet, and she responded without hesitation. Caroline turned my short kiss into a very long one. And after it, a thousand more followed.

And once again, the starry sky was the only witness to our innocent love.

EPILOGUE

Spring seemed to arrive faster that year than I had anticipated, and to my great relief, things slowly got back to normal.

We still hadn't heard anything from the Elders, and none of us was eager enough to request another audience with them. We looked at their absence like a well-deserved timeout from all the events of the past six months.

We decided that we already had enough problems in such a short amount of time that we were going to trust the natural unfoldment of things, thanks to Lerato's encouragement.

Every moment is perfect just as it is, he explained during one of our training sessions in his library, and if it doesn't appear that way, then we must be looking at it from the wrong point of view.

By March, Caroline and I were already halfway through our

practices. They were so complex, mostly consisting of long talks with Lerato and demanding a great deal of mental effort, and we still had a long way to go.

Classes at the university were also intense. I survived exam season thanks to Caroline's help, and we were looking forward to Easter break.

Caroline and her family had originally planned to spend Easter in Spain, but they ultimately decided not to because of a combination of factors: The Elders were still deciding about our situation, I still hadn't been assigned a new angel of death, and no one knew where Corbett's wife was and if she was planning to attack us. I encouraged them to go numerous times, but Caroline refused.

As time passed, I realized that her appearance in my life had never been the slightest coincidence. There was a reason why our physical paths had crossed. And it occurred to me that I needed to find out why, so I could move forward with my life utilizing my entelechy, with the power I was gifted with from within. I needed to understand aspects of my life I would never have been able to understand if I hadn't seen Caroline the first time when she healed me after the car accident.

When Caroline explained to me that angels trigger healing from within their hearts, I understood why she had been able to completely heal me after Corbett's attack in the forest.

Caroline's love had lifted me from the claws of death and brought me back to life.

***

When I met her in the park on a sunny Sunday afternoon, I reached for her hand. My lips anticipated the touch of hers with an excitement that provoked a warm feeling in my stomach.

Her hair was curled and loose. She was wearing tight jeans, black boots and a vibrant red coat. The sunlight played beautifully in her eyes and cast a perfect glow on her hair.

"Every minute spent away from you is a waste of time," I said as we merged into the crowd of pedestrians.

Her smile was perfect as she intertwined her fingers with mine.

"Any news from the Elders?" I inquired.

"Nothing at all. I guess we'll have to keep waiting until they get back to us."

Every time I asked her about the Elders I felt slightly uneasy. I secretly hoped they would take as much time as possible.

I was lost in my thoughts when we came to a square in the park where children were playing with soap bubbles that turned into iridescent rainbows in the sunlight. We paused there, and I took both her hands into mine.

"There's something I'd like to ask you," I said.

We both blinked a few times when a bubble popped just above our heads.

She looked up at me with her beautiful sunny eyes and said, "I'm listening."

"That day in the forest…when you were healing me…do you remember what you said to me?"

Another bubble popped as it touched her hair.

"I remember," she said, still smiling.

"Right before you healed me, you asked if I could keep a secret."

"I remember that, too."

"What secret were you talking about?"

At that moment, all the children blew their bubbles at the same time, and it looked as though we were standing in the middle of a shower of sudsy, soap bubbles.

She kept smiling, but with an air of mystery about her.

The bubbles were still floating all around us, and she leaned toward me, whispering a promise in my ear with her sweet, angelic voice.

"I will always heal you."

Acknowledgments

I would like to express my gratitude from the bottom of my heart to the following people:

My family, who always believe in me: Mom, thank you for making this dream possible. Dad, thank you for always being there for me. My sister, Jelena, thank you for inspiring me. Words cannot express how much I love you. My brother, Nenad, without whom this book would still be unfinished; thank you forever. You believed in me even when I was about to give up.

A huge thank you to Angelika Whitecliff. I don't know how this book would have ever turned out without your guidance and mentorship. You brought the right people into my life just when I needed them the most.

Thank you to Aliene Hughes for your valuable feedback, editorial suggestions and copy editing. You made me see important details of the story that needed to be tidied up.

An enormous thank you to Tanja Capuder for allowing me to use your poem "Historia Magistra Vitae" from your book, *Entelehija Spirit*. Parts of this novel would not have been possible without your generous permission.

A big thank you to my editor Christy Walker for all your treasured edits and for making *Unattainable* into a better story than it originally was.

John Grant, from John Grant Studios, thank you for the maestros front cover.

Thank you to Aylem Merino for such a wonderful back cover and all the designs you have so bigheartedly provided for *Unattainable*.

Thank you to Feslyan Studios for composing the official reading soundtrack for *Unattainable*.

And last, but not least, thank you to Olivia Kim not only for being an awesome proofreader, (and future world's best doctor), but also for being my best friend. Your feedback and suggestions will always be part of this story. Thank you for believing in me until the end.

©Paul Martin K F. @paulmartinkf http://www.paulmart.in

MILOSH ZEZELJ was raised in Switzerland and has lived in New York City since 2012. He holds a degree in economics from the College of Commerce in Switzerland and has studied acting for film at the New York Film Academy. He is multilingual and fluent in five languages. *Unattainable* is his debut novel.

www.unattainablebook.com
www.facebook.com/unattainablebook
www.twitter.com/Miloshzezelj
info@unattainablebook.com